D0794429

CHANCES

Nowak, Pamela.
Chances /

c2008.
33305213842291
gi 04/14/08

Chances

Pamela Nowak

FIVE STAR

An imprint of Thomson Gale, a part of The Thomson Corporation

THOMSON

GALE

Detroit • New York • San Francisco • New Haven, Conn. • Waterville, Maine • London

THOMSON
GALE

Copyright © 2008 by Pamela Nowak.
Five Star Publishing, an imprint of The Gale Group.
Thomson and Star Logo and Five Star are trademarks and Gale is a registered trademark used herein under license.

ALL RIGHTS RESERVED

This novel is a work of fiction. Names, characters, places, and incidents are either the product of the author's imagination, or, if real, used fictitiously.

No part of this book may be reproduced or transmitted in any form or by any electronic or mechanical means, including photocopying, recording or by any information storage and retrieval system, without the express written permission of the publisher, except where permitted by law.

Set in 11 pt. Plantin.

LIBRARY OF CONGRESS CATALOGING-IN-PUBLICATION DATA

Nowak, Pamela.
Chances / Pamela Nowak. — 1st ed.
p. cm.
ISBN-13: 978-1-59414-637-4 (alk. paper)
ISBN-10: 1-59414-637-3 (alk. paper)
1. Women telegraphers—Fiction. 2. Undertakers and undertaking—Fiction. 3. Suffragists—Fiction. 4. Women—Colorado—History—Fiction. 5. Denver (Colo.)—Fiction. I. Title.
PS3614.O964C48 2008
813′.6—dc22 2007035071

First Edition. First Printing: January 2008.

Published in 2008 in conjunction with Tekno Books.

Printed in the United States of America on permanent paper
10 9 8 7 6 5 4 3 2 1

To Tim and Katrina, who daily teach me the meaning of love. Without you, I would not have had the courage to take a chance on following my dream.

ACKNOWLEDGEMENTS

So many people helped me make this journey, and I cannot begin to thank them for their support. From that first encouragement to write through those rough years of learning that writing is a skill that must be developed, their support and guidance have been treasured greatly.

I owe so much to my husband Tim and daughter Katrina. Tim has put up with me all these years as I spent hours with my fictional characters instead of with him, ever encouraging my dream and loving me. Katrina has been unfailing and vocal in her faith that I would someday have my novel published and her love and support have meant more than she will ever know. Without either of them, I would not have been able to do this.

Deepest thanks to my parents, Dick and Vauna, for fostering a home in which imagination, confidence, and my love of history could flourish; to my sister Judy for encouraging me from the very first moment, and her husband Dave for enthusiastically sharing all his books on Denver; and to my brother Mike for his support. And, of course, thanks to my dear friend Terry for always cheering me on; it has meant the world to me.

I am eternally grateful to all those who helped me refine my writing skills. Many thanks to my early critiquers, Dawna and Tim, for seeing potential amid the roughness of my craft and for encouraging me to continue. I am forever in debt to the Rocky Mountain Fiction Writers for all I have learned through their organization. My RMFW, Cheyenne Area Writers Group, and especially my Celestial Sisters, critique partners who all taught me so much and inspired me to keep on learning, are close in my heart: Sharon, Janet, Sue, Robin, Liz, Kay, Peggy, Alice, Teresa, Jennie, Tina, Heidi, Anita, Deb, Leslee, Margaret, Vicki, Mary, Mike, Heather, Jeana . . . thank you all.

Finally, I owe my appreciation to Thomas Jepsen, whose research of female telegraphers and publication of Ma Kiley's story sparked the idea for this book.

Chapter One

Denver, 1876

Sarah Donovan tapped out the final few dots and dashes of the telegram in her usual rapid tempo. Sharp voices rose in a ruckus outside the bare window of her small office in the Kansas Pacific Railroad Depot, and she spun toward the sound.

Jim Wilson, the wiry stationmaster and ticket agent who shared the tiny cubicle with Sarah, stood at the lone double-pane window. "Sounds like somebody's havin' a good time," he commented dryly. He adjusted his dusty spectacles and peered out the open casement.

"What Denver needs is a few less saloons and a few more policemen," Sarah observed. "It sounds like a riot out there."

"You want I should shut the window?"

She tugged at the collar of her shirtwaist and shook her head. "No, Jim, we'd be stifled by the heat. I can't believe this kind of weather in October."

"Yep, you got that right." Jim returned to his stool behind the ticket counter and began sorting through the morning's ticket stubs.

Sarah pushed the noise from her mind and focused her attention on the stack of telegrams she'd just received. She logged them and stuffed them into envelopes, then marked each for delivery. If deliveryman Frank Bates was any good at his job, he'd be halfway across town with the first of the messages by now. Instead, he was likely standing in front of the depot, watching the doings out on Depot Street.

Sarah stood and gathered the pile of telegrams into a bundle. "Cover the wire for a couple of minutes, Jim?"

The stationmaster nodded and pushed his eyeglasses back up. "I got it, Miss Sarah."

Crossing the sparse office, Sarah entered the more elaborate passenger waiting room and spotted Bates lounging on one of the leather padded benches.

Bates sat apart, his dark eyes alert under the visor of his cap, his attention riveted on a salesman in a checkered suit and the fashionable woman caught in his spiel.

Sarah crossed the well-lit room, her shoes clicking on the polished wooden floor. The sound blended with the pockets of conversation. She paused a few feet away from Bates and brushed her wilting hair from her forehead. "Got a batch to be delivered," she told him.

Bates looked up with annoyance. "Sure you got the right addresses? Can't never be too sure with lady folk." He snatched the parcel of telegrams and rifled through them. "Can't deliver to Petterman, he ain't in town." He stood, tossed the envelope back at her, and stormed out of the depot.

Sarah's anger roiled. In the two weeks she'd been in her position, Bates had shown nothing but contempt for her. Men like him were the ones who made it so necessary for women to gain the vote. She'd told her friends, Miriam and Lise, the same thing, back in Saint Louis. Somehow, though, she sensed they hadn't quite shared her passion for the cause. Enrolling in Western Union's telegraph operator training academy had been one way of taking action to prove women capable. She'd taken the position in Denver with high hopes, only to encounter Bates. Slighted that he'd been passed over for promotion, the man was not only skeptical of her abilities, but was openly hostile.

Sarah sighed and unclenched her fingers, knowing she needed to calm down before she returned to her office. Across the depot yard, a crowd had gathered around a stray yellow dog. Bounty hunters, probably, arguing about who had the right to claim the animal.

Among Denver's many growing problems was an overpopulation of dogs. The city fathers had recently decided to offer a bounty of a quarter for any dog brought in, dead or alive. Sarah moved away from the door in disgust.

On his perch behind the ticket counter, Jim sipped at a cup of steaming coffee. He turned as she entered and smiled, her one unexpected ally in the station. "Wire's been quiet."

Sarah settled back at her desk and examined the telegram Bates had tossed at her. It was a body notice. She sat up straight and leaned over to read the note. A body was coming in on the 10:20 for Daniel Petterman, undertaker.

She didn't have long. The train was due soon. With quick finger taps, she relayed that the message was undeliverable. Rules were strict on bodies in transit: transfer immediately to an undertaker. The last thing Kansas Pacific needed was a deteriorating corpse sitting in baggage claim overnight.

It was the first unusual situation she'd encountered since taking the job, and she was relieved Bates had bothered to inform her Petterman was gone. So far, her performance record was spotless, and she aimed to keep it that way. A man might be able to weather a few demerits, or "brownies," as railroaders called them, but she was sure the dispatcher would have his eye on her, the sole female telegrapher in the region.

The Kansas Pacific dispatcher's response was swift and to the point. *Find another undertaker.*

Sarah took the message, recorded it, and glanced at Jim.

"Know any good undertakers?" she asked.

Jim looked up and grinned. "Bates getting to you that much?"

"We've got a body coming in on the next train, and no one to claim it."

"Can't say I'm too familiar with them, myself. Just send it to Silverman, he's the closest."

Sarah shrugged. She'd seen Petterman around. The tall, well-groomed undertaker was known for his professionalism. She wasn't so sure about Silverman. Sarah marked the telegram with his name anyway, flagged it as urgent, and stuck the message in the delivery pile.

Outside, the arguing voices became louder. Sarah frowned. The clicking of an incoming telegram drew her attention, and she bent to decipher the message. Two gunshots echoed through the air, followed by pained whimpers and a child's scream.

"Holy mother of God." Jim jumped from his stool and ran to the door. "That sounded like a kid."

Sarah forced herself to sit still until the telegram was done. Then, she rushed to join Jim. "What happened?"

"Looks like that gang of boys shot some kid's dog."

Across the depot yard, a dark-haired girl had crumpled beside the yellow dog and lay sobbing, her arms clenched around the dog's neck. An older girl stood above her, dazed and motionless. The dog's limp body showed no sign of life.

Sarah's heart lurched for the girls—they couldn't be more than either side of ten years old. "That's downright cruel," she muttered through clenched teeth. "Damn that bounty law and the gang along with it."

Beyond the train yard, the rotund little German who ran the closest saloon emerged from the darkness of his establishment and slapped a wet towel at the group of boys. Sarah caught a few angry curse words amid the stream of guttural German he tossed at them. The boys laughed in his face.

Sarah's anger intensified. Nobody deserved to be treated that way, not the saloonkeeper, and especially not those little girls.

She sucked in a breath and strode across the yard. Her long skirt swayed and her sensible shoes kicked up dust with each determined step.

As she neared, the gang's laughter dwindled. Sarah had known it would. She was used to it. No one ever expected such righteous fury from a little thing like her.

She marched up to the boys, noting they were youngsters themselves. The oldest of the five was thirteen-year-old Cyrus Gall, well known for his mistreatment of others. She eyed their single gun, then dismissed it. They were kids. Bullies, not outlaws. With a lightning quick motion, she grabbed Cyrus by the ear and twisted. He squirmed once, yelped, then stilled.

"What in heaven's name are you doing?" she demanded. "The bounty is on stray dogs. *Stray.* I ought to twist this ear off and feed it to the next dog I see. How dare you shoot someone's dog for a measly two bits?" Sarah twisted his ear again.

Cyrus spat at her shoe. "Weren't nobody tendin' that dog. Makes it fair game, far as the law goes." He winced and pulled away from Sarah's grasp, rubbing his ear.

Sarah planted a look of stern reproach on him. "By the time I get done talking to city officials about this, there won't be a cent paid to any of you. You shoot one more pet, and I'll see to it you never reap another bounty. Ever."

Cyrus met her gaze, weighing the situation. The other boys shuffled their feet as they pondered her words, a low murmur of discontent rising from their midst. Sarah stood with her hands on her hips, daring them to voice their complaints to her. Instead, Cyrus spat again, then sauntered away down Depot Street. The other boys stuck out their chins in insult before turning tail and following their leader.

"Ach, like *mein* own *Mutter,*" Gottlieb praised, his fatty jowls widening into a smile. "It is *gut* you come for the *Kinder.* Here is for der tears." He tossed the towel to her and nodded at the smallest girl, still despondent and clinging to the dog. The older girl stared, mouth agape, at Sarah.

"But I'm not—" Sarah stopped in mid-sentence. Gottlieb had already scurried into the saloon, apparently satisfied in his assumption that she was the girls' mother.

Suddenly unsure, she glanced down at the children.

The older girl swallowed once, hard, and big tears began to flow down her cheeks. "Thank you," she said in a choked voice.

Sarah peered at her and searched her mind for the right words. "Are you all right?" she finally asked.

The girl nodded gravely. "Those hoodlums ought to be horsewhipped." She clamped both hands over her mouth, her hazel eyes wide with surprise.

Sarah fought back a smile. "Do you need someone to accompany you home?"

The girl shook her head, brown curls swaying. "No, thank you. We don't want to trouble anyone. Molly? It's time to go home. Papa wouldn't like us making a scene."

The younger girl stiffened. "Well, *Papa's* dog isn't dead. I guess a person can make a scene if their own dog is dead, can't they, Kate?" She stuck out a petulant lip.

"No, Molly, that's enough. We need to be dignified now. Biscuit's dead and no amount of tears will bring him back. Stand up so we can go home."

Molly pressed her lips against the dog's head and offered it one last hug, then rose. As she stood, bright red drops of blood dripped from the front of her once-blue dress and splattered the dirt around her feet.

Kate's gaze froze, her eyes widening again. "Ooooh, Biscuit, they killed our Biscuit." Her dignified tears erupted into sobs and she threw herself at Sarah.

"I want my mama." Molly wailed out the words and launched into Sarah's arms as well.

Sarah glanced back at the depot in desperation. She was good with causes, but children were another story. Jim stood in the entry. He shrugged his shoulders, his hands in a helpless open-palmed gesture, then pointed to his watch. The 10:20. Its whistle sounded in the distance. She was on her own.

Lord, what in the world had she gotten herself into? She should be in the station, minding the wire so Jim could do his own job. She'd get a brownie for sure if anyone realized she'd abandoned her duties.

She patted the girls awkwardly and waited for them to stop crying. "Shhhh," she said. "Is your mama nearby?"

"Mama died when we were little," Kate explained in a choked voice.

Molly tightened her hold around Sarah's upper legs and sobbed louder. Her head bobbed against Sarah's waist. Kate burrowed her face into Sarah's bodice, staining it with wet tears.

"Oh." Sarah frowned. "Well, is your papa around?"

"He's at work, up Blake Street."

Sarah sighed. She *was* on her own. How did one comfort little girls, anyway?

Lise's frequent advice on the value of hugs flashed through Sarah's mind, and she tightened her arms around the girls, squeezing them as she brushed her hands across their backs.

"I'm so sorry. You must have loved Biscuit very much."

"He was our best friend." Molly sniffled.

Sarah squeezed the girl again then pulled out of the hug. "I think a friend like that deserves a decent burial, don't you?"

Kate and Molly nodded, their faces solemn.

"Then we'd best make our way over to the depot and see about talking my boss Jim into carrying Biscuit out of here before someone claims the bounty, and the dog wagon shows up."

She ushered the girls toward the station and offered a silent prayer that she'd be able to get their situation settled soon. As it was, she'd have a stack of telegrams to tackle, and her favorite work skirt was stained with Biscuit's blood.

"You work here? At the train station?" Kate asked as they neared the door.

Sarah nodded.

Inside, Jim glanced up, his eyes widening at their appearance. "Them boys sure did leave a mess."

"Kate and Molly here would like to take Biscuit home and bury him. Can we get him off the street?"

"You just mind the ticket counter while I load him up in the wheelbarrow and bring him back. You got four wires in."

Kate watched Jim exit the building, then turned to Sarah. "Ma'am, I think Molly needs a drink and somewhere to sit."

Sarah pointed to the ceramic water cooler in the center of the now empty waiting room. "Help yourselves," she said. "Take any seat." She smiled at them and entered her small office.

A stack of four papers lay on the counter next to the telegraph key. Sarah scanned them, noted that Jim had carefully recorded them in the logbook, and prepared them for delivery.

"Ma'am?" Kate's refined voice interrupted from the doorway.

Sarah turned. "Yes?"

"I don't think Molly should sit on these leather seats, ma'am. Not with her dress all stained. May she sit in here?"

Sarah sighed and nodded. "Just move those boxes off that stool."

Moments later, she heard the box hit the wooden floor and the rustling of cloth as Molly climbed onto the stool. She hoped the child didn't chatter. It was late morning already, and she had several telegrams scheduled to be sent before noon. Taking the first of them, she counted the number of words it contained and added in the category "Day Letter," then began clicking out Morse code.

"Miss?" Molly's polite tone was an echo of Kate's.

"Yes, Molly?"

"What are you doing?"

"I'm sending a telegram."

"But it's just a bunch of clickety clack."

"Molly, mind your manners," Kate chastised.

"It's all right, Kate." Sarah finished the letter, then turned to the girls.

Molly sat on the wooden stool, watching Sarah with bright brown eyes. Her brown hair, like Kate's, was curled into tidy ringlets. Kate stood beside her, craning her neck toward the telegraph.

"It does sound like a bunch of clickety clack unless you know what to listen for. Every letter in the alphabet has a certain pattern of dots and dashes, short clicks and long clacks, if you will. You just need to know what's what."

"How come you know all that?" Molly asked.

"I went to school just to learn it."

"I've heard of telegraphers before," Kate added, curiosity finally getting the better of her. "Papa gets telegrams, sometimes. But I've never heard of a lady telegrapher before."

"There aren't many of us, Kate, but our fingers can transmit code as well as any man's can."

"Papa says ladies belong in the home."

Sarah nodded. She'd heard that comment many times. "Well, Molly, some ladies do and some ladies don't. It all depends on the lady."

"Sorry to interrupt your little suffrage meeting, Miss Sarah, but Biscuit's all loaded up. I reckon it's best to get him and the girls on home before the one o'clock rush starts."

Sarah shook her head at her friend's familiar teasing and smiled. "Thank you, Jim."

"I covered him up with an old blanket."

She nodded, then shifted her glance to the telegraph key.

"Go on, take them home," Jim told her. "I can't be leaving the station for that long. I know more about telegraphing than you do about ticket selling anyway. Shouldn't be too heavy, and I know better than to assume you can't handle it."

"Thanks." Sarah turned back to her young charges. "Now, Misses Kate and Molly, I need to know who your papa is and where to find him."

"His name's Daniel Petterman and he—"

"Petterman? The undertaker?" A twinge of foreboding began to gnaw at Sarah.

"Yes, ma'am." Kate nodded.

"And he's at work?"

"Yes, ma'am."

"He's not out of town?"

"No, ma'am."

Sarah bolted to the basket of telegrams waiting for delivery. It was empty.

"Bates came back and took them out while you was across the way," Jim explained. "There a problem?"

"I had a wire for Petterman. Bates told me he was out of town."

"This about the body you were talking about?"

Sarah nodded.

"Silverman came for it just after the train pulled in. Said the body had no name, and he'd take it right on up to the graveyard and bury it with the rest of the unidentifieds." He glanced at Sarah and raised his bushy eyebrows. "Something tells me Petterman knows who it is and that he don't belong in Potter's Field."

Sarah followed Kate and Molly up Blake Street to a tidy white building. At the front, a lettered sign declared it to be the establishment of Daniel Petterman, Undertaker, the man who should have received the body from the train.

She set the back of the heavy wheelbarrow down and waited as the girls called out for their father. Biting her lip, she cursed Frank Bates for playing her for a fool. He'd told her Petterman was out of town, and she'd taken his word. Now she'd need to confess to making a mistake that she hadn't really made and pray that Petterman was an understanding sort.

The front curtains wavered slightly, then a slender, chestnut-haired man burst from the door of the coffin shop and down the front steps, two at a time.

"Molly, Kate. Are you hurt?" He knelt next to the girls, touching them and eyeing Molly's blood-soaked dress with concern. "What happened?"

Kate shook her head. "Molly's fine, Papa, but Biscuit's dead." Her lower lip trembled and tears glistened in the corners of her eyes.

"Biscuit?"

"Miss Sarah's got him in the wheelbarrow," Molly added, pointing. The tears poured down Molly's face but the little girl held her earlier sobs.

Petterman drew his daughters close. "Thank you for taking care of my girls," he said hoarsely. He hugged them for a moment, then glanced up at Sarah, staring with the most amazing eyes she'd ever seen, an unremarkable hazel in color, but piercing and intense.

Sarah fussed at her stained brown skirt for a moment, then straightened. Lord, she hated it when men perused her that way, like she was some *thing* rather than an intelligent and capable woman. And she hated even more that she had reacted by immediately fretting about how she looked.

She wiped her dusty right hand against her thigh, then offered it to him. Let him think what he wanted. "Sarah Donovan, Mr. Petterman."

"Daniel Petterman," he answered, somewhat warily. He stood, eyebrows raised, then shook her hand. She saw disapproval in his expression and bit her tongue. If he didn't like women introducing themselves, he should have offered his hand first.

"I'm afraid one of the local gangs caught up with Biscuit and claimed him for the bounty," she explained, "and I also need to—"

"They shot him?" Daniel barked, stepping toward her.

Sarah nodded. Clearly, the explanation about the body would have to wait. "Twice."

"In front of my girls?" He paced until his breathing slowed. Once again composed, he turned back to Sarah. "I apologize for the outburst, Miss Donovan."

Sarah glanced at Molly and Kate. Kate's earlier words echoed through her mind. *Papa wouldn't like us making a scene.* Heavens, somebody shot their family dog, and he was worried about being angry? Though he should, he'd probably never think about the girls' needing more than just physical comforting.

She leveled her gaze on Daniel and sighed. "I thought Kate and Molly might want him to have a proper burial instead of him being hauled off."

"Thank you, Miss Donovan." His probing eyes took in her disheveled clothes. "It looks as if my girls made quite an impact on your day. May I arrange for someone over at Hop Alley to clean that skirt?"

Sarah shook her head at his businesslike tone. "Oh, that's really not—"

"Yes, it is, Miss Donovan. I don't shirk from my responsibilities. I only hope the stain will lift out. Send it to Su Ling, and I'll take care of the costs."

"Papa?" Molly tugged at Daniel's hand. "Can Biscuit have a casket?"

Daniel stiffened and shook his head, his face full of unease. "Well, Molly, I'm not sure—"

"I don't think Biscuit would be very comfortable in a casket, Molly," Sarah interrupted, wondering where in the world the sudden urge to rescue Daniel from his discomfort had come from. "When he gets to heaven, I'm sure he'll want to run and play. Does he have a favorite rug? That would be real nice for him, a familiar place to sleep."

"Oh, Miss Sarah, what a grand idea." Kate hugged Sarah impulsively then quickly pulled away, straightening her dress. "Isn't that a fine idea, Papa?"

Daniel glanced at Sarah, as if trying to figure her out.

"Papa?" Kate prompted.

Daniel's attention returned to his daughter. "It sounds like the best one offered so far. Why don't you take Molly in and see if Mrs. Winifred will help the two of you get changed into clean dresses? We'll get Biscuit settled temporarily out back. We can bury him this evening, maybe say a few words."

The two girls disappeared around the building to the side door of their private quarters, leaving Sarah and Daniel alone. "I'll haul him around back," he announced.

He lifted the back of the wheelbarrow, and his muscles tightened under his crisp white shirt. He straightened and the cloth stretched over his biceps.

Sarah smiled in appreciation. Daniel Petterman was obviously a fit man, his body molded by hard work.

"You managed to bring this all the way from the railroad yard?"

Sarah bristled. "I'm not a bird, Mr. Petterman, however slight I may appear."

He ignored her and pushed Biscuit around the end of the

wood frame building. Sarah kept pace, matching his long strides with quick steps of her quite-a-bit-shorter legs. It was time to tell him the other reason she'd come.

"Mr. Petterman?" she said hesitantly. "I have something else—"

"Yes?" He tipped the wheelbarrow, the dog slid forward and the blanket slipped away. The animal was a mangled mess. Ragged holes tore its flesh and its yellow fur was matted with dried blood. Daniel stared, his mouth tight. "Jesus, my girls watched this?"

Sarah's heart caught at the emotion in his voice, and she wished she were able to offer more comfort than quiet words of explanation. "I think they tried to stop it. I didn't pay much attention until the shots."

"What a damned idiotic statute. A bounty on dogs. Does nothing but encourage hoodlums to kill family pets. They could have easily shot Molly or Kate." He settled Biscuit onto his side and recovered his remains with gentle reverence.

"Then why hasn't the statute been changed? Have you considered doing something about it?"

"I'll file my complaint with the City." He straightened and turned to her. "Good enough?"

"For a start, but why stop there? Don't just complain. Write a letter to the editor of the *Rocky Mountain News,* go to the next City Council meeting, start a petition, march in front of City Hall, throw rocks at the dog wagon, refuse to allow anyone to pick up the dead dogs."

"My, aren't you the hotbed of ideas?" Daniel shook his head and reached for the wheelbarrow again.

"Ideas lead to action, Mr. Petterman, and action leads to change. Things don't change when people sit quietly at home." She followed him around the building.

"Well, I'm afraid I don't do any of those things, Miss Donovan."

Sarah stopped, dumbfounded. She couldn't imagine not taking action. "Why not?"

"Businessmen use proper channels. They do not cause problems."

"Problems? A few moments ago, it sounded as if you thought the law was a problem. Businessmen carry a lot of power, Mr. Petterman. Perhaps you ought to use it. They shot your dog, for crying out loud. What if they'd hurt your daughters?"

Daniel stopped and marched back to her. "The law *is* a problem, and I know they shot my dog." His voice was tinged with hostility, surprising her. "It is an absurd law which incites situations like the one that killed Biscuit and endangers the public. I will handle it in my own way, not with some radical knee-jerk reaction. Don't you dare imply that I don't care about my girls or that I take this lightly."

"But you won't do anything about it?"

"I said I would handle it in my own way. I don't *do* any of the things you mentioned, Miss Donovan."

"Sarah, please," she prompted, knowing he'd use her first name if she were a man. "And why don't you?"

"Because I prefer to avoid the bother it would cause. I live my life quietly. Besides, it isn't dignified."

"Dignified? What kind of answer is that? Either you care about changing the law or you don't. If you don't care enough to do something about it, then you clearly don't care, period."

"We elect city councilmen to make these decisions. Our actions are taken at their meetings and at the polls. If we don't like their decisions, we've only ourselves to blame."

Sarah felt her anger rise. "Elect? I certainly didn't elect anyone, Mr. Petterman. *I* don't happen to have a vote."

Daniel sighed and shook his head. "Of course not, Miss Donovan. You're a woman."

The remark bit into her like a slap. "This *woman* was the very one who stood out there and made sure those hoodlums left your daughters alone. This *woman* dealt with their tears and the blood and the remains. Don't you dare tell me this *woman* doesn't possess the ability to vote. If women had suffrage or the right to stand for office, stupid laws wouldn't even exist."

Daniel's jaw tightened, and his gaze bore into her. "No, if women voted, the whole City Council meeting would turn into a tea party."

Sarah stomped her foot in frustration. Men were all the same. "Oh, of all the hare-brained, ludicrous statements! No wonder men never get anything done."

"Are we finished here? I have a body to locate."

"Oh, my goodness, the body." How could she have forgotten? Now he really *would* think her nothing but a bumbling female.

Daniel tensed. "You know something about Mr. Harding?"

"I tried to tell you earlier." She paused, then composed herself and looked him straight in the eye. "I'm the new telegrapher. Cheyenne sent a wire, but I thought you were out of town so I sent the message to Silverman. The body came in on the 10:20. Silverman already picked it up to take it to Potter's Field."

Anger washed across Daniel's face, running roughshod past his self-discipline. "And *you* think women possess the brains to vote? If that body is buried already, *you* can inform the family and work out the legal issues involved with exhuming what's likely to be a badly deteriorated corpse. If he's six feet under, you're going to get yourself a new job because I'll personally see you fired. How's gravedigger suit you?"

Chapter Two

Daniel watched Sarah's plainly clad figure disappear up Blake Street with her wheelbarrow. He hated the position she'd put him in, and he hated having lost his composure. He'd yelled, at a woman, in public. The quick crunching of Sarah's footsteps lingered behind her, further aggravating him.

Frowning, he entered his shop and slammed the door. Wincing in regret at the sound, he crossed to the expensive mahogany casket that lay waiting for Wilson Harding. Snow-white satin lining shimmered beneath the etched glass of the lid's viewing panels, and polished brass hardware graced its sides.

Harding's family wanted the best. He'd had the coffin shipped in special from the Stein Manufacturing Company in Rochester, New York, their top-of-the-line model. The funeral itself was scheduled for tomorrow morning. He sure as hell hoped Silverman hadn't put Harding in the ground yet.

Daniel crossed the spotless workroom and checked on the corpse cooler. This afternoon, he would prepare the body it was keeping chilled. Lifting the lid, he noted that the top chamber was still full of ice. He had time to head to Silverman's.

Opening the rear door to his family's private residence, he informed the housekeeper, Mrs. Winifred, that he was headed out, flipped the "open" sign to "closed" and left the shop.

Daniel hurried through the busy business district of Blake Street. Merchants displayed their wares from glass storefronts and carefully arranged boardwalk cases. He ignored their inviting offers, intent on the distasteful task ahead of him. All he wanted to do was collect Harding and get home, without any further complications.

Silverman's establishment was located just a scant block from the Kansas Pacific Depot. He was one of the less professional of the Denver undertakers and not well known for his quality of work. He probably didn't even have a cooler. Even if Silverman hadn't buried Harding already, Daniel hated to think about the possible decomposition the lack of cooling might have prompted in the unusual autumn heat.

Rounding the corner of Blake Street, Daniel crossed 21st Street to Silverman's squalid little building. Located less than a block off Market Street, Silverman catered to a lower class clientele, often providing burials to the working girls of "the Row." Daniel wrinkled his nose in distaste and entered the bare wooden structure.

Silverman stood behind a rough wooden plank in heated discussion. On the street side of the makeshift counter was a petite blonde, none other than Sarah Donovan herself. Daniel's jaw clenched as he approached.

"You don't understand, Mr. Silverman. The body was supposed to go to someone else." Sarah punctuated her words with her hand.

Silverman chewed on a wad of tobacco, indifferent to her vehemence. "Didn't though. Notice was delivered here. Makes it my responsibility, and ain't no way I can release it to you."

Daniel sighed and marched to the counter to rescue the situation. "But you *can* release it to me," he stated with firmness.

"Well, if it ain't Dan Petterman. You slummin'?"

Sarah looked at both men, then turned back to the proprietor. "Mr. Silverman, it seems—"

"I'll handle this, Miss Donovan, if you don't mind."

"But I—"

"I said, I'll handle this." Daniel shook his head. What in God's name was she doing here? If she'd made a further mess, he'd file a report with her supervisor. In fact, he might just do so anyway. He reminded himself to stay calm, then shifted his weight and moved in front of her. "Silverman, Miss Donovan made an error. The body should have been delivered to me."

Silverman's mouth lifted in a wry smile. "She already covered that. You got paperwork?"

Sarah pushed Daniel's elbow out of the way. "And why wasn't my paperwork satisfactory, Mr. Silverman?"

"Be quiet, Miss Donovan. This is no longer your affair."

"It is my affair, Mr. Petterman. You have implied that I made a mistake when I was, in reality, misinformed and unable to take any other action."

Once again irritated to the verge of outburst, Daniel drew himself away from the counter and faced Sarah. The little spitfire looked riled at the implication that she had erred. He peered down at her, bit back a scathing comment about her professional abilities, and discovered a pair of big violet eyes that could just about melt an iceberg. Somehow, with the girls and the dog, he'd missed seeing them earlier. God Almighty, but the woman was pretty, too pretty for that forward personality.

He sighed and switched tactics. "Miss Donovan, will you cease your chattering? I don't care how or why it happened. I can't straighten this out until you're quiet."

"You two about done?" Silverman interrupted. "Paperwork looks in order, and you're welcome to take the body. You best run, though, 'cause it's halfway up to Potter's Field by now."

Sarah glanced at Daniel. His jaw muscles were twitching again, and she knew he was fighting to control himself. He glared at her, then crossed the room and exited without a word.

By the time she made it to the door, he was halfway down the block, headed southeast, toward Cemetery Hill. Sarah watched him ease into a loose trot and knew he was likely hating every embarrassing minute of it.

The cemetery lay some two to three miles distant, past the meandering City Ditch. It'd take Daniel forever to get there. Why the dickens hadn't he just borrowed a horse?

Sarah turned northwest and entered the Kansas Pacific yard. Frank Bates's company horse stood at the rail, waiting patiently for his next delivery. Glancing into the depot, she spied Bates again lounging on one of the benches, his mouth stuffed full and a sandwich in his hand. He wouldn't need the horse for a while. She untied Buck, flipped the reins over his head, and glanced around before hiking up her long skirt. She mounted the horse and settled the brown serge around her legs, then trotted toward Broadway after Daniel. By now, he was starting to look winded. Goodness, men had no sense whatsoever when they had their minds full of themselves.

Sarah came abreast of Daniel and slowed the horse.

"You going to run all the way or would you like a ride?"

Daniel glared at her, then halted for a breath. "Th-thank you, Miss Donovan. I should be delighted to ride." He waited expectantly.

Sarah inched forward on the horse. If he thought she was dumb enough to dismount and have him take off without her, he had another thought coming.

"Do you need help down, Miss Donovan?"

"Look, Petterman, if you want to get to the cemetery before they put that body in the ground, you'd better get on. Otherwise, I'll go without you. I have a stake in this, too. Until that body is safely in your hands, I cannot clear up the paperwork with Western Union or the Kansas Pacific."

Daniel glanced around the area, then let out a huff and swung himself up behind Sarah. When Sarah continued to grasp the reins herself, he slid his reluctant arms around her waist.

"This is hardly proper. Why didn't you bring a buggy?"

"You ought to be thankful one of us thought to bring a horse. If there had been a buggy available, you can be sure I would have thought of bringing it instead."

She felt him stiffen behind her, and she knew she'd hit a nerve. It served him right. She hoped he stewed in it. Why in the world was it so difficult for men to accept that they were fallible, and that, sometimes, women could do things better than they could?

Sarah kept Buck at a controlled trot as they left the business district. Daniel's warm heat coursed through her as his arms bounced up and down, occasionally bumping against her breasts before settling back around her waist. He shifted, his firm chest hard behind her back.

She should have let him take the horse himself, after all.

Just past the capitol building, they spotted Silverman's burial wagon. Sarah reined in Buck. Daniel slid down and approached the driver. They spoke quietly for a few moments, giving Sarah time to wonder why she had felt so compelled to come along. This was now an issue between the two undertakers and, truth be told, she didn't actually need to be present for the exchange of the body.

She glanced at Daniel's trim figure. His broad shoulders merged into a strong, tapering back. His pressed white shirt disappeared into the waistband of tailored black pants, which were molded over a well-formed derriere.

Sarah's face grew hot. She was scrutinizing him in the same maddening way that men did her. She was looking at the man's backside, for heaven's sake. She spun Buck away, no longer wishing to witness any of Daniel Petterman's activities.

"Whoa, there," Marshal McCallin called from his approaching horse.

Sarah pulled Buck's reins and slowed to a stop, face to face with the Chief of Police.

"You got a fair amount of explainin' to do, gal. Frank Bates and the Kansas Pacific just reported this horse stolen."

The following morning, Daniel stood next to his fine black funeral carriage and watched the pallbearers carry William Harding's coffin to his cemetery lot. It had been precisely two hours since he'd made his appearance at municipal court in Sarah Donovan's defense, and it was his first quiet moment.

He was glad to be rid of her and happier yet that he'd never have to meet with her again.

Court had cluttered up his already busy morning, and he'd spent the hour during the funeral service checking on the gravesite, something he normally did far in advance of the actual burial. Thank God, the gravediggers had done a proper job.

Fortunately, Harding hadn't been too badly deteriorated. With a little molding, some powder and rouge, he looked as distinguished as he had in life. The family was pleased. The funeral was crowded with Denver's elite bidding farewell to a favorite banker. Daniel smiled at the thought of the positive impression he'd made today.

Watching them now, as the minister led a final prayer, Daniel was glad word hadn't gotten out about the trouble with Sarah. She sure was a high-falutin' little busybody. He'd never met a woman quite like her. Much as he hated to admit it, a few of the things she'd said even made sense.

Whoever would expect such spirit from a tiny little thing like her? Heck, she couldn't be more than a little over five feet tall, and that thick blond hair looked like spun cornsilk. And those big violet eyes—a man could drown in them. Her whole appearance was at odds with her attitude.

After this morning's court session, he'd told her to be sure and send all telegrams by messenger. He didn't want anything more to do with the woman, violet eyes or not.

Across the cemetery, a distinguished bearded man broke away from the lingering crowd and approached. Daniel recognized him as William Byers, owner of the *Rocky Mountain News.*

"Fine funeral, Petterman," he said, offering his hand.

"Thank you, Byers. I fear Denver's lost one of her finest."

Byers nodded. "He was well-liked."

"It meant a lot to the family, seeing everyone come out like this. They went through a lot, getting him shipped back from Wyoming Territory."

"Speaking of which, word has it you had your share of trouble receiving him back." Byers's eyebrows rose expectantly.

"Am I speaking on the record or off?" Daniel countered.

The newsman smiled in appreciation. "I'm not working today, Daniel."

"You heard about the trouble, huh?" How many others had heard? Daniel cringed at the thought of the rumor mill invading his privacy and slandering his well-guarded morals.

"Heard that new female telegrapher got her wires crossed."

Daniel chuckled at Byers's joke, then nodded, one eye still on the funeral party. "She said somebody told her I was out of town. The body went to Silverman, and I ended up having to chase it halfway up Cemetery Hill."

"Riding double on a buckskin horse," Byers supplied, "stolen by the lady with the quick fingers."

Daniel groaned. "Is that going to make the front page?"

"No, but I was real tempted."

"I'll just bet."

"So, what's she like?"

Daniel glanced at the dispersing crowd and relaxed a little. Everything had gone well, and no one but Byers was paying him the least attention. He leaned forward and kept his voice low. "She's a hellcat, Bill, a hellcat through and through. Spouts off like a geyser on women's rights and such. Pretty little thing, but she sure doesn't know her place."

Byers smiled. "Sounds a lot like my Libby."

Daniel arched his eyebrows in surprise. "The hellcat or the suffragist?" Everyone had heard about Elizabeth Byers and her causes, but he certainly hadn't expected Bill to be so cavalier about the issue.

"Both, I'm afraid." He grinned and shrugged his shoulders in mock helplessness. "Seriously, though, Daniel, I already heard most of the story. Newspaperman's sources, you know. What I'm really curious about is the incident with the gang. Is it true Cyrus Gall and his entourage shot your daughters' dog?"

Daniel offered a sober nod. "Right in front of the girls. They're just children. Kate's eleven and Molly's only nine. They aren't old enough to comprehend the reasons behind what happened. All they know is that those boys shot their dog."

They crossed the now empty cemetery toward their waiting vehicles. A set of matched bays stood in front of Bill's elegant buggy. Daniel's funeral carriage was hitched to an equally appealing set of Morgans.

"The bounty?" Bill asked.

Daniel stopped and spoke earnestly. "When the City Council passed the ordinance, I didn't think much of it. But now, I've seen the impact, and I think it's a lousy answer. I know the dogs are a problem. There must be a better way to address it."

"Couldn't agree with you more. You ever consider writing a letter to the editor on the subject?" Once again, Byers raised his eyebrows.

Daniel shook his head and laughed. "Funny. That was one of the things Miss Donovan suggested." He thought about tiny Sarah, almost running to keep up with him, lecturing him all the while on civic action. She probably espoused anarchy, too.

"She's right, you know. The *News* has a pretty large reader-

ship. Get the issue out there. Out of respect to you, I'll hold back the story and let you bring it up in the letter. It has the advantage of getting the message out there without some snoopy reporter bringing in any embarrassing details."

"You son of a gun. You're just itching to get this out there." Leave it to a newsman to agree with a suffragist.

"I am, Daniel. I happen to agree that the practice of awarding bounties on dead dogs is barbaric. Your daughters' experience is a newsman's delight. It teems with drama and heartache. What a way to launch a cause."

"I'm not so sure I want to launch a cause." What in the world would people think of him? His father's stern lectures on public image crowded his mind.

"Do you want somebody else's kids standing there bawling their heads off when their dog gets shot? Better yet, do you want to go home and tell your girls you had the chance to do something about poor old whatever his name was, and you didn't?"

The image of his daughters' tears flashed through Daniel's mind. Damn, he hated making a scene. He told himself that his daughters were safely done with such situations. It wasn't about his kids anymore. Then Sarah's harping voice flooded his thoughts, shaming his lack of action, and again, the image of his girls crying. Damn.

"Biscuit. His name was Biscuit, and I'll write the damned letter."

Chapter Three

Sarah took her lunch break on the back stoop of the station at half past twelve. Lord, she was glad Frank Bates had finally left the station for a while. He'd been a boor ever since court. He was none too pleased about the charges being dismissed.

"You got another one of them good ham sandwiches again?" Jim asked, his bushy eyebrows standing at attention.

Sarah laughed and handed her friend the other half of her sandwich. "I'm not going to have the guys from freight and baggage up here begging, too, am I?" she teased.

Jim smiled and shook his head, then settled down next to Sarah. "Wouldn't share these for the world," he said, between bites. "Sure do wish my landlady would learn to bake a ham without it tastin' like shoe leather."

Poor Jim. Of the six employees at the station, Jim was the only bachelor, and his constant woes over his landlady's poor cooking had the baggage master and freight agent's wives sending food for him. Sarah supposed she ought to do her part, too.

"How about I just start bringing two sandwiches?"

"That'd be just fine with me." Jim grinned and pushed his glasses further up his nose. "Bates givin' you a hard time?"

"He'd rather I spent another night in jail, or more."

"They treat you all right, girl?"

She shrugged. "McCallin keeps a clean jail, and they fussed over having a proper lady in it. Leave it to Bates to try to press charges. I sure am glad Buck belonged to the Kansas Pacific,

though. Once the judge found out I was using Buck for official business, he laughed Bates out of the courtroom."

Jim sobered and glanced around the station before facing Sarah, concern filling his eyes. "Yeah, and now Bates is gonna add that to his list of complaints. You watch out for him, Sarah. You're the best telegrapher to hit this place in a long time, and there ain't no way he's ever gonna admit that. Best decision I ever made was hiring you instead of promoting him, even if he does have experience. Makes him sore, though. He'll just keep trying to do you in, one way or another."

"Thanks, Jim, I'll be careful. I aim to make first-class op by spring." She eyed her friend, waiting for his reaction. It took some operators several years to gain the speed and skill necessary to earn the coveted title. She planned to do it in less than one.

"Well, like I said, you're the best I've seen. I'd guess that's why KP hasn't been in much of a hurry to have me fill the manager's position. You're already doing the work. You just ain't getting paid for it." Jim wiped his hands on his faded blue handkerchief, folded it, and placed it in his pocket. "Gotta head back to the freight room and check on things there."

Sarah frowned at his departing figure. Jim was right. The Kansas Pacific was saving a pile of money. The first-class op had transferred out the minute he heard the railroad had hired a woman. Since her arrival, she'd been handling both jobs at a fraction of what they would pay a man to do either one of them.

The click of the telegraph broke into her thoughts, and she returned to her post. Once she made first-class operator, she'd be eligible for manager's wages instead of being a lowly assistant. From there, she'd have the opportunity to supervise a commercial office.

The afternoon proved busy. The wire clacked away at a steady rate. Jim scurried from the ticket counter to the freight room to the rail yard, assuring that the station operated with brisk efficiency, while Sarah sent and recorded messages, logged them in, created switch lists, and relayed siding orders. In between, she rushed to deliver the orders to Jim. Then he made sure the signals were set correctly and the heavy siding switches were thrown so the "inferior" trains were diverted onto sidings, and the "superior" trains could pass safely. By the time six o'clock rolled around, the delivery basket was full, and Bates was still nowhere to be seen.

Sarah frowned and rubbed her aching back. Her fingers throbbed after ten hours of almost constant work. As it was, she would barely have time for dinner before the suffrage meeting started. She narrowed her eyes at the basket, anticipating the added delay that would result from having to deliver all those messages herself.

At the ticket counter, Jim slammed the drawer of his desk and muttered under his breath. Bates's absence had netted him extra work, as well.

The door of the station clicked open, and Sarah glanced up, expecting Pete Sanders, the evening relief man. Instead, Frank Bates sauntered across the empty waiting area.

Jim rose from his desk and adjusted his glasses with deliberate determination. "Mr. Bates," he said tiredly, "it has been a long afternoon. You've a pile of telegrams to be delivered, and I've had to run all over the rail yard doing your job. The boys in the freight room missed you, too. It's time we had a talk about whether you're movin' on."

Sarah hurried to gather the stack of telegrams. She'd slip quietly out the door and leave Jim to chastise Bates in private.

"Yeah, well, I was busy taking care of business."

"Personal business, Mr. Bates? You failed to return to your duties and, as stationmaster—"

"They ain't my duties no more," Bates muttered. He moved

to the ticket counter and leaned his elbows on the wooden shelf, staring down at Jim. "I figured Kansas Pacific ought to know about the mess here. I wired the main office from the Broadwell House to fill them in."

Sarah stopped at the door. What had Bates done? She turned and watched the exchange with foreboding.

Jim stood, shaking his head while Bates grinned at him.

"They decided maybe they need a head telegrapher after all, seeing as the assistant is stirring up trouble. Sorry about going over your head, boss, but I didn't see much choice. I ain't your delivery boy no more, Jim. You're looking at your new first-class op."

"Not until I get word of it. Things don't work that way."

Bates's grin widened. "They do if your uncle has a hand in it."

Jim's face clouded, and a shocked silence settled over the station, broken only by the click of Bates's boots as he moved away from the ticket counter. He stopped at the office door and peered quizzically at Sarah.

"What are you doing just standing there?" he barked. "Those telegrams should have been delivered hours ago. You know this is going to result in brownies, don't you, *Miss* Donovan?"

Sarah swallowed hard. Oh, she knew it all right, knew it without a doubt, and there wasn't a thing she could do about it.

Two hours later, Sarah dropped off the last of the telegrams and headed toward the residential district and whatever was left of the suffrage meeting.

Despite the horse and her efficient pace, the deliveries had taken twice as long as she had hoped. Most of the businesses had closed, and she'd had to track down several of the telegrams' recipients, costing her precious time. Curse Frank Bates and his scheming.

Sarah moved down 17th Street at a steady clip, leaving downtown's bright gas lamps behind. She pulled her shawl closer. The days might be hot for this time of year, but the nights sure did cool off. Here and there, leaves skittered across her path, but they were few and far between, like the trees. She crossed Broadway and angled east, her mind doing somersaults. Somehow, there had to be a way around Bates.

Despite Jim's assurances that he'd investigate in the morning, she felt like she'd had the wind knocked out of her. How was she going to get the practice she needed to improve her accuracy if all she ever did was deliver messages? She had no doubt Bates would see to it that she did nothing but run all over town. He'd never let her near the wire.

Still, there'd been no official word from the main office. Jim would wire his supervisor tomorrow, they'd discover it was all a bluff, and Bates would be removed from her life forever. She would still have her chance to prove herself. She'd make primary op and become the first female manager in the district. People would know she was more than a pretty little blonde. They'd see she was a woman to be reckoned with. They'd look at her achievements and know she was worthy.

But she knew better. She kicked at a rock and watched it roll away into the darkness. Jim's expression had said it all, that and his lack of argument. Bates had paraded out of the depot like a banty rooster, and Jim had confirmed that Frank's uncle, Walter Bates, owned a controlling interest in the KP, shaking his head all the while.

At the corner of Sherman Street, Sarah stopped in her tracks, remembering Frank's words. He'd told the main office that there were problems, that Jim couldn't handle them. Whatever he'd said, it was enough to get himself promoted as well as casting doubt on Jim's management abilities. No wonder Jim had remained silent. Lord, did Bates have enough pull to put Jim's position in danger?

The last thing she wanted to do was jeopardize her friend's job. She wouldn't ask Jim to defend her. If her only choice was being an errand girl, she'd ask Jim to transfer her to the graveyard shift. That way, Bates would think he won, and she'd still get her practice time. It wasn't the way she'd planned to get there, but she'd make primary op status any way she had to.

Mounting the front steps of Elizabeth Byers's stately brick mansion, Sarah noted the dimmed lights. Drat it all, she was too late. Before she could decide whether or not to knock, the door opened.

An attractive woman in her mid-forties stood inside the lavish foyer. Her brown hair was styled in the latest fashion, and her elegant dress was a clear indication that this was not the downstairs maid.

"Mrs. Byers?" Sarah queried.

The woman nodded. "Call me Elizabeth," she offered, abandoning propriety in the manner of a true suffragist. "I'll wager you are Sarah Donovan?"

Sarah nodded.

"We missed you. Everyone was looking forward to meeting Denver's only female telegrapher." She stepped back and gestured for Sarah to enter. "They've gone but come on in, anyway. I'm dying to hear about your adventures and pick your brain about suffrage movements back East."

"Goodness, how did you—"

"Nothing's a secret in this town, my dear, nothing at all. Especially not in this household." She smiled and closed the door, then led the way into the front parlor. A host of empty chairs indicated the meeting had been well attended.

"It looks like I missed a good meeting."

"We're gathering steam all the time. Tea?" She indicated a fragile china pot. "Or perhaps sherry?"

Sarah's glance followed Elizabeth's gesture. Two crystal decanters sat on a polished table. "No thank you, I'm not much of a sherry drinker." Her gaze drifted to the second bottle, half full of amber liquid.

Elizabeth noted the motion. "Brandy it is," she announced. "My preference anyway." She gathered two snifters, filled them, and passed one to Sarah. "Sit."

Sarah gathered her plain brown skirt and perched on a red velvet settee.

Elizabeth sat across from her in a floral side chair. "We're organizing rallies on a monthly basis for now, weather permitting. The Colorado Suffrage Organization will meet again in January. Our goal is to persuade the legislature to call for a referendum on suffrage. From there, if we succeed, there will be a host of rallies and, hopefully, an appearance from Miss Anthony herself. For now, my husband has agreed to run a weekly column in the *Rocky Mountain News.*"

Sarah sipped at her brandy. At last, a group of women who took things seriously. She was so tired of undirected action. You couldn't get noticed if you didn't produce results. She leaned forward. "You sound so organized, so full of purpose. In Saint Louis, all we did was listen to speeches. A group appeared in local parades, but the ladies lacked a clear goal."

Elizabeth popped out of her chair, her face animated. "Well, we have some very active suffragists in Colorado. You know Mrs. McCook. Her husband, Edward, was the territorial governor. And then there's Eliza Thompson, her sister-in-law. Together, they lead the state suffrage movement."

Excitement leaped through Sarah. With the strong organization Elizabeth was describing, her efforts could truly make a difference. She would be able to do something important, be someone that mattered. She rose to join Elizabeth.

"What can I do?"

"Since we won't know about the referendum until January, things will be quiet these next few months. We're asking that everyone find other ways to make an impact. We're hopeful you'll speak on your position as telegrapher, a clear message to convey how capable women truly are."

Remembering how much more difficult Bates had made her goal, Sarah sighed. "I'm afraid I haven't felt very capable these past couple of days."

Elizabeth reached for Sarah's brandy snifter. "Bill mentioned you had a bit of a problem with Daniel Petterman." She moved across the room.

Sarah cringed. "You weren't kidding when you said there were no secrets, were you?"

"Heavens, no. I get to hear all the latest gossip first, even when I'm the object of it."

Sarah caught her easy smile but knew it belied a great deal of pain. Like everyone else in Denver, she'd heard all about last spring's incident with Hattie Sancomb. According to the rumors, Bill Byers had broken off an affair with Hattie only to have her appear on the street, firing at him with a revolver. Elizabeth herself had rescued her errant husband, but the scandal had cost him the Republican nomination for governor.

"It must be very difficult."

"There are difficulties in everything, my dear. Benefits and drawbacks fill every aspect of life. Here's your brandy, drink up." She grinned. "Being in the public eye isn't always easy, but it does have some positive associations. Where else would I be able to pursue so many different causes?"

"You're involved with more than suffrage?"

"Heavens, yes. I've been head of the Ladies Relief Society for years. We work to raise money for the underprivileged. I'm involved with several cultural organizations, and I firmly believe this city needs to be doing something about the problems caused by our rapid growth. Worthy endeavors abound."

"I guess I've been too focused on my career and suffrage."

"Oh, Denver has a host of problems, my dear, plenty for you to become involved with until the suffrage campaign begins in earnest. In addition to all those pompous men we have to deal with and our lack of rights, we have poor sanitation, runaway crime, abandoned children, destitute families, streets of vice, and gangs of hoodlums who shoot children's dogs."

Sarah's eyes widened. She'd seen the dog shootings first hand, but she hadn't realized there were so many other causes. "Are there efforts to correct all these problems?"

Elizabeth shook her head and sipped from her brandy. "Plenty of discussion, limited effort. What we need are more people willing to step forward and take leadership. I say, let's get women involved. Show the men we can make a difference, that it's about so much more than voting rights." She nodded at Sarah. "What about you? You've encountered at least one of the problems yourself. How do you feel about pushing our citizens to action?"

A small thrill crept through Sarah. Elizabeth Byers thought she had leadership potential. "What did you have in mind?" she asked, curious to hear more.

"I propose you could take on the dog issue. You watched those little girls lose their dog, after all. And you've met Daniel Petterman."

Sarah grinned at Elizabeth's tone. "I take it Daniel is one of the 'pompous men' you're referring to?"

"If anything is to be accomplished from that incident, Daniel Petterman needs to be put on the spot."

"Well, I certainly shook him up when I made him get on that horse behind me."

Elizabeth snorted, then covered her mouth. "Oh, my, I'll wager you did. I wish I'd been there to see it. Bill says Mr. Petterman's agreed to write a letter to the editor about the dogs, though."

"I'm sure it will be very polite and cautiously worded." It would be the dullest letter Bill Byers ever published.

"Which will get the cause nowhere. It'll die on the editorial page without stirring any response. You can't rally the public to action unless your initial effort enflames them. Daniel Petterman is clearly not capable of starting a fire under Denver's public. No, I don't think that is going to work."

Elizabeth was exactly right. Daniel's letter would stir no one. "Why bother with Daniel's letter at all? Perhaps your husband could write an article on what happened."

"Letters about real incidents have more power. People ignore general articles. They need their heartstrings pulled. They need the tears of little girls and the righteous anger of a father." Elizabeth's voice dropped. "Was he even angry?"

"Well, he *did* get a little incensed about it when pushed."

"He did?" She clasped her hands together, intent.

"Well, it took quite a bit of pushing, actually." Sarah wondered what was on her new friend's mind. She could just about see the wheels spinning in her head.

"But, he did get fired up?"

"Yes, but—"

"Then, we simply need to do it again." Elizabeth poured more brandy into their glasses and smiled at Sarah as though they were fellow conspirators.

"We? Don't look at me. I'm not going anywhere near the man. He's one step away from reporting me to the Kansas Pacific, and my new superior won't hesitate to have me fired if he does."

"Nonsense, my dear. Daniel hasn't the grit to raise enough of a stink to get anyone fired, and you know it. How about it, Sarah? You never answered me. Are you game to spur another cause? Will you lead us? Shall we get these bullies off the street and let children's dogs live in peace? Shall we find a sensible alternative to control the problem of wild dogs? Will you join us, Sarah Donovan, and show this town who you are, or will you sit by and watch the cause falter?"

Sarah stared at her. "Good heavens, Elizabeth, what do you want me to do?"

Elizabeth stared back, a smile twitching at the corners of her mouth. "I want you to help Petterman write that letter."

Chapter Four

The door to the coffin shop creaked open, sending late morning sun streaking across Daniel's desk. He glanced up, expecting a customer.

Instead, Sarah Donovan stood in the doorway, framed in the sunlight. "Elizabeth Byers says your letter won't work," she said. She held what appeared to be his letter to the editor in her hand and peered at him with that no-nonsense look of hers. "She thinks it could use a little polishing."

Daniel groaned. "What do you mean, Elizabeth thinks it won't work?"

"She thinks the message is flat." Sarah stepped farther into the coffin shop and closed the door behind her.

"Flat? It's a finely crafted letter." Daniel stood, more aggravated by the minute. Last night, he'd labored hours on the missive before having it delivered to Bill Byers. It irritated him that Bill's infernal busybody wife had seen fit to step into the middle of it. He sighed and shook his head. "What does Elizabeth have to do with it, anyway? It's Bill Byers's paper."

Sarah approached his desk as if he'd invited her. Her blond hair was pinned back in a strict style that emphasized her brusque manner. Her big violet eyes looked out of place, somehow too soft for a take-charge woman like her. "Bill Byers doesn't run that paper alone, and you know it. Elizabeth knows how to stir a cause."

God save him from demon women. Daniel took a step

forward, just to prove she wasn't in control of what happened in *his* place of business. "Are you implying that Bill Byers is a puppet?" he asked in an even tone.

"Of course not." She sounded irritated, as if she shouldn't need to explain. "What I'm saying is that Bill is a smart man. His wife has a tremendous sense of what it takes to rally the public. He'd be a fool if he didn't use her skills."

The idea intruded, making sense, however unpalatable. Daniel bristled. "So you think Bill runs every idea past his wife?"

"I think Bill uses Elizabeth's expertise when he thinks it will help his paper the same way she uses his when it helps her cause." Sarah's voice had risen, and she punctuated her words with quick hand movements, a habit Daniel found annoying.

He looked down at her tiny frame. Such vehemence from a little bird of a thing. He stood firm, hands on his hips, and fought against the smile that threatened to lift the corner of his mouth. She had gall, he had to give her that. "So now you're here to help me?"

"Daniel, read your letter." She thrust the envelope forward. "How does it make you feel?"

"Feel?" What was she getting at?

"Bill Byers wants a letter that will make his readers angry. He wants something that will make people pound their fists on the table and denounce the bounty." She slapped the envelope against the palm of her hand. "He wants people so upset that they get up out of their chairs and do something."

There she went again, blathering away. Daniel sighed a second time and drew a breath. "Look, I hardly think—"

She stomped her foot and glared at him. "That's the point."

Daniel's patience thinned, and he moved forward, heart pounding. "What gives you the right to march into my shop and insult me?"

"Seems to me as though the Bill of Rights gives all of us the right to insult anyone we want," she snapped.

"Sarah Donovan, you need a husband."

Her mouth dropped open and she blinked her eyes for a moment. "What?"

"You need a husband. You're far too free-mouthed, and I think it'd do you good to have someone issue you a little discipline." Daniel heard his voice, louder than he'd intended.

"Discipline? Like that code you live under? Little rules that keep you from experiencing life?" Her tone had risen as well, but she retained control, and it struck Daniel that she knew exactly what she was doing.

His annoyance turned to anger at the attack on his ordered code of conduct. "My life is none of your business."

She stepped closer. "You *have* no life."

"I have a fine life."

"I'm sure. You polish your coffins and lay out your dead and remind your daughters to behave when all they really need to do is be children."

The words stung. "Don't you dare bring my daughters into this."

She stepped even closer, toe-to-toe, and glared up at him. "And why not? Don't you realize what all that imposed self-control is doing to them? You're forcing them to grow up too soon. When was the last time they had any fun? They're so busy being perfect that they hold in their feelings. Do you realize they were so worried about appearances that they couldn't even grieve over Biscuit the way they needed to? They should have been sobbing their heads off instead of worrying about what you or anyone else would think."

Daniel fought to ignore the fire in his head. "Who the devil do you think you are?" he yelled.

Sarah smiled benignly. "See? Didn't that feel better?"

Good God, he'd yelled at her, cursed even. Daniel turned

away, embarrassed. He hadn't intended to do that, but it *had* felt good. That bothered him immensely. Losing control wasn't supposed to feel good.

He breathed deeply. He hated her words, hated them because they pricked at him, because he didn't want them to be even remotely true. Lashing out at the stab of guilt her accusation had provoked had been the only way he could deal with it. Such outbursts went against everything he'd always stood for, a forbidden self-indulgence that could lead to God knew what. Calming himself, he turned back to her and kept his voice level. "It felt like I lost control."

She nodded, her gaze softer than he'd ever seen it. "But just for a moment, you wanted to do something, didn't you? You reacted. That's what this letter should accomplish. It should make people angry enough to do something about the idiotic bounty. I can't do it alone, and you most assuredly aren't going to do it. Think how many people read the *Rocky Mountain News.* If even half of them step forward, that's a great many people spurred to action."

He knew she was right. Much as he hated to admit it, most of the world *did* respond to emotion. Pushed, even he resorted to reaction. She'd certainly proved that. Still, he liked his letter. It appealed to logic, not emotion. He glanced at the envelope, still clutched in her small hand, though it was considerably less crisp than it had been when she came in. "And now you want to rewrite this letter, so it makes people angry?"

"I don't intend to rewrite it, Daniel. I plan to help *you* rewrite it." She opened the envelope and unfolded the letter.

"It's perfectly fine as is," he hedged.

"It's too perfect. It doesn't incite change."

Daniel heaved another sigh. The woman was an aggravation, bent on leading him astray. "If I agree to this, you'll leave me alone? I won't have to listen to your half-baked comments about my character, and you'll quit insulting me?"

She shook her head with a smile that lit her entire face. "I speak my mind. I can't promise you won't be insulted by my comments, and I'm not about to start pussy-footing around because you can't handle the truth." She sobered. "I'm not enthusiastic about working with you, either. But I do want to get the community to stand against random killing of family pets. If that takes a few hours of your company, so be it."

Daniel glanced at her, his mind on the words she'd uttered earlier. He still wasn't sure if it was that she had insulted him or that there was a grain of truth in what she had said but, for some inexplicable reason, he needed her to know that he loved Kate and Molly; that he did the best he could for them.

"Sarah? I really do care about my girls. Don't slander my affection for them and don't question how I raise them. That isn't your business. Agreed?"

She nodded. "Agreed. But that doesn't mean you've changed my mind."

"I didn't think I had."

They stood in uncomfortable silence for a moment, then Sarah cleared her throat.

"Let's take a look at the letter, then," she said.

Daniel gestured to his desk and watched her move away. Her plain brown skirt was unflattering at best. Most women with coloring like hers wore soft hues. But, then, there was nothing soft about Sarah Donovan. He pictured her in strong colors, shades suitable to her attitude but wholly different from the faded brown. Good God, but she'd be striking.

"Oh, my."

He drew his attention back to the business at hand and peered over her shoulder. "What?"

Sarah stared at the letter, reading. "This letter is intended to serve as this writer's complaint about the current bounty being placed on local dogs?"

"Standard form. You can look it up in Hill's."

She turned, her eyes wide and disbelieving as she crumpled the letter. "You used a social and business form manual? No wonder it's formal."

Daniel threw up his hands. "Standard business form isn't correct?"

"Correct, but far too distant." She motioned for him to sit and waited for him to settle into the oak captain's chair. She drew his inkwell close and pulled out a fresh page of stationery. "Let's start with what happened. What went through your mind when you looked out that door and saw your daughters?"

He turned around in his chair. What did she *think* went through his mind? "I feared they'd been injured," he said, keeping his voice even.

"Well, yes," she sighed and rolled her eyes. "But what did you see? How did you feel? You flew out that door."

"I . . ." He stopped, unsure of how to describe his feelings.

"Say it," she commanded.

His mind replayed the scene, awakening the feelings he'd stored away, until the words tumbled out. "Blood. I saw Molly's dress soaked with blood, and I thought it was hers. I thought my little girl was going to die. All that blood. Good God, she had to be in pain. And then, I realized *she* was all right, and I thought it was Kate." He paused and turned back to the desk. "It all happened so quickly and was over and done with by the time I reached them."

"When the practical Daniel took over again?" There was no goading this time, just a simple statement of fact.

"That's right."

"So start the letter with that."

He shook his head. "Sarah, I can't share that with the entire population of Denver."

"Why not? Because it isn't correct to do so?" She tilted her head in challenge.

He pushed the paper away and slouched in the chair. "Emotions are personal."

Behind him, she stood silent. Then she slowly and deliberately rested her hands on his shoulders. "But don't you see? Those emotions are what elicit response. People think, 'My God, what if it were my children?' "

Heat from her hands penetrated his shirt. Daniel tried to ignore her touch. Her firm fingers squeezed, offering reassurance. But it wasn't the reassurance his mind rebelled against. He fought the instant defense that screamed against being touched so boldly by a woman and against the sudden jolt of attraction that poured through him.

He shrugged away from her hands and pushed back his chair, then stood and faced her. "I can't do this."

She tipped her head and caught his glance with her own. "You can," she insisted. "What if Molly had stepped in front of Biscuit, and what if I had brought her home in the wheelbarrow? What would you be feeling then?"

He shut his eyes and brought his hand to his mouth, hating it that she could stir up visions he didn't want to imagine. "Good God, Sarah."

"You need to open that letter with a description of what you saw and felt in those first few seconds. Tell them about the red blood on Molly's blue dress. Tell them about the tearstains on your daughters' faces. Tell them about Kate's shaky voice when she revealed that Biscuit was dead and that she and Molly had seen the whole thing. Let the readers feel the shock and fear and anger."

Daniel listened to the earnestness in her voice and knew she would have no trouble pouring out such thoughts. He gestured to the chair. "You write it."

She only stared up at him. "You need to write it. You're the one who felt it."

He shook his head and turned away from her. He couldn't. Such things were private, not meant to be shared with anyone, an indulgence in self-pride that would once have netted him a full day of meditation on his knees.

He knew Sarah was waiting. He shook his head again, unable to fully explain. "Writing that down in a letter the public is going to read goes against my rearing, against everything my father ever taught me. I can't."

"Your father must have been quite a man," she said, a challenge in her voice.

He turned on her sharply. "Oh, for Pete's sake. You make him sound like the devil himself. He was a good and pious man, who knew well the dangers of wallowing in the cesspit of emotions. He was the pillar of the community, the yardstick everyone measured themselves against."

"That's a pretty heavy responsibility," she countered.

"My father served as the one and only minister in Sutton, Indiana. His character was above reproach, and I'll thank you to quit using that tone when you refer to him."

They were face to face, Daniel not knowing where his vehement defense of his father had come from. He certainly hadn't felt that way growing up. Still, everyone had held the Reverend Ebenezer Petterman up as an example. He was right to defend him. He was.

Sarah lowered her gaze and took a deep breath. When she looked back up, her big eyes were once again empty of accusation. "Then I guess we'd best leave the subject." A beguiling smile filled her face. "But he sounds like a self-righteous stick-in-the-mud, if you ask me."

"I didn't ask you," he said softly. "Good God, Sarah, why do you dig so?"

"Why *don't* you?" Her eyes were luminous.

An overwhelming urge to touch her cheek coursed through him, then away. He knew he should move back, but didn't. "Enough. You are trying my temper."

"Really? I'd hardly noticed."

He hated her sassiness, and he loved it. Good God, what was she doing to him? "You write the letter."

She raised one blond eyebrow. "Your temper's showing."

"Write the blasted letter," he ordered, trying to escape from the emotions she was stirring.

Sarah's eyes widened even more, but she didn't back away,

Daniel felt as if he were drowning. She was too close, her eyes too captivating, his feelings too jumbled. He'd barely moved and all of a sudden she was in his grip, his mouth descending on hers in an impetuous kiss.

Her lips were soft and slightly parted in surprise.

He pulled away and stared into those big violet eyes.

Aw, hell. He hadn't meant to do that. He hadn't meant to do that at all.

Sarah slammed the cup of lukewarm coffee down on her desk and slumped forward, cradling her chin in her hands. The kerosene lamp's weak light cast an eerie glow over the cluttered telegraph office. She glanced at the clock. Lord, it was only two a.m., with hours yet to go before her new shift was over. Curse the men in her life for making things difficult.

She was tired and cranky and sick to death of kowtowing to Frank Bates and mollycoddling Daniel Petterman.

Or was it herself she was mollycoddling?

Sarah scowled at her coffee. Lord, not only was Daniel aggravating, but he was getting under her skin. She should have belted him across the face right then and there. And she would have . . . except . . . she couldn't.

She settled her head on her arms. It had happened so quickly, the heat of Daniel's strong hands on her upper arms, the sudden warmth of his body as he pulled her close, the surprising touch of his lips on hers. She'd felt that brief kiss to the tips of her toes. Even the memory of it brought goose bumps to her flesh.

She didn't slap him because she enjoyed it, and *that* bothered the daylights out of her.

The realization hit her hard. She'd spent the evening trying to convince herself that it was the shock that had immobilized her, or perhaps Daniel's surprised response, the confusion in his penetrating hazel eyes as he drew away from her. Daniel hadn't meant to kiss her any more than she'd meant to peruse his body after she rode double with him through the streets of Denver the other day. Her face grew hot with the memory. Something drew them together, and she didn't like it.

The man was maddening, with all his burdensome concern with decorum. How in the world did he ever accomplish anything productive? And his outdated and uninformed view on women irritated her to no end.

Yet he kept intruding into her thoughts.

He hadn't even looked her in the eye. He'd paced around the coffin shop with his hands stuffed uncomfortably into his trouser pockets, muttering his regrets and soliciting her forgiveness.

Even though they both knew the kiss wouldn't have happened without her prodding, she was sure of it.

She'd poked at his emotions, stood there and blatantly soothed his tight muscles, urged him to surrender to his feelings, put her face so close to his that they could feel one another's breath. She all but invited his kiss.

Maybe she should have hit him just to clear the air.

Except that she'd enjoyed it. It kept coming back to that.

In the end, he didn't say a word about her behavior. He simply shooed her out of the shop, refusing to work any further on the letter. He instructed her to write it herself, the way she wanted it, and to sign his name.

That was easier said than done. Her most recent draft of Daniel's letter stared up at her. She glanced at the paper on the desk and read the words. Frowning, she crumpled the page and tossed it across the room. It landed on the floor, near the stool, with the other five pages she'd started and discarded.

Sarah kicked the desk with her sturdy work shoe and cursed. Lord, wasn't it time yet for the next train to come through? She peered into the coffee cup, worst coffee she'd ever had.

No wonder Bates hadn't protested when she requested the transfer. Jim had done some checking, and it didn't look like Bates would be removed as primary op anytime soon. Jim had already filed an official protest and sent it on up the line. Bates's uncle held just enough company stock to make things complicated. But, as Jim told her, Bates would prove his own inadequacy, given time. It wouldn't take too long before the man hung himself. Meanwhile, Jim would put her on the night shift. She'd still get her secondary op time in and it would distance her from the errors Bates was sure to make.

But the late shift, or trick, was a miserable one. The wire stayed unbearably quiet, except for routing orders. The leftover coffee tasted like it had been there for days and the great empty depot resounded with eerie echoes. Sarah sighed into the silence, then crossed the small office and tossed the stale coffee out the window.

The signal lantern sat in the rail yard, where she'd forgotten it, beside the main switch. She grimaced and rotated her aching shoulders. Throwing the switches was by far the worst of the shift's duties.

As the sole employee on duty, she was now responsible for

both relaying the routing orders and carrying them out. The heavy levers of the siding switches were harder to push than she had anticipated. It took every ounce of her strength to move them. She'd be sore for days.

Sarah rubbed her eyes and returned to the desk. She might just as well write the letter and get it over with. Her thoughts scattered. Was Daniel sitting in his tidy white house behind the coffin shop, unable to sleep? Was he tossing in his bed? Maybe the kiss hadn't even bothered him.

She should have insisted that he write the dratted letter in the first place.

Men! Bates had delayed her rise to primary op by at least a month, and then Daniel had balked at writing the letter. How in the world was she ever going to get anything important done?

Sarah plopped into the chair and pulled out a fresh piece of paper while she thought over Daniel's clipped comments about his father. No wonder he was such a stick-in-the-mud. How could someone live his entire life within those narrow confines? How could he subject his daughters to the same stifling rules? It was time Daniel learned there was more to life than that coffin shop and his stuffy little world of self-denial.

How, heaven help her, was she going to keep Daniel involved with the cause if he wouldn't even write a letter?

He was so concerned about public appearances. If she could just force his hand a little. Smiling in spite of herself, Sarah dipped her pen into the inkwell and began the letter again.

Daniel Petterman was about to challenge the good citizens of Denver to join him at the next City Council meeting where he intended to make a public protest against the dog bounty.

Four days later, Sarah sat on a hard-backed chair near the front of the City Council gallery. The place was packed. Grim-faced parents filled the seats, muttering angrily about the bounty issue. At the rear, a group of grocers complained about the problems caused by the stray animals. A bespectacled doctor wandered in, nodding at those he knew. Since Daniel's letter to the editor had appeared, the *News* had published a flurry of ever more hostile letters on both sides of the issue.

Bill and Elizabeth drifted in, a triumphant smile gracing Elizabeth's elegant face. Bill's glance darted around the crowded room, no doubt taking note of who was present. They spotted Sarah and settled next to her.

"Where's Petterman?" Elizabeth asked.

Sarah shrugged her shoulders. "He hasn't made his appearance yet. Do you think he'll really show?"

Elizabeth nodded. "Without a doubt. That challenge was a stroke of brilliance, pure brilliance. Look at the response. And yes, Daniel will be here. He issued the call to action, after all, and a professional businessman can't go back on such a public statement." She lowered her voice to a whisper. "I just wish you could have written his speech, too."

"There's our man," Bill announced. He rose and gestured to Daniel.

Daniel glanced at the trio, his face filling with distaste.

"We've saved you a chair," Bill called with a wave.

Daniel moved across the room with reluctance. His hazel eyes bore into Sarah and she was glad for the buffer of the crowd.

Pumping Daniel's hand, Bill made short work of introductions. "My wife, Elizabeth—I call her Libby." He gestured to the women. "And you already know Sarah Donovan."

Daniel curled his lip and Sarah held back a smile. Lord, he was angry.

"Unfortunately, yes," Daniel replied. "How do you do, Mrs. Byers?"

"Oh, please." She waved her hand dramatically. "Call me

Elizabeth. Bill, move over. You'll have a better view next to the aisle. Daniel can sit next to Sarah."

Daniel stood stone-faced as the newspaperman and his wife shifted to the right. He took the empty chair, then glared at Sarah. "You have some nerve," he whispered.

Sarah batted her eyes at him and smiled innocently. "I?"

Daniel's face darkened and he leaned toward her. "You overstepped your bounds, Sarah, and you know it."

"And you overstepped yours." She let the statement sink in, refusing to take all the blame, even if it was deserved. Besides, it was a good enough excuse. She'd be hog-tied if she'd reveal her true reasons to him. "I don't think I was quite clear about that the other day. This should clarify things nicely, I should think." She gave him a smug smile.

"Is that what this is all about? Good God, Sarah, I apologized."

Elizabeth peered at them, her eyebrows raised.

Sarah kept her voice low. "Yes, you did. But I forgot to slap you. I figured this would be a good substitute punishment."

"Punishment?" Daniel whispered, incredulous. "Oh, now, that's low. I would have thought you a bit more open-minded."

"I am. I just thought that a backward thinking man such as you might misinterpret my tolerance. I didn't want you to assume a lack of morals on my part."

"Oh, for God's sake." He threw up his hands in a helpless gesture.

"Have you ever noticed how often you curse around me?"

"That's it, right there, around *you.*" He was pointing now, more animated than he'd been in their previous discussion. "You can ask anyone in this room if they've ever heard me speak that way before, and they'll tell you it isn't my habit. You have this uncanny ability to make me do things I do not do."

Sarah glanced around the room, realizing others were beginning to stare. She dropped her voice again. "And if you quit feeling guilty about doing them, you'd realize it makes you feel better to say what you mean and be done with it."

"Just because you say anything that pops into your head doesn't mean we all have to." The words came out in a hiss.

"I'll have you know that most of the time I give a great deal of thought to my words before I say them." She straightened and smoothed her dark-green skirt.

In front of the room, the city councilmen were entering and taking their seats.

Sarah leaned toward Daniel, tossing him one last challenge. "Speaking of thoughtful words, I'm quite sure you have a stirring speech planned for the folks tonight."

"Hmph," was all he said.

"Shush," Elizabeth admonished. "It's time."

The audience murmured quietly as the councilmen went about their business. Coughs and sneezes filled the air as they moved down the agenda. A few seats away, a lady with a baby stood and left the room, the odor of the infant's soiled diaper lingering in their wake. Elizabeth pulled a packet of lemon drops from her purse and passed them down the row. Daniel popped one into his mouth. Sarah smiled at the pucker that appeared on his face as he sucked on what was likely a forbidden treat.

"We now move to our final item of business. The Council has received a petition requesting repeal of the dog-bounty statute. Are there public comments at this time?" The chairman tapped his gavel, silencing the muttering crowd.

The petition had been an unexpected godsend, lending more legitimacy to the public outcry. Sarah wasn't sure if Elizabeth had played a role in instigating the action or not, but she was pleased nonetheless.

Daniel sank into his chair and Sarah leaned toward him. "Your public is waiting."

He frowned at her.

"What if it had been Molly or Kate in the wheelbarrow, Daniel? What if those boys had shot your child? All that blood. Would she have lain there, suffering, calling for her daddy? Could I have kept her alive until I pulled that wheelbarrow, dripping blood all the way down the street, to your house? Would you have held her lifeless body in your arms only to carry her inside and make her coffin with your own hands?"

"Good God," he muttered as he stood and waited to be recognized.

The City Council Chairman nodded at him solemnly. "State your name and address for the record."

Sarah crossed her hands and waited for Daniel to begin, hoping he was stirred up enough to deliver a rousing speech.

Daniel cleared his throat and introduced himself, then closed his eyes and drew a breath. "Last week, my daughters trudged into my front yard, blood covering their usually neat dresses. It was enough to pull me to their sides immediately. My first thoughts centered on them. Were they hurt? What had happened? By the time their protector explained that it was their beloved dog, Biscuit, whose blood covered their clothes, my concern had turned to anger. Those of you who know me know that I am not a man given to displays of emotion. But I tell you now that I was scared and I was angry. What kind of law encourages ruffians to kill family pets and endanger this community's children? Has the City of Denver sunk so low?"

Silence reigned as his words hit home, then shattered as he sat and one after another in the audience vied for attention.

Elizabeth patted his arm and offered her praise while Bill nodded his assent.

Daniel slouched in the chair and closed his eyes.

Sarah granted him his peace. Lord, he looked overwhelmed. What came so easily for her must have been a monumental effort for him. She'd pulled off her letter assignment well and, despite her worries, he hadn't muffed it. Elizabeth would make sure the local suffrage leaders knew of her abilities. Next time, they would offer a bigger assignment, one she could carry out easily, without involving anyone else.

What's more, Daniel had done the unexpected. He'd stood up and voiced his opinion with fire and determination. It was a good first step. She hoped he'd gained from it, that he'd be able to take it home and apply it with his girls.

She concentrated on the debate. There was much more to the issue than she'd realized. One of the grocers was telling the crowd about the number of times the strays had gotten into his produce when a red-faced butcher jumped up and added his complaints. There *was* a problem with dogs in the city; that was clear. One of the physicians even pointed out the health hazards of so many loose animals.

By now, Daniel sat quietly listening and Sarah wondered what he was thinking. He nodded from time to time, his brow wrinkled in thought.

The audience was growing restless. There were points made from all corners. People were tiring and tempers grew short. Twice the chairman had to bang his gavel and call for order.

Daniel glanced at her. To Sarah's surprise, he stood.

"I've listened to all of you as you've added your insights to my concerns and learned a few things. It seems clear that Denver has a problem with strays. I'll concede that we need to address the problem and that we need to continue to round up the strays from the city streets. I remain unconvinced, however, that offering a bounty for any dog brought in is the best way to address the problem. I'd like to call for the appointment of a committee to explore alternatives."

Elizabeth started the applause. Sarah sat in amazement, then joined in.

"Excellent idea, Mr. Petterman, excellent idea. I hereby establish said committee and appoint Daniel Petterman to serve as its chair. Mr. Byers, will you serve?"

Bill Byers nodded his agreement as other appointees were named. Elizabeth leaned toward him, whispering.

Daniel glanced at Sarah, uncertainty in his expression.

"You can do it," she told him.

He sat, wearily. "I'm not so sure."

"From here on out, it's as simple as managing a meeting. You won't even need to push people."

"I guess you got even, all right, huh?"

"Guess I did," she said quietly. "Now we can go our own separate ways."

A few chairs down, Bill was standing. "Mr. Chairman," he said. "In the interest of being fair to everyone in the community, I'd like to call for the appointment of a few women to the committee. My wife Elizabeth has generously offered her services, and I'd also like to nominate our female telegrapher, Sarah Donovan."

"Point well taken, Mr. Byers. Ladies, consider yourselves appointed."

Sarah caught Elizabeth's triumphant grin and saw the move for what it was, an effort to more actively involve women, a further weapon in the suffrage arsenal, a way to show the men of Denver that women could contribute politically.

Beside her, Daniel ran his hand through his hair. "Oh, God, not again."

Sarah grimaced. Daniel Petterman had a way of messing up her plans. The last thing she needed was his mule-headed concern for decorum getting in the way of her political action.

"You just run the meeting, Daniel, that's it. Don't jump in, don't get involved, don't even join the discussions."

Bewilderment flashed across his face. "But, Sarah, I think I rather like this involvement you've shoved upon me. People actually respect it. I'm going to do this, Sarah, and you're going to show me how."

Sarah dropped her head into her hands. Would she never be rid of the man?

Chapter Five

The events of past week had surprised Daniel more than he thought possible. Whistling, he gathered embalming fluid, a bottle of M. & L. Flesh Tint, and a collection of bulbs and syringes from the cupboard, then headed into the small rear room of the coffin shop to begin his day's work.

He'd mulled that regrettable kiss over in his mind for several days before finally settling on a shaky conclusion. It happened, it was no one's fault, and he wasn't going to feel guilty about it anymore.

The unexpected decision left him feeling rebellious.

That night it had happened, guilt had made sleep difficult. A lifetime of imposed self-restraint told him his actions were ungentlemanly, improper, and immoral. He couldn't decide what bothered him the most—the impulsive loss of control, the act itself, or his pleasure at the softness of Sarah's lips.

At one point, he tried to justify the kiss by telling himself Sarah had asked for it. She'd pushed at him to let his emotions take control, after all. But deep down, he knew that was no excuse. Sarah hadn't behaved seductively. Even her shoulder massage had been innocent, despite how it made him feel.

Then, after he read that damned letter in the paper, he tried to convince himself she'd plotted his downfall. Yet he survived the meeting and had discovered a thing or two in the process.

First, there was Sarah herself, or, more to the point, her view on the kiss. She sat there and lectured him about his behavior all the while smiling and batting her eyes until he finally realized that she wasn't truly insulted. He suspected she was more pleased by his impulsiveness than angry. He should have expected as much from a suffragist. And if she didn't care, why the devil should he beat himself up about it?

Then, there was his speech. Sarah and her perky little challenges had goaded him into voicing feelings he hadn't wanted to reveal. Yet no one considered it the least improper that he'd shared them with a room full of people. In fact, they'd applauded him and made him chairman of a committee.

He'd sinned several times over and no one had been harmed. The world did not look upon him with horror and distaste. He'd garnered respect and he was accomplishing good.

It all made feeling guilty a pretty big waste of time.

He'd made his peace with his impulsivity, forced his father's voice to be silent on the matter.

"Papa?"

At his daughter's searching voice, Daniel glanced up. "In here, Molly." He moved to shield the body he'd been working on from her view.

She entered the back room of his shop and peered at him with wide eyes. "You were whistling. I thought we weren't supposed to—"

"We're not," he confirmed. Had he really been whistling? It was an old habit, long abandoned at his father's insistence.

"Then why are you?"

Now how in the dickens did she expect him to answer that when he hadn't even known he was doing it? Sometimes his daughters, especially Molly, vexed him. He shrugged and offered a weak excuse. "I decided to break the rule."

Molly's eyes widened again. "You did? But, we're not supposed to break the rules."

"No, Molly, we're not." He set the embalming syringe on the

table and peered at her. "Is there something you wanted?"

"Oh! I'm supposed to tell you Mr. Byers is waiting in the parlor."

"Thank you, Molly. I'll be right in."

She scampered back into the house while Daniel turned, injected the last of the fluid, and covered the body. He wished more families would allow him to embalm. He was convinced the technique was the way of the future and a solid step ahead in the preservation of bodies. Still, many remained skeptical.

Wiping the ill-smelling liquid from his hands, he left the room and moved to the front of the shop, wondering what Bill was doing in the parlor. The carefully lettered "will return" sign hung on a small nail next to the doorframe. He reached for it, noticing that the "closed" sign still hung in the window. He'd never even opened up. No wonder Bill had gone to the house.

He replaced the sign and retraced his steps, through the two-room addition that comprised his business shop, and into the parlor of the house itself.

Bill Byers sat on a neat but well-used sofa, flanked by Kate and Molly. Mrs. Winifred stood in the kitchen doorway, shaking her gray head at the trio. Molly's tiny china tea set decorated the table in front of the sofa.

Goodness, he hadn't seen that tea set for ages. His wife, Mary, had bought it for the girls just before she died, some five years ago. He didn't recall them ever playing with it in the time since. He'd forgotten they even had it.

Bill held a dainty hand-painted teacup between his thumb and forefinger. He grinned at Daniel and raised the cup.

"May we offer you some tea, Papa?" Kate asked in her best grown-up voice. Her hazel eyes glistened with pride.

"Why, thank you, Kate. It was thoughtful of you and Molly to serve tea to Mr. Byers." Daniel settled into a chair while she poured a second cup, then accepted it on its fragile saucer.

"Of course, we served tea. A good hostess always offers tea. I'm sorry we have no crumpets."

Molly nodded her brown curls in solemn agreement. "Besides, I never get to use my tea set otherwise."

The innocent comment hit Daniel squarely in his gut.

When was the last time Kate and Molly had played with other children? They should be having tea parties with other little girls, not entertaining their father's guests.

Daniel drained his rapidly cooling tea. On the sofa, Bill handed his cup to Kate with a satisfied sigh, his eyes twinkling. Molly collected Daniel's cup and saucer, placed them on the tiny silver tray, and beamed at her sister. Kate nodded. The girls stood primly and carried the tea set into the kitchen.

"Lovely girls, Daniel, very mature," Bill praised.

Perhaps more mature than they should be, Daniel thought. Hadn't Sarah said much the same thing? He shook his head to clear the thought and leaned forward. "Thanks, Bill. What brings you away from the paper?"

"Planning, my good man, planning. I wanted to get a grasp on your vision for the committee. Have you any bright ideas in mind?"

Daniel nodded, more assured than he'd been the last time Bill had been around to prod him. "My mind has been reeling with ideas."

Bill raised his eyebrows. "And?"

"I think what's most important here is finding a way to compromise. I listened to the comments at that City Council meeting. Denver has a problem here, one of many. Stray dogs are a nuisance to business owners and private homeowners alike. They are also creating a sanitation problem. They become wild and pose a physical danger. All of that impacts the whole community and threatens the children. It's clear that we need to do something to reduce or eliminate these strays."

"Well said."

Daniel released a deep breath. "But offering a dead-or-alive bounty is encouraging hoodlums to shoot dogs without regard to ownership or safety. We need to find another method to solve the first problem or we've only created a second one."

"I thoroughly agree." Bill stood, his eyebrows furrowed in thought. He turned back to Daniel and anticipation lit his face. "What do you propose the committee do?"

Daniel rose, knowing Bill had likely figured out the answer for himself already. "We need ideas, lots of ideas." He stated the obvious. "Our first meeting should consist of just that. We need to explore all options. List every conceivable idea then pick each one of them apart until we've examined the good and the bad related to each. Once we've done that, we pick the best of the bunch, refine it, and present it to City Council."

Bill shook his head and chuckled. "I never would have thought it."

"Thought what?"

"That you would come up with a plan like that. You've got to admit it's not your usual style."

Daniel chewed at his bottom lip. It felt good, taking an unexpected step, stating what he felt. He'd always assumed the only respectable way of doing things was the one his father had dictated. "Maybe I'm coming to learn there's more than one way to skin a cat. I didn't look for this appointment and never would have placed myself here. But, it seems the fairest, most efficient method, as well as a thoroughly dignified way to get things done, much to my surprise."

"And you're not angry about my suggestion to include Sarah Donovan?" Bill crossed his arms and grinned.

"She's a shrewd woman." Daniel shrugged his shoulders. "Combine her with your wife's insight on how to get those ideas into action and we've probably got the most powerful committee we could ever hope to have. A week ago, I'd have dismissed both of them. But, now, I'm seeing things a little differently."

Bill laughed. "Tut tut, do we have a burgeoning suffrage supporter?"

"Hah!" The thought made Daniel shudder. "I might listen a little closer but I wouldn't let either one of those manipulating females anywhere near a ballot box."

"Speaking of my dear wife, she'd like me to offer our house as the site of the first committee meeting."

"Sounds fine. I'll need to arrange for Mrs. Winifred to stay with the girls. Did Elizabeth set a date and time?"

"She said to tell you to plan for dinner on Friday evening, seven o'clock. She'll take care of the invitations."

Dinner? Daniel let the suggestion settle. It sounded more like a social event than a meeting. What was Bill's wife trying to finagle this time? He shook the thought off. There was nothing improper about meeting over dinner. Dinner at the Byerses' would be a highly respectable affair.

"Took it for granted I'd agree, didn't she?"

Across the room, Bill sobered. "Elizabeth takes nothing for granted, Daniel."

Daniel's thoughts drifted to Sarah and the surprises a formal dinner might offer. Maybe. As long as no one took anything for granted.

Nodding, he signaled his agreement to the idea, then sealed it. "Then she might make sure Miss Donovan knows she should dress for dinner. Have Elizabeth lend her something if she has to. Otherwise, she'll show up in that ugly work skirt again."

"I'm sorry I had to call you in like this, Sarah. You want I should boil up another pot of coffee?"

Sarah stifled a yawn and smiled weakly at Jim. She was more

than a little sorry herself. The long sleep-filled morning she'd looked forward to had vanished with Jim's summons. Still, it was good to be back on day shift. She wondered if Bates could be fired for failing to show up. She yawned widely and thought about Jim's offer, then shook her head. "More coffee I could use but I think maybe *I'll* boil it up this time."

Jim grinned and had the good grace to look chagrined. "That bad?"

" 'Fraid so." She dumped the old coffee then filled the pot with fresh water from the pail near the door. She ground a handful of beans and added the new grounds, then placed the pot on the small iron stove in the corner. Eying the growing pile of messages in the delivery basket, she wondered if she'd get stuck distributing them, too.

Jim caught her glance. "The new boy's a little slow but he should be back soon." He paused, then issued a benevolent smile. "I sure do miss having you around here, girl. There's more than one good reason I didn't willingly put Bates on as primary op. The man might have the experience, but he sure makes a mess out of the wires and he ain't particularly neighborly. Wouldn't even have put him on as delivery man if I hadn't been forced to."

Sarah couldn't agree more but she figured it would be best to keep her opinions to herself. "Where is he, anyway?"

Jim shrugged his shoulders. "Haven't a clue. The man gets more worthless every year." He paused and shook his head. "Time was, he wanted to take on the world. He just never had the skill to do it, I guess. I hear he lost every job he's had up to now, and I still don't know how he passed his primary op test. Probably why he resents you so much."

"Because it comes easy to me?"

"Yep." Jim pushed at his glasses. "I imagine he'll throw another fit when the brownies get tossed into his file, but I'm going to toss 'em just the same. Far as I'm concerned, failure to report for duty ought to be enough to release him from his position. The superintendent is going to hear about this, you can count on it. I'm running everything through his office, just to be safe."

Sarah nodded, knowing Jim hated the administrative layers that existed because of Bates and his uncle. Despite being the stationmaster, his decisions were no longer independent. Without the superintendent's approval, he left himself open to Bates's insinuations. But running things up the ladder often delayed action for days at a time.

"You sure you can handle doing a double shift?"

"I told you before, you can count on me. Besides, it's good to have more to do than simply listen to the depot groan all night, especially since I don't have to throw any switches."

Jim's face paled. "Wish you didn't have to do that." He frowned and moved back to his own stool at the ticket counter. Unexpected silence drifted through the station as he sorted through ticket stubs.

Sarah checked the logbook, comparing Bates's scribbles to her own careful penmanship. Jim should have the superintendent go through the log. Some of the entries were almost illegible. The dispatcher would have a fit if he saw them.

Her slender finger ran down the page, stopping as she came upon gaps in the record. Several times, she noted that he'd neglected to indicate whether or not wires had been delivered. If that kept up, Western Union would take their business elsewhere. He'd even forgotten to record a signal order.

"Jim? Have you seen the log?"

"Sent word up the line yesterday. Shame, isn't it? You get a bad apple and you can't even toss him out unless you jump through the hoops like a circus dog."

Sarah nodded and set the book aside.

"Noticed your log entries are pretty sparse. You ain't just sitting all night? You practicing like I told you to?"

It was common for night operators to send private messages back and forth, in between official wires. Most were petty correspondences, meant only to keep the fingers active and the ear well trained. Still, it was good practice, and she'd already discovered she needed to work on her translation skills. Some of the operators were rough, but a primary op had to be able to decipher their messages as well as those sent by the more precise operators. "It's tough to get used to."

"Yeah, but it's about the only way anybody on the late trick can get any finger work in."

Sarah thought about last night's messages, each a mystery in itself, signed with an operator's sine, or identifying code. She'd go over them later, searching out her errors. "It just seems strange to be exchanging personal wires with folks I don't even know," she said.

"Yep, that's true. But it'll keep you busy for hours, if you find somebody as bored as you are. As long as the KP don't mind, keep firing those messages away. Keeps the fingers nimble, and you're going to need that to make primary op."

"You know they've all figured out which one is me by now."

"Figured they would." He nodded. "Don't take too long to link your sine with Denver and Denver with 'that female op.' Pretty soon, they'll know you just by your tapping pattern, too. They giving you any trouble?"

Sarah grinned. "I had two proposals last night."

"Marriage proposals?" Jim pushed his spectacles up and peered at her with curiosity.

"Not exactly." Leaving Jim to sort out her meaning, she turned to the wire and began to record an incoming message. She picked out a distinctive tapping and recognized the operator. "It's from Bean," she announced with pride. Recognition of her fellow operators by their unique styles was the first mark of primary op skill.

The message finished, she recorded it and handed it to Jim, instructions for the next siding. He rose from his stool, then headed out the door to pass it on to the men in the yard.

Sarah smiled as she watched him through the window. She definitely liked the day shift better. Pouring herself a cup of freshly brewed coffee, she returned to her counter. The first cup wasn't the best either, but it sure beat that day-old paste she'd dumped earlier.

Jim reentered the station, pushing at his glasses. "You never said how things are going on the suffrage front."

"Slow. Things are pretty much at a standstill until the legislature's decision in January. The upper echelons are handling all the meetings with them, so I've been focusing on other things for a while."

She tidied the counter as Jim watched.

"Heard you got yourself nominated to a committee the other night," he prompted.

Sarah turned in exasperation. "Elizabeth Byers got me nominated. I'm not too thrilled about it myself."

Jim frowned. "Why, a committee sounds like just the place you'd want to be."

"Not that one."

"A little testy about it, are you?" he observed as he found his stool.

Sarah sighed. She still didn't like the idea of serving on a committee with the monster she'd created. Daniel had been easier to work with when he'd been predictable. That infernal kiss and his new enthusiasm threw her off balance.

She glanced at her friend and decided to confide in him. "Elizabeth wanted me to get involved in local politics, her strategy for demonstrating the capabilities of women. She gave me an assignment, I carried it out, and now I'm stuck on a committee I don't want to be on, and if I don't give it my all, I'll fail. Yes, I'm a little testy."

Jim turned at the sharpness in her voice and set his hands on his lap. "What's eating at you, girl?"

She pulled in a breath and slowly let it out. "Daniel Petterman."

Jim nodded solemnly. "Ah."

"Ah?" she choked out. She should have kept her mouth shut. "What's that supposed to mean?"

"Nothing." He turned back to the ticket counter and reached for his coffee cup.

Sarah stood and crossed the room, her shoes clicking all the way. "Now wait just one danged minute. When a person says 'ah' in that tone of voice, it isn't nothing."

Jim ignored her temper. "You got some problem with Petterman?" he queried.

Sarah fought to stay calm. Jim was clearly baiting her. She refused to be drawn into an argument about Daniel, and she certainly was not about to admit that there was more bothering her than business. She smoothed her faded work skirt with her hands and picked up Jim's coffee cup. "Only that I assigned his corpse to another undertaker and ended up with a few brownies in my file. You know that as well as I do."

Jim was momentarily silent as she turned to the stove and filled his cup. "Riding double down Broadway Avenue don't have anything to do with it, then?" he finally asked.

"Of course not," Sarah snapped.

"Heard you two were whispering together the whole City Council meeting, too."

"We were not."

"Seem to recall readin' it in the paper."

"No!" She turned away from the stove with an audible

swoosh. Hot coffee splashed over the edge of the cup and she shook her fingers to cool them. "It wasn't!"

"Yep, it was." Jim grinned.

She marched to Jim's counter and plunked down the coffee cup. "Why, of all the low-down, dirty, rotten little—"

"Bill Byers ain't above a little juicy gossip."

"I'll throttle him," she announced.

"He make it up?" Jim peered over his glasses.

"No."

"Then why make a fuss? You raise a stink and I'd wager Bill'll do it again."

Sarah sat down on her stool and crossed her arms. "You're right." Jim's grin annoyed her. She leaned forward and waved her finger at him. "But just so it's clear, I'm not having anything more to do with Petterman than necessary. One or two quick meetings and that's it."

"Same go for his girls?"

"What?" What did his girls have to do with anything?

Jim nodded at the window. "His daughters are about halfway across the rail yard, and I doubt they're looking for me." He stared pointedly at Sarah. "Third time this week they've been here."

Sarah's thoughts scattered, as she remembered the last time she'd encountered Kate and Molly and the trouble it had led to. "Oh, Lord. Just what I need."

She spun back to her counter, wishing that she could somehow fade into her work. Behind her, she heard the light clatter of their footsteps and knew wishing was useless. Putting a sunny smile on her face, she turned toward the door. She'd greet them, exchange pleasantries, and send them on their way.

Molly and Kate stood just inside the threshold.

Kate took the lead, her hazel eyes bright and hopeful. "Miss Sarah, you're here."

Not to be outdone, Molly stepped forward. "We almost didn't come. Mr. Bates was cross with us last time."

Sarah's resolve crumbled. What had Bates said? They were only children, after all. "Mr. Bates is cross with everyone," she sympathized.

The girls nodded wordlessly.

Jim slipped from his stool and crossed into the station's waiting area.

Sarah stared at the girls, at a loss.

"We've come to watch you telegraph again," Kate supplied.

"Oh, well, it's mostly just the same thing."

"Well, *I* think it's exciting. We don't know any other ladies who do it." The eleven-year-old's facial expression was filled with awe.

"Kate, we don't know any other ladies. 'Cept for our teachers and Mrs. Winifred, and I'm not sure she counts."

Sarah looked at the girls questioningly.

"She's our housekeeper," Kate explained.

"She's cross, too."

"Molly!"

"Well, she is."

Sarah listened with interest. They'd been more reserved on their last visit. She found their enthusiasm refreshing. Perhaps Daniel hadn't ruined them yet. Still, she wasn't quite comfortable being the object of Kate's adoration. She smiled and decided to try again. "I'm not sure you girls should—"

"Aw, take 'em in and let them watch a bit," Jim interjected from across the waiting area. "Long as they don't interrupt your work, I don't care."

Sarah glared at Jim. "But your father—"

"Oh, he's so busy putting 'balming fluid in some dead lady that he won't think of us for hours."

"Molly," Kate chastised.

Sarah stifled a giggle at the image and felt herself caving in. "Well, I guess if Jim doesn't mind, you may sit and watch. I'll get another stool." She busied herself with clearing a crate from the extra seat and moving it close to her counter. The girls removed their hats and gloves and climbed onto the stools, chattering all the while.

"So how come you haven't been here?"

"Molly, please phrase things properly." Kate stared at her sister with a stern scowl of reproach.

Molly puckered her face into a frown, then continued properly. "*Why* haven't you been here?"

Sarah fought a grin. "Oh, well, I've been working the late shift. I'm here at night when you're at home sleeping."

"Except for today."

She nodded. "Mr. Bates couldn't be here today so Jim asked me to work an extra shift."

"Gosh, doesn't it get lonely at night?" Molly's brown eyes were wide and curious.

"Yes, Molly, it does indeed."

"How come—why—do you have to be here at night? Isn't everyone asleep?"

My, but she was full of questions. Sarah turned and placed her hands in her lap. She might as well forget about getting anything worthwhile done. "There are still the railroad telegraphs," she explained. "Sometimes, there are two trains that need to use the same track. The telegraphers let each other know so one of the trains can be routed to a siding. Otherwise, the trains would crash."

"Gosh, I guess you must be the most important person we know, huh, Kate?" Molly slid off her stool and wandered around the office while Kate sat at prim attention.

"I'm going to mosey around the baggage room, see if anyone's noticed that darned delivery boy," Jim called, then disappeared through the door at the end of the waiting area.

"What are these, Miss Sarah?"

Sarah glanced over her shoulder. Molly stood in front of a wooden shelf, her gaze focused on Sarah's stack of personal messages.

"Those?" she queried, wishing Molly would move on.

"Do you need us to fold them up so they can be delivered like you were doing the last time we were here? We could help," Kate offered politely.

"I'm sure you could. That stack, however, was just for practice."

Molly reached for the top sheet. "Who's Lark?"

Sarah sighed and decided she'd better put the messages away before Molly got any nosier. Perhaps the girls were a little too enthusiastic this time. "That's my persona, my sine. All the telegraphers use a special name to identify themselves."

"Big John sounds sweet on you."

Sarah strode the last few steps to Molly. "Give me those," she commanded.

Molly surrendered the papers and gazed up at Sarah. "Are you sweet on him, too?"

Sarah sighed. "I don't even know who the man is."

"Then why does Molly think he's sweet on you?" Kate chimed in.

Sarah stared at her, flustered. "I don't know. Maybe because he found out that I was a woman and he thinks I have loose morals because I'm a telegrapher."

"But how come you saved his letters if you aren't sweet on him?"

"Because I need to go back through them and look for any decoding errors I made." Sarah tossed the papers into a drawer, slammed it shut, and turned back to the girls. "Are you sure your father isn't looking for you?"

They shook their heads and Molly clambered back up onto her stool.

"That was a pretty big stack of letters, Miss Sarah," Kate noted, then paused. "Are those all from beaux?"

"They are not my beaux," Sarah snapped.

"How come they like you so much?"

She looked from one to the other. "Molly, Kate, I am not going to discuss this with you. You are prying into things that don't concern you."

They both sobered. Kate's hazel eyes, so like Daniel's, blinked solemnly. "I'm sorry, Miss Sarah."

"Me, too," Molly added, her voice wavering. "Are you going to tell Papa?"

Guilt drifted through her. She hadn't meant to make them feel bad. Lord, but talking to children was difficult. She offered a reassuring smile. "No, I won't tell your papa."

"Is Papa your beau?"

"Molly!"

"Girls, that is enough." Sarah's hands flew to her hips. "I don't have a beau, and I don't *want* to have a beau. Even if I did, it would not be of concern to either of you. We are no longer going to discuss the topics of my correspondence or my personal relationships."

The girls' eyes pooled with tears as Sarah's words hit home.

A deep "Ahem," interrupted.

Sarah spun around at Bates's familiar voice, willing the girls to stay quiet.

"I think you ought to be discussing both of those things with Jim. Seems a good station manager would want to know what his night telegrapher is doing with her time."

"Well, the long lost Frank Bates," she parried. "What brings you to work?"

"I got called away. Had a meeting, you might say." He curled his lip at her. "Wish I'd a known about all your little affairs before I seen my uncle. Guess that's the sorta thing that happens when you put a woman on the night shift."

How long had he been standing there listening? Sarah fought to stay calm. Lord, how it must have sounded.

"Mr. Bates, I can assure you—"

"You ain't gonna assure me nothin', missy. Looks to me you got a mess of trouble, kids hangin' around a place of business, a stack of telegrams that ain't been delivered, and an even bigger stack of illicit messages."

Sarah fought against telling him to go to hell. "The children were about to leave," she announced in a professional tone. She handed them their hats and gloves. "Furthermore, the delivery boy is missing. The 'stack' consists of practice messages."

Bates scowled. "Just what are you practicing here all alone at night?"

"I don't like your implication, Bates." She ushered Kate and Molly quickly out the back door, then turned back to Bates.

He raised his eyebrows with a smirk. "And I don't like what I been hearin' from the other ops."

"I don't know what you're talking about, Bates. I haven't done anything to be ashamed of."

"Word is your 'favors' are for sale."

"What?" Sarah asked, incredulous. "That is the most ludicrous thing I've ever heard. Who told you that?"

"It ain't a matter of who told me, missy. It's a matter of who *I've* told."

Chapter Six

The next morning, Sarah stood in front of the beveled oval mirror in Elizabeth Byers's guest room, tugged at the neckline of the bright lavender gown, and wrinkled her nose.

"Oh, stop it," Elizabeth chided. "You look fine."

"I look all trussed up. I'm almost falling out of this thing. My shirtwaist and work skirt are fine."

Elizabeth dropped her face into her hands, took a deep breath, then lifted her head tiredly. "Your work skirt is not fine. It's a work skirt."

"Isn't it bad enough that you've turned the committee into a dinner party? I don't need to look like a strumpet." Sarah turned from the mirror and glanced at the mound of satin and faille and crepe de Chine. She didn't want to do this. She didn't want to have dinner and she didn't want to abandon her comfortable, no-nonsense clothing. She pulled at the bodice again and shook her head at the pile. "Ruffles and lace? No, thank you."

"Fashion is a tool of power."

Sarah bit her lip, memories clouding her mind. She'd had the same discussions with Miriam and Lise, back in Saint Louis. It had never made a difference. Being beautiful and fashionable had netted her mother nothing but heartache. Men, even her father, had complimented her then dismissed her from their discussions as nothing more than what they saw. Sarah crossed her arms and offered Elizabeth a half-hearted smile in lieu of sharing the remembrances. "I'd prefer to rely on my skills."

Elizabeth plopped onto the bed and raised her eyebrows at Sarah. "Used in the right way, femininity can be an asset, sometimes even a shrewd advantage."

"Hah. Just *being* female gets me into trouble, let alone being feminine."

Elizabeth's face clouded. "Is it the ruffles and lace or is it something else? If you yank that bodice up any higher, you'll rip the ruffles right off of it. I wouldn't have thought you a prude, yet here you are trying like the devil to hide your cleavage. What's going on here, Sarah?"

Sarah sighed and sat down next to her friend. Truth be told, even if she liked low-cut gowns, Frank Bates and his innuendoes begged more modest attire. She suspected Elizabeth would be more satisfied with that explanation, anyway. "The male telegraph operators are speculating about my morals. They can't believe a woman would be an op unless she were depraved."

"Oh, dear."

"They've begun wiring suggestive offers and Frank Bates pretty much accused me of selling my favors."

"Pshaw. That's so unbelievable that it's ridiculous. Is Frank Bates that bitter?"

"He thinks I stole his position."

"Poor Frank. All these years, he's never amounted to anything. I think he fails worse with every job he takes." She shook her head. "I imagine it's easier for him to believe you're immoral rather than to admit you're better at your job than he'll ever be."

"Unfortunately, most folks won't find Frank's ravings that tough to swallow. Will they believe a woman is employed as a telegrapher because she's good at what she does, or will they nod their heads at the suggestion that I've slept with someone important?"

"Perhaps it's time they learn just how capable you are."

"Elizabeth, if I put on one of those dresses, I'll never even have a chance to prove myself. The clothing will just fuel the rumors. People on the committee who don't know me will assume the worst." She eyed the pile of gowns. "Look at them. They might be the height of fashion, but they're far too revealing. I can't afford to even suggest relaxed morals."

"All right, all right. You do have a point. First things first. What have you done about these innuendos?"

"I went to Jim right away. He took the pile of 'proposals' to see if he could isolate whom the comments were coming from. He's also having a few trusted ops from around the area check into it. He said I should just ignore the messages and not to respond to anything sent by those operators."

"Good advice." Elizabeth patted Sarah's hand and offered a cheery smile. "I say you go forth with your head held high and no one will believe anything that wretched man says. Modesty might indeed be your best bet, though. I'll be right back."

Elizabeth disappeared into the large walk-in closet. Creaking trunk hinges and sounds of rustling fabric filled the silence. She swore quietly then emerged with a deep indigo watered-silk gown. Unlike most of the other dresses, its high-necked bodice was bare of the irritating trimmings Sarah so disliked. No complicated frills interfered with the gown's simplicity. A touch of lace, a box pleat at the bottom, and the draped bustle were the only decorations.

"Half-mourning garb, definitely the most modest, unadorned thing I own."

Sarah eyed the dress, reluctant yet attracted. Despite the deep hue and conservative styling, the gown was elegant. It bespoke quality, gentility, respectability. She nodded her assent.

"Then put it on, my dear, and we'll see what needs to be adjusted." She tossed the gown to Sarah and reached for a paper of pins.

Sarah gathered up the dress and headed toward the folding screen at the corner of the room. "One dinner dress solved," she announced, "and with no hint of impropriety. Just let anyone say that I am anything but above reproach."

By the time Friday evening arrived, Sarah had endured a week of bothersome suggestive messages and she was more than ready for the diversion of a dinner party. She crossed Elizabeth's grand front porch and rapped on the polished mahogany door.

A uniformed butler appeared and nodded to her with stiff formality. "Madam?" he queried, extending his palm.

Sarah handed the man her invitation, her name scrawled across it in Elizabeth's firm hand.

"Ah, Miss Donovan. Do come in." The butler stepped back, pulling the carved door wide open.

She stepped into the elegant foyer and waited for the servant to take her wrap. Modern gaslights lit the house, each creating a warm circle of light to beckon guests down the hall. The butler took her cape and invited her to follow him through a set of sliding doors into the front parlor. Across the room, Elizabeth wiggled her fingers in greeting.

Sarah's gaze swept the room. Mrs. Anderson, conversing with an elegant matron, brushed her hands down her worn Sunday dress and smiled in recognition. Bill Byers stood amid a well-heeled group of businessmen, all of them in tense discussion. Ladies in every shade and shape filled the room, gracing the arms of their husbands. All in all, the committee appeared to have grown.

She maneuvered her way through the crowd, exchanging pleasantries with those she knew, until she neared Elizabeth.

"Who *are* all these people?" she whispered.

"People we need, dear. Brandy? Or are you opting for a more conservative sherry tonight?"

"Ha ha. It's been a long week of watching every word for hidden, unintentional meanings. I'd like to let my guard down a bit, but . . ."

"Well, unless it's lemonade, you're damned either way."

"Elizabeth, really."

"Here, have a drink, quit worrying, and get your bearings. Over there, we have the mayor and his wife. He's not technically on the committee, but we'll need his support. Lavinia Morgan, president of the local suffrage chapter insisted on attending. Watch her, dear. She rules the chapter like a queen bee, and she can be vicious when crossed. She also boards at the same rooming house as Frank Bates and is quite a gossip. Frank trails her like a sick puppy."

"Frank Bates and a suffragist?"

Elizabeth nodded and leaned toward Sarah's ear. "Frank's so besotted with her that he wouldn't care if she was an ax murderer."

Sarah laughed, then followed Elizabeth's gaze as she further scanned the room. "You recognized Lucy Anderson from the council meeting? She's joined the suffrage movement, is a mother of six, and owns three dogs. She rounds out the female viewpoint. Bill persuaded some of the leading businessmen to join us." She smiled at Bill's group and blew her husband a kiss. "We also have the policeman in charge of the bounty system. All in all, just a few more people." She pointed out a couple more notables then excused herself to welcome new guests.

Elizabeth flowed through the room, commanding attention, garnering it with both her elegance and her presence. Men nodded in appreciation and women chatted purposefully with her. Though Sarah hated to admit it, it was obvious that femininity definitely wasn't holding Elizabeth back.

Sarah smiled at the realization, then searched the room for the police department's bounty officer. It would be good to find out his views before the meeting began in earnest. Spotting his white head, she moved toward the library only to have the mayor engage the policeman first. She stalled just inside the open door, reluctant to interrupt.

"Looking for someone?" Daniel's strong voice queried.

Sarah glanced to the side. Daniel stood, lounging against a black leather side chair, a near-empty glass of brandy in his hand. He raised his eyebrows and smiled, for once relaxed.

"Your committee seems to have multiplied," she commented.

"So it seems. I half expected it to. Besides, I have a hunch it's Elizabeth's committee. I'm just a figurehead."

"She does tend to dominate, doesn't she?"

"As if you don't." Daniel's hazel eyes twinkled, taking her by surprise.

A smile tugged at Sarah's mouth. "Why, Daniel, whatever do you mean?"

He shrugged, the movement hinting at the silent strength lying beneath his brown serge jacket. "You manage to get things accomplished when you want to."

"I make my own way."

"That you do," he teased.

The comment sparked between them, provocative in its simplicity. Lord, the man was appealing when he let down his guard. Sarah's gaze drifted to the mayor and policeman just outside the library door, and she stiffened. Bates would have a field day if he got wind that she was flirting with the committee chairman.

She glanced back at Daniel and armed herself against his charms. "And you find something wrong with that, do you?"

"Not wrong, just unexpected." He pulled himself upright and drained the last of his brandy. "Look, Sarah, I'm trying not to argue with you tonight. Do you have to take offense at everything I say?"

"You usually mean offense with everything you say," she snapped, at once regretting her tone.

"My, what wit," he countered, ignoring her barb.

She arched an eyebrow at him. "Is that a sense of humor hiding in there?"

"It might be. I think a second snifter of brandy might be in order before I answer that."

"Are you sure that would be proper?"

"No, I'm not. But I'm one glass past proper right now and determined not to find my way back there for the rest of the night." He let the comment drop then turned and left the room.

Daniel nodded attentively to his dinner partner, but his gaze slid catty-corner across the square table to where Sarah sat engrossed in conversation with the bounty officer. Damn the woman for bewitching him. He'd anticipated the night with an uneasy eagerness, imagining how she'd look, all the while dreading the temptation she was sure to stir.

The deep indigo of her gown shaded her violet eyes to a dark, dusky hue and magnified the highlights in her golden hair. Mounded high on her head, it invited touching and drew attention to the hint of neck just visible above the high lace of the dress. Devoid of any other frills, the dress molded her shapely body. She lifted an escargot to her mouth with a dainty fork, full lips accepting it, savoring it. She closed her eyes in appreciation. Daniel felt his loins tighten.

What the hell am I doing?

Maybe his plan to savor the evening hadn't been such a good idea after all.

He set down his fork and reached for a glass of water.

His code of conduct contained little guidance on how to behave at dinner parties. Instinct told him to retain his professional demeanor. Common sense screamed that such formalities didn't apply. Elizabeth had moved the dinner from the realm of business to a social event, after all. Tonight, he would remain loose, he would experience, he would not let his father's rules interfere with his enjoyment.

And so he sat with a snail in his mouth and a stiff cock.

Good God, but he needed another drink.

Efficient waiters cleared the appetizers and brought the next course while he forced himself to pull his thoughts away from Sarah. He needed to begin discussion of the issue at hand. He glanced across the table at her, caught a question in her eyes, ignored it, and cleared his throat.

"Fellow committee members, I beg your attention, please."

Conversation dwindled as attention shifted. Sarah smiled and nodded encouragement.

"While I hate to interrupt, Elizabeth has given us rein to forego proper etiquette and focus our dinner discussion on the business at hand, namely dogs. Our committee has been expanded so that we can have a more rounded approach to the problem. I think it would be pertinent to hear from Officer Jenkins, Mrs. Anderson, and some of the shop owners who have been affected most. Once we've heard about the situation, I'd like us to generate ideas. We are not here to argue the merits of those ideas. Once we've all been heard, we'll narrow the list and select the most practical ideas for further discussion. Who would like to start?"

Down the table, Jenkins raised his hand. Daniel nodded to him and settled back into his chair as the meeting moved on. He'd done it. He had now only to moderate as necessary and let the others have their voices. He reached for his glass of wine and stretched his legs out under the table.

Sarah tipped her own glass of wine at him in salute.

The woman ran hot and cold tonight. At times he swore she hated him, then she opened up with warmth only to shutter herself up again. Did she want to flirt or to argue?

And why in the world did he care? Mary had never once flirted with him, not in all the years of growing up together or during their marriage. She'd been refined, not one to stir up dangerous thoughts and images like Sarah seemed to do with every breath she took.

He shook her from his mind and tried to concentrate on the meeting. The main course slid into dessert as waiters placed plates of grapes and cheeses, bowls of ripe strawberries and confectioner's sugar on the table. Speakers moved on to Mrs. Anderson, who made a few valid points before sliding into a soliloquy on her six children.

Sarah's mouth grew broad with restrained humor and she winked at Daniel, one violet eye closing beneath thick blond eyelashes.

A smile tugged at his own lips. Humorous as Mrs. Anderson's tales were, it was time to move on. He straightened and tried to look official. "Thank you, Mrs. Anderson. Are we ready to list ideas?"

At the far end of the large table, Elizabeth stood and smiled to her guests. "I would be delighted to list our ideas. If we'd like to let things stew for a while, give more thought to the solutions, I'm sure Bill could print the list up at the newspaper. Then, we could all look things over and reconvene to discuss the ideas in a week or so."

Several heads nodded in assent.

"Then we have just one task remaining as we finish dessert," Daniel said. "I'll turn things over to Elizabeth so she can keep us from getting ahead of her pen."

Ideas were offered from several committee members. Daniel listened, sliding back to the relaxed slouch, an unusual position for him, but oddly comfortable. His stretched-out legs bumped against Sarah's skirts and her eyes widened at the touch. He waited, gauging her reaction.

Her breath caught, then she relaxed, her legs still in place under the table, touching his. She peered at him, blinked wordlessly, and picked at the food on her plate. She fingered a deep red berry, vivid against the white of the china, then leaned forward and dipped it into the bowl of sugar.

She brought the fruit to her mouth, lips parting in expectation, and bit into it. Appreciation lit her face. She chewed, savoring the berry, then took a second bite.

Daniel's heart tightened. *Good God, watching her eat food is one of the most sensual things I've ever seen.* The thought jolted him and he reached for his wine.

His leg pressed against hers and she peered at him, realization filling her deep violet eyes and shifting across her face like a shadow. Her lips parted, the remains of the strawberry suspended in her fingers as she inhaled. Her leg pressed back, a fleeting response, then she pulled away, set the strawberry on her plate, and turned her attention from him.

The hunger in Daniel's eyes shook Sarah to her core. The remainder of dinner passed in a blur. She quietly excused herself and slid into the dark recesses of the butler's pantry.

Her heart thumped audibly in the small space.

When had Daniel Petterman shifted from a narrow minded, self-righteous annoyance to the incredibly attractive man with smoldering eyes and a drop of red wine clinging to his upper lip like an invitation. Lord, she'd never left a room for lack of control in her entire life, yet here she was hiding in the pantry. Would she have run if her fears about Frank Bates and his rumors hadn't intruded?

A creaking door broke the silence. Sarah straightened, smoothed her dress, and tried to appear as though she were casually searching for something in particular.

"Sarah?" Daniel's clear voice penetrated the closeness. His thick brown hair looked rumpled, as if he had run his hand through it. He looked about as unsettled as she felt. "Are you all right?"

She pasted a bright smile on her face. "Of course. Why wouldn't I be?"

He sighed. "I think perhaps I was out of line earlier. Too much wine and brandy, I suppose." He looked at his feet, then at her.

"I don't know what you're—"

"Yes you do." He moved toward her, his eyes searching, piercing. "You're a lousy liar, Sarah."

She backed against the cupboard and drew a shaky breath. "All right, I do. I was just trying to give you a way out, save us both a little embarrassment." She knew she needed to stay calm, in control, but her knees felt weak.

Daniel moved closer, leaning toward her until his hands rested on the small counter behind her. He smelled of mingled scents, soap and cedar, red wine and strawberries. His muscled shoulders bunched under the brown suit jacket.

Sarah stared in fascination. If she touched them, would they ripple beneath her fingers?

"I figure the embarrassment won't set in until tomorrow, Sarah. I've breached my code so far tonight, a little farther wouldn't be much of a stretch. We're not done, not yet." His words came softly, luring her.

She eyed the pantry door.

"You never had any grapes, Sarah," he whispered, pulling a linen napkin from his pocket. He unwrapped the bundle and the room filled with the scent of fresh grapes.

Her breath quickened as he drew her into his spell. Her lips parted in surrender.

Daniel's hand brushed across her cheek, hot and intense. He

set the grape in her mouth. She took it from him, feeling his fingers slide against her lips before cupping her chin and tilting her face upward for his kiss.

His lips were soft, far softer than she remembered from their last brief touch. He kissed her lightly, a gentle greeting before the onslaught. He groaned and her own voice answered him mindlessly as he devoured her, ravishing her mouth with hot, hungry kisses. Their tongues danced together, touching and retreating.

Her bustle hit the hard counter behind her as Daniel pressed closer, hard and hot against her lower abdomen. His hands stroked her face, her neck, her hair. One by one, he slid her hairpins out until the heavy tresses tumbled downward.

As if in answer, her own hands raked through his hair, feeling its thick softness, smelling the cedar from the shavings of his shop, touching his face.

In the recesses of her mind, she recognized the creak of the door at the same time she heard the sharp intake of breath that accompanied it.

Lavinia Morgan's sharp voice broke the interlude. "Mercy! The rumors were true. Heaven help us all."

Chapter Seven

After a morning of tossing and turning, Sarah gave up on restful slumber. She'd fretted about the mess she was in, worrying about Lavinia Morgan and Daniel's kiss through the entire night shift. She'd penned letters to Miriam and Lise, then crumpled them. The sleep she'd hoped for never came. She needed some air.

Rising, she dressed in haste. The deep blue gown she'd worn last night was draped across the iron railing at the foot of her bed. She frowned at it. She should have stuck with her practical brown work skirt.

What in the world had she been thinking?

She slipped on her plain woolen stockings and reached for her worn brown shoes with sharp, quick movements. Yawning, she pulled them on and tugged the laces tight. Lord, she was tired. Worse, she was confused. She wound her thick braid into a bun, pinned it, and made a face at her reflection in the small oval mirror atop the dresser. It would have to do.

She moved through the deserted boarding house, and crisp November air hit her as she emerged into the day. It was the kind of air that helped a person think. She smiled at the wind and drew a deep breath.

Sarah moved away from the crowded neighborhood of the station, hiking toward the isolation of the meandering City Ditch. The irrigation canal wound past unpopulated stretches, perfect for soul-searching. She kept a brisk pace, crossing smaller, rancid-smelling ditches as she neared outlying areas.

Her rapid steps chipped away at the dreadful confusion that had haunted her for the past twelve hours. Lord, she hated it when things weren't clear to her.

Sarah frowned at the thick brown water in the ditch. It was the color of Daniel's hair. Visages of its softness filled her, his hazel eyes, more intense than she'd ever seen them, his lips, unexpectedly demanding, and the incredible way she'd melded with his body.

She kicked at a rock and watched it tumble into the canal. It landed in the water with a plop, sending a fleeting odor of waste into the air. Sarah stepped away from it, disgusted.

Daniel was nothing but an annoying, irritating, pompous man and she should hate it that he'd made advances.

Except she didn't.

Daniel had her weak-kneed and out of control. Last night, he had been the master of the game and she'd been unable to resist him, even if she'd wanted to.

She nodded to herself, accepting the realization, and moved away from the ditch, across the brown prairie. There was still the matter of Lavinia Morgan.

Sarah bit her lip. She'd never, ever, in her entire life worried about what anyone else thought of her. She should simply enjoy whatever she chose to pursue with Daniel instead of worrying about Lavinia. Still, for some reason, the thought of Lavinia rankled. Elizabeth had hinted Lavinia could be a dangerous woman, and a strange knot of worry had stayed in Sarah's stomach all night.

Maybe it was the dreadful realization that someone had really paid attention to Bates's horrid tales that bothered her. Judging by Lavinia's shocked reaction to what she'd seen, Frank had more than likely fed his rumors to Lavinia over dinner at the boarding house and she'd eaten up every crumb. Sarah had dismissed Frank as less than credible. Yet Lavinia's comments last night indicated she'd formed an opinion before she ever even opened the door of the butler's pantry.

Sarah pulled her winter shawl closer and turned back to town, wondering how dangerous Lavinia could really be.

The gossip would be juicier now, but she'd be damned if she let a lifetime of trying to prove she possessed the skills to do anything she wanted get washed away by the rambling of a gossipy old hen. Truth would prevail. All she had to do was meet the rumors head on and those spreading them would see her abilities.

That's what Elizabeth would do. Her friend had been dragged through the mud any number of times, often because of Bill's indiscreet behavior. But she'd stood tall and the rumors had lost credence. It had been difficult for her, but Elizabeth had emerged as one of the most respected women in town. Sarah neared the residential neighborhoods at the edge of the city with new resolve. She would carry herself with character and the public would see it. If she hid in shame, shame is what they would see. She'd fight Bates and those old toads who sent the irritating telegrams. She'd quit denying rumors and simply turn them back on the men, force them to explain the idle talk away. Put the men on the defensive for a change.

And she would not mix any of Frank's insinuations up with her attraction to Daniel. Proving she could succeed was a lot lonelier business than she'd expected. There was absolutely no reason she shouldn't explore the relationship further, as long as she set the pace instead of allowing Daniel to catch her by surprise again. Besides, what better way to prove Bates wrong than to live her social life *her* own way.

A sharp rap pulled Daniel's attention from the simple casket on the table. He frowned, set the container of rouge on the counter next to the tin of caked powder and moved toward the door. There went his quiet, contemplative morning.

Lifting the curtain, he spied Bill's familiar face and turned back the lock to open the door.

"You look a little grim this morning, my friend," Bill chided.

Daniel scowled. The last thing he needed was yet another reminder of last night. "I'm busy. What do you want?"

"Testy, too. Rough night?" Bill moved past him with determination, glancing around the shop. He leaned against the counter and offered a wry smile.

"I think you know the answer to that. You here to confirm a story or fish for more news?"

"Neither."

"That would be a first." Daniel eyed his friend with suspicion as he moved back to the coffin. By now, most of the town had probably heard the gossip from that wretched Morgan woman. He hated the prospect of Kate and Molly hearing rumors. And then there was the position he'd placed Sarah in.

Bill threw up his hands in a helpless gesture. "I already got the scoop, Daniel. Of course, if you'd like to confirm the details, I'd be more than happy to hear your side of things."

"You're not really going to print—"

"Easy, Daniel. I popped over to fill you in on information you might be unaware of. Got a few minutes?"

Daniel fought to bury his frustration, focusing on routine. "If you don't mind me putting the finishing touches on today's burial." He nodded to the body and retrieved a container from the counter, knowing Bill would stay whether he continued or not. "She needs to be ready to go in twenty minutes."

"Not at all. That rouge?"

"Folks don't like seeing the color of death on their loved ones. A little touch-up makes the body more lifelike. Less shocking."

He rubbed a small amount of the coloring into the woman's cold, lifeless face. The pastiness blended away and she looked a little less dead.

Bill watched with rapt attention. "Interesting. You might consider touching up your own face a bit. You seem a little pale this morning."

Daniel set the rouge down, weary of battling himself over what had happened. Sometimes, he hated being alone. Maybe talking to someone about it might help. "Mrs. Winifred maintains a dry household here. I'm afraid the brandy carried a little more punch than I'd remembered it having."

"Yeah, I seem to recall you were loosened up a bit."

"So loose I was almost tight."

"You weren't drunk, Daniel. A drunk, I can spot. But you were a whole lot less inhibited than usual."

Daniel shook his head and put his supplies away, then turned back and closed the lid of the coffin. Last night definitely stripped away his inhibitions. But at a price.

"Makes me wonder if my father's admonitions on the evil of liquor weren't correct after all."

"Easy, no need to take the pledge, my friend. There's nothing wrong with letting your guard down every now and then." Bill grinned and settled himself into Daniel's desk chair. "In fact, there are times it can be damned enjoyable."

"It was that obvious?"

" 'Fraid so."

"Damnation." He slammed the cupboard door shut and ran his hand through his hair. What a mess he'd made out of things.

"Whoa. Cursing from you, Daniel?"

"Seems I've been doing a lot of it lately." He paused and stared at Bill for a few moments, then went on. "I had no business letting myself get that far out of line. I behaved like an ass and I compromised Sarah's character. As soon as I get this funeral out of the way, I intend to make my apologies and assure her it won't happen again."

Bill's mouth dropped open. "Are you an idiot?"

"Now what's that supposed to mean?"

"You think she wasn't offering you invitations all night? Flirting? From what I heard, she wasn't exactly resisting your kiss."

"Oh, hell." Sarah's reputation was being dragged through the mud already. How could he have been so careless?

"You'd be a fool to assure her it won't happen again."

Daniel sighed. Aside from the fact that he'd twice stepped across the line with Sarah, she wasn't even the right kind of woman for him. He stared at his friend. "Neither of us needs this right now. She's an outspoken suffragist. I don't want that kind of influence on my daughters, and I'm sure she'd rather not have her name hooked up with mine. We're not exactly made for each other."

Bill nodded but didn't look convinced. "You got a point there. But, hell, a liberal-minded woman like that, I'd take what she has to offer."

Rumors about Bill's affair with that pretty little milliner, Hattie Sancomb, had run rampant a few months back. Daniel didn't know if he believed all the gossip, but Bill sure as blue blazes didn't deny his interest in women. Daniel just couldn't picture himself playing around like that. "I'm not you, Bill."

"You might be more discreet than me, but I'd be hard-pressed to believe any man would turn down a free offer." Bill offered a knowing smile.

Something about Bill's words gave Daniel pause. Good God, Bill thought Sarah had initiated this. How the blazes had he gotten an idea like that? He eyed his friend, leaned against the counter, and forced his voice to be casual. "What makes you think she made an offer?"

"A little visit I had earlier from Lavinia Morgan. I thought you'd appreciate hearing what she told me."

"Damned old busybody."

Bill laughed. "You pegged her on that one, but she's got reach. She's also got lots of sources. Seems she lives at the same boarding house as Frank Bates over at the Kansas Pacific. According to Bates, Sarah's reputation is more than a little sullied. That plain-girl image she tries so hard to project may be just that, an image. Bates hinted that there's only one way a woman gets a job like that and told Lavinia that Sarah uses the wire to arrange illicit meetings with the men on the line."

"Aw, come on, Bill. You know better. Check your sources. Bates has had it in for her since she got the job he wanted. He made that pretty clear when he accused Sarah of stealing that horse. You heard how he rambled to the judge."

Bill leaned forward. "What about her request to move to night shift?"

"Request?" Daniel's mouth tightened into a scowl. "I think she's on night shift because I threw a fit about the misdirected corpse and Frank Bates used it against her. Jim Wilson himself said it'd go easier if I revoked my complaint."

"And did you?"

"I was mad. I told him I thought she was incompetent and deserved what she got." A fresh wave of guilt swept through him. He had dismissed Jim's insistence that Sarah was the best young telegrapher he'd seen in years. He hadn't wanted to believe it, and he'd pushed the whole matter out of his mind.

"You sound less than convinced."

"I get the unsettling feeling I was wrong. The Sarah I've seen seems pretty skilled at everything she does. It goes against everything I believe about women, but she probably is a good telegrapher, too. I interfered, and she got moved to nights. Is it her fault she's getting ribald letters from men she doesn't even know? You print one word of Lavinia Morgan's trite little gossip and you set Sarah up for more."

The comment drew Bill's attention. "You sound pretty convinced. What makes you believe she's so innocent?"

Daniel searched Bill's face and debated with himself. Self-revelation was damned uncomfortable. An image of Sarah, her breath catching as comprehension dawned, filled him. He shifted his feet and took a breath. "Last night, as seductive as I found her, she was completely unaware of what she was doing to me. I saw it in her eyes, the moment she realized what was happening. I felt it in the way she tried to resist and I ignored her."

"It's a pretty juicy tale." Bill shook his head. "I hate to pass it up."

Daniel pounded his fist on the counter. "Damn it, Bill, giving in to my anger and my lust put her into this, not her actions. I suggest you keep this issue out of the *News* until I get a chance to fix it."

It was far past time he stepped forward and did the right thing. He'd have to start with contacting the head officials at Kansas Pacific, and he'd probably need to do something honorable about that kiss. Damn, but people were going to talk.

The November meeting of the Denver Suffrage Association was packed. Sarah glanced across the crowded basement of the Lawrence Street Methodist Church, searching for Elizabeth's familiar face.

Several of the ladies from last week's dinner were clustered together in the center of the room. Their busy chatter smacked of their pride in helping resolve the bounty issue and their confidence that they had contributed.

Sarah noted their self-assured bearings, their plucky tones and steady voices. These, indeed, were ladies of action. She approached her comrades, determined to keep her head high. Her comfortable, no-nonsense shoes and plain brown skirt lent her confidence.

The ladies parted. Five sets of intelligent eyes focused on Sarah and conversation stopped. Two of the women had grace enough to look away. The other three stared at her as if she had sprouted horns and a tail.

A thick cloak of discomfort settled about Sarah.

Lavinia Morgan emerged from the crowd and clicked her tongue with disgust.

Sarah slowed her step, unsure of how best to respond to the women's scrutiny. She had to maintain control. Unfamiliar anxiety hung over her. Each piercing gaze hit her like a rock. Her mastery of the situation slipped, and she fought to keep it in her grip.

Elizabeth stepped into the light and offered a smile of encouragement. Calm confidence leapt from her, giving Sarah strength. If Elizabeth could face gossip and emerge this nobly, how could Sarah run from it?

Sarah drew a deep breath, moved purposely toward Lavinia, and pasted a gracious smile on her face. "Good evening, Miss Morgan. How nice to see you again." She forced a level of self-assurance that she no longer felt.

Surprise flickered across Lavinia's face, then disappeared. She glared at Sarah and pointedly ignored her as she moved grandly past to greet someone else.

A low buzz crept across the room.

Elizabeth swept forward into the void and reached for Sarah's hands. "Sarah, dear. We're so pleased to have you." She turned to the women who had attended the dinner. "Ladies, you remember Sarah Donovan. She contributed a number of ideas toward solving the dilemma with the dog bounty."

Several of the more well-dressed women held back, waiting to take their cues from other people. Elizabeth raised her eyebrows at them. Finally, Mrs. Anderson nodded her head and offered a shaky smile. "That she did. I was there."

"Then you should be able to confirm Miss Donovan's indecent behavior." Lavinia's pinched face emerged from the crowd.

"I . . . I didn't see anything such as that." Mrs. Anderson's voice shook.

Good for her, Sarah thought. She might not be half as wealthy as some of the other women in the room, but she sure wasn't afraid to hold her ground.

"Well, of course you didn't, dear. You were rambling on about your children at the time." Lavinia's tone was condescending. Mrs. Anderson blanched.

Elizabeth's face hardened. "Lavinia, I hardly think—"

"Let me, Elizabeth." Sarah heard her own voice, bold and much more plucky than she expected. Letting Elizabeth fight her battles wasn't what she had in mind. She stepped forward until Lavinia had little choice but face her. "Miss Morgan, your battle seems to be with me. I don't think Mrs. Anderson needs to be the brunt of your insults."

Lavinia stared as if she'd been slapped. "H . . . how dare you," she sputtered.

"How dare *you.*" Sarah flung the words at her. "Who made you judge and jury of Denver's women?"

"Sarah, I don't think—"

"Stay out of this, Elizabeth," Lavinia snapped. "If the little upstart wants to fight, I'll give her a fight. I suspect it's time the other ladies learned the truth about her."

Sarah tried to process her words. Upstart? Good heavens. Lavinia was threatened by her. Empowered, her anger surged ahead. "The truth? Would that be *your* version of the truth?"

"What do any of you know about Sarah Donovan?" Lavinia whipped around, addressing the room. She marched forward, questioning the nearest women. "Anything?" Not waiting for an answer, she flung her arms wide. "We all heard Elizabeth's glowing stories at the last meeting, all about the new female telegrapher. Well, she forgot to tell you how Sarah got the job. She and Jim Wilson, the stationmaster, are thick as peas in a pod." Lavinia's eyes narrowed. "Why, to hear Frank Bates tell it, they can hardly keep their hands off each other."

Sarah pulled back her shoulders and stepped into the battle. "Perhaps that's the key to the real truth, Miss Morgan. Would you like to tell the ladies how angry Frank Bates is because I was hired for the post he wanted? Surely the ladies want to hear about how he set me up, how he went behind Jim Wilson's back to complain to Kansas Pacific officials."

"He wouldn't have had to if you hadn't had Wilson in your pocket, dear. But one man's not enough, is it?"

"Lavinia, Sarah, this is getting a little out of control." Elizabeth's commanding voice broke into their clipped debate.

Lavinia leveled a momentary stare at her, then addressed the crowd. "You should all see the messages this woman is exchanging with other telegraph operators."

Sarah glanced around the room. Curious eyes waited for her denial. She counted to five, unwilling to let the anger consume her. Satisfied her fury was under control, she directed her words to the whole group rather than to Lavinia.

"The logbooks at the station are open for review. They provide a written record of all messages sent and received. I make no attempt to deny that distasteful messages are being sent to me. After all, we all know men will be men. I have no control over what they send to me. You will find no record of outgoing wire either inviting or responding to such messages."

"Poppycock, I tell you. Mr. Bates has copies."

"There can't be copies because there were no messages. Ladies, I invite you to—"

"Is this the kind of woman we want as part of the suffrage movement, ladies?" Lavinia demanded, her face dark with rage. "Do we want all our reputations sullied by the immoral actions of this Jezebel?" She pointed an accusing finger at Sarah.

Sarah stood firm, unwilling to be drawn into a catfight.

Mrs. Anderson glanced from one of them to the other, then nervously began to speak.

"Lavinia—"

"I seen her," a voice called out from the back of the room. "I seen her talkin' to men all over the city. Lord knows what they're arranging."

"Oh, for heaven's sake," Elizabeth said. "She delivers telegraphs. I know Sarah, and I know she's earned her position honorably. This is nothing but vicious gossip made up by a man who resents the fact that Sarah is more skillful than he is."

"Drivel, Elizabeth. Where there's smoke, there's fire. It's time to cut her loose." Lavinia threw out an arm, encouraging others to comment.

"She'll drag us all down," a haughty voice chimed in.

"It's taken us years to gain credence. We surely don't need the men raising morality as an issue," another woman said.

"Morality? And men? Don't make me laugh." Elizabeth's gaze hardened and the crowd tittered, half hysterical. "We all know what men will do, and we know even better what they'll say when they're threatened. Sarah doesn't deserve any of this."

Lavinia stepped forward. "Mrs. Bean hit the nail on the head, ladies. Think about it. Those same men will be calling the whole association immoral. We'll lose the referendum."

Those around her began nodding as the comment sank in. Sarah's gaze drifted over them as control shifted away from her. Elizabeth's face registered shock and Sarah realized Lavinia had played a trump card, one she didn't think she could beat.

Lavinia's wicked smile mocked Sarah's silence. "Shall I tell you the rest? Shall I tell you what happened last week?"

Sarah's thoughts flew to Daniel. One word about what happened in the butler's pantry and Daniel's carefully crafted reputation would be ruined, his image tarnished in his daughters' eyes. She sent a beseeching look toward Elizabeth as Lavinia watched with hawk-like interest.

"Shut up, Lavinia. You are affecting innocent people," Elizabeth hissed, her genteel graciousness abandoned.

Lavinia smiled with smug satisfaction. "I will not. These ladies need to know. The public needs to know that the suffrage movement does not stand for this kind of behavior. That we condemn it. If your husband won't publish the story, I'll go to the *Tribune.*" She paused, letting the full impact of her threat hit home, then raised her voice until it filled the room. "I am not about to let Sarah Donovan destroy everything we've worked for, ladies, are you? Are you willing to let all our efforts die? Die, when we are so close to gaining the vote?"

Sarah felt the sting of accusing eyes. Women who had worked for years to gain the vote stared at her, considering her a threat to all they'd accomplished. Hostility filled the room.

"Last week," Lavinia continued, "she took her loose morals out in public, ladies, in public, do you hear? In all my born days, I've never seen the like. This, this *adventuress*—"

"Stop it." Sarah heard the command in her voice and wished she could shrink away from it. Her heart stung.

A few more ill-placed words from Lavinia and the local suffrage movement would shatter, Sarah's career would be gone for good, and Daniel's good character would be destroyed.

God help her, none of those outcomes was acceptable.

She closed her eyes, praying Lavinia would keep quiet. Rustling fabric filled the room with sound and Sarah forced her eyes open. Lavinia neared, a venomous aura surrounding her. She leaned forward and hissed into Sarah's ear. "You want my silence? Step down from the association and walk out that door. This is *my* movement and you're not needed here. Resign and I won't say another word. Fight me and I'll see to it that undertaker and his family never know respect again, their own or anyone else's."

Chapter Eight

Sarah stared at Lavinia, measuring the threat in her steel-gray eyes. The mixture of fear and determination lurking there gave credence to her words. A chill crept through Sarah.

Lavinia Morgan was not just spouting words. Not at all. She was as vicious as Elizabeth had warned, perhaps even deadly.

"Shall I ruin him, dear?" Lavinia whispered, the threat shrouded in overtly genteel tones.

Sarah bit back the retort that threatened to erupt and forced herself to think before she spoke.

Lavinia's smile thinned and she leaned closer. The stale odor of onion lingered around her and Sarah fought the urge to step away. She could not, would not, give Lavinia the satisfaction.

"And what of those dear little girls who so mindlessly worship you? How will people treat them once word is out that their father is a lecher? Perhaps Denver needs to know he's not the fit parent everyone thought he was. I can make this as big as I need to."

Sarah shivered and pulled away. Curious stares filled the room, each one attempting to decipher the situation. Among them were women who had trusted Daniel to bury their loved ones, perhaps cried on his shoulder as they pondered coffin styles. Surely they wouldn't believe he was that kind of man.

She caught Elizabeth's gaze, one of just a handful that held reassurance instead of blatant curiosity or fear. In the whole room, only a few even knew Sarah. To the others, she was no longer a potential leader. She was a threat to the cause, her credibility tattered to the point of hampering the movement.

A few well-chosen words from Lavinia and the gossip could spread far beyond what was or was not happening at the depot. In the ladies' eyes, she and Daniel would be whatever the rumors made them. She hadn't any doubt that Lavinia would build the entire situation into something it wasn't. Like a cornered cat, Lavinia would lash out with all her claws, ripping and tearing without discretion.

Even if it meant shredding the lives of two little girls.

Sarah sighed. Somehow, she had to find a way to prevent what was happening, appease Lavinia before she mentioned Daniel's name aloud to the others. The only loss would be to her own reputation and her active involvement in the movement. Deep down, she knew she'd lost both already.

Swallowing the pride that screamed for defense, Sarah nodded then lifted her head and faced the room. "Are any of you listening to yourselves?" Her measured words bore into the void until several women dropped their stares. "You're letting malicious gossip run rampant over our honor and our cause, yours as well as mine. I don't want to sacrifice Colorado's chance for women's suffrage because of in-fighting. Good heavens, ladies, what a field day the men would have with that."

A few of the women laughed nervously as the truth of her words hit home. Sarah waited, watching them begin to nod in agreement, gauging the crowd. Low murmurs of agreement surfaced and the mood shifted.

Sarah smiled, an offering of quiet sincerity, and chose her words with care. "I'd rather give up my active involvement in the movement than have that happen." She scanned the group, pinning her gaze on Lavinia's most vocal supporters. "But even without me here, if you continue to repeat Lavinia's empty accusations, you'll destroy the cause on your own."

"Hear, hear," Mrs. Anderson chimed in.

"But what about everything she's done?"

"Oh, hush up," Elizabeth chastised. "Good gracious, ladies, you've torched her honor enough. Unless you want to sacrifice the vote, you'll quit wagging your tongues and give the woman a little respect. Besides, why push one of our best campaigners out the door?"

Sarah held her hands up in a gesture of nullification and shook her head. Elizabeth had earned their respect with years of community involvement and charitable giving. It wasn't Sarah's due, not yet, and demanding it would only make things worse. "Thank you, Elizabeth, but I've made my decision. Let's not argue any further. I feel I've caused dissent, and no movement needs that within its ranks. My further involvement will only make things difficult."

Lavinia nodded, her shock hidden behind a cheery smile of support. "I think Miss Donovan is being quite noble. Perhaps I misjudged her." She patted Sarah's arm and leaned forward toward the crowd. "I do have a tendency to let gossip get the best of me." She beamed as she once again turned to Sarah. "Are you quite sure, dear, that we can't all work together?"

Sarah pasted a contrite smile on her own face and shook her head, wondering if Lavinia's pacification was all going just a bit too easily. "I think it would be better if I weren't actively involved."

"Quite right. We do need to preserve the cause, and there is always the lingering chance that others in the community would look poorly on us." Lavinia glanced at Elizabeth. "Perhaps there are other ways Miss Donovan can contribute, outside of the organized movement. We do want to be fair, after all. We'll put our heads together and see what we can find for her."

Elizabeth crossed her arms and stared back. "How decent of you."

Sarah groaned and shook her head at her friend.

Lavinia waved a hand through the air and squeezed Sarah's arm again. "Don't be catty, Elizabeth. I believe Miss Donovan is more than happy with the way things have turned out, aren't you dear?"

Sarah choked back a derisive snigger. Lavinia Morgan had to be the shallowest woman in the room. But she was also the most dangerous and Sarah knew better than to assume the threat was gone. A sudden idea formed in her head and she offered a silent prayer that her intuition was right.

Leaning forward, she lowered her voice for Lavinia's ears only. "It's a compromise, Lavinia. If it works, we'll both be happy and your leadership of the movement will succeed just fine. But just so we *both* know, this works only if we both do our share to squelch the gossip. If it continues, you will lose this movement and your role in it. What's done is done, and we both know the rumors about the telegrams aren't going to simply disappear. But I'd hate to hear them grow to involve anyone but me. I'm sure you won't start any new gossip—about Daniel or about me. As long as things are quiet, I'll make sure any little tidbits about you and Frank Bates are nipped in the bud. Are we understood?"

Shock skittered through Lavinia's gray eyes, confirming Sarah's hunch that Frank and Lavinia were more involved than Lavinia would have anyone know. Lavinia offered a reluctant nod of agreement. "It appears we understand each other quite well."

The following afternoon, Daniel stood, kicking at the dirt on the floor of the Kansas Pacific depot while Jim Wilson finished with his line of customers. He didn't much like eating crow, but he figured he owed it to Sarah. Much as he hated admitting it, he'd been wrong to hold her responsible for that body fiasco in the first place. Filing the complaint with the railroad had been reactionary and totally uncalled for.

He shifted his stance and glanced about the station. It sure was a busy place. A frazzled woman sagged on the leather bench, two cranky toddlers at her knee. Their vocal complaints filled the room. In front of the ticket window, two old-timers argued over which day they wanted to depart. A young boy pushed a floor broom across the wooden planks, stirring up dust devils. Luggage handlers carried a trunk away and the distant sound of a train whistle caught the attention of waiting passengers.

Good God, what it must be like to work among such noise, trying to concentrate on deciphering the dots and dashes of a telegram. It was all such a stark contrast to his quiet coffin shop where the grate of sandpaper on cedar was the only intrusion on one's private thoughts.

Still, he could picture Sarah here, content with all the fuss and bother. Because of his actions, she'd been removed from it and now pulled her duty during the quiet night shift. The silence must be eerie for her.

The last customer turned away from the ticket counter and shuffled toward the open doorway that led to the platform. Jim Wilson followed, pushing up his glasses and reminding the boisterous little ones not to step too close to the waiting train.

Daniel watched them board, fingering the carefully scripted letter in his pocket until Jim reentered.

"Sorry about the delay, Mr. Petterman. You wanted to talk to me?" Jim wiped his hand on his pant leg and extended it.

Daniel shook it, then presented the letter. "I think I made a grave error in issuing that complaint against Sarah Donovan. I acted in haste, without seeking to discover the facts of the situation. I'd like to retract the complaint."

Jim raised his bushy eyebrows. "You would?"

"Yes. After some observation, I've noted that Miss Donovan

has a much higher level of professionalism than I originally thought."

The stationmaster nodded. "Like I told you when you issued the complaint, that li'l gal is the best telegrapher I've ever had here. Didn't seem you wanted to hear it much then. Anything in particular change your mind?"

"Yeah. I got stuck on a committee with her and she put me in my place." He rued the stupid grin inching its way across his face. Wilson acted like he was enjoying his discomfort. But he seemed a good sort and Sarah spoke well of him.

"She does tend to do that. You want this letter forwarded on up the line, then?"

Daniel nodded. "It needs to go wherever the original complaint went."

"Will do, Petterman." Jim stuffed the letter into his vest pocket and eyed Daniel.

"Any chance this will get her transferred back to days?"

Jim paused as if weighing his words. "It'll help. No guarantees, though. It's complicated, and I reckon she'd rather stay on nights than be bossed by Bates. But what with him not showing for his shift, it might just be enough to do the trick at that."

"Thanks, Wilson."

Jim glanced around the station then turned back to Daniel. "She tell you she stepped down from that suffrage association of hers? Told me she just lost interest. Seem right to you?"

A sense of foreboding crept through him. It just didn't fit with the Sarah he'd seen. "Lost interest? Hardly. That woman doesn't just *lose interest* in anything, let alone women's suffrage."

"Heard from Bates that she got in a tussle with that Morgan woman."

"Lavinia." The name was sour on Daniel's lips. "That old bat ought to have her wings clipped."

Jim snorted in agreement, then pushed at his spectacles.

"Whatever it was that got them two tangled, it must have been something to make Sarah step down from fightin' for the vote."

"And whatever it was, Jim Wilson, is none of your business." Sarah entered the open doorway of the depot and glared at them, hands on her hips. "Don't you two have better things to do than stand around gossiping?"

Daniel's mouth went dry. Sarah was once again clad in plain brown, her golden hair drawn into a severe bun. Funny, all he'd seen before was the brown skirt. Now, all he saw were the curves she was trying so hard to disguise, curves he had no right even thinking about.

"Afternoon," Jim nodded.

"Sarah," Daniel said, not trusting himself further.

"Well?" she demanded.

Daniel stared back at her and shook his head. "Well what?"

"If you two will just excuse me, I sure got a pile of ticket stubs to file away." Jim hustled into his office.

Sarah crossed the room toward him, heels clicking, and Daniel groaned. The hellcat was back.

"What in the world are you doing here?" she snapped.

"It's a train station, Sarah. Last I heard, anyone was welcome in here." His voice was sharper than he'd intended and he wanted to kick himself. He needed to make things right with her, not antagonize her again. Damn, but she needled him.

"Jim doesn't like folks to loiter. Was there something you needed?" She stopped in front of him, violet eyes flashing like it was his fault she'd stopped by.

"I've already taken care of my business with Mr. Wilson."

"Then I guess you can be on your way." She turned away and he caught her arm.

"It's a little early for your shift, isn't it?"

"And why is that your business?"

Daniel sighed and forced his mouth into a smile that didn't

have the slightest thing to do with the way he was feeling. "It's not. But then, it wasn't really any of your business what I was doing here." He silenced her retort with a finger to his lips. "I just thought maybe you might have time for a walk."

"With you?"

Good God, she was sassy. He should just turn around and walk away and let her stew. He should, but he owed her, especially if that Morgan woman was stirring things up. "No, with the next customer that walks in. Of course, with me."

Sarah wiped her hands on her skirt, glanced at Jim's ticket counter, and took a deep breath. "Look, Daniel, I have enough problems as it is—"

"So do I, but I figure we have at least one or two in common." He softened his tone and caught her gaze. "Could we at least go somewhere quiet to talk about what happened the other night?"

She shook her head. "I don't want to talk about it."

"Well, I do. Shall I talk about it here where Bates is liable to walk in and cause us both an upset stomach, or will you come with me?"

Sarah glared at him, her eyes once again full of fire. "I take my walks along the City Ditch," she said, then turned and stalked away.

One corner of Daniel's mouth lifted. Most women he knew took their strolls along the respectable paths in front of the city's larger homes. But Sarah wasn't like most women he knew. He shrugged and followed her out the door and into the fading light of late afternoon. "Sounds fine to me. It'll give me a place to throw you if you keep up with that mouth of yours."

She turned and stared at him, incredulous. "You didn't seem to mind my mouth too much when you cornered me in the butler's pantry."

A smart retort formed on Daniel's lips and he swallowed it.

"Truth be told, Sarah, neither of us minded, and that's exactly why we need to talk." He paused, pondering her sour face, then decided to drop the subject until her mood softened. "Are you sure you want to walk all the way to the ditch? It must be three miles. Why don't we just take my buggy?"

"Ah, the elusive buggy. Too bad you didn't bring it last time we needed one."

He recalled the warmth of her body surrounded by his arms, and the swell of her breasts as the horse jostled him against her. Even then, when he'd been angry as hell, she'd possessed him. Forcing the thought away, he smiled at her and arched his eyebrows. "As I recall, you're the one who fetched the transportation."

Sarah planted her fists on her hips. "Only because you were short-sighted enough to run off on foot and leave your own horse and buggy sitting at home."

He paused at the polished black runabout and turned to offer Sarah his hand. "Well, I brought it this time, so let's use it."

She shook her head with an exasperated glare and marched past him. Placing a worn black boot on the high iron step, she grasped the leather seat back and swung herself upward in one fluid motion.

"Stubborn woman," Daniel muttered into the crisp air, then stepped up and into the seat beside her. "Put the blanket on, it's cold."

She eyed the coverlet at the edge of the seat then stole a glance at him. "I'm not stupid, Daniel."

"I never meant to imply you were." She sure made things difficult, always putting her own spin on what he meant. He let the silence stretch between them for a moment, then breathed deeply and searched for a calm, even tone. "Look, I'm trying to do this your way. I didn't put the blanket over you and I didn't tuck it in around you like I would for any other woman. You'd just toss it off if I did. But I happen to think it's cold and the blanket's on your side. Put the blasted thing on yourself or pass it over to me."

"Sorry." She gathered the wool plaid lap blanket and placed it over them.

Daniel watched her without words, noting the care she took to avoid frightening the horse as she distributed the blanket. Most women, expecting a man to tuck the robe around them, would have flung it out as if they were at a picnic. She was stubborn, but she was smart. He snapped the reins and threaded the buggy down 22nd Street and onto Broadway. They approached Colfax and turned east, leaving most of Denver behind them.

The buggy rocked with a steady rhythm, accenting the clip clop of the horses' feet. They rode in silence with the prairie, devoid of trees, stretched before them.

"There's 'the Folly.' " Sarah pointed to Bill and Elizabeth's grand house on Brown's Bluff. "What do you think, Daniel? Was it folly to build way out here?"

"Smart, I'd say. Look at the other fancy homes going up. Brown even wants to donate land for a new capitol building."

"So I heard."

Daniel bristled at her tone. "Are you going to keep this up the whole drive?" he finally asked.

"Me? What'd I do?"

"You're snappy. Even in the middle of a conversation about other people's houses, you snap."

She rolled her eyes and made a soft sound of frustration. "Maybe I snap because I'm not very happy with you right now. Your complaint made it easy for Bates to get himself promoted over me. My reputation is compromised to the point that I had to step down from the suffrage movement. But, then, that really wouldn't matter to you, would it, because you don't believe in suffrage in the first place."

"Now wait just a minute." He jerked the horse to a stop and turned toward Sarah. "You're telling me you wouldn't complain if I loused up an important telegram?"

Her breasts rose and fell, stretching the fabric of her shirtwaist as she took a measured breath, then two. "I'd take the time to find out the facts, first."

Daniel felt the corners of his mouth twitch at the thought of Sarah taking the time to gather facts. Somehow, he just couldn't picture that happening. "You'd jump right in with your own assumptions, just as I did, and you know it. Sarah Donovan, you are not a saint. You are an opinionated, hell-bent-on-taking-charge woman and you would have marched right up to my boss and complained. No doubt about it."

"So maybe I would have. But that still doesn't—"

"Quiet." He'd be damned if he'd let her temper redirect what he'd come to do. It'd taken him far too long to work up the nerve and self-control to do it. He closed his eyes, willing himself to remain calm, then opened them to find her staring at him. He smiled and touched her hands briefly. "I apologize for the action and for the consequences of it. I never did ask questions and I should have. I'm not so pig-headed that I won't admit I was wrong. I think I made a mistake and you suffered for it. I'm sorry."

She swallowed, her violet eyes large above her pouting mouth. My God, but she was pretty.

"And," he continued, "I'm sorry about being so careless at the party. Jim Wilson said you'd stepped down from the movement. What did that Morgan woman do, anyway?"

Sarah waved her hand in a gesture of insignificance. "She hissed some threats in my ear and raised a stink about how it would pull down the movement if I stayed." Her airy dismissal didn't quite hide the slight catch in her voice.

Something wasn't right. Sarah had too much spunk to have been quieted by a few threats. Hell, she liked raising a stink. Daniel caught her hand and she peered at him in surprise. "Sounds to me like a challenge that should have had you fighting back. You don't give up so easily, Sarah. What really happened?"

"She has the power to embarrass a lot of people."

Sarah turned away, leaving her quiet words on Daniel's mind. Realization hit him slowly, like a lazy summer wind. Lavinia had done a great deal more than threaten just Sarah.

"Me? Sarah, you didn't step down because—"

"I stepped down because she would have ruined the movement." Though her voice was even, she avoided his glance.

"Sarah?" He rubbed his thumb against her hand.

"I just didn't want the movement to suffer."

"Then why the blazes won't you look me in the eye unless you're arguing with me? What else happened?"

"Nothing."

"What happened?"

Sarah paused, then turned her hand in his, clasping it, and caught his gaze. "She hinted that she'd raise doubts about your fitness as a father and make your life miserable with rumors and insinuations."

Daniel shook his head. "No one would believe her."

"They wouldn't have to believe her. All they'd have to do is repeat what they heard until it reaches far enough around town. Or Lavinia could hand pick some self-righteous biddy who doesn't know you to take it on as her personal mission. She didn't stop with threats to you, Daniel. She included the girls, and I have no doubt she'd stir at it until Kate or Molly came home from school in tears."

Anger surged through him. "She'd do that?" he questioned.

"On purpose?" His fist clenched. "Somebody ought to throttle her."

"Elizabeth told me that Lavinia's father disinherited her years ago and she's all alone. Her whole life centers around being president of the Suffrage Association. The attention I've received recently hasn't set well with her. My guess is she's unsettled and jealous. However it came to be, her threats were enough to scare me."

The words were sobering. He'd never realized the stakes had been so high. "So you stepped down? Because of Kate and Molly?" Their not-so-little kiss had cost her much.

She nodded again, this time more slowly. "It's the weakest thing I've ever done."

"That's what's got your goat, isn't it? You think you did something weak? Good God, Sarah."

Puzzlement crept across her features. "What?"

"It wasn't weak. It took guts, a lot of guts. Don't you know that?" He stroked her hand, small in his, but not weak, never weak.

She shrugged. Her face clouded, then she shook the heavy-heartedness off. Daniel waited for her tirade, anticipating the blame in her words. Instead, she sat, saying nothing, until he realized it wasn't vengeful anger she'd been expressing earlier. It wasn't Kate or Molly she blamed, or even him, but herself.

He released her hand and let the silence surround them for a while, as he guided the horses farther from the city. Bleak brown grass covered the plains and rolling hills. He let the horses drift out across it, seeking the last vestiges of withered green. Beside him, Sarah's teeth chattered, reminding him of the chill. He reined in the horses, turned them, and headed back toward town. They reached the City Ditch, brown and sluggish, and he paused. A stale odor hung in the air above the ditch. Quite a place. Only a woman like Sarah would take her walks at a place like this.

Glancing at her from the corner of her eye, he tried to gauge her emotions, then gave up. "You all right?"

"Of course I'm all right."

What in the world was he supposed to say to her? He doubted she'd be reassured by trite gestures of comfort any more than he'd be comfortable offering them. But he couldn't very well just let the matter go without saying anything. She'd want him just to say what he meant, straight up, whether it was the proper thing to say to a lady or not. He exhaled and tried to find the right words, then gave up and blurted out, "If it makes you feel any better, I didn't exactly plan to kiss you, and I'm not much happier about it than you are. The indiscretion just didn't mess up my life the way it did yours."

She looked surprised, appreciative, and concerned, all rolled into one. "Daniel, I'm sorry. I know it wasn't planned. On either of our parts."

"But it happened, nonetheless."

She nodded and offered a tiny smile. "That it did."

"It was totally irrational," he added.

Her smile widened. "Totally and completely inappropriate."

"And I should be begging your forgiveness for it and all the heartache it caused." He took her hand again, hoping she wouldn't pull it away.

"But you're not?"

"No, I'm not." The admission surprised him. He plunged on, letting the moment drive his words. "It's the first time I've behaved with such abandon since the time I bit the end off a candy stick the shopkeeper gave me at the mercantile when I was five years old."

"That's a long time ago."

He shrugged, wishing he'd never mentioned the incident.

"My father was a minister. There were rules."

"And if you broke them?" She rubbed his hand with her thumb.

Daniel closed his eyes, remembering the punishments he'd endured until he'd finally learned to obey. "I didn't," he evaded.

"You ate the candy stick."

He glanced at her, wanting to trust. "One bite, then my father made me give it back, then thrashed me and sat me in the corner with the Bible, which I couldn't even read yet. I never did find out why it was wrong to accept what was given to me." He paused, then surged ahead, before he lost his nerve. "If it was wrong to take that kiss, then I'll apologize, but if it wasn't, I'm not going to do it this time."

She squeezed his hand in understanding. "It wasn't wrong, Daniel. It was reckless. We were both reckless."

Daniel grinned, letting the mood carry him further from his self-restraint. "Reckless? Me? I don't think I've ever been reckless before."

She laughed, a portrait of freedom, so different from him. Or was she? He sensed her carefree attitude covered something deeper, a part of herself she preferred to keep hidden behind a mask of outspokenness. "Is that why you were so mad, because you were reckless?"

For a moment, he thought she might not answer. But she nodded, offering admission, a tiny bit of herself. "Being reckless put me in a vulnerable position. You don't get places in this world when you do that. I know better."

Oddly, the words made sense. Except that his father had preached denial as the preferred method. Control yourself and your behavior, and you shall win God's favor. Practice civility and you shall win respect. Thinking about it, he wasn't all that sure so much self-restraint was worth it.

He smiled at Sarah and decided to blatantly ignore his

father's directives against being too direct. "So, we've established that it was reckless and that we both knew better and that no one's to blame. Do you think we can get past it and figure out what is going on between us?"

"I don't know if I want to figure it out. It's getting in the way."

"Do you propose we try to ignore it?"

"I think we need not to make more of it than it is. We're from two very different worlds and I really don't—"

"You're right, we are, and maybe that's part of the attraction." Daniel pushed on, refusing to let the subject lie. If they didn't discuss it now, it might never get discussed. And damn it, it *demanded* discussion.

"And maybe the appeal is in the forbidden aspect of it. Did you ever stop to think maybe you kissed me like that because it *was* improper and reckless? Or because I'm enough of an independent spirit that you knew I wouldn't slap you?"

He pondered the thought. She might be right, but there had to be more to it. "So why did you kiss me back?"

She grinned, mischievous, and shrugged her shoulders. "The challenge of leading you astray?"

"It was a hell of a kiss."

She sighed. "That it was."

They sat, cold air nipping at their faces. That it was a hell of a kiss was a bit of an understatement, and Daniel sensed she knew it as well as he did. Her eyes had hungered for him, inviting his lips on hers. Her mouth had been soft and sensual, demanding and responsive, hot and liquid and amazing.

He shifted on the seat and wondered what to do next. God, he wanted to kiss her again, to see if the desire was as molten now as it had been before, if the hardening in his loins was as real as he thought it was. But this moment, too, of pure understanding, was theirs and he didn't want to lose it.

He shifted again and peered out at Sarah's favorite walking place. "You ever get tired of looking at this wretched ditch?"

"All the time. But it's quiet out here. Empty enough to sort out my thoughts."

"There's talk that folks want to clean it up, before it gets any worse. Imagine how it reeks in the summer heat."

"It *does* reek. When I first got to town, it was horrid. I tried one walk out here then quit until fall."

She must have fussed like crazy about it, probably cursed up one side and down the other. He smiled at the image. "They'll never get folks to stop dumping in it."

"Never say never. Look at abolition. Look at what ladies are gaining with suffrage. Look what the temperance movements are doing. Look what we did with the dog bounty. Take a group of dedicated people, a worthwhile cause, toss in some leadership and enthusiasm, and you can accomplish anything."

Daniel eyed her animated face. She could fire up the whole cause all right. She should be in the midst of it. He'd just tell her about the efforts already afoot and let her plunge in while he went back to his simple, uncluttered life. After all, this sort of agitation was right up her alley and not at all up his, the sort of thing he hated.

"The *News* said there's a town meeting to discuss the city water system scheduled for Monday evening," he announced. He glanced at her and discovered an ocean of longing in her eyes that melted his resolution to remain uninvolved. "Would you care to join me?"

Chapter Nine

Sarah sighed, closed the logbook and set it aside, glad the wire was quiet for a while. She'd spent the week rehashing Daniel's invitation. He was the most intriguing man she'd ever met. His businesslike appearance couldn't hide his well-toned body. Beneath those crisp white shirts lay rippling muscles shaped by years of woodworking, evident each time he stretched. And he hid a complicated personality behind his professionalism.

That she couldn't get him out of her mind unnerved her. She should be deep in plans to clean up the City Ditch. But here she was, unable to think about anything but Daniel himself.

She glanced around the telegraph office, glad she didn't have to stay much later. Late afternoon shadows were already darkening the windows. Rising, she crossed the room and lifted the lantern from its hook near the door. Ernie, the new night telegrapher, would need it before too long. With the early evening telegrams and the last two trains of the day, it would be handier for him to have it nearby. She set it next to the sending key and gathered her winter shawl and gloves.

"Y'all set, Miss Sarah?" Ernie's tinny voice squawked from across the lobby. A gust of cold air swept through the empty depot as he closed the outer door behind him.

"Just getting my things," Sarah called.

Ernie entered the office and grinned at her with a toothless smile. His tall, lanky frame filled the doorway, his unruly black hair full of cowlicks. "Sure is mighty nice havin' y'all back on day shift. Didn't know how much I missed you till you was gone."

"I'm glad to be back, too. Frank doesn't like it much, though." In fact, Frank Bates had protested quite a bit when Jim informed the staff of their new assignments.

"Frank don't like much of anything. He ought not to harp about it, seeing how he's always pitchin' a fit about havin' too much to do. Jim shoulda put you both on days from the start." Ernie settled onto the stool and reached for the logbook.

"Well, I'm glad he finally did. I didn't much care for nights." Sarah smiled at the bony telegrapher, glad he'd agreed to rearrange the shifts. Ernie worked the lonely night shift while she and Frank split the hours between four a.m. and six p.m., overlapping shifts at midday. Jim had announced the new schedule at the end of last week, citing heavy daytime telegraph activity, but she'd known Daniel's actions had made it easier.

"You sure you don't mind coming in early?"

"Just an hour. Don't make me no never mind. Got nothin' to do and nowhere to do it. I heard how that other committee you was on picked a plan to register folks' dogs and all. Figured you'd be lookin' for somethin' else to do. Go on and git goin' to that meeting of yours." He grinned again and wedged his long legs under the counter.

"Thanks, Ernie. I'll see you tomorrow night."

He waved his fingers at her, opened the logbook, and began his review of the day's activity.

Sarah pulled on her wraps and headed out, her mind again drifting to Daniel's invitation. The cold air stung and she increased her pace, reviewing what she'd read about the issue in the *News*. A local doctor had written in about the risk of typhoid, complaining about all the folks dumping waste in Cherry Creek and the City Ditch. The new sewage pipes that had been laid just last year were already too small to handle the demand, and property owners were bickering about the possibility of more assessments. It had all the makings of a wonderful controversy.

A familiar flicker of challenge bubbled through her and she smiled to herself, feeling somewhat better about the meeting. Daniel had known she'd be unable to resist being in the middle of it all. Perhaps she'd just been too busy to get excited, what with the shift changes and the distraction Daniel created.

His involvement surprised her. He'd protested and balked at every turn of the dog bounty fight. Maybe his success there was just what he'd needed. Still, she hadn't expected that he'd voluntarily step forward a second time.

She strode through the thinning downtown crowds, the wind chafing her cheeks. Shopkeepers, shutting up their stores, waved and hustled back inside to the warmth. Heavens, here she was, thinking about Daniel again. Maybe she was worrying too much. Just because she'd slipped once, it didn't mean things would get out of hand again. Besides, if it hadn't been for Lavinia opening that door, there wouldn't be a problem. Daniel was right; she was mad at herself. It hadn't been the kiss at all, but the weak position it had put her in.

She liked Daniel. He'd let his guard down and she'd discovered an intelligent, passionate man. They'd work well together; she knew it.

But, by God, she wasn't about to let Elizabeth Byers truss her up in any more ball gowns.

She didn't need any more complications in her life. Daniel piqued her interest and there was nothing at all wrong with them spending time together. They could forget about that kiss, keep things professional, and pour their energies into more important things. After all, they'd gotten it out of their systems.

Two hours later, Sarah sat in a stiff wooden chair, listening to

James Archer, president of the Denver City Water Company, drone on about his plans to improve the city's water system. Archer's long bushy beard bobbed below his balding head and his lined face accented stern features. From the crowd's lack of argument, it was evident that Archer would dominate this committee, just as he dominated Denver's growing utility system.

Sarah glanced at Daniel from the corner of her eye.

He shifted in his chair, then slid into a slump.

"What do you think?" she whispered.

"I think this is a waste of time. Let's go."

Sarah nodded.

Daniel rose, gathered their wraps, and waited for Sarah. They squeezed their way down the row and out of the room.

"I'm not sure what I expected," Sarah announced as soon as they were outside. "Certainly not Archer dictating everything."

"Truth be told, Sarah, I didn't expect it either, though I should have. Archer's water delivery system made life a lot easier in this town. Folks aren't likely to turn against him now. Besides, if he says he has a plan to carry the wastewater away, he'll get it done. I guess I'd rather he told us more about it, though." Daniel's forehead creased. "You aren't angry I suggested we come, are you?"

Sarah shook her head. "No, I'm just not used to having everything all arranged. I rather like getting in with both hands, figuring out the best course, taking a direct role."

Daniel smiled, a quiet hint of laughter surfacing then fading, almost before it could be heard. "You don't like being in the background, do you?"

She caught the slight sparkle in his eyes and smiled back. "Is it that obvious?"

"You're not much of a wallflower."

"Thank you, I think."

They shuffled through the empty street, evening darkness

surrounding them. The air was braced with moisture, hinting of snow, and Sarah tugged her shawl more closely around her.

Daniel buttoned his overcoat and glanced in her direction. "I'm sorry there wasn't more opportunity for you."

"It's all right, Daniel. Archer's water company seems on target. The plan for using a bigger pump should take care of the complaints about capacity and the supply problem will be solved. There's not much for the public to do on that end."

"I guess I expected this meeting to focus more on the disposal problem." His voice was full of apology and something that almost sounded like disappointment.

"I think Dr. Denison is still going to attempt to organize a subcommittee. I'm going to join his efforts to focus on fighting the sewage while Archer and the city fathers deal with fixing the system. We'll need to raise money for a flyer campaign and increase the letters to the editor. It wouldn't hurt to organize a few groups to get out and literally clean things up. That'll be men, I suspect, though the women could do door-to-door visitation to explain the risk of disease. The people we most need to reach may not even read. We've got to get word out to them."

They neared the steps of her boarding house, and she debated with herself over whether to ask for his help or wait for him to volunteer. Daniel was new to all this, and she doubted he'd budge too far without a little prompting. They'd stopped, waiting. She hated the absurd uncertainty over asking him for even surfacing and pushed it away, then turned to him. "Would you sound out interest among the businessmen for a clean-up day? It would be so much more effective coming from one of their own."

He shrugged with obvious discomfort. "No promises, Sarah. Cleaning ditches would be dirty work, and I'm not such a skillful persuader as you are." He caught her gaze, his features softening under the light of the gas lamp. "I'm sure I can drum up interest for some political pressure, though. Maybe push Archer faster on his design to carry the waste away?"

She rolled her eyes at him, hating the way he dodged involvement when it became uncomfortable. "The health of this city is the concern of everyone in it," she said, her hands punctuating the air of their own accord.

"Eight days ago, I couldn't have cared less about the stench of the City Ditch or the number of cesspools in town and I was getting along just fine." His words were edged with controlled crispness, an obvious attempt to keep Sarah's fellow boarders from overhearing and peering out the windows.

She pinned her gaze on his and changed tactics. "How many lower-class people do you prepare for burial?"

"What?"

"How many poor people do you bury?" She knew the answer already, just by the confused look on his face and the increasing indignation in his voice.

He stared at her for a moment, then threw up his hands. "What does that have to do with whether I should be involved in city sewage?"

"Maybe you don't know anyone who has a cesspool behind their house. Maybe you've never noticed the families who overflow their cramped, dismal hovels and the muck outside their back doors. Maybe you're just too high and mighty."

"You're the one sounding like she's high and mighty."

"Come Saturday, I'm going to be out along the worst part of Cherry Creek, picking up waste. What are you going to be doing?" A twinge of self-reproach poked at her. She wasn't high and mighty. She wasn't. She was simply dedicated, committed to her cause. She planted her hands firmly on her hips and drew herself up to her full height and ignored all the crazy, mixed-up thoughts running roughshod through her resolve. "I'd invite you to join me but you might get your hands dirty, and we all know Daniel Petterman is above that. If you care to prove me wrong, you can ask Denison where to find me."

She left the challenge hanging, turned and pointedly left him standing at the bottom of the front steps, mouth agape.

How in heaven's name had she ever thought she would work well with such a pompous, unimaginative, stick-in-the-mud?

Daniel approached the Larimer Street Bridge wishing someone had died so he would have an excuse to avoid Sarah's project. Of all the dismal ways to spend a Saturday afternoon, this had to take the cake. And to top it all, he didn't know why the heck he was doing it in the first place.

Cherry Creek stretched through the city, a narrow ribbon of mucky brown water. Looking down the creek, he spied an area of small, run-down cabins, and headed in their direction. Serious businessmen hadn't built close to the creek since the floods of the sixties, but the open lowlands and usually placid water had attracted the newcomers. Their small homes were as Sarah had described. Daniel felt a stab of self-recrimination and sighed.

Why did that woman have to be right about everything?

"Well, would you look who finally showed up," Bill Byers observed from the middle of the creek. "You joining me or that pack of slowpokes back there?" He gestured to the group clustered on the creek edge, a few hundred feet away.

Daniel waved to his friend and picked his way closer to the creek. The area was scattered with decaying newspapers and empty glass bottles. A slight odor of decay hung in the air, but not nearly so thick as it likely would in the summer. He approached the edge of the water and noted a stronger stench.

"C'mon in, the water's fine," Bill challenged. He stood in the ankle-deep stream, clearly enjoying himself. "Thank God it's low."

Daniel eyed the muck, skeptical. "Aren't you afraid you'll catch something?"

"I'll just have Libby draw me a nice hot bath. She owes me for letting her host another of those damned suffrage meetings this afternoon. As long as I don't drink the water, I figure it should be all right."

Already, Daniel's shoes were mired in thick mud. Thank goodness he'd donned a pair of old brogans before he'd left home. He marched farther into the creek, felt the cold water seep over the tops of his boots, and pushed up his sleeves. "What exactly are we doing?"

"Trying to pick up floating garbage," Byers indicated a gunnysack dangling from his waist. "I got fish heads, scraps of oilskin, and a few corn cobs, among other things."

By now, the others were moving closer. They, too, carried burlap sacks but focused on picking up the scattered debris along the banks of the creek. They stretched across the flat area that filled with water in the spring of the year. Dry now, it was host to rotting refuse, clear remnants of emptied slop pails.

Among the group, he spied Sarah's small frame. She bent to snatch up a handful of old watermelon rinds, then rose and caught his gaze. Her expression registered surprise and she stared for a moment before marching over. Not bothering to peel off her stained work glove, she stuck her hands on her hips.

"You're late." Her voice held a trace of pleased warmth but the words nettled at him.

He glared at her, wanting to tell her she ought to be happy he was here at all. Bill Byers was the only other businessman present. The realization was somewhat hollow, though, and of little satisfaction. Any minute, she'd point out that they'd failed to invite any of the others and he'd have to admit she was right again. He shifted slightly, sloshing in the water.

"You never did tell me what time."

"The time was announced in the *News,* and don't tell me you didn't see it because you obviously read enough of the notice to know where to find us." Her voice held chastisement, but not as much as he'd expected. In fact, he thought he detected a carefully hidden note of admiration. He glanced at her and found a spark of humor in her eyes.

"Glad to see me?" he teased.

"Extra hands are always welcome." She straightened, the lightheartedness disappearing in the shadow of brisk efficiency. "Here, take my extra bag. You're on your own for the gloves. Either help Bill here or join the rest of us on the shoreline."

"I think I'd prefer Bill's company, thank you." Plowing further into the chilly water, he mucked his way to the middle of the creek.

"Lover's quarrel?" Bill queried, reaching for an empty patent medicine bottle.

"Hardly." Daniel glanced at his friend. "She just hates it that I'm not as enthusiastic about the dirty work of this project as she is. The only time I seem to do anything right is when I flaunt what's expected. If I tease at her, I can't tell if she likes it or hates it. If I behave like a gentleman or think like a businessman, she's insulted."

Bill laughed heartily. "Women make an art of it, old boy. Libby can twist me around her little finger when she puts on that hurt attitude. 'Course after this many years, she usually gets what she wants without all the bother."

It didn't quite seem like something Sarah would do. "I don't know that it's a game with her and I'm not sure she's trying to get anything. She just flat doesn't like the fact that I'm not extreme."

"You're here, aren't you?"

Bill did have a point. Daniel scooped up a section of newspaper and stuffed it into the bag. Was he really here because

Sarah had acted hurt and betrayed?

He shook his head. She'd made him realize a thing or two maybe, but it sure wasn't female manipulation. "It's for the good of the community, not some radical cause."

Bill nodded sagely, accepting the answer, then switched gears. "So, who defines radical?"

"C'mon, Bill, you know what I mean. Quit being philosophical."

"Just let me play the devil's advocate for a minute. This is for the common good so it's not radical? What *is* radical?"

Daniel shrugged. He'd play along, for the sake of discussion. "Well, if you're looking at it along those lines, I guess I'd venture radical would be something that is promoted either by or for the benefit of a small group."

"So if the issue concerns a large group, it's not radical?"

"I guess." What the hell was Bill getting at?

"Then I guess I'm going to have to tell Sarah you're in support of women's suffrage after all." Bill stood up and grinned from ear to ear.

"Now just wait one danged minute—"

"Relax. I'm just trying to roil up your thoughts a bit."

Daniel let it rest. It'd take more than a little bit of questioning by Bill Byers for anyone to figure out his thoughts, himself included. Still, Bill did have a point. Could be his lifelong definition of extreme was a smidgeon off-center. "How long have you been out here?" he asked, ready to switch topics to something a little more comfortable.

"Couple of hours. I never knew the creek had gotten this bad. Back when the *News* was located in this neighborhood, things weren't so filthy. 'Course there were a whole lot fewer people then, too." He glanced up. "Look out, here comes your radical. Ask her who gets to define the word." He slogged his way through the creek water, leaving Daniel alone.

Sarah marched down the creekside, her boots thick with caked mud. The hem of her tattered brown skirt was soiled and blond curls escaped from her bun, spilling alongside her face in wispy tendrils. On Sarah, the disarray looked perfect.

She stopped and took a determined breath. "Daniel, look, I'm glad you're here and I'm sorry I snapped at you."

"You usually do." He kept his voice light, hoping she wouldn't get her hackles back up. "Why should today be any different? Funny thing is I keep coming back for more."

"I didn't expect you."

"Truly, Sarah, I didn't expect to come. But you have this uncanny ability to make a man feel about two inches tall." He waded out of the water until he reached her side.

She looked up at him, eyes full of sincerity. "I didn't mean—"

"Yes, you did," he told her in a quiet tone. "You knew exactly what you were doing when you uttered that little challenge. I haven't been so involved in things that are none of my business since I was in knee britches. I've lost all sense of polite gentility around you and most of the time, I can't keep a civil tongue. Folks are going to start thinking I've lost my mind."

"Maybe you're just finding it."

He thought about the comment for a moment, watching Sarah's petite rear as she bent after garbage. What was it Bill had said? Ask Sarah to define radical? Maybe he had a point. Maybe they were both a bit off in their opinions. He hated to risk her getting angry, but if he didn't bring it up now, he probably wouldn't at all.

He waited while she plucked the last blackened orange peel from the ground then caught her arm and pulled her upward. "Do you think, though, that you might have a little consideration for my point of view? You don't need to dismiss my opinions simply because they are not identical to yours. Do you?"

"Was that really what I was doing?"

"If you spent a little more time discussing things with me and a little less time judging me, perhaps you might discover a few things yourself."

"But, Daniel, there are times when you are so wrong."

He tipped his head, accepting the possibility. "Only when we use your definition. But if it's narrow-minded for me to fix my thoughts on a certain way of looking at things, isn't it narrow-minded when you do it, too?"

"Me? Narrow-minded?" She dismissed the thought and, for a moment, Daniel worried she'd taken the question wrong. She took a few steps then turned and walked back to him. "A person who looks at the far-reaching consequences and considers different alternatives is anything but narrow-minded."

Daniel felt his mouth stretch into a smile at her stubborn pride. "Even when she refuses to consider that someone else may not look at things in the same manner?"

She stared at him, eyes widening. "I do that?" The question came out in a quiet breath.

He nodded, reluctant to reveal too much of himself but needing her to understand. "You have made me feel, at various times, heartless, backward, and childish. Yet, I consider myself none of those things and neither would most people who know me."

Her eyes clouded, her bag of garbage falling at her feet. With an uncharacteristically tentative movement, she touched his arm. "Goodness, I didn't intend to make you feel that way."

"You are very adept at stirring people to action, Sarah, even when they don't wish to be stirred."

"You give me a great deal of power." The comment hung between them, its impact unsettling.

"I don't give you anything," Daniel sidestepped. "You take it."

The moment passed and Sarah pulled her hand from his arm, offering her attention to the last remaining remnants of refuse. A group of fellow garbage collectors passed them and drifted away from the creek. Sarah waved to them and turned back to Daniel. "I've charged right into things for years. Mother always told me I had to make myself known, leave a mark on the world, prove I was a leader and not just another pretty face."

"But you are a pretty face. Why would you want to downplay it?" He marveled at her complexity. What other woman would dismiss her own beauty that way? In his eyes, it only served to increase her appeal.

"Because I'm more than that. I *can* do whatever needs to be done and I can do it well."

"Did anyone ever say you couldn't?" He watched her, waiting for her to point out that he had said that very thing, and wondering how the devil he could ever deny it.

"No, but most people assume women are frail-minded creatures who don't know what they're doing. They think of us as decorative without a care to our capabilities."

Daniel mulled her words, needing her to understand, and chose his own words carefully. "I was always taught that women were superior to men's baser instincts, the personification of all that was fine and good, and that men should treat them as such, not place burdens on them. Doing so is an indication of respect."

She nodded, digesting the explanation but clearly not agreeing with it. "But what if we see it as an indication that you feel us incapable and unworthy?" she offered. "Besides, you may all be fooling yourselves into thinking that you do this as a symbol of supplication, but we all know such behavior has come to mean more than that. Pick up any etiquette book, homemaker's guide, or pamphlet on the 'facts of life,' so to say, and they will all tell you that a woman is to be subservient because she has fewer mental and physical faculties."

He wrinkled his eyebrows, puzzled. "I don't think I've ever looked at any of those items."

She sighed. "Well, most women are indoctrinated with such garbage. Is it any wonder I'm trying to prove such beliefs wrong?"

She had a point. Again. "Yet you persist in doing things flamboyantly and your behavior draws attention."

"Precisely. Do something out of the ordinary and people take a closer look."

"Sometimes they dismiss you as too radical."

"Then they miss the point entirely. They're the same people who would refuse to consider the issue no matter how it was presented to them."

"Like me?" he prompted, already knowing the answer.

She offered a soft smile. "Yes, like you." She kicked at a rock, sending it toward the creek, before gazing directly at him. "You don't like it when life is not how you expect it to be, do you?"

"No. But, then, you don't like it much when it is."

She laughed. "Goodness, we are quite an unlikely pair, aren't we? Do you know we've managed to have a whole conversation without yelling at one another?"

"I could fix that."

"I'll just bet you could." She hugged herself against the cold and offered a disarming smile.

"You're shivering. How long have you been out here?"

She shrugged. "A few hours, I suppose."

"Look, our sacks are full, folks are starting to drift off, and the wind is picking up. Let's head over to the cafe for a cup of something hot. We could stop and get Kate and Molly."

Sarah's eyes brightened. "Cocoa would be wonderful," she glanced down at her muddy clothing, "but we're hardly fit for the cafe."

Daniel laughed. "True enough. How about my kitchen?"

Sarah wavered, then nodded. Waving at the few scattered remaining souls along the creek, they turned toward Blake Street. Within a few short minutes, their muddy shoes were on the back porch and Mrs. Winifred was tsking about the mess.

"It'll clean up," Daniel told her.

She shook her head and set cups of cocoa on the table before exiting the kitchen.

"Gosh, you and Papa must have worked very hard," Molly piped up. "Papa never lets us make such a mess unless we're so tired we're gonna drop."

"Molly, be polite," Daniel cautioned.

Sarah detected a hint of nervousness in his voice, as if he was unsure about inviting her now that it was all said and done. Perhaps he was as unsure as she was about coming.

"It's all right, let her chat. I don't mind. I suspect, Molly, that you've managed to hit the nail squarely on the end. We're very tired." The comment seemed to satisfy Molly, and Sarah was glad when the tension of the moment drifted away.

"We're very glad you decided to stop by," Kate said.

Sarah smiled at her and nodded, recognizing that Kate never seemed to need the response that Molly always courted.

"Here's to you, ladies," Daniel announced, lifting his cup high into the air. Sarah noted just enough surprise in Kate's raised eyebrows to realize that his abandon was unusual.

"Mrs. Winifred says Papa's gonna be running for mayor, next thing."

"Molly."

Sarah laughed at Daniel's chagrin. "Well, I don't think I'd lay my bets on that one if I were you. I don't believe your papa is quite ready for politics. I think you'd more likely find me running for office than you would him."

"You can't be a mayor, Miss Sarah. Only men can be mayors and stuff like that."

Sarah raised her eyebrows. She shouldn't be surprised that Molly would believe such a thing was true. Obviously Daniel hadn't offered her any other alternative. "Did you know women can vote and serve on juries up in Wyoming Territory?" she queried, her eyes on Daniel, gauging his reaction.

"Sarah," he cautioned, just as she had expected.

She ignored him as Kate and Molly shook their heads, then she pasted a smile on her face and stared at him. "Is there something you wanted, Daniel?"

"Must you discuss suffrage with the girls?"

"I was making conversation. Besides, what on earth is wrong with exposing them to suffrage?" She widened her eyes at him. "Or are you back to being narrow-minded again?"

"I am not being narrow-minded," he announced. "I am sharing a cup of cocoa with my daughters and I am allowing them to converse with an adult despite the fact that most folks advise that children should be seen and not heard." The teasing left his voice, indicating she'd crossed some invisible line he'd neglected to tell her about. "Don't you dare tell me that now I'm a stick-in-the-mud because I do not want to have them embroiled in a political discussion."

"But you are a stick-in-the-mud," she reminded him with a lilt. Goodness, toss in the girls and he lost all sense of the progress they'd made. The man was absolutely maddening, but she'd be hog-tied if she was going to get drawn into another argument.

"And you're—"

"Papa?"

Sarah and Daniel both started at the strict note in Kate's voice.

"I'm sorry, Daniel. I'm not used to conversing with children." She smiled at Kate and Molly. "I'm sorry, girls."

Daniel's eyes softened. "My apologies, as well. Perhaps I'm a bit protective."

A bit? The thought fluttered, unchecked, through her mind. Heavens, the man was sheltering the girls so much that they'd never be able to develop an independent opinion about anything. She wondered momentarily if he'd do the same if they were sons rather than daughters then shooed the idea away. She was judging again, drat it all.

"Miss Sarah?" Molly's voice pulled her back to the trio at the table.

"Hmmm?"

"If you aren't much used to children, maybe you ought to come help the other ladies up at our school. They're gonna help us put on a recitation."

"Oh, please, Miss Sarah," Kate chimed in, abandoning her usual reserve. "Our teacher said she could use extra hands. You could get used to us and help out at the same time."

Daniel looked from his daughters to Sarah, his expression one of apology merging with worry. "Now, girls, I'm not sure Miss Sarah—"

"It's all right, Daniel. I think it might be good for me and I'm sure I could help somehow." She offered a reassuring smile. It *would* be good for her. Besides, what possible trouble could she cause at a recitation, for heaven's sake?

Chapter Ten

Sarah shifted in her too-small seat in the primary classroom of the Arapahoe School. She glanced at the sparse group of mothers, some with toddlers at their knees, and resisted an urge to get up and flee. She wasn't anyone's mother and had no soapbox on which to stand, and everyone here knew it.

She drew a breath and reminded herself it was a meeting, like any other. Despite the unfamiliar territory, there would be things to do, things she'd be good at, things that had nothing to do with children. There must be something associated with recitations that needed a firm take-charge person.

Miss Clay walked to the front of the room, her ample hips swaying with each step. The distinctive scent of lemon verbena followed in her wake.

A willowy mother in the next line of seats leaned toward Sarah and whispered, "Best teacher in the city but she hasn't a clue how dull this thing is." She offered a wry smile and extended her hand. "Margaret Lassiter, mother of five."

"Sarah Donovan, mother of none, recruited by the Petterman girls." She shook Margaret's hand and shrugged her shoulders.

Margaret laughed and shifted her gaze to the front of the room.

The plump teacher clapped her hands together twice and beamed at the group. "Good afternoon, ladies. I see we have new faces, just as I had hoped when I asked the students to invite family friends as well as mothers. Our numbers have so dwindled these past few years. Please welcome those who are not among our usual group." She clapped her hands again, this time in a brief show of polite appreciation. "I've prepared a list of our entertainments as well as the tasks needed to support them." She waved at the blackboard behind her.

Sarah read the list. Kate and Molly hadn't been kidding when they'd called the show a "recitation." The long list contained one poem after another. The second list, tasks, was devoted to refreshments and setting up chairs.

"My hope this year is to attract a wider audience," Miss Clay explained, clasping her hands in front of her rather large bosom. "We seem to have dropped off in that area, as well."

Mrs. Lassiter rolled her eyes.

"Isn't this the same list as last year?" an unkempt young woman asked. She smoothed a few errant hairs from her face and crossed her arms in a defiant gesture of complaint.

Miss Clay stood straighter and leveled a gaze at the woman. "Classics, tried and true, Mrs. Benson. McGuffy's standard offerings. The framework of great literature."

"Great literature, yes, Miss Clay," Mrs. Lassiter said, "but must we always use the same ones?"

Mrs. Benson nodded. "I was thinking we should offer something new this year?"

The teacher's plump face twitched. "Changing the content would alter the intent of the exercise. Besides, I've already assigned the poems. Perhaps we should expand the refreshment table. Maybe more of the fathers will come."

A twinge of sympathy welled in Sarah's heart. Distasteful as the poems were, Miss Clay seemed attached to them, and there was no mistaking the hostility between her and Mrs. Benson.

"Miss Clay, if I might be so bold," Mrs. Lassiter said, "I've had four children come through your class and each year, it has been the same recital. Those that continue to attend do so only because they do not want to disappoint their children. We need to look at change."

Mrs. Benson scowled. "These poems are flat-out dull."

A well-groomed older woman stood and glared at the group. "I think Miss Clay is doing an admirable job and we ought to just stay out of it unless we can propose something better." She tossed her head at the group and resumed her seat.

Sarah shifted in her seat, more sure than ever that she did not belong there. Her mind leapt into action, seeking solutions that would end the growing sense of conflict filling the room.

"Aren't there any new poems?" Mrs. Benson asked.

Miss Clay shook her head. "These pieces are classics."

Tired of the bickering, Sarah stood and smiled at the group. "Perhaps the poems could be taught in class rather than used as the recitation pieces. That way, the children would still be exposed to them. Miss Clay could then explore something more entertaining for the presentation, perhaps forego poetry altogether."

"Hear, hear," Mrs. Benson added. "My husband says we ought to just let the kids make up limericks."

"The recitation is intended to expose the children to literature, to foster memorization skills, and to allow them to present in front of people. Limericks are out of the question." Miss Clay's voice shook and her chubby face had stiffened in defensive resolution.

Sarah glanced around the room and saw the same fierce expressions deepening on others' faces. "What about a play?"

The teacher stared at her as though she'd proposed a song and dance routine. "Oh, no. I hardly think . . ."

"It's not a bad idea. The men hate poetry and the children are not fond of it themselves." Mrs. Lassiter sat down at her desk and raised her eyebrows at the teacher. "Why not?"

"Oh, my, a play? I . . . well . . . I couldn't. I mean, I've never done such a thing. I wouldn't know how."

"Nonsense," said the woman who had earlier defended her skills. "You'd do fine."

Miss Clay's lower lip trembled. "As fine as I do with poetry recitations? I can teach a play, but I do not possess the skills to direct one. Do not put me in that position."

Sarah swallowed. "What about allowing someone else to direct? Miss Clay can teach about the play and utilize her talents to educate the children on drama and its history while organizing the other aspects of the event."

Miss Clay stood at the front, looking oddly relieved. "What a grand idea," she declared. "Would anyone like to serve as director?"

The room filled with silence for what seemed like an eternity. Finally, the well-dressed woman who had earlier defended Miss Clay raised her hand. "Mrs. Elliot is an ardent supporter of the theatre. Perhaps we should ask her."

Mrs. Lassiter snorted. "If Mrs. Elliot directs, we shall have nothing but melodrama, with her little darlings in the midst of it."

"Well, we all know that the very best of the roles will go to your children if you take on the job," the woman said, shaking her head.

"I don't want the job." Mrs. Lassiter stood with her hands on her hips. "Why does it even have to be one of us? Ask someone who doesn't have children." She turned and pointed to Sarah. "You, Sarah Donovan. It was your idea. You direct it."

Nine sets of eyes focused on Sarah and a wave of panic washed over her. She didn't even know how to talk to children. "I'd be happy to do what I can to assist, perhaps secure props or arrange advertising but—"

"You're good enough to come up with the idea but not to see it through."

"That's hardly the case, Mrs. Lassiter, and I think you know it."

Mrs. Lassiter pinned her with a stare. "Or is what they say true? That Sarah Donovan got her job through no skill of her own, that she is not truly as accomplished as she would have people believe?"

Sarah's breath caught and her jaw stiffened. Was that really what people were saying?

She glanced at the blackboard, with its list of poems. A play was definitely the right answer, for the children as well as the audience. Still, a poorly directed play would be as disastrous as the worn-out recitation.

Could she do it? It would be a whole new test of skills, something she'd never done. With children. But wouldn't it be something to pull it off?

Sarah straightened her back, feeling the familiar irresistible lure of a challenge, and nodded her acceptance.

Seconds later, she caught Mrs. Lassiter's satisfied smile and realized she'd been suckered.

Frank Bates lay on the rumpled bed of his sparse room in Mrs. King's boarding house. He peered at the tiny gray mouse in the corner and smiled.

"You like that cheese, huh fella?" he whispered.

The mouse tensed at the sound and waited without movement.

Frank smiled and sketched whiskers on his charcoal drawing of the rodent. As sketches went, he reckoned this one wasn't too bad. He didn't much like charcoal, but his pastel crayons were across the room, in their metal tin. Squeaky didn't pose for him all that often. He'd make do with the tools at hand.

He waited while the mouse snatched up the last crumb of cheese and scampered off behind the dresser. Then he rose and looked up at the high shelf that held his other drawings. Mostly all animals, they peered down at him, wordless friends.

If he'd had the nerve all those years ago, he'd have told his father to go to hell. Maybe one of his sketches would be hanging in some fancy museum somewhere. Maybe he'd be wealthy and famous and recognized everywhere he went.

Instead, he was working at a shit job in a railroad station. As jobs went, it was just one more shit job in a long line of shit jobs, all of them ruined in one way or another. He'd have been good at all of them, if it weren't for bad luck.

Frank slammed his sketchbook and charcoal pencils on the dresser and snarled at the reflection in the mirror. "Spineless, cowardly little bastard," he muttered. "No account little sissy. Be a man." He growled his father's words, crumpled the sketch into a ball, and threw it across the room.

Stupid drawings would get him nowhere. If he wasn't on his toes, Sarah Donovan would turn this job to ruin, too, and his father would be right. She'd signed up to take her primary operator test. He'd be out on the street, sure enough, and through no fault of his own, except that he'd let it happen. This time, he'd show some spine, prove he was a man.

Empty ideas slid through his mind until one stuck. All he had to do was send off a few telegrams to Big John, hint around that any and all proposals would be entertained, for a certain sum, and use Sarah's sine. Little Lark wouldn't know what hit her. Big John would pass word around and she'd have more propositions than she could shake a stick at.

Then it wouldn't be no time until she was gone, bad luck along with her.

"What do you mean there's not going to be a recitation this year?" Daniel asked, following his daughters up the stairs. Kate and Molly's brown curls bobbed in excitement. They were so animated he could hardly get a word in edgewise.

Molly jumped up and down, her black button-shoes tip-tapping on the upstairs hallway's polished wood floor. A small oval portrait bounced, frame and all, against the wall.

Kate frowned, censure in her hazel eyes. "Be careful, Molly." She straightened her back and tried to look official, brushing off her blue calico dress for effect. "We're going to put on a theatrical instead," she announced.

"A real live one," Molly added.

Daniel crossed his arms and bent to Molly's level. "As opposed to what, a dead one?"

Molly shattered into giggles while Kate rolled her eyes. "Papa, that truly wasn't very funny. I'm not sure you're very good at teasing."

Daniel frowned. There wasn't much he was good at, when it came to the girls. He tended to either treat them like small adults, because it was easier, or push too far, like now, only to have Kate recognize, and call attention to, his over-effort. "Molly thought it was funny."

"Molly thinks everything is funny."

"Perhaps Molly has good taste."

"Perhaps she doesn't." Kate shooed Molly into their bedroom and eased the door shut. "We'll be just a minute, Papa, and then we'll tell you all about the play Miss Sarah is going to help us put on."

The door closed completely, leaving him to digest Kate's words. So Sarah was going to direct a play. For years, Miss Clay had been presenting the same tried and true poetry recitation and now that Sarah was in the midst of it, they were going to do a play. He wondered how long it had taken her to convince Miss Clay and the group of mothers that they should let her refurbish the entire show.

He should have put his foot down when Molly issued the

invitation. But he'd been loath to protest, especially when he'd almost ruined all the progress he and Sarah had made that day. She just had so many newfangled ideas. Heaven only knew what sort of child-rearing notions she had.

Reminding himself to stay objective, he knocked on the girls' door. "Are you two ready in there?"

"Yes, Papa."

"Come in."

He opened the door and peered into their room. Their school dresses were hung, each on its own hook, just as he'd taught them. Shoes sat, paired up, in a straight row underneath their dresses. Kate was brushing out Molly's brown curls.

"So tell me about this theatrical," he prompted, seating himself on the bed next to them.

"Oh, it's gonna be so much fun. Lots and lots better than those same old poems we always do." Molly turned and smiled at him with excitement gleaming in her eyes. "Miss Sarah said so."

"Now, girls, there's nothing wrong with poetry." The words sprang more from loyalty than a sharp preference for odes and sonnets, and Daniel fought to keep his face serious. Kate and Molly needed to learn to appreciate fine literature.

Kate nodded in agreement. "That's what Miss Sarah said. She said poetry is special but that this year, we were going to do something different so we wouldn't get tired of things. I think that makes sense."

"It seems to."

"Miss Sarah says we're not gonna do a regular play, on account of most plays being for grown-ups," Molly added. "She says we're gonna read a book and then act it out."

"Don't you think that's a good idea, Papa? That way we're 'killing two birds with one stone.' " Kate slid off the bed and placed the hairbrush on the dresser, then turned back to Daniel, waiting for his opinion.

Daniel weighed the information, finding its logic more sound than he'd expected. "It certainly seems like a good idea. Did Miss Clay think so?"

"Oh, Miss Clay is very pleased. She's going to be in charge of refreshments and she's got all sorts of fancy baked goods planned." Kate winked at him knowingly.

Daniel stood, waited for Molly to climb off the bed, and turned down the blankets. "So, Molly girl, what story are you going to read? A fairy tale?"

She shook her head. "Oh, goodness no, Papa. We're going to do a 'piece of literature.' "

"Miss Sarah has lent Miss Clay her copy of *Little Women,*" Kate explained.

"*Little Women,* hmm? Why does that sound like something Miss Sarah would recommend?"

Kate curled her bare toes and gazed at him as if he'd said something wrong. "My friend Dorothy said her sister read it and it's a real good book about four sisters."

Daniel shrugged his shoulders. For the life of him, he couldn't recall a thing about the book save for its popularity these last few years. "I imagine it must be, then," he agreed, pointing to the open bed. "Come on, let's get you tucked in."

The girls crawled into their double bed and pulled up a worn scrap-quilt. Daniel bent to whisper a goodnight to each of them and kissed them on their cheeks, then turned and blew out the lamp. Pulling the door half shut behind him, he started down the stairs wondering what in the world Sarah had up her sleeve this time.

Near the end of the week, Sarah opened the door of the depot and rushed in. Between writing the script for the play, practicing for the primary op test, and work itself, she'd done nothing but rush all week. She should feel overwhelmed. Instead, invigoration filled her. She stomped her boots to shake off the morning's wet snow and waved to Jim.

"You got company, Sarah," he called from his perch behind the ticket counter.

Sarah glanced around the waiting room and spied two familiar brown heads. Kate and Molly sat on one of the padded leather seats, book in hand, intent on what they were reading. Goodness, they hadn't even heard her come in. She hung her cloak on a hook and crossed the room to where they sat.

"May I help you, ladies?" she asked.

"Oh, Miss Sarah, we've been waiting for you."

"We've come on an errand for Miss Clay. She wanted you to have a list of the parents who have signed up to help with costumes and set construction so you can start on things as soon as Thanksgiving is over. She doesn't have Papa's name down but we think you ought to add it."

"Why, thank you, Kate. And Miss Clay let you out of school to bring this?"

"Not 'xactly."

"What Molly means is that it's lunch time and we figured it would be better to catch you now, when you're just coming to work, instead of later when you're more busy."

"And does Miss Clay know you've left school to do this?"

"Not—"

"Lots of kids leave to take lunch at home. We don't need to get permission just as long as we're back in time."

Sarah nodded, accepting Kate's explanation for the sidestepping it was, and watched Frank Bates leave the telegraph room and saunter over to them. Leave it to Frank to add his two cents' worth.

"Figured it had to be you out here yakking," he stated with cocky sureness. He gestured at the girls. "Them kids was in the office yammerin' at me afore I sent 'em out here. They ought to be in school, seems to me. You about ready? I got a pile of messages to deliver and I want to get 'em done before the snow starts fallin' again."

"I'm sure Kate and Molly offer their apologies for disturbing you, Frank."

"Yeah, yeah. You ready? Jim sure lets you get away with straying onto other activities during work hours, don't he?"

Sarah glanced at the girls. "Not now, Frank."

He stepped closer to her and lowered his voice. "Get them kids out of here and make 'em stay out. You don't wanna mess with me." He stumbled back into the office, still muttering under his breath.

Sarah shook her head and turned to Kate and Molly. "Never mind him," she told them. "I have ten minutes before I'm officially on duty. Have you girls eaten? If not, come grab part of my sandwich before you go. Otherwise, your stomachs are liable to growl and Miss Clay will discover you didn't go home for lunch after all." She smiled at them, sealing their secret, and moved across the waiting room.

They followed her into her office while Frank glared at them and puttered around collecting telegrams and stuffing them into envelopes. Jim offered a smile, shoved his glasses higher onto his face, and whistled his way back to the freight room.

Sarah turned her attention to the girls, leaving her review of the logbook for later. "So, is that *Little Women* you were so involved in reading when I came in?" She handed each girl a half sandwich and gestured to the stools they'd sat on before.

"It is." Kate took a bite of the sandwich and settled herself on one stool while Molly clambered onto the other.

"I thought Miss Clay was reading it to you in class."

"She is. We just got impatient. We checked our own copy out at the public library so we can read ahead."

" 'Cept Kate hogs it all the time." Molly swung her legs back and forth against the legs of the stool, garnering another sharp glare from Frank and a look of reproach from her sister.

"That's only because I'm the better reader. It takes you too long."

Sarah grinned. "How do you find it, then?"

"Oh, it's very good. I can't decide who I like best. I like Meg but I like Beth, too."

"I like Jo," Molly announced between sandwich bites.

Frank bundled his stack of messages with a leather strap and reached for his worn overshoes. He buckled them on and Sarah tried to ignore his too obvious eavesdropping.

"I've always liked Jo, too," she told the girls.

"You're lots like Jo."

"You are, Miss Sarah. You aren't afraid of anything and you have lots of spunk."

She smiled at Molly's observation. Spunk? She supposed it was a fair assessment, but not quite the way she would have chosen to describe herself.

"Do you suppose Jo wants women to vote, too?" Molly continued.

"I wouldn't be half surprised, but I'm not going to tell you. That would be spoiling it. But I will tell you that Miss Alcott, the author of the book, is very much a supporter of women's suffrage."

Kate stopped eating and grew wide-eyed. "Oh, my, is she a radical, then?"

Sarah laughed. "Goodness, I'd never have thought of her that way, but perhaps she is. The Alcott family was very supportive of the abolition movement in New England."

Frank shook his head with a grunt and began fussing with his wool plaid overcoat. He shuffled out of the office, turning at the door. "You mind what I said, Sarah Donovan. You've crossed the line, messin' with me, and you're gonna be mighty sorry you ever did."

Sarah looked up at him. "Don't be so melodramatic, Frank."

"Don't say I didn't warn ya. I ain't having no more bad luck and I ain't gonna let you make me out no spineless coward. If you knew what was good for you, you'd have listened instead of flouting what I said. You just wasted the last chance I was offerin'."

He stared at her for a moment, intense anger pouring from his eyes, then turned and left her in stunned silence. The banging of the depot's outer door punctuated his lingering words and Sarah shivered.

Chapter Eleven

Sarah stood outside the front window of Daniel's coffin shop. Despite the "closed" sign on the front door, soft light poured out into the early evening darkness. If she was lucky, she'd catch his attention, get his commitment to help build the set for the play, and be on her way back home in no time. She peered through the glass.

Within the glow of the lantern, Daniel hunkered beside a half-finished wooden casket. His dark brown hair shimmered in the lamplight. Jacket and vest were draped over a chair, and his white shirtsleeves were rolled high on his upper arms. Tools were scattered on the floor. Concentration filled his face, sharpening the angle of his jaw as he sighted along the top of one side. He bit his bottom lip, knitted his eyebrows, and frowned. His thigh muscles tensed as he crouched lower, then eased as he stood in a single fluid movement.

Appreciation flowed through Sarah, warm in the early winter chill, and she stayed her hand. She'd knock in a minute.

Daniel grasped a plane and shaved it across the edge of the coffin, biceps rock-solid with the effort. He slid the plane again and blew at the wood shavings. They drifted through the air, floating like golden leaves in an autumn wind.

Sarah backed away from the window. Maybe this wasn't such a good idea, after all. Some other father could chair the construction committee. It didn't have to be Daniel.

The door swung open and Daniel leaned out into the night. "Sarah?"

Heat flowed into her face, and she shifted briefly, then masked her discomfort with a smile and stepped forward. "Hello, Daniel. I wanted to speak with you about the school program. Do you have a moment?"

His shoulders lifted in a slight shrug and he nodded, then stepped back, gesturing her in. "I was working on a coffin." He grinned at the obviousness of the comment, noticeably more at ease with her than he'd been a few weeks ago. "The room's a mess."

He closed and locked the door, and she entered the shop. The mellow scent of fresh cedar filled the air, lingering in the warmth of the small Franklin stove.

"Smells good in here. I thought coffins were made of plain old pine."

"Most. I usually keep one cedar in stock and a few families request something special. I don't make too many at all, anymore. With the big companies back east and the new metal coffins, it's easier to order them in. I just can't seem to stop making them altogether, though. There's something about working the wood that satisfies." Contentment crossed his face and drifted away. "Let me move those."

Sarah glanced at the jacket and vest on the chair. Already, he was rolling down his shirtsleeves, following society's rules. "No need," she countered. She picked up the garments, sat down, and laid them across her lap.

Daniel's unsettling hazel eyes widened almost imperceptibly and his lips parted, then closed. "All right." He fumbled in his pockets, pulling out gold cufflinks.

Sarah felt another wave of warmth creep into her face at his discomfort, but she left his clothes on her lap anyway. "You can keep working," she blurted out. "Please, don't stop on my account."

He glanced at her and held her gaze. Then a grin burst onto his face and he shook his head. "You want the cufflinks over there, too?"

You could just take off the shirt.

Sarah snapped off the thought. "I don't want to interrupt you. Just go on as you were and pay me no mind."

"You do bring out the worst in me, Sarah. You know that?"

He inched the white sleeves back up his arms. The fine brown hairs on his forearms glistened in the golden lantern light. His gaze again centered on Sarah and a smile tugged at the corners of his mouth.

She let the comment pass, enjoying his rare abandon too much to risk saying the wrong thing. She sat up straighter, purposely prim, and crossed her ankles daintily. His deliberate disregard of propriety was seductive, and she wondered if he realized it. She swallowed hard, unsure of his intent. Maybe he was just making a conscious effort not to be stuffy.

"Did you have a nice Thanksgiving?" he asked.

She shrugged. "Quiet, working the telegraph. Did you?"

"Quiet, too. Mrs. Winifred cooked a turkey before she left on Wednesday. Among the three of us, we put together a decent meal."

Daniel stared at her for a moment longer, then reached to the floor for his sanding block, rose and slid it back and forth along the cedar. His muscles rippled in a myriad of patterns with each different movement. Sarah watched him, her heart pounding, as the scratch of sandpaper against wood filled the shop.

"So, are you going to tell me what you stopped by for, or is this it?"

"Not originally." Sarah warmed at the unbidden comment,

and she fought for control, her mind in conflict over what she really wanted. Lord, she needed to state her business and get out of here. But all she could think about was Daniel and the passion lurking behind those piercing eyes, within his hard muscles.

"And now?"

Now I could watch you all night, waiting for you to grow hot enough to take off your shirt, hot enough to . . . "And now, I've had a chance to see a little more of what you do here."

"You ought to stop by when I'm laying out a body."

Only if it's mine. "I think I'll pass on the dead bodies."

"So, what did you want?"

"I came to ask you if you would be in charge of building a stage for the school play."

"One more thing you're getting me involved in?"

"You're the logical choice. Your girls attend the school, will likely be in the play, and you know how to build things. Besides, your daughters insisted I add your name to the list."

A twinkle lit his eyes. "Oh, they did, did they?"

"Were they wrong in thinking their father wanted to help and support their efforts?"

"Their efforts? Isn't this your play?"

Sarah shrugged. "Surprisingly, it isn't. I'm not quite sure how it came about, but I truly want this to go well so the kids can feel good about it."

"This mean you're abandoning the sewage fight?" Pausing, he pulled a wrinkled white handkerchief from his back pocket and wiped it across the glistening skin of his forehead.

Sarah's shoulders rose in a silent sigh. "I don't abandon anything. Sewage reform is a good cause, but I don't really think I'm the best person to head it up. Archer and Denison need to take the reins or it won't work. I still plan to help Denison and his committee."

"Good, since you managed to get me into it." He grinned for a brief moment, offering a light challenge.

"You invited me, much as I know you hate to admit it." She smiled at him, fighting an inexplicable urge to stick out her tongue. "So will you help with the set?"

"I'll help. Kate and Molly said the play is about a family of sisters. It *is* something suited to a school play?"

"Of course. I'm pulling bits and pieces from a wholesome, well-written novel. The children will like it as well as their parents, and it's literary enough for Miss Clay to deem fit for the classroom. Just a simple story of four sisters growing up and learning about life and themselves."

"Good." He resumed sanding the coffin, gritty scratching taking over their conversation until he paused, blew away the sawdust with a soft breath, and caressed the wood.

Sarah's own breath caught at the lightness of his touch.

He turned and caught her staring. "Sarah?"

"Hmm?" she said, words escaping her.

"You do realize I would've said no if you'd pushed your way in and demanded I help?"

Softly uttered, his honesty took her by surprise, another side of what was turning out to be a much more complicated personality than she'd expected. Arrogance and propriety she knew what to do with. "I know," she ventured, tentative in her frankness. "I've decided I'd rather have you on my side than try to push you around."

He smiled. "Me, too."

Sarah offered a small smile in return and rose from the chair, uncertain in this new facet of their relationship. "I need to be getting home. I have some scenes to draft." She laid his jacket and vest on the chair and moved across the room.

Daniel followed, hands in his pockets. "It's cold out there, bundle up." He paused, then pulled his hands free and adjusted her shawl, his cedar-scented hands resting on her arms.

She caught his gaze. "Thank you, Daniel."

"Sarah . . . next time, you don't need a reason to stop by." He swallowed and leaned his head forward. His hands caught her face, lifted it back and his mouth met hers, cautious and gentle.

Sarah's chest tightened, and her mouth opened. The insistent thump of her heartbeat filled her head until she couldn't even think. She drank in the kiss, drowning, until he pulled back.

"Goodnight," he whispered, his voice husky in the expectant void that surrounded them.

She heard herself respond in kind before she opened the door and stepped into the night, her mind searching for answers that were not there. She moved toward the dark street, out of the shop's meager light. Behind her, the door closed, and she realized her heart was still pounding.

Daniel had taken her by surprise again. Somewhere between his hard muscles and quiet teasing, images of his hands caressing her body had consumed her. When he'd blown away the sawdust, all the resolutions she'd held about pursuing this relationship at *her* pace had scattered into the air along with it.

It wasn't at all what she'd expected, and she almost wished she hadn't stopped at all.

Daniel sat in the rear of the classroom with several other parents, unable to take his eyes off Sarah. Dimly aware of the hum of voices, his mind scrambled. He should have stayed at home, away from the temptations that plagued him every time Sarah walked into a room. He willed his heart to be still and forced his attention to the reason he had come. Surely, in a room full of glowing gaslight and crowded with other parents, he could be objective about her, forget about her parted lips and wide violet eyes. He took a breath, seeking assurance that wasn't quite there, and glanced up.

Sarah stood in front of the room, fidgeting with her brown work skirt while she waited for the children to settle into their seats. Darkness graced the large windows just behind her. Before her, the seats were filled for the first "Wednesday evening rehearsal," as Sarah had chosen to call it. Frankly, Daniel was surprised at the turnout. Miss Clay had never held an evening rehearsal in all the years she'd been doing class presentations.

Sarah's glance darted around the room then settled on Daniel and she smiled for a moment before inhaling deeply and making eye contact with each of the students in turn. "How many of you have ever had your parents go away on a trip?" she asked.

Several students raised their hands and Sarah's shoulders relaxed. Confidence lit both her violet eyes and the wide smile of encouragement she offered to the group. "Good. Let's start with a discussion about how you felt."

Daniel settled back into the desk, more comfortable now that she'd quit fussing, and stretched his legs out from under the cramped desk.

He had to hand it to her; she sure knew how to work with a crowd. She'd been nervous, but he doubted anyone else had even picked up on it. But once she found her confidence, it surrounded her.

"I almost cried when Mama went to see Aunt Bess," one of the girls said, drawing his attention back to the discussion.

A freckle-faced boy shook his head with bravado. "Not me. Pa left me in charge and I had to watch over Ma and my sisters."

"Why do you suppose two people had different feelings about the same sort of situation?" Sarah prompted, her question personalized with soft sincerity.

Daniel felt himself drawn into her query, wanting to answer himself. How could she think she didn't know how to talk to children? She'd managed to convey genuine interest in every movement, every word.

Several children shrugged in unison. Expressions of tentative understanding crossed some of their faces. A few hands inched up, mostly those of adolescents ready to be heard.

Sarah nodded at one of the oldest girls, a redhead with errant curls and her own aura of self-confidence.

"I think it depends on what kind of person it is and what is being expected of them. Older kids, especially boys, are supposed to watch over others. But younger children, or those given less responsibility, depend more on their parents."

"That's right. Any other reasons?"

"Maybe it's how close you are to the person who's gone." The observation came from one of the few boys in the room and was delivered in a voice that couldn't quite make up its mind whether it wanted to be twelve or fourteen.

Grins crossed parents' faces and a few of the younger children chuckled at the sound. The boy's face reddened. Sarah nodded encouragement to the boy, a smile of acceptance lighting her face, as if she hadn't even heard the shift in pitch, and the boy's blush faded.

Appreciation for this new side of Sarah Donovan spread through Daniel, warming his heart, confirming what he already knew. He'd kissed Sarah because of who she was, not merely because he'd drowned in her eyes.

"All these observations are very good," Sarah stated, smoothing over any discomfort. "In a few minutes, I'm going to have you take turns at reading one of the scenes from our play. It's from the very beginning of the story, when Mr. March is away at war at Christmas. I want all of you to keep in mind how each person in the story might be feeling and how those feelings would show. You've read this part of the story in class, so everyone should be familiar with Meg, Jo, Beth, Amy, and

Marmee, and understand that they all felt and acted differently, even though they were all missing Mr. March. I will decide who will be each of these characters based upon how well you portray their feelings and how you fit together based on sizes and ages and coloring. Then we'll read some other scenes for the other characters."

She assembled the children into small groups, handing out scripts to each group. She'd sweet-talked Bill Byers into printing them up, just like she'd maneuvered the Odd Fellows into lending their hall for the event. She'd set up a construction day for Saturday and Daniel suspected most of the fathers would be there, building the stage, all of them feeling good about it, himself included.

Her blond head bobbed amid the children, her laughter ringing out as she sorted them and prepared them for the audition. The kids laughed with her, their enthusiasm sparking smiles among the parents.

He'd never in the world expected it, but Daniel was glad Sarah was here. Somewhere along the line, her forwardness had turned into a breath of fresh air.

He just hoped it didn't turn into a hurricane.

Sarah rushed into the depot, shedding her cloak as she crossed the waiting room. A cozy fire filled the room with warmth, drawing the waiting passengers close about it. An elderly man lounged, asleep on the leather-padded bench closest to it. A family of five sat on the other side with a picnic basket and sandwiches. Except for a couple in the far corner, the remainder of the large room was empty and Sarah's boots echoed on the wooden floor. The three tow-headed children looked up in surprise, then returned to their makeshift dinner.

"You're late," Frank Bates muttered from the doorway of the telegraph office.

"I know. I'm sorry, Frank. Rehearsal at the school ran longer than I expected."

He waited until she passed, then moved to the telegraph counter. "Yeah? Well, maybe you ought to just move on over there full-time, solve all our problems."

She turned away, biting back a retort, and hung her cloak on a bare wooden peg. Frank had been making snide comments all week, ever since finding out she'd filed to take the primary op test. She sure didn't need to ruffle his feathers any further. She pasted a smile on her face and crossed the room. "I'll come in early tomorrow. Anything unusual I need to know about?"

Frank lifted the corner of his lip in a barely perceptible sneer, then shook his head. "Wire's been quiet this morning." He paused, staring for a moment, then raised his eyebrows. "Ernie had a busy night, though. Ol' Big John's been missing his little Lark."

Sarah groaned. Not again. Things had been quiet since her blunt message a few weeks before. She didn't need this kind of attention, not just before the op test.

Frank picked at his front tooth with a fingernail for a moment, as if waiting for a comment. He stared at Sarah in the stretching silence.

She shrugged and picked up the logbook. Frank Bates could just stew for all she cared.

A gust of cold air swept through the building, telling her Jim had entered the waiting room, followed by his official announcement. "Train's boarding, folks."

Sarah glanced out the ticket window. In the lobby, passengers rose from their seats and stretched. The woman at the rear offered a chaste kiss on the cheek to her companion and straightened his tie. Fabric rustled as coats were donned and packages bumped together with soft thuds. Sarah smiled at the hustle and bustle of it all.

A bothersome tap on her shoulder pulled her attention away from the scene. Annoyed, she turned back to Frank. Lord, how she detested that man.

"There were a few more little notes, too," he said, his voice low enough to keep from carrying into the lobby. "Ernie tossed 'em all but I managed to find 'em in the trash can."

Sarah's heart thumped and she steadied her response. "You'd have done better leaving them where you found them."

"Maybe. But they might come in handy. You never know."

Pompous little fleabag. "They're my property, Frank." She damned the edge of anger that had crept into her voice and tried to ignore the knot forming in the pit of her stomach.

Frank grinned at her discomfort. "Yeah? Guess Ernie shouldn't have tossed 'em, huh?"

"Where *are* they?"

"All tucked safe away." He patted the pocket of his suit jacket. "You ain't got no business running personal messages out of this office and you know it. Figure that makes the messages the property of Kansas Pacific."

"And how does that happen to put them in your possession?"

"I'll just get 'em to the right folks. I got connections, you know."

It didn't take much figuring to reason out that Frank would have the news to his uncle before the day was done. A second report of misconduct, especially misconduct of this nature, would not sit well. It might even be serious enough to disqualify her from the primary op testing.

Damn that man.

"And what about Jim?" she ventured, glancing toward the lobby where her bespectacled friend was still ushering passengers out the door. Surely Jim's word would have some pull. He'd straightened things out before, hadn't he? Hadn't Frank been given his own warning to follow proper channels?

"I imagine things might just be bigger than Jim can handle. Who's to say he ain't got his own hand in the cookie jar?"

Anger surged through Sarah, hot and intense. She fought the urge to slap Frank's face. She wouldn't give him the satisfaction. "That's a bald-faced lie, and I resent the insinuation."

"Don't matter none how much you deny it. Them messages say otherwise. You had things hushed up there for a while, but Big John must have been talkin' you up good with all them 'inquiries' what came in last night."

The knot in her stomach tightened, churning and nauseous. "What are you talking about?"

"Ain't no way Kansas Pacific is going to let some randy little strumpet conduct her business from inside their station." He paused and let the threat settle. "Might be the best thing for both you and Jim if we was to make a little deal. What d'ya say, Lark?"

Chapter Twelve

Sarah glanced across the spacious meeting room of the Odd Fellows Hall. Surrounded by bare white walls, the hall was empty of its usual tables and chairs. Children milled about, most chattering away like members of an aimless committee in need of leadership. Sarah shook her head and reminded herself they were children. She wasn't on a mission and this wasn't a crusade. As soon as her assistants arrived, they would get busy. For now, let the children have their fun.

With the cast members who had shown up to run lines and those hammering away on set construction, there were more than twenty children in the room. Added to the mix were five fathers who tutored their sons on the finer points of square corners and how to brace the stage support legs. A steady drone of male voices, punctuated by the pounding of hammers, kept pace with the lighter voices of the cast members. Except for the lingering scent of sawdust in the air, the bustle was little different from the depot.

Surrounded by the comfortable noise, Sarah surveyed the group at the back of the room and spotted Daniel. He stood, bracing a two-by-four with one foot, a saw in hand. A brief smile graced his mouth before he bent to cut the lumber. The fabric of his white shirt shifted with each movement of his biceps. She watched, anticipating how the cotton would cling to his chest after a few hours of labor.

She filed the image away in her mind. Perhaps later, she'd

write a few lines to Miriam or Lise. Gracious, if either were here, she'd tease Sarah to no end for mooning away over a man.

"Miss Sarah?" a small voice beckoned with a tug to her skirt.

Sarah turned her attention to Molly. "What is it?"

"Everybody's here now. Are you ready for us to start?"

"I'm as ready as I'm going to be. Did you get everyone in their groups?"

Molly's chest puffed with pride. "I sure did. And every group has a leader. We told 'em we aren't going to give them full lines today. I don't think they liked it much."

Sarah's mouth lifted into a smile. She leaned forward and whispered in a quiet aside, "I'm not surprised."

Molly offered a sage nod of agreement, basking in her role of junior assistant.

Sarah hesitated a moment, then patted her on the back. She suspected she'd made the right decision, choosing Molly as a helper, despite her initial doubts. Though young in age, Molly's take-charge attitude made her a natural leader. She rivaled the other assistants in self-confidence and did her job as well as the older students.

The children were, as Molly had reported, assembled into small groups, each with an able prompter. Sarah's gaze drifted to each assistant in turn with a silent nod of confidence.

"All right, everyone," she began, "as promised, today we run lines. Each group will practice until they have their assigned scenes memorized a bit more. That way, we can spend our next rehearsal working on acting instead of figuring out what to say next. I'll also work individually with some of you on your characters. I'll start with you, Kate."

Kate looked up, her hazel eyes shocking in their resemblance to Daniel's.

Sarah drew a sharp breath. In many ways, Kate was so much her father's daughter. She'd mastered her lines quickly, already reciting them by rote. Yet she kept her emotions controlled, hidden under the surface. Sarah beckoned to her with an enthusiastic gesture.

She was conscious of Daniel's observant gaze as Kate approached, and she fought to keep her attention on the task at hand. She needed to pull Kate's passion out. Sarah had cast her as Jo, an unusual choice for a girl more suited to be Beth, but one in which she had faith. Underneath that cool exterior lay great intensity, she was sure of it.

"Hello, Kate. Are you ready to start exploring Jo?"

Kate bobbed her brown curls in a serious nod. "I have all my lines memorized," she announced.

"That's perfect. It means you can focus more attention on how you say those lines." Sarah spied an empty area on the stage, near Daniel, and led the way across the room, seeking her next words with care. Children were an unknown course and she didn't want to dampen Kate's enthusiasm. She brushed sawdust from the corner of the half-constructed stage, sat, and turned to Kate. "Jo is a very outspoken young lady, quite a bit different from the Kate I've seen."

Kate tipped her head, as though searching for her own response. "Molly would have made the perfect Jo. I don't know why you picked me." She stared at Sarah, her hazel eyes demanding an answer.

"Because you will put everything you have into the role, whether you are like her or not. Besides, I think you're more like her than you realize."

"I'll try, Miss Sarah," she said, sitting. "I don't want to disappoint you."

"You won't."

Kate digested the comment, her expression shifting from polite conversationalist to excited child. She leaned forward, hands grasped together in her lap. "Do you truly think I can learn to do it?"

Sarah chuckled. "I have a hunch you'll learn a great deal more than just how to do it, Kate. Shall we get started?"

Kate nodded.

Around them, sporadic pounding and the grating of saws merged with the low hum of voices. A few yards away, Daniel continued his work. His glance skimmed over the rough planking on the sawhorse and darted to Kate before returning to the task at hand. Sarah sensed his thoughts were divided, his ears ready for snatches of Kate's conversation. He paid the board only cursory attention, his fingers performing their tasks while his mind focused on his daughter.

Unsettled, Sarah took a deep breath. Lord, she was nervous, of all things. She pushed her strange lack of surety aside and plunged ahead. "All right then. First, let's look at the ways in which you are like Jo. Do you see any of them?"

"No, Ma'am."

"Well." Sarah itemized with her fingers. "You're very bright, and you always pipe up in class with an answer, and I've never seen you hesitate to remind your sister when she steps out of line."

Kate looked dubious. "I don't think I do those things at all like Jo."

"No, you don't do them like Jo." She touched Kate's hand briefly, drawing her attention. "But you do them. You have self-confidence. The difference is that you control very carefully how you express that confidence while Jo just lets it all pour out, like Molly does. For Jo, you need to let go of your control and let things tumble out. Or perhaps, use that control to *make* things tumble out."

"But Jo does lots of things I'd never do. She gets her hair cut off without permission, and she doesn't care about wearing gloves, and she arranges plays and writes books." Kate's voice took on a panicky edge, loud in a momentary ebb of noise.

From his nearby work area, Daniel stared, his eyebrows edging up in concern.

Sarah ignored him and nodded to Kate in what she hoped was calming reassurance. "Yes, she does. Do you have any thoughts on why she does those things?"

"Why?" The question seemed to puzzle her.

Sarah paused, then clarified. "Does she do them just because she gets a bee in her bonnet?"

Kate laughed, her panic gone as fast as it had appeared. "Of course not. She does them because she cares about people. And because she doesn't care that doing those things might not be proper."

"I think you're on the right track. Jo doesn't do outlandish things in *order* to misbehave. She takes action to meet the needs of people she cares about. But she doesn't care about following rules. You will need to think about how her enthusiasm needs to show and forget about all the rules you've been taught are important."

"But Jo doesn't write because of other people, or strike out on her own."

Surprised at Kate's perception, Sarah tried to explain. "No, she does those things for herself. She makes a decision that she cannot have the life she wants if she marries Laurie. Writing is her dream, and she follows it to New York and makes friends with Professor Bhaer. At that part of the story, she learns to be true to herself, even if it means breaking the rules to do it."

"That's a lot of rule-breaking. Papa wouldn't like it."

Sarah glanced at Daniel. His mouth was stretched into a thin line. She smiled at him, wondering what she'd done to garner his disapproval this time.

"No, I suspect he wouldn't." She turned back to Kate and threw up her hands in an open gesture. "But this is Jo. And Jo realizes she needs to be true to herself. She discovers that most when she quits writing the stories she thinks other people want and writes the stories that are a part of her. It's somewhat of a symbol. When you start living for yourself instead of for other people, you discover your own happiness."

"This story means all that?"

"It does, sweetie." She placed her hands on her lap and leaned forward. "Maybe it's even one way for you to figure out what road *you* want to take. Maybe you need to look at life's rules for yourself."

"Papa still wouldn't like it."

"Maybe your papa needs to break a few rules, too."

Kate smiled and shook her head. "So how do I turn all that into being Jo?"

Sarah pondered the question. Being spontaneous would be an effort for Kate, she knew. But she also suspected Kate was capable of anything she put her mind to. "You will need to use that self-confidence you have and let it show through in everything Jo does. But you will need to do it in a new way, without hesitating to think about the rules. It will be like answering the teacher's question without raising your hand first. It will be like going out of the house to do something good but not asking permission first. It will be like admitting that you want to do something, something that is not a bad or dangerous thing, and then doing it even though it might not be exactly proper."

"Oh, my goodness." Kate looked horrified again, a proper, dignified expression except for the hint of melodrama that leapt across her face so fast that Sarah wondered if she had seen it at all.

Heavens, Sarah thought, what made a child feel she needed to choke off the rare whimsical moments of life? Perhaps Kate needed this role more than the role needed Kate.

Sarah again chose her words with care. "Do you remember,

on the day we met, how you cried and let out everything you were feeling for just a moment before you thought about it and kept the rest bottled up inside because somebody said it was a rule that you weren't supposed to cry in front of people?"

Kate nodded, her eyes misting briefly.

"Didn't it feel good to cry when you felt so horrible?"

Kate nodded again.

"Then there shouldn't have been any reason for you not to cry. Jo would have cried, and maybe even screamed and hollered and stamped her foot a bit. It wouldn't matter to Jo what other people thought or what the rules were." She offered Kate a smile and grasped her hands while she let the words sink in, then continued. "To convey Jo, you must be able to say Jo's words without worry over speaking out of turn, to take action without hesitating. If you stop to think about rules, it will show, and the audience will see Kate Petterman and not Jo March."

"Do you truly think I can do all that?"

"I think so. You already have the confidence." Sarah stood and tentatively rubbed Kate's back. "Just start thinking about how Jo would do things each time you do something and it will be easier to act like her when the time comes."

"Jo March is just like you," Kate noted, standing. "You don't like rules much, either. Otherwise you wouldn't be a suffragist. Or a telegrapher."

Sarah laughed. "I've never thought much about it, but I suspect you're right." She leaned closer. "But I think, sometimes, I just like to break rules."

"I think it's because you think independently."

"Perhaps it's because I don't think at all." She glanced at the back of the room and caught Daniel staring at them, his mouth still tight and his fingers clenched around the handle of his hammer.

★ ★ ★ ★ ★

Daniel placed the last of his tools into his worn pine toolbox and shifted his weight while Sarah stood at the door of the Odd Fellows Hall, her soft laughter echoing through the nearly empty room.

The woman was as much a mystery as anything he'd ever come across. Every time he thought he had her figured out, she did something unexpected—unexpected and unpalatable. He slammed the toolbox onto the floor and tugged at his tool belt.

Damned if she didn't have Kate and Molly so caught up in her spell that they swallowed anything she tossed at them. Involving Kate in a play, up there on stage in front of everyone, was one thing. Filling her head with all sorts of ideas about breaking rules was altogether different. He scowled and threw his tool belt against the wooden box at his feet.

The click of the door brought abrupt silence, and he realized the last of the students and parents had left. He glanced up at the sudden quiet.

Sarah stood at the doorway, brushing her ever-busy hands across her brown work skirt. "Are you upset about something?" she finally asked.

"Should I be?"

"I don't think so, but a carpenter doesn't bang his tools around like that unless something's bothering him, does he?"

Daniel swallowed against his anger and told himself that it didn't matter that she was once again right, or that she'd caught him in another public display of temper. "You've got a lot of nerve, you know that?"

"What is it I've done this time?" Her voice dropped in resignation. "You've been stewing practically all afternoon, tossing wood scraps and glaring at me. It must be pretty awful for you to have sent the girls on home alone."

He raised an eyebrow at her. Sarah's expression shifted, her mouth dropping open with a soft sound of exasperation, and her violet eyes widened. She raised her hands in a puzzled gesture.

Daniel crossed his arms and pinned his gaze on her face. How could such a lovely woman be the cause of so much trouble? He inhaled, refusing to be distracted, and summoned the words. "I thought you knew my views on suffrage, Sarah. I thought you understood how I felt about Kate and Molly being exposed to it."

Her mouth dropped further open, then pinched shut. "What are you talking about?"

"How can you use this play as a platform to expound on suffrage? This is supposed to be a children's play."

"It *is* a children's play." Sarah's hands bobbed in the air, punctuating her words. "Wherever are you getting the idea that it's related to suffrage?"

Daniel's heart pounded in his chest, and his jaw tightened. Had she no idea? "Disobey the rules. Disregard propriety. Cut your hair, take off your gloves, turn down marriage proposals, and strike out on your own, doing the sorts of things normal women don't do. That's what I'm talking about."

"Oh, for pity's sake, Daniel. This story isn't about women's rights, or even about disobedience, for that matter." She frowned. "It's about the love of a family and one young person's journey as she discovers who she is and finds the courage to think for herself. Or aren't your daughters supposed to think?"

"I'll decide what's best for Kate and Molly. They're good girls and you know it. How dare you question how I raise them?"

"I never said that." She paused, her voice even but firm. "You did. Maybe that says something in and of itself."

"You're out of line." The words felt hot in their vehemence.

Sarah touched his arm. "Am I, Daniel?"

A tinge of guilt shifted through his anger, begging for his attention. A chill crept over his skin, borne of sweat and the cold December air. He shoved his hands in his pockets.

"Look," she said with uncharacteristic patience. "I know they're good girls. They're wonderful girls, very well behaved. Like you. As for whether or not that's the right way to raise them, I don't know. What I do know is that you aren't even giving them the chance to be themselves. Is a parent who dictates every moment of his child's life doing what's best? You tell me."

Daniel shifted and took his hands out of his pockets. His heart still pounded, but the hot anger had dissipated into an uncomfortable void. He stared back at her, shoved his hands back where they'd been, and ignored the gnawing discomfort.

"How can you begin to question what I do?" he asked instead. "When have you taken the time to get involved in someone else's life, to share their laughter or their pain? You're so caught up in making the world into your vision of right that you've never tended a sick child or sat up half the night calming nightmares. This is just another avenue for making one of your points, an agenda for women's rights."

She colored, silent. Then she swallowed and marched forward, stirring up sawdust with each clipped step. A foot short of Daniel's chest, she stopped.

Daniel stared down at her. This wasn't going at all as he had intended. Those big eyes held him fast, stilling his words, forcing him to consider her side of things.

"This isn't an effort to promote anything," she said. "Have you even read the script? Or the book? You can't just take isolated scenes and draw a conclusion. How much of my conversation with Kate did you actually hear? Scattered bits and pieces? You should have listened to the whole thing, Daniel. Maybe you need to go talk to your daughter about what she thinks we discussed and read the book. Then, if you still feel this is about suffrage, I'll step down."

He nodded, accepting the truth of her words. "I guess that's fair enough. You're right. I didn't hear the whole conversation." He settled onto the edge of the stage, his elbows on his knees. "But what I did hear concerned me."

She smiled and sat down next to him, legs dangling. "I imagine it bothered you quite a bit."

"You knew?"

"I suspected. I think perhaps there's quite a bit of what I said to Kate that applies to you as well. Maybe more. Sometimes, I think you're so tied up trying to meet your father's expectations that you've never discovered yourself."

"Sarah—"

"What? Don't say it? Don't say it because it might be true?" She paused, watching his face, and touched his arm. "When's the last time you thought for yourself, Daniel? When's the last time you tried something new? When's the last time you did something on the spur of the moment, without analyzing it to see if it was considered proper?"

He shrugged. "I'm just not a spur-of-the-moment type person."

"How do you know that? You told me yourself that you hadn't done anything spontaneous since you ate that candy stick when you were a kid."

His mind drifted to the conversation, the one at the City Ditch, and the events before it. His heart stirred and a rush of heat flowed through him. He caught her gaze. "Until I kissed you."

Her eyes softened and she smiled. "Until you kissed me. Look how guilty you felt. Daniel, no one should feel guilty about enjoying life."

Her words poked at him. He'd spent almost his whole life worried about feeling guilty, avoiding his father's wrath and admonitions until doing what he thought he was supposed to do had become second nature. He'd quit even evaluating things on his own, or maybe he'd never done so. His breathing slowed as the silence stretched.

Next to him, Sarah swung her legs. Her skirt billowed, the fabric's rise and fall the only sound in the room.

Daniel glanced at her, weighing his thoughts. Truth be told, he figured Sarah had her own demons. Demons he should leave well enough alone. But the moment beckoned, and Sarah's own words pushed at him, urging him on.

He reached for her hand, surrounding her cold fingers with his warmth, and drew it into his lap. "And what about you?" he asked. "Do you always hide? I've never once heard you talk about having fun with folks instead of trying to get something done. When's the last time you let go of your vision of what the world should be and enjoyed just spending time with people, pure and simple?"

"I enjoy people." The smile that flitted across her face wavered.

Daniel stroked the back of her hand with his thumb and measured his words. "Sarah, this play is the first thing you've done with children in your entire life and we both know it. Maybe you need to spend a day playing make-believe, just doing something for the fun of it. You're just as much stuck on one way of doing things as I am."

"I like my life."

"And I like mine," he reminded.

"But you don't even know what you're missing."

"Neither do you."

Her hand shifted beneath his, slowly opening, responding to his touch. She leaned against his shoulder and sighed. "So, if I agree to try something different, will you do the same? I doubt you spend many days playing make-believe, either, much less doing anything even the slightest bit outrageous."

"And just what would you have me do? March around with signs protesting some thing or another?" He laughed softly, feeling Sarah's silent chuckle shake her body. He wrapped his arm around her and pulled her to his side.

"Close down your shop and spend the afternoon at a circus. Go to the theater and watch a scandalous dancer while downing a beer. March into a bar, stare at the nude painting above the bar, and play a game of poker. I don't know, Daniel, anything but sit at home and lecture others about impropriety."

He tried to place himself into the images and curiosity jabbed at him. Scandalous dancers and nude paintings? He reckoned his father would turn in his grave.

Uncomfortable with his attraction to the suggestion, he tipped Sarah's chin up and peered down at her face. "And what do you get to do? How about taking a week off your campaigning for this or that and going to the circus yourself, or maybe reading fairy tales? Have you ever been to a tea party with dolls?"

"Have you?"

The stab of curiosity became insistent, poking at him until he knew he could no longer ignore it. He took a breath and gave in to it. "You want to make this a challenge?"

Sarah smiled. "One challenge, Daniel?" She raised her feathery eyebrows. "Too easy. How about you do one non-Daniel thing every day for a week?"

"A week? One activity per day?"

"Minimum."

He debated, looking for the trap. "Nothing illegal or immoral?"

"Whose morals do we get to use?" Her smile softened. "Nothing illegal. We can negotiate on morality."

"And what about you? Could you handle a week of doing things with other people, with them at the center, no special causes allowed?"

She straightened and pulled away, once again beaming with self-confidence. “That doesn’t sound so difficult. I can do that, hands behind my back.”

“And how do we keep track of one another so you don’t cheat?”

“Me?” She looked up at him, her lips parted, then shook her head. “As if I would need to cheat. If you’re so worried about it, we can just stick together. You watch me, and I’ll watch you. That way, neither of us can cheat.”

A sudden chill crept through Daniel’s mind and crawled down his back. “A week? Together? Sarah, really—”

Her face lit up in animated challenge. “You can’t even do one, can you?”

What had he started? This was supposed to have been about Kate. Spontaneity? Hell, no wonder his father had insisted he think everything out.

He shook his head and tried to capture Sarah’s attention. “Look, this wasn’t ever about you and me—”

“Oh, but it is now.” She laughed, soft ripples of humor filling the room. “If Kate can get up on that stage and portray a girl who breaks rules, then surely, you can try one week of new experiences.” She sobered and pinned him with a solid stare. “Or are you afraid of what you might discover?”

Chapter Thirteen

Sarah stood in the Petterman kitchen, noting the evidence of Mrs. Winifred's expert housekeeping in its sparkle. Her survey swept from the immaculate counter past Daniel's lean frame, straight into the expectant gazes of Kate and Molly. Bright afternoon sunshine lit the tidy room, bouncing off the girls' faces. Taking a deep breath, she stepped forward and smiled at them. She was going to do whatever it took to have fun at this challenge, even if it killed her.

"Papa said you wanted to do something special with us," Kate said, a rare hint of playfulness lighting her eyes. "He suggested you might like to bake cookies."

"Oh, he did?" Sarah lifted an eyebrow in satisfaction. While baking cookies wasn't her favorite activity, it was something she knew how to do. Given an adequate recipe, she could make a darned good cookie, maybe even one that would melt in Daniel's mouth. If the other challenges were this easy, the week might not be so bad after all. "Shall we get started?"

Kate's mouth stretched into an uncharacteristic grin. "Papa said he didn't think you'd like spending your Sunday afternoon in the kitchen."

A tiny prickle of foreboding jabbed at Sarah. Things couldn't be this uncomplicated. "Your father's right. Baking cookies is a perfect challenge for me. I'm not exactly a kitchen kind of person."

"I thought as much," Daniel said from the doorway, "so I

told Mrs. Winifred to show you to the kitchen. After all, this isn't really about what you'd *like* to do." He leaned against the doorframe and crossed his arms. "I think a day in the kitchen will work fine for both of us."

Sarah felt her mouth go dry. Drat it all, it *was* too easy. She'd forgotten about this being Daniel's challenge, too.

Daniel's eyes narrowed. "We did have to do these things together, didn't we?"

She stared at him. If she didn't know better, she'd swear the man looked smug. Smug. Displeasure picked at her. Play her for a fool, would he? She marched across the kitchen and glared up at him. "Are you trying to cheat already?"

His mouth fell open with a huff of air. "I'm not trying to cheat. You're the one who said we had to do things together."

Sarah shook her head and paced across the room, ignoring the girls' questioning expressions. "Baking cookies is hardly the sort of challenge I had in mind for you. It's too conventional and you know it."

He shrugged. "So, we do separate activities."

"I think not."

"Then we bake cookies. It will be a new experience for me. The girls will tell you that." He uncrossed his arms in a gesture of frustration. "Besides, it's Sunday. This is about as unconventional as we can get on a Sunday."

"I'm sure there are plenty of other things to do."

"Such as?" He stared at her, waiting.

"How am I supposed to know? Something besides staying in your own house doing something as wholesome as baking."

"Papa?" Molly interrupted. She stepped forward, her brown curls swinging in defiance, and gazed up at him. "Does this mean we're not gonna make cookies?"

Daniel rolled his eyes. "Miss Sarah thinks baking cookies is too ordinary."

Molly turned abruptly and peered at Sarah. "But he never bakes cookies with us, so how can it be ordinary?"

"There." Daniel grinned. "See?"

Sarah looked from one girl to another. Kate stood with her head tipped, eyebrows arched and expectant, her grin faded into a thin, stoic line. Molly, with her hands on her hips, tapped one foot against the wooden floor, its steady beat filling the void of silence. Sarah glanced at Daniel's unsuccessful attempt to hide his smile, and bit back the retort that crowded her tongue. Instead, she bent her knees until she was eye-level with the children. "Did your papa explain any of this to you?"

"Sarah," Daniel warned.

"Daniel."

"I'm not sure the girls—"

"Oh, for heaven's sake. Quit being so stuffy." She sent him a silent reprimand with her eyes and turned back to Kate and Molly. "Do you girls know what a dare is?"

They nodded.

"Jimmy O'Brien dared Henry Graham to put a tack on Miss Clay's chair, once," Molly explained.

"Well, I've dared your father to spend a whole week doing things that he doesn't usually do, things that aren't stuffy and proper. Cookie baking won't work because it has to be something that he wouldn't do because he'd be too worried about whether or not he *should* do it."

Molly rolled her head on her shoulders. "Just take him to a suffrage meeting."

Sarah laughed and stood. "That would work for me."

"Oh, but Miss Sarah has a dare, too." Daniel leaned back against the wall, shoving his hands into his front pockets. "She has to do things that have nothing to do with any of her causes. It can't be a meeting and she can't talk about suffrage, water systems, telegraphing, or even about the play. It should be something without any big purpose where she doesn't get to be in charge of anything."

Molly's brown eyes lit up. "Oh. How about if Kate and I get to pick?"

He leaned forward, hands emerging in empty protest. "Well, I'm not sure—"

"I think that's a wonderful idea. That way, we're both giving up control." Sarah smiled in triumph at the wonderful solution. The girls would pick something harmless, and they'd both be off the hook. "What do you say, Daniel? Seem fair?"

"Oh, Papa, can we?" Molly jumped up and down. Even Kate looked interested.

Daniel glanced sideways at Sarah, his eyes filled with uncertainty.

"How about Kate and Molly choose a couple and we work the rest out together?" Sarah suggested.

He nodded with a sigh. "Sounds good enough to me. You girls understand the rules?"

Kate stepped closer, taking charge. "I think so, Papa. Molly, let's talk."

The girls huddled together, whispering for a few moments, then turned to Daniel and Sarah with frivolous smiles. Kate moved forward and glanced at her father. "We've picked something we aren't allowed to do on Sundays because it isn't quiet or reflective like Sundays are supposed to be." She turned to Sarah. "It's not exactly improper, but Papa won't like it much. And it's something fun, something we don't think Miss Sarah ever has time to do. It should be—"

Molly jumped in front of her. "We're going ice skating," she announced.

Sarah's stomach tightened. Fun? Memories stabbed at her as she recalled sitting on her rear, cold seeping through her bones, other children laughing at her inability to conquer the simple act of skating on ice, shunning her for her inadequacy.

How long would it take the good citizens of Denver to realize she was incompetent?

Sarah tightened the buckle on the leather strap that fastened the skating blade to the bottom of her brown work shoe and wobbled to her feet, wondering where Daniel was hiding.

He hadn't said a word since Kate's announcement, confirming the girls' assessment that he wouldn't much like their proposal. Well, that made things just about even, she supposed, because she was a far cry from satisfied herself.

Ice skating, of all things.

"Come on, Miss Sarah," Molly beckoned from the ice.

Sarah glanced around the small Sunday crowd that had gathered along Cherry Creek and breathed a sigh of relief. No one was watching her. Mostly young people, they huddled around a small fire, their carefree laughter filling the crisp winter sunlight, their attention drawn to their own activities. A few tentative couples joined mittened hands, gazing shyly at one another. She crunched carefully across the snow, step by step, until she reached the ice.

"Hurry up, Miss Sarah."

She offered a weak smile to Molly, took a deep breath, and glanced upstream. A group of children practiced fancy swirls while an isolated trio glided into the distance. Her heart jumping, Sarah placed her right foot onto the ice. Maybe it wouldn't be so hard after all. Everyone was intent on their own business. No one need ever know she was a miserable fool on the ice. She gritted her teeth and took a step.

"You're supposed to glide, not walk."

"Yes, Molly, I know. I'm just moving out a bit to where the snow cover is thinner."

"Oh. I always start skating right away. The skates just slide right through the snow, anyhow." Molly slid past her, her blades kicking up tiny shards of ice, her cheeks pink with cold. Poised and perfect, she kept her hands snugly inside her fur-lined muff.

Sarah forced her foot forward and stretched her arms out for balance. Ankles shaking, she pushed first one, then the other foot across the ice. Already, her legs were numb with the cold, and she wished she'd worn an extra petticoat under her gray plaid skirt. She wavered and fell with a thud onto the cold, hard ice.

Molly giggled.

"It isn't funny."

"Need help?" Molly pivoted with grace and grinned.

"I'm just fine. I'm having a little trouble finding my balance is all."

"Well, at least you're not still sitting on a log, festering."

Sarah followed Molly's gaze to the edge of the creek, some thirty feet downstream.

Daniel sat on a log, half hidden by a trio of evergreens. He had one blade strapped on. The other lay in Kate's hand. She thrust it toward him and he shook his head.

Sarah's blood stirred. If she had to strap on these stupid blades and let everyone see how inept she was, there was no way Daniel was going to simply sit on a log and avoid his end of the bargain. She placed her gloved hand on the frozen stream and rolled onto her knees. The snow-covered ice nipped at her through her woolen skirt. She bit her lip and steadied her feet, then rose upward, ruing the sight she must make, her rear end poking out. She stood, one foot slipping forward as if it belonged to someone else. She teetered, arms circling madly, then found her equilibrium.

For a moment, she stood still, feeling the strain on her ankles as her feet tipped inward, fighting for balance. The thin blades caught the ice and held. She looked down and saw the tips of her shoes, pigeon toed like some knock-kneed puppet. If anyone so much as giggled, she'd die.

Downstream, Kate had made little progress with Daniel. Sarah gritted her teeth and inched forward, sliding choppily toward them. Her jaw tightened, and she increased her stride. The sudden movement sent her left foot skittering and she plopped back onto the ice.

Daniel stood, his expression an odd mixture of concern and amusement.

"If you laugh, I swear you will live to regret it."

"Are you all right?"

"No, I'm not all right. I'm sitting on my backside in the middle of a lousy creek. How about you?"

"Oh, I'm all right."

"Of course you are. You've been sitting on a log. Put that stupid blade on your foot and get out here."

"I think I'll just sit here and watch for a little while."

"That doesn't count."

"I don't skate on Sundays, Sarah."

"And I don't skate at all. Now put the blade on and get out here on this ice."

"It doesn't seem right."

"Oh, for heaven's sake, Daniel, relax a little. It's just ice skating. How ridiculous can you get?"

"We should be at home, reflecting on God's goodness."

"So reflect on it here. Look around at nature and marvel at its frozen wonders."

"But—"

"Enjoy time with your girls. That seems like it would qualify as reflecting on God's goodness."

He glanced at her, humor replacing the uncertainty in his eyes. "You're right," he said. "It is ridiculous." He grabbed the blade from Kate's hand, strapped it on, and rose to his feet.

"Are you going to skate or sit on the ice all day?"

"I think maybe sitting here would suit me just fine."

"Oh, no, you don't. If I'm going to skate, you're going to skate." Daniel glided unsteadily to her and stared down.

"Help me?"

Daniel grasped her hand and pulled. Pushing off the ice with the other hand, Sarah wavered to her feet. Kate and Molly beamed in triumph, then raced off across the ice, their bright-green skirts bobbing with each graceful movement.

"You do have a knack for putting every rule I've lived my life by in a different light. You know that, don't you?"

"I guess I just believe in defining individual ways of doing things, interpretations of life's rules, if you will. And, I prefer a very generous interpretation." She poked him playfully in the ribs to emphasize her point.

Daniel acknowledged the action with a brief, gentle smile. "My whole upbringing was nothing but rules. Everything was either right or wrong, mostly wrong. It's a part of who I am."

"But you don't like it."

His eyebrows knitted. "What makes you think that?"

"Because I've seen you struggle against that control you work so hard to maintain."

He glanced away from her, shrugging, then sighed before his gaze returned. "And what about the control you strive for?"

"Me?" She stared up at him, incredulous.

"You literally sparkle when you run things. When you don't, like out here on the ice, you fidget and fuss like crazy."

She shook her head, ignoring the disturbing comment. "I simply don't enjoy doing things I'm not good at."

"You avoid them."

"I do not." She turned and forced one wobbly foot in front of the other. How could he accuse her of running from things? She took charge. She accomplished things.

"So, why didn't you learn to skate?" His voice was even, but every fiber of Sarah's skin prickled at the implication. "You grew up in New England, didn't you? Seems like skating would be something folks there do."

"Pennsylvania, and, no, I didn't learn to skate."

"Why not?"

She stopped and jerked around. "Because I was lousy at it and I looked like a helpless fool." The words tumbled out before she could stop them.

Daniel's gray eyes softened. "So what's wrong with being helpless?"

"What's wrong with it? Nothing, if all you want is to have people dismiss you as insubstantial." She opened her arms in a gesture of nonchalance, hating the small tremor in her voice.

He reached forward, his gloved finger touching her face. "Ah, there it is. You're afraid of what people think, just like you say I am. We're pretty much alike."

A small chuckle forced its way out of her mouth.

Amusement lifted Daniel's lips and he dropped his hand in a gesture of invitation. "Come on, let's quit standing still and skate. If you don't need to be successful at it, then who cares how many times you fall down or how silly you look?"

"You do realize, don't you, that I skated all the way over here?" She issued a grin of challenge. "You're the one who sat there on that miserable log refusing to put his skates on."

Daniel shrugged and smiled back. "I haven't been sitting on that log for quite a while." He glided away from her, then turned back. "You going to skate, or not?"

"Maybe. Maybe not."

"What was it you said earlier? Something about interpreting life's rules and making things individual? Just change the rules. Instead of looking at it in terms of how well you can or can't skate, look at it in terms of how much fun you can make of it."

"Fun? Falling down and looking silly?"

"Sure. See how much silliness you can achieve."

"That's ridiculous."

"Is it?" He raised his eyebrows and tipped his head to one side in inquiry.

She sighed, knowing he'd turned the tables on her. Besides, he had a point. She cocked her head in response. "Are you willing to join me?"

He laughed. "Do I have a choice?"

"Well, come on, then. We're off to see how silly we can be." She issued the challenge before moving past him, her choppy steps kicking up ice and snow.

Daniel turned behind her, his skates scratching the ice with his movement. He glided past her, not exactly with grace, but with much more finesse than she possessed. Heaven help her, even Daniel skated better than she did.

"Too slow, Sarah. You're never going to get anywhere at that rate." He grasped her hand and pulled.

Sarah felt her balance shift. She wobbled, her free arm waving in circles, while her body bobbed with uncertainty. "You'll pay for that," she chided.

"Move. If you keep the forward movement, your natural momentum will help keep your equilibrium." He pulled her along, his long stride forcing her to abandon the choppy steps she trusted. "Turn your back foot out, just a little, and push off."

Fighting the urge to tell him she didn't need his help, she did as he instructed. The blade caught and she slid forward with little conscious effort.

"I'm doing it."

"Now keep it up. Just push off every few glides." He smiled in encouragement and tugged at her arm.

"I can do it." She shook from his grip and moved away.

"See?" She glided past him and the smirk in his eyes. Challenged, she lifted her head and kicked at the ice with her left leg. Her right leg wobbled as the left shot out to the side and she plopped onto the ice.

Daniel's hearty laugh erupted into the crisp air. His body jerked as the laughter took control. Arms waving and his legs flying, he landed beside her.

A riot of giggles exploded from her throat. "Serves you right."

Molly skated past with a precise turn. "It's ice skating not ice-sitting," she shouted before speeding away to rejoin Kate. Once there, she pointed and they laughed together for a moment, then headed toward a group of other children.

"My own children are laughing at me."

"As well they should." Sarah shivered. "This ice is cold."

"Upsy-daisy, then." He turned and braced one knee on the ice. The cloth of his gray trousers tightened with the pull of his thigh muscles.

Warmth spread through Sarah and she smiled in appreciation.

Daniel's eyes twinkled. "You ready?"

Images of his biceps rushed through her mind and she wished they weren't out in the winter cold where his heavy cloth coat hid them. "I guess."

He reached forward and pulled her up, standing with her in one fluid movement. She stumbled and he reached around her, steadying her with both arms. Their gazes locked and Daniel's mouth lifted in a gentle smile.

Sarah shivered.

Daniel's smile widened.

Beneath her own coat, Sarah's heart quickened. Her breath caught.

The bright twinkle in Daniel's eyes shifted into a hot, intense light and he pulled her forward.

Surprised, she stepped into the embrace, her feet tangling, and she slipped sideways.

The sudden movement caught Daniel by surprise and he lunged forward, tumbling them both to the slick surface of the creek. Sarah landed on her rear, Daniel atop her.

A chorus of laughter rang through the sunlit air and Sarah groaned. "I'll never live this down."

Above her, Daniel's gaze softened. "New rules, Sarah. We set new rules." His voice was thick, intense.

She stared up at him, her breath heavy and expectant. "New rules for both of us?"

The question hung between them. Daniel inhaled, his gaze never leaving her face. "For both of us," he whispered and lowered his mouth to hers.

Frank Bates sat at Mrs. King's crowded Sunday dinner table absently stirring a pile of lumpy mashed potatoes. A hodge-podge of voices filled the landlady's dining room and the stale scent of tobacco mingled with the overcooked liver and onions that still sat on most of the boarders' plates. Across from Frank, Lavinia Morgan's chair remained empty.

"You gonna save that food, or is it up for grabs?" Alvin, the chubbiest of the boarders, and the only one with an empty plate, asked.

Frank bristled. "That there's Miss Morgan's and I reckon Miz King oughta be saving it for her."

"I'd say that answers it," Harry Bowers commented with a tip of his whitened head. "Have some pie." He pushed a rather burned dried-apple pie at Alvin and blinked his baby-blue eyes.

Frank lifted his lip in distaste. Bowers, with his high-powered position in the Chamber of Commerce, was as annoying as Alvin. Between the two of them, they hadn't left any of the pie. It was a good thing Lavinia wasn't much on sweets. He'd saved her back a generous portion of the liver and a pile of droopy onions, knowing it was her favorite.

If he remembered right, the last time Lavinia ate apple pie, it was the night her father gave her that damned ultimatum. She'd refused to marry his handpicked dandy and lost her share of the family money all in one fell swoop. That was the night Frank knew she was sweet on him. He just had to prove himself; that was all. She was just waiting for him to make good.

The sharp clap of the front door broke through the lingering dinner conversation followed by the sound of Lavinia's heels as they clicked across the wooden floor of the hallway.

"I do apologize," she announced and paused as her fellow boarders shifted their attention to her. "I was rather delayed by the Morton sisters and all their tired gossip." She smoothed her long hands down the sides of her narrow black skirt, emphasizing her thin form, marched grandly to the table, and waited with impatience as Bowers pulled out her chair.

Frank fought back a grin. For all her fuss and bother about suffrage, Lavinia still wanted to be treated like a lady. She always had. She didn't want no sissified dandy and she didn't cotton to men who treated her as unimportant. Once his spell of bad luck turned, he'd show her a fine time for sure. He'd treat her like she was governor, if that's what she wanted.

"Is something amusing, Mr. Bates?"

"N-no, ma'am," he stuttered, hating it that she made him quiver. "I saved you some liver and onions."

"Why, how very kind of you, Mr. Bates. I do like my liver and onions." She peered around the table, her gaze seeking the plate of meat. She smiled and waited for Alvin to pass it to her. The plate came quickly around the table and she transferred two slices of liver, then covered them with piles of sautéed onions.

The other boarders drifted away from the table, one by one, as Frank watched Lavinia eat. She chewed the liver with quick but dainty precision, thirty-two times per bite. The onions, however, she tended to slurp, sucking each one fully into her mouth before chewing.

Frank squirmed in his seat.

Lavinia swallowed and leaned forward. "I heard a bit of news you might find interesting."

Frank nodded.

Lavinia arched her eyebrows and inhaled another onion.

He reckoned she'd make him wait all night. She did that kind of thing, his Lavinia. She dangled it out there in front of him, just to make him ask.

"Of course, I don't need to tell you."

"But I reckon you will."

"Maybe. Maybe not."

Frank smiled at the game. She'd tell him, in the end. If he managed to convince her he didn't care, she'd even tell him without being begged.

"It's about the little strumpet at the station," Lavinia baited.

His heart skipped a beat. "Sarah Donovan?" His worst piece of luck, yet. In fact, he was beginning to believe she'd targeted him on purpose.

Lavinia put another piece of liver into her mouth and began to chew. She arched her thin black eyebrows again and waited.

Frank swallowed, leaned toward her, and gave in. "What'd you hear?"

Lavinia leaned back. "Didn't you say she was preparing to take her primary something or another test?"

"Primary op." His mind flew to all the months of practice he'd put in himself. How she could be ready to test so soon baffled him. It had to be a conspiracy.

Lavinia patted his arm. "That wouldn't be very good for you, would it?"

"No, ma'am." The way she'd stacked things against him, the

little busybody would pass the damned test and he'd be out another good job. Ain't no way she was gonna do that to him. His jaw quivered and he reminded himself there was a lady present. "What was it you heard?"

Lavinia lowered her eyelashes. "You know, Frank, she tried to take over my suffrage association. Can you imagine that?" She smiled and patted his arm again. "Thank goodness you had shared that bit of information about those solicitation wires."

"Damned interfering little nobody sure does seem to be crowding her way into things."

"Did you take my advice, Frank, about those wires she tossed away?"

He thought about the thick bundle he'd retrieved from the trash, all on gut instinct, and how Lavinia had gushed with praise when he'd told her. They were all tucked away in a lock box, up in his room, just in case, just like Lavinia had advised. "Sure did."

"Good." Lavinia bobbed her head in satisfaction, her severe black bun acting as an exclamation point.

Frank waited, on the edge of his seat, while she reached for another bite of liver. "Dagnabbit, Lavinia!" He pounded the table for emphasis. "You gonna tell me or not?"

Lavinia straightened in her chair and glanced about the room. "Don't make a scene, Frank. It won't do."

He followed her gaze. There wasn't a soul in sight. Still, he figured he might have overstepped a little. Lavinia didn't much like it when a man spoke his mind. She liked her men strong, but not so strong that folks forgot about her. "I'm sorry, Lavinia," he said.

"I forgive you, Frank. I think I know how you feel, after all she tried to take from me. I'd like to see her gone, you know. Before she tries it again."

Frank nodded in solemn agreement. Lavinia had been upset

ever since Donovan had come to town and started horning in on things at the suffrage movement. Getting rid of the bitch would win him Lavinia's heart for sure. Ruining him on two fronts was just about more than he could handle, anyway.

Lavinia moved toward him, glancing furtively at the diners who had drifted to the parlor. "Frank Bates, you're not going to let that upstart take your job, are you?" she whispered.

"Hell no." He pounded the table in defiance.

"I didn't think so. That's why I thought you'd like to know what I heard." Lavinia lowered her voice further. "She was out today, with the undertaker, Petterman. They were out on the creek, down on the ice, in broad daylight, with him all over her and her driving him on. Very improper, very nasty, Frank."

"You're sure?"

"Of course. I think that confirms her reputation, don't you? I'd consider acting on that rumor we discussed a few weeks back, the one about her and the stationmaster."

"It's all true then, what I was thinkin'?"

"Oh, my dear Frank, I'm afraid it is." Lavinia shoved another onion into her mouth and sucked it in with slow deliberation. "Wouldn't things be so much easier for both of us if she were out of Denver entirely?"

Frank nodded, afraid to trust his voice.

Lavinia touched his cheek with her hand. "Then I can depend on you?"

He nodded again. "I'll do whatever it takes."

Chapter Fourteen

Daniel sat in the empty parlor, listening to the evening wind knock against the side of the house. In the kitchen, his daughters' voices mingled with clinking dinner dishes.

In the silence, his father's voice echoed with unwanted chastisement. His stern face intruded, as it had throughout the day, to offer yet another reminder that polite society frowned on public displays of affection.

No one cared. The earth did not swallow me up and heaven did not rage with fury. Go away.

In fact, no one had said a thing. Well, no one except Bill, who had popped into the coffin shop to convey the suggestion that it was about time Daniel loosened up a little. In the cafe during lunch, a couple of old ladies had whispered together, offering half-hidden smiles whenever they looked at him, but no one had berated him for having loose morals or for making a spectacle of himself.

Kissing a gal while tangled up on the ice-covered creek did not seem to be the sin he'd been led to believe it was.

Daniel rose and crossed to the mantle. He picked up his father's framed picture. The Reverend Ebenezer Petterman's dour countenance peered out of the hinged, gold-encased tin-type.

Go away, old man. I kissed her and she laughed and we got up and had fun. Daniel snapped the tintype shut.

He'd had enough fun that he'd agreed when the girls suggested inviting Sarah over this evening to play board games. Enough fun that he'd invited Bill and Libby to join them. Enough fun that he was considering telling old Ebenezer that he might very well play something else besides The Mansion of Happiness. He might even open the reverend's picture for it.

Except it was the only game in the house, a tired version of the sole game approved for Petterman use, a worn-out board whose faded squares featured virtues and vices. The vices, of course, brought punishment to the lonely pawns who worked their way around the spiral path seeking only the rewards of virtue.

"The girls are just putting things away, Mr. Petterman. If you've nothing more for me, I'd best wrap up and head home." Mrs. Winifred stood in the arched doorway, waiting.

Daniel nodded to the housekeeper. "Bundle up. The wind's nasty."

"Always is, this time of year." She lifted her wraps from the coat tree, then disappeared down the hall and into the kitchen. Moments later, the back door clicked shut.

The clatter of dishes continued in the wake of Mrs. Winifred's exit. On the front stoop, someone stomped his feet, and Daniel moved across the parlor and into the foyer in anticipation of the knock. He swung open the door to a gust of cold air and the wind-reddened faces of Sarah and the Byerses.

"Mighty cold out here, Daniel. You order up this wind?"

"Been here since before me, and you know it, though I can't quite figure how it stays so cold with all your hot air."

Bill chuckled as he waited for the women to enter, then stepped inside and shut the door. "Figured maybe it was the frost from those body coolers you use out in the shop. 'Course, maybe you forgot to bring home the ice yesterday, being preoccupied as you were."

Sarah's face colored, sending a brief warmth coursing through

Daniel's veins.

Then Libby gave Bill a playful slap, breaking the moment, and the group pulled off their assorted wraps. Kate and Molly emerged from the kitchen, Molly's eager chatter joining the mix. Kate slipped into the role of hostess, hanging up coats and shawls before finessing the group into the parlor.

Sarah and Libby settled into the floral side chairs while the girls perched on tasseled ottomans.

Bill stood, eying the game Daniel had placed on the polished oval table. "The Mansion of Happiness?"

Discomfort crept over Daniel. "It's . . . uh . . ."

"It's the only game we have," Molly announced.

"You couldn't even update to the Game of Life?"

"Bill—" Libby cautioned.

"I don't mean to insult you, but I haven't seen anybody play this game since I was a kid. I s'pose you play it by the book?"

Daniel felt a grin creep across his face. He pointed to a small, cloth-covered booklet of moral verses lying next to the game board.

Bill grinned back and shook his head.

"Why don't we just have some cocoa and Bill and Libby can update us on the new water system progress," Sarah said, from her side chair. Her big violet eyes lit her face with hope.

"Sounds fine to us, doesn't it Bill?"

Daniel cleared his throat and shoved his hands into his front pockets. "Oh, no, you don't."

"What?" Sarah lifted her eyebrows with the question and Daniel fought to keep from laughing at her mock innocence.

"You know what. This is purely social. No causes."

Libby's face tilted in confusion, and Bill glanced from one of them to the other. Obviously, Sarah hadn't told them anything about the challenge during their walk over.

"Papa, you and Sarah should go to the kitchen and bring out

the cocoa. Molly and I already put it on the stove. I think we need to explain the dare to Mr. and Mrs. Byers."

Daniel glanced at Sarah and shrugged his shoulders.

Sarah shrugged back. "You heard her." She rose from the side chair and moved toward the kitchen. Her tiny figure slipped through the doorway, and Daniel followed.

In the kitchen, Sarah's efficient footsteps filled the room with quick clicks. Her dark-green skirt swung on her hips as she moved away. The fabric was pulled back so that it draped at the rear but clung at the front and sides, moving with each step she took. Daniel smiled, pleased at the lack of a large bustle.

She turned and caught him staring. "What?"

"I like the dress."

She blushed again, just a hint of pink filling her cheeks. "It's new. They called it a tie-back."

"It's flattering." He watched her turn away, avoiding the compliment, and it dawned on him that she didn't get too many of them. In fact, she seemed to go out of her way to hide her beauty. His heart stirred with an unexpected need to know more. "You don't do that very often, do you?"

"Do what?"

"Buy yourself something new."

"No." Her hands paused in their busy collection of spoons from the silverware drawer.

"Why?"

"Fancy clothes make me disappear." The words came out so softly that he could barely hear her.

"What?" Daniel cringed at the incredulity in his voice.

Sarah busied her hands again, rummaging through the silver. "Nothing," she said.

Waves of disbelief rumbled through him. "How could looking like that make you disappear?"

"Never mind." She slammed the drawer shut.

"You think people will miss you for the clothes? Who told you a fool thing like that?"

Sarah dropped the spoons on the counter with a clatter and turned to him. "Why are we talking about this?"

He stared at her, unable to stop himself, and struggled to contain his sharp response. He didn't want to start an argument with her. He softened his voice, steering it between his anger and any trace of pity. "Because it matters."

She shook her head. "No, Daniel, it doesn't."

He smiled at her, unsure of what to do next. If he reached out to her, would she run? She was so different from Mary. Always predictable in her gentle way, Mary had never seemed unsure or in need of anything, except molding him. He swallowed hard, acknowledging his own need to soothe Sarah's discomfort.

He laid a pile of napkins next to the spoons, the casual action conveying none of the concern he felt. "Is that why you always wear that infernal brown skirt? So people will see you and not your clothes?" He turned and caught her gaze, wanting to touch her but afraid she'd misinterpret the action. "This isn't part of what you said yesterday, is it?" He softened his voice. "Did someone make you feel you didn't matter?"

Sarah's eyes clouded and she drew a shaky breath. Then, she laughed and the moment slipped away. "You, Daniel, are getting touched in the head and it doesn't become you. That cocoa needs tending or it's going to have such a film on it that it will take you years to skim it off. Go and stir."

Daniel gave the hot chocolate a swirl then turned to watch Sarah. She reached for ivory mugs, aligned above her in a perfect row on the cupboard shelf. The cloth of her bodice pulled across her breasts, and her thighs tightened as she rose on her tiptoes.

Yeah, he liked the dress, the way it clung to her curves. But, hell, he liked the rest, too, the sass and intelligence, all rolled up together with those big violet eyes and silky blond hair. And he liked the soft vulnerability she tried so hard to hide underneath it all.

His heart clamoring, he reminded himself of the group waiting in the other room. He sighed and fought the maddening urge to step to her, slide his hands along those curves, and show her how desirable she was. Deep down, he knew the moment wasn't right, not with her skittish as the kittens down the alley. He removed the cocoa from the stove and focused on filling the mugs Sarah had placed on the counter.

In silent tandem, Sarah shifted the filled mugs to a silver tray, then led the way back to the parlor.

"Well, now we know what possessed the two of you to go ice skating," Libby teased from across the room.

"And we've decided on this evening's activities."

Daniel glanced at his friend. The oval table in front of him was bare, the faded Mansion of Happiness game on the floor under the sofa, its morals clearly no longer welcome. Above the table, Bill's face was filled with a devilish grin.

"No more prim and proper. We're playing charades."

"Charades is improper?"

"Hush up, Sarah, you know what I meant. Shoving a bunch of markers around a painted board just reeks of boredom. Something a little more lively seems the ticket, wouldn't you say, Libby?"

"Bill's right. Besides, Daniel knows full well that playing a proper moral game doesn't satisfy the challenge. And before you know it, Sarah and I would be knee-deep into discussing causes. Kate and Molly tell us Daniel finds charades undignified and I suspect Sarah doesn't have time for such whimsy." Libby raised her eyebrows at the two of them. "Hah, I'm right and you know it." She smiled in triumph and explained the rules of the game.

Daniel glanced at Sarah. It was a game devoid of purpose and the dubious wrinkle of her mouth told him she was not comfortable. His thoughts drifted to the reverend and he felt a smile tip his lips. He was no doubt going to look like an ass, but it wouldn't matter. Not when the amusement lit Sarah's pretty face and laughter filled those vibrant eyes. Self-indulgence, Ebenezer would say. But this time, Daniel figured he might just refuse to stand in the corner.

Frank Bates waited, drumming his fingers, at a corner table in the deserted Broadwell House dining room. The place wasn't fancy, but it was clean, and Frank was more comfortable in its homey surroundings than in the more elaborate restaurants of the larger hotels, even if Uncle Walter hated the place. He checked his pocket watch. Uncle Walter was late, as usual. A tinge of resentment nagged at him.

A frazzled waitress cleared luncheon dishes from a nearby table. She cast a furtive glance toward the manager's desk in the lobby, then scraped breadcrumbs from the wrinkled red-and-white-checked tablecloth with careless disregard. The crumbs landed on the floor and she kicked at them with a worn shoe until they scattered.

Frank shook his head. She was courting bad luck, that one. One day, someone was going to see to it that the manager looked her way at the wrong time and she'd be out on the street. He ought to know. Seemed like he'd been dodging bad luck and folks who wanted to ruin things for him all his life. He figured it was time he took charge and made his own luck.

Frank picked at his slice of gingerbread cake and watched the waitress cart her tray of dirty dishes past him and into the kitchen. A soiled cloth napkin leapt from the overloaded heap and perched on the floor in her wake. Filled with droplets of gravy, it stared up at him. Frank wrinkled his nose in distaste and stretched out a too-short leg to kick it from his sight.

"Wouldn't it be easier to just ask someone to pick it up?" Walter Bates's refined baritone asked from behind Frank.

Frank cringed and looked up at his uncle's imposing figure. Shit and hellfire. It was like he'd been caught by his father. "Weren't nobody around," he explained.

Walter shrugged. "It's a hotel restaurant. I'm sure someone will be along to pick it up before long. You're making more work for the waitress." He frowned and sat down opposite of Frank. "But, then, foresight isn't your strong suit."

Frank's skin prickled. It wasn't his fault the waitress was inept. "Is this going to be a lecture?"

"Should it be? Your father lectured for years and it didn't do a bit of good."

Frank shifted with the memory. "Look, Uncle Walter—"

"What is it this time, Frank? What is so urgent that you wire me with a cryptic summons?" Walter leaned back in his chair and pulled a pipe from his jacket pocket, kindling it with piercing arrogance.

Frank sat up straighter. "I think there's more problems at the station."

"You made me travel all the way out here so I could listen to you sputter about the station? You've complained ever since I got you the job." He sighed. "What is it you're going to whine about this time? Somebody picking on you? More Sarah Donovan trouble?"

A knot of apprehension formed in Frank's stomach. "She *is* trouble."

"You put me in a very embarrassing situation last time, Frank." Walter drew on his pipe then leaned forward. "I took your ramblings about her poor job performance to heart, called in some favors, and ended up looking like a fool. Not only did

Jim Wilson file an official protest, but that undertaker Petterman revoked the complaint you claimed he made. Then I find out *your* job performance is miserable, after I backed your promotion."

"There's more goin' on, here. There's reasons Wilson and Petterman are defendin' her."

Walter waved a dismissing hand. "Don't waste my time, Frank, or my position. I'm not finding you another job. You fail again and I'm washing my hands of you."

A bead of sweat trickled down Frank's forehead. He was not going to fail, not this time. He wasn't gonna let nobody ruin things for him anymore. This time, the luck was his. He centered his thoughts on Lavinia, then plunged ahead. "She's sellin' her favors. I got the wires to prove it."

Walter raised an eyebrow. "Proving she's been solicited or that she's soliciting others?"

"Well . . ."

"You want me to go to the other directors and tell them what? That my nephew has telegrams that offer nasty invitations to Miss Donovan? And just what does that prove?"

"She's whorin' on the telegraph."

"I know all about the wires, Frank. Jim Wilson reported on it the day after it happened and sent in a copy of the logbook. Those wires were incoming. All recorded outgoing messages are requests for such comments to stop." Walter tamped his pipe and waited with an expectant gaze.

Frank shifted in his chair, trying to recall everything Lavinia had revealed to him. "What if she sent some invites and Wilson's coverin' for her?"

"You have evidence of that?"

"I might," Frank stalled, "I'm tryin' to find it."

Walter set the pipe down and leaned across the table. "Are you saying the logbook has been doctored?" he asked, his voice low in the empty room.

Frank nodded. He hadn't thought about the logbook when he'd sent the fake messages, but he reckoned it wouldn't take much to ink out a few of the real entries, make it look like something was being hidden. "That's what I think, yes."

"Well, that would make this a whole different situation. The last thing I need is trouble bringing down the value of my stock." A worried frown formed on his face. "You sure this isn't just you being jealous of Miss Donovan? Word is she's doing a fine job of it."

"I ain't jealous." Frank heard the sharpness in his voice and collected himself. "But I ain't going to just sit around and have her make her way, ruining everything, just because she's willing to sleep around to do it."

"Lay it out, Frank. What are we looking at?"

Lavinia's revelations filled his head and his chest puffed with hopeful pride. This time, she'd realize how much spine he really had, how much he loved her. He wiped his sweaty hands on his trouser legs and leaned in toward his uncle. "Petterman withdrew his complaint because Donovan's offering up her attentions. Folks have seen 'em together in whatcha might call 'compromising situations.' As for Wilson, word is that he's gettin' some, too. He not only hired her, he does her job and covers up her mistakes. It's all set up to make her look good."

Walter sank back, his mouth slightly open. "Dear God. Decent folks would boycott us for the Union Pacific."

Frank nodded. "That's why I figured you'd want to know."

"Frank, I'm not taking this up without proof. Not after last time." He shook his head. "I can't."

"If I can prove it?"

"You get me the proof, boy, and I'll see to it Wilson and Donovan never work in the telegraph business again."

★ ★ ★ ★ ★

In the darkened main theater of Occidental Hall, Daniel exhaled with the last strains of "Professor" Wilson's brass band music machine and watched Miss Evie, the featured entertainer, take a final bow. He should never have agreed to come to the variety hall. Having done so, he needed to get through the evening and rethink this week of challenges. He shifted in his chair while Miss Evie exited the cramped stage, applause lingering in her wake. The Tuesday evening crowd was small but raucous, and several catcalls begged for an encore. Miss Evie reappeared, blew a kiss to her adoring fans, and began to climb back up the ladder to the tiny trapeze platform teetering high above.

Across from him, Sarah shifted her attention to Daniel, a smirk tugging at her perky mouth. "You don't look very comfortable."

He offered a wry smile. "I'm not." He picked up the pint tumbler of beer Sarah had coaxed him into ordering and drained it.

"It's quite a bit different from *Little Women,* but you have to admit, she's very good." Sarah waved an arm dramatically. "The audience loves her."

Daniel tipped his head at the obvious truth of it. "The audience would love her if she fell flat on her face. She's half dressed." He shrugged. Miss Evie's antics on the trapeze had been less than sensational, but her curves were a whole different matter.

"So enjoy the show." Sarah raised her arm, two fingers lifted in silent request for more beer. The movement stretched the fabric of her pale-green bodice, pulling it tight across her breast.

An image of Sarah, clad in revealing pale-green attire skittered through his mind. Bare arms, a short, torso-hugging costume, shapely legs in clinging tights. He sighed. "It's not—"

"Not what?" Sarah prodded. "Not right?"

Feeling sheepish, Daniel shrugged. Miss Evie and Occidental Hall's Variety Extravaganza hadn't put the images in his head, after all. Of late, there had been far too many images of Sarah lingering in the corners of his mind, all of them waiting for opportunities to express themselves. All of them prickling at the ghosts of his conscience. "Point taken," he said, ignoring the path of his thought. "I guess I just didn't know what to expect."

Sarah's violet eyes sparkled with a hint of mischief. "You truly have never been to a variety show?"

The din of the crowd rose as busy waitresses moved to refill beer glasses before the intermission ended. A pale blonde in worn clothing plunked two more pints on their table and picked up the correct change from the collection Sarah had advised Daniel to leave on the tablecloth.

"Obviously, you have."

"I attended a few shows with Miriam and Lise, at the academy, back in Saint Louis. Heavens, I haven't done much of anything like that since I got to Denver."

"You haven't said much about them. Were you close?"

"Lise and I started there at the same time. She's part Indian and her desire for justice fell right in with my crusading. Miriam's younger, the daughter of a military family. She's back with them now, far more independent and outspoken than a few years ago." A smile lit her face. "I think I dragged both of them more places than they truly wanted to go."

"A woman on a mission, no doubt."

She frowned briefly, then nodded. "I didn't see it that way, but it's likely true." She reached for her glass of beer and took a sip.

Daniel smiled at her effort to avoid the issue and lifted his own glass. The beer was warm and slightly bitter, reminding him why he seldom imbibed. "What took you from Pennsylvania to Saint Louis?"

"Adventure, independence, a boarding school with an open-minded headmistress." She grinned.

"I should have known. Did you always want to telegraph?"

Delicate laughter filled the air. "My only goal was to make my mark on the world. When I discovered the wire, it seemed a logical choice. Passing next week's primary op test ought to prove it."

Daniel sensed a larger story behind her words. Her history beckoned him, urging him to probe further but her sidestepping of personal issues last night weighed on his mind. Like him, she preferred to avoid discussion of the past. And like him, she was just itching to put an end to any exploration of it. They were two of a kind, all right.

He sipped again at his beer, a mockery of his father's temperance that probably had Sarah wondering quite a bit. Probably enough to start digging at it. And if she didn't fire any pointed questions, his past would pick at him anyway. Damn it, he couldn't even ignore things anymore.

He took a breath and plunged ahead. "My father considered alcohol and variety shows among the major evils of the world."

"And here you are, defying him on both counts." Her voice was soft, cautious.

"He never liked it that I had an occasional drink." He drained the glass and set it back on the table.

"Why did you?"

Daniel mulled it in his head, unsure of whether or nor he wanted to explore the issue. He could detour around the subject, as she had. Hell, they could dance around their pasts forever. He caught her waiting gaze and held it. "Rebellion."

"Excuse me, did I hear you correctly?"

"Rebellion. Pure rebellion."

She grinned. "I never would have thought it."

He nodded, a memory picking at him. "Mary hated it."

Sarah's grin faded. "You've never talked about Mary."

He nodded, waiting for a wave of guilt to surface. The deep loss he'd felt when she died had long since dissipated but she lurked in the recesses of his mind, offering memories whenever he focused too much on Sarah and the turmoil she was stirring in his soul. He closed his eyes briefly, shooing the tightness away from his heart.

"Daniel?"

He looked into Sarah's gentle violet eyes, stilled his heart, and took a breath. "Mary embodied every virtue I'd been raised to honor. She sanctioned every rule, rewarded every principle and somehow made it all a matter of integrity rather than the self-righteous blather my father preached. We grew up together, our parents grooming us for marriage. I never considered any other option. When my father had a stroke, just after we were married, she cared for him without complaint until the day he died. I don't think she ever complained about anything, not even when she was ill and dying herself."

Sarah's breath was audible, and disappointment pooled in her eyes.

Daniel reached for her hand, grasping it amid the yeasty beer spills on the table. "I never questioned the lack of passion in our lives, not ever." His thumb circled her delicate skin. "Maybe I should have."

"She wouldn't have liked you being here."

"No, she wouldn't. But, then, being here wouldn't have occurred to Mary. Or to me."

"And she wouldn't like me."

"She's not here."

She squeezed his hand and offered a wavering smile. "Isn't she? Daniel, don't you see? Both of them are here. The question is, are you going to let them stay?"

Chapter Fifteen

Daniel's jaw clenched and Sarah regretted her words. She'd pushed too far, again. Next to Mary, she was nothing but an oddity. No wonder he was put off by her. Amid the clatter of the variety hall, they sat in silence while her heart pattered.

"Daniel?"

He lifted his head, meeting her gaze. His eyes were full of distant thought but void of anger.

Sarah breathed easier.

The next act began, a melancholy ballad in sultry tones by songstress Lola Ferrangetti. She crossed the stage with languid movement, her heavily darkened eyes emphasizing the sad song. A hush fell across the room as she cast her spell on the audience.

Daniel's eyes closed and his shoulders rose and fell with each weighty breath.

Sarah squeezed his hand. "I'm sorry."

He squeezed it back. "Don't be," he said, his voice thick. "I have a couple of ghosts living inside my head."

"I never meant—"

"I know. But they're here and they don't want to leave. I need to decide whether or not to banish them for good." He exhaled and offered a tentative smile.

A prickle of warmth spread through Sarah, relief that, for once, she hadn't pushed him away.

"But, Sarah . . . if I'm going to exorcise my ghosts, I'm going to expect you to confront a few of yours, too."

Lavinia Morgan surveyed the crowded basement of the Lawrence Street Methodist Church, taking note of the swelling membership of the Denver Suffrage Association. The spare whitewashed walls were nearly hidden behind the faithful entourage. Her faithful entourage.

She'd crafted the organization, almost since its founding, pouring her heart into making it strong and influential. Here, if nowhere else, she reigned as master of her own fate. Losing her inheritance hadn't mattered any more than losing that horrid young man her father had chosen for her. If her father were here, she'd spit in his face and claim her victory. And tonight, she would reign supreme in the unveiling of her greatest coup, a rally they would laud for years to come, a perfect rally handcrafted to make her shine.

She stepped forward, pulling herself to her full height behind the lectern, and struck the gavel. The sharp sound reverberated through the room and the multitude turned their eyes to her and silenced.

"Good evening, ladies. Tonight, we have before us the final planning for next week's suffrage rally." She peered out over the crowd, nodding to the most recent recruits, currying their loyalty. "We have received word that the Colorado Suffrage Organization will indeed hold their meeting in conjunction with the rally. Further, we will be honored with an appearance by Miss Anthony herself."

Lavinia paused, allowing the group to digest her announcement. A shiver of anticipation raced through her as the ladies heralded her coup with a burst of avid applause.

"An added reminder, ladies: the state suffrage referendum will occur within the month. With the agreement of the state organization to run their meeting during the rally, we have before us the most important two-day event in Colorado's move for suffrage. We will split into committees for final planning. I urge all of you to put forth the extra effort to make this rally a premier event which will set the tone for the election."

"Miss Morgan?" A tentative voice interrupted her instructions.

Lavinia searched the room and finally placed the voice. "Mrs. Anderson."

"With all those extra doin's, do we need to ask Marshal McCallin to put on an extra man?"

"An excellent point. I suspect there may be a significant increase in public unrest, especially with Miss Anthony's presence. Our usual small group of drunken men may become more numerous and vocal. Perhaps it would be wise to alert McCallin. I'll personally attend to it."

In fact, with the referendum vote upon them, dissenters would swell in number. Lavinia shivered. The men would be livid. Their drunken slurs would grow loud, intimidating, and more than a few would approach the suffragists. The women's hand-painted signs would be smashed on the ground, and violent threats would be made. One or two might even strike out and be carted off to jail. It would create magnificent press, if presented correctly.

"Elizabeth Byers, are you present?"

"I am."

"We will place press coverage in your capable hands, as usual. I trust Mr. Byers will devote a fair amount of space to unbiased coverage of the event."

"I'm certain he will."

"You may wish to speak to him specifically about the potential for more than the usual amount of trouble. We wouldn't want careless violence to reflect badly on the ladies or the movement, after all. I'll ask McCallin to cooperate fully with the *News* so that any sordid background information associated with such troublemakers is revealed to the public."

"Mr. Byers will do his best to include the information."

"Thank you, Elizabeth. Now then, is there anything else we need to discuss as a whole?"

"We're going to need more speakers."

Lavinia peered out in search of the voice. An attractive young woman stood in the rear of the room, a newcomer. Lavinia bit her lip. How in heaven's name had someone new stepped into a committee leadership role? Gracious, had Frank's plans for that Donovan woman distracted her that much? She drew a smile and beamed at the woman. "I'm sure the officers of the state organization would be happy to oblige. Has everyone met you, dear?"

"I . . . uh . . . Amelie Parsons. I'm just filling in for Mrs. Noble. She's ill." She blushed under the unexpected scrutiny of the other women, then drew a deep breath. "Shall we round out the state officers with a few additional orators to fill the slate? Do you wish us to present the list for approval?"

"I'm sure Mrs. Noble's committee is doing a formidable job." Lavinia nodded, secure that Parsons wasn't worth worrying over. "Time is getting away from us and we really do need to split up and pursue our remaining work. Ladies? Move approval?" Lavinia nodded at the quick motion and second, then called for the vote. As expected, the ayes carried. "Motion approved. Carry on as you see fit, Miss Parsons. Committees, let's get busy."

Women swarmed, moving folding wooden chairs into smaller cliques. A busy chorus of voices filled the room, and Lavinia smiled at their industry. Without her tutelage, the group would have floundered long ago. Now, they were a force to be reckoned with. Her force.

She strode through the noisy room, stopping to check on

each committee. Refreshments were assigned, transportation and accommodations arranged for visitors, a tent and folding chairs secured, and two hundred painted signs committed. Her ladies were doing well.

The crowd thinned with each committee's completion of its task until Lavinia alone remained in the now empty basement. She straightened a few last chairs and collected the lists her diligent groups had left for her. Everything was neatly penned out, firmly planned, and sure to catch the attention and admiration of the state organization.

She scanned the last of the lists, the guest orators. It was a fine collection of the best Colorado had to offer and even a national figure or two, a list the association could be proud to have approved. Even the names penned below Mrs. Noble's original list showed foresight. There were long-time suffragists, a female photographer, wives of businessmen and politicians, and Caroline Churchill, that young journalist who kept talking of opening her own suffrage paper.

Lavinia's gaze halted on the last name and a tight acid knot formed in her stomach.

Miss Sarah Donovan was scheduled to discuss her exploits as Denver's first female telegrapher.

Twilight descended, darkening the sidewalk next to the double front doors of Orchestrion Hall. Daniel sat on an icy wooden bench and wondered what he'd gotten himself into this time. German music leaked from the establishment and he grimaced at its ribald audacity. He shouldn't have suggested coming. Not at all.

He pulled up the collar of his overcoat and exhaled into the cold January air. He suspected he was going to be even more uncomfortable tonight than he had been last night. A German beer hall, for God's sake, with dancing. He had to be out of his mind. Mary would have steered him away, gentle reminders about the dangers inside falling from her lips. Ebenezer would have sermonized, pounding his fist on the pulpit, or on Daniel. A few days ago, he'd have simply avoided the place. And he would have tonight, too, except he wasn't sure of anything anymore. Besides, he'd told Sarah he was a new man, ready to take risks, and he wasn't about to let her know otherwise.

Boasting is a sin, Daniel.

God shall smite the deceiver, boy. And woe to those who tempt the devil and court evil. Do you hear me, son? They shall be swallowed by wickedness unless they are willing to seek forgiveness and endure the punishment they are due.

He slammed his hand on the bench, shutting the voices out, refusing to believe he was doing something wrong by walking into a perfectly respectable German establishment and enjoying himself.

These challenges had turned his thoughts in directions he didn't want to chase any further. His life had been just fine until Sarah raised all those questions and left them lingering in his mind. He'd found enough ghosts to last for a while. Tonight, he intended to shift the focus. Enough was enough.

He had to make Sarah believe the challenges had worked. He'd told her more than he'd ever revealed to anyone about his childhood, or Mary, and he didn't intend to bare his soul any further. Sarah had a way about her, a fiery temper that covered up such softness that a man's heart just about melted. Or he'd melted, at least, and he'd melted about all he wanted to. Tonight, if anyone melted, it was going to be her.

He crossed his arms against the chill and glanced down the street. Sarah had rounded the corner, looking half-frozen herself, curiosity lighting her big eyes.

"A beer hall?" she asked, sounding doubtful. "Are you sure?"

Daniel grinned, a projection of the new man he'd told her

he'd become. "I figure maybe my father's ghost won't even set foot inside." He rose from the bench and shrugged in feigned nonchalance. "I've spent the whole day telling myself that some fine people frequent the place. I thought of every German I know and not one of them seemed to be any less respectable for drinking beer and dancing. They're all good people. And Bill Byers is among the non-German regulars down here. Orchestrion Hall doesn't seem to have smudged his reputation any. My common sense says this won't be my ruin."

It was true enough. There *wasn't* anything wrong with the place, not really. Places like this were only temptations of evil when people allowed them to be. And he didn't have any intention of letting himself do anything he'd regret. He'd have a couple of beers, dance a little just to prove the ghosts were gone, and convince Sarah it was her turn to field the questions.

Sarah laughed. The sound came out far too unnatural to pass muster and, for a moment, Daniel feared he'd overdone it.

"Nervous?" he asked. At least she seemed convinced that *he* was comfortable.

"I am not dancing," she told him in flat tones.

Ah, dancing. He should have known. "It's a challenge, Sarah. It's meant to stretch us, remember? Both of us. Last night, I got stretched a whole lot, and if I can do it, so can you. Now, let's go in." He opened the bright red door and the polka music poured out, engulfing them. Sarah stepped into the darkened room, and he followed her, pausing to let his eyes adjust. In the rear corner, behind the crowded dance floor, a flamboyant machine blasted forth.

Sarah stood, staring. "Good Lord."

The machine was close to eleven feet high with horns, drums, and a xylophone all built in. Next to it, a small group of musicians, accordionists, mostly, were warming up on a makeshift stage.

He laughed, a bit shocked by the gaudiness of it, despite having been forewarned by Bill earlier in the day. "Want to go take a closer look?"

Sarah shifted her attention to Daniel and shook her head. "It's loud enough from here. I don't know if I want to get any closer. Maybe we should just go for a nice quiet walk."

"Oh, no, you don't. We're trying something new. Tomorrow night, I get to watch *Little Women* so tonight is my choice."

Sarah swallowed. "And this doesn't bother you?"

Daniel lifted his palms in a no-care gesture. "Not a bit."

God hates a liar, boy. Do you hear me, son?

"Can I buy you a beer?" *Take that, old man, and leave me alone.*

"I guess you might as well. I doubt they have anything else to offer."

He caught the barkeep's eye and raised two fingers, then looked at her and winked. "See, I paid attention last night."

A warm smile lit her face, releasing the tension that had surrounded them since her arrival.

Daniel led the way to one of the few remaining empty tables that edged the dance floor and they sat. In the center of the room, couples spun together, legs frantically pumping to keep up with the music.

A plump waitress, her hair bound in a halo of braids, set two beer steins and a small loaf of rye bread on the table and waited while Daniel counted out payment. The woman's ample bosom strained against the white cloth of her traditional German dress. "On da bar, we have pretzels und blutwurst und sauerkraut, *ja?*"

She strode on to the next table, her bountiful posterior swaying.

Daniel tasted his beer, finding the forbidden hops and barley more pleasant than usual, then leaned forward. "What in the world is blutwurst?"

Sarah shrugged. "Some sort of sausage, I think." She lifted her beer, drank, then added, "Something guaranteed to make you thirsty."

"More sage knowledge from your Saint Louis days?"

"Just common sense." She shifted in her chair and offered a bright smile. "You know, like yours."

The smile did little to fool him. She evaded discussing herself, sometimes even more than he did. And he'd allowed her to get away with it. "You don't like talking about yourself, do you?"

Sarah sighed. "There's not much to tell."

"Then it wouldn't take long to tell, would it?"

She shrugged her shoulders. "I was raised by loving parents and had a tranquil childhood. Papa owns a bank and served several years in the state legislature."

"And your mother?"

She held his gaze and drew a breath. "Mama was his elegant wife. She died just before I left home." Her eyes clouded and she looked away.

"You were close to her?"

She nodded and drank again.

"Tell me about her."

Wariness fill Sarah's eyes. "Oh, I don't think we need—"

"I didn't think I needed to talk about my past, either. Or are we back to not playing fair?"

"I've been playing fair, and you know it." Her voice had taken on a defensive tone. She crossed her arms and sat ramrod straight in the chair.

"Then why do you always get to change the subject when you don't like it? I told you last night that you were going to have to face a few ghosts, too. Is this one of them?"

"I don't think that's fair. Mama gave me nothing but love." She fingered the locket at her breast. "Don't you *dare* put her in the same category as your father."

Daniel held his tongue, surprised at Sarah's vehemence. He'd struck a nerve; he just didn't know what the hell kind of nerve it was. "Is that her picture?"

Sarah pulled her hand away from the locket and nodded, then drew the chain that held the locket from her neck and handed it to him. He opened it to reveal a miniature painted portrait. A remarkably attractive woman gazed up at him. Her hair, like Sarah's, was spun gold, but dressed elaborately. A jeweled amethyst comb matched her vibrant eyes. A finely tailored gown told him she was also a woman of fashion. He glanced at Sarah and closed the locket softly. "She was beautiful."

"Her name was Hannah. She was the saddest person I've ever known."

He waited but she supplied no further information. End of conversation. He changed tacks. "What about you being a telegrapher? Did you have their blessing?"

Sarah weighed the question with another swallow of beer. "Papa's skeptical, waiting to see if I make good. With Papa, it's never a matter of what a person does, just how well they succeed with it. Mama never knew but I think she would have been proud, maybe even a little awed." She paused and glanced at the bar. "Could you go get us some of that blutwurst and we'll see what it is? Maybe some pretzels?"

Definitely the end of the conversation, but he was beginning to understand some of her comments from earlier in the week. Not enough, but a beginning. Still, she'd avoided pushing at him too much and he owed her the same courtesy. "Sauerkraut?" he asked.

Sarah nodded. "More beer, too."

Daniel worked his way to the bar. For whatever reason, being beautiful hadn't brought happiness to Hannah Donovan, and he suspected it was at the root of that plain facade Sarah insisted on for herself. The monstrous machine wound to a halt and the band took over, their steady oom-pa-pa resounding through the hall. Daniel heaped a plate full of hearty German fare, signaled the waitress and returned to the table.

The waitress followed with four steins of beer. "You will want more beer, *ja?* Dat is food for two beers. You will be thirsty, *ja,* I know." She grinned and hustled away.

Across from Sarah, Daniel slid into his chair. "She looks like she knows what she's talking about. At least, how many beers for the amount of food, *ja?*"

A sharp giggle rose in Sarah's throat, obviously hell-bent on running straight into the sip of beer she'd just taken. She slammed her beer stein onto the table and slapped her hand across her mouth.

Daniel's shoulders shook. He'd forgotten to tell her the German beer was a bit stronger than the swill they'd had last night.

Sarah rolled her eyes, swallowed the beer, and stuck out her tongue.

An image of Mary, prim and proper, filled Daniel's head. *No, Mary, let me be. I never had any fun. This is my chance. I promise, it won't hurt anybody.* He glanced around the crowded room, caught himself in the habit, then downed half a stein of beer, raised his eyebrows, and winked at Sarah. Drawing on her wide-eyed reaction, he slurped again at the beer and issued a loud burp.

She snorted and reached for her own stein. She gulped at the beer, emitted a surprisingly loud belch, and raised her eyebrows in challenge.

Daniel tipped his head at her and chugged again. He readied himself and forced out an even louder burp.

Sarah snorted again and finished her beer. Forming her mouth into an "o", she stretched out the sound of her belch, until it trailed off into a gasp of empty air.

They dissolved into laughter, tears filling both their eyes. "Heavens, Daniel, I don't believe you did that."

He shrugged and tried to ignore the pain in his side. "I don't either. Thank God I don't know anyone here." He leaned forward and lowered his voice. "I looked." His mouth widened into a grin. "Wanna dance?"

Sarah stopped laughing. "Oh, no. Thank you, but no."

Daniel cocked his head to one side. "Scared?"

"No."

"If I can do what I just did, surely you ought to be able to get out there and dance. Of course, if you want to just call it quits, say I won the challenges, we can forget all about it."

She exhaled in disbelief. "I think not."

"Then on your feet. It's polka time." He stood and offered her a hand.

Sarah placed her hand in his. "Don't say you weren't warned." She reached for the second stein of beer, took a gulp, and allowed Daniel to haul her to the dance floor.

"You know how to do this?" he called over the din of the accordions.

"Barely."

"Well, all I know is what I've watched during the last three beers. I guarantee you'll look better than me." He swept her into the circling crowd, their feet hitting the ground in maddening rush of one-two-three.

She stumbled, her foot landing on his. She bit her lip and for a brief moment, Daniel thought she might cry.

"Whoa, sweetheart, that's my move," he called, offering her an encouraging smile.

She smiled back, tentative at first, then broader as he pulled her back into the dance.

Moments later, Daniel misstepped himself and jarred them both to a halt. A German couple plowed into them, sending the whole group to the floor.

The older couple stared for a moment, then burst into good-natured smiles. The men rose, extending hands to the ladies as the two gray-haired strangers spoke back and forth in rapid German. Once standing, the rotund man brushed his dusty hands across his even dustier overalls, cleared his throat and turned to Sarah.

"Ach, you come wit me, Gunther Muller. Frau Muller, Helga, goes wit him. Enough we all look like *Dummkopfs.*"

Helga grinned at Daniel, revealing a partial set of yellowed teeth, and snatched him into her powerful arms. "I lead." Seconds later, she was steering him around the room, counting *"ein, zwei, drei"* as they stepped. She pointed at Gunther and Sarah. "Ach, your *liebekin,* she is a good *Schuler,* look how she learns."

At the edge of the dance floor, Gunther was nodding to the count of the music, pulling Sarah along with him as he spun circles. Sarah's feet scrambled to keep up then settled into an even but rapid pace. Daniel grinned and focused on following Helga. He should have felt every shade a fool. But he didn't.

Helga paused, her frizzled gray head bobbing up and down with the beat of the accordions. "*Ja,* you are learning. Now, you lead."

Daniel nodded, then took the plump woman in his arms and led her awkwardly around the floor.

Helga continued to jabber, most of her accented words mingling with the music. He caught bits and pieces, enough to realize she'd misinterpreted his relationship with Sarah.

The polka ended with them near the table and Daniel downed the last of his beer. Then, Helga pulled him back onto the dance floor, jabbering about another go-around.

Sarah and Gunther had ended up in front of the band. Sarah looked as winded as Daniel felt, but her face beamed. Gunther crossed to the stage and exchanged words with the musicians. They nodded and announced the next number.

"Now, you learn to schottische, *ja?*" Helga's yellow teeth grinned at him. Not waiting for his response, she pulled him toward another couple and they formed a quartet, a pair in front and back, all linked together with arms and hands. "Step, step, step, hop," Helga instructed.

Daniel heard the beat and repeated the actions. The music shifted and the others switched steps and changed positions. Daniel soloed his own step, step, step, hop, then exploded into laughter as he realized he'd been left behind.

"Step-hop, step-hop," Helga supplied, her own laughter swallowing half the words.

Daniel lifted his feet, a giddy sense of play settling over him. He felt like a child, like the child he'd never had the chance to be.

On the other side of the dance floor, Gunther had pulled Sarah aside and was demonstrating the pattern. His heavy pot belly bounced with each step-hop. He moved aside and waved for Sarah to repeat her moves. She grimaced slightly, shrugged, then took a step. Gunther dictated the count, his finger bobbing to the music. Sarah circled by herself, her skirt held up to prevent stumbling, silly in her shuffle steps and completely ridiculous in each step-hop. Then laughter consumed her, and Gunther escorted her back to the table. Halfway there, Sarah paused and offered the German a quick hug.

The music stopped and Daniel bowed to Helga. "Frau Muller, it has been a pleasure."

She bobbed her head. "*Ja*, it was *gut*. Now, we get some beer, *ja?*"

"*Ja.*"

He escorted her to his table, now absent its chairs, where Sarah and Gunther stood, waiting. He knew he looked a mess, sweat dripping from his temples. But, then, everyone else was dripping, too. He grinned at Sarah, then shook Gunther's hand. "Thank you. You and Mrs. Muller are good people."

"*Ach,* we just didn't want to fall no more. It's *gut* you had some fun, *ja?* Come on, Helga, let's get some blutwurst." He grabbed his wife's hand and the two drifted off to the bar.

Sarah wiped her hand across her brow and blew at the wisps of hair that had fallen from her once tidy bun. Her eyes sparkled with an abandon Daniel hadn't seen before, a complete lack of purpose, he realized.

She caught his gaze and giggled.

"What?"

"Herr Muller thinks we're married."

"*Ja?*" He grinned. "Well, Frau Muller thinks we're lovers."

Sarah's mouth formed a silent "oh" and her eyes grew wide.

Daniel was dimly aware of a small scuffle, two drunks shoving at each other, behind Sarah. They left his consciousness as the deep amethyst pools in her eyes pulled him in. He imagined her in his arms, bare, soft, willing. Sarah, full of abandon as she'd been on the dance floor, directing all her passion to him.

The drunks passed, knocking her off balance, and she tumbled into his arms.

"Look at this. Sarah Donovan at a loss for words." Daniel stared down at her, tightening his hold. His heartbeat quickened and his thumb caressed the bottom of her breast. He lowered his head, his mouth meeting hers in a slow kiss of invitation as he pulled her flush against him.

Sarah arched into his arms, against the hardness of his body, making him ache with desire. Her lips opened and she drew his mouth closer, her tongue teasing at him.

Daniel nipped at her tongue, then pulled it into his own mouth. He delved into her mouth, seeking, finding, demanding.

Distant catcalls and whistles sounded from behind him,

reminding him they were standing in the middle of Orchestrion Hall.

Sarah pulled out of his arms, her breath in ragged spurts, like his own, her eyes registering an odd mixture of shock and regret. "Oh, Daniel," she whispered.

Inside Daniel's head, Mary frowned and Ebenezer pounded on his pulpit while Sarah turned and walked out on him.

Chapter Sixteen

Sarah approached the corner of 15th and Larimer, glad the afternoon was bright and sunny. Horses, buggies and people crowded the busy thoroughfare, more than a few making Joslin's their destination.

It wasn't really much of a day off, not with the final rehearsal of *Little Women* this morning and tonight's performance still looming. With the remnants of a headache and last night's loss of sleep, she should be taking a nap. But when Miss Clay had announced a shortened day of school, the children had all chattered nonstop about visiting Joslin's Dry Goods Company.

The temptation of coconut dainties and chocolate fudge had swayed her to do the same. Today was a chocolate day, if ever there was one, and Sarah intended to drown in the sweet confections. Between Daniel and the play, she'd had all the strain she could handle and a relaxing afternoon sampling Thursday candy specials was just the ticket. She'd make her purchase, go home, and spend the afternoon getting fat.

She crossed Larimer and stepped into the busy store. Here and there, she recognized children she knew. She waved but didn't dwell to speak with them. Instead, she made her way to the back of the store, thoughts of Daniel filling her head.

Lord, her emotions were tumbling over one another, and the jumble scared her. Last night, she'd slid from all nerves to exhilaration then somehow to raw desire. And somewhere along the line, her heart had gotten wrapped up in the mixture. And that kiss and the haunted look in Daniel's eyes that shattered her so badly she'd left him standing there alone in Orchestrion Hall.

She wasn't any good at this, any of it. She'd kept her deepest self bottled up for so long, she'd forgotten how to share. Besides, no good came of revealing vulnerability. She felt like a fool for losing control of the situation.

The store was crowded with bustling shoppers and she drifted among them, anonymous. A display of hats caught her eye and she imagined herself wearing one of the fancy things, birds and flowers perched on top. She smiled and dismissed the image. Silliness.

Rounding a corner, she almost ran into Kate and Molly, their brown ringlets bobbing as an enthusiastic clerk demonstrated a bright hand-painted marionette. They caught sight of her immediately.

"Oh, Miss Sarah, isn't it something?" Molly asked.

Sarah eyed the marionette with skepticism. "It looks complicated, to me."

"But you're a telegrapher and your hands are used to doing complicated things."

"I suppose they are, Molly, but it still looks pretty involved for a toy and liable to break if you use it much."

"See, Molly? I told you it wasn't a good purchase." Kate crossed her arms sagely.

The clerk shrugged, set the puppet on the counter, and turned to his next customer.

Sarah glanced around, anxious to be on her way. "Well, girls, I need to get going. Where's Mrs. Winifred?"

"Mrs. Winifred didn't bring us," Kate explained.

"I did." Daniel's familiar voice sounded behind Sarah and her heart jumped.

"Daniel, I didn't expect . . ." She let the words trail off, self-conscious. The banished thoughts of his kisses flooded back into her mind with all the confusion they could muster.

He smiled, hesitant, and she realized he was as unsure as she was. "I didn't expect to see you here, either."

"I was really on my way to the candy section."

"Us, too. C'mon." Molly led the way to the back of the store where the confectioner displayed his wares.

Sarah followed, keeping pace with the girls, their proximity her insulation against having to discuss last night with Daniel. What in the world could she say?

At the counter, they eyed the selections. There was the usual assortment of peppermint sticks and cinnamon drops, anise and horehound candy, even lemon drops. But it was the specialty confections that drew her attention. Nestled at the top of the case were the bonbons, delicate pastel creations of cream cheese sugar rolled in coconut next to rolled balls of chocolate sprinkled with chopped walnuts. Candied fruit squares were next, each a delectable combination of fruit, nuts, and coconut. There were pralines and sugarplums, caramels and divinity, taffy and maple sugar candy. Finally, her gaze rested on the fudge in all its varieties. This was what she had come for.

"Something catch your eye?" Daniel teased.

Sarah licked her lips. "I'll thank you not to interfere with my chocolate party, if you don't mind." She kept her voice light and hoped it didn't sound as forced as it felt.

"Forewarned is forearmed." Daniel smiled, playing her game, and crossed to the other end of the counter where Kate and Molly were absorbed in their own selections.

She purchased a pound of fudge, assorted maple cream, white chocolate, and almond roca along with a half-dozen each of chocolate-covered cherries and coconut delights. Popping a cherry into her mouth, she savored the sweet combination of flavors and the syrupy texture.

"The girls want to look at new hair ribbons for tonight. Do you feel like coming along?"

"I really need to—"

"C'mon. It's a dry goods store. Let's look at the ribbons and set things right. Then you can go."

"All right," she said, before she could start picking his words apart and analyzing them. It was only fair that she offer some explanation. She forced another smile. "As long as you don't mind me nibbling chocolate."

They followed the girls up a flight of stairs. Bolts of cloth and rolls of ribbons were arrayed behind a long counter. On the opposite side of the aisle, dozens of ready-made dresses were displayed. Daniel was silent until the girls had skipped far enough ahead.

"Are you all right?" he asked, his voice for her ears only. "You ran out on me."

Sarah nodded, not willing to share the jumble of emotions that were gnawing at her. "I'm sorry. I got rattled, I guess."

"I got rattled, too."

She'd realized it the moment she had looked into his eyes. "Those ghosts you kept insisting were banished?"

He shrugged. "I—"

"Papa, look, isn't it grand?" Kate stood among the dresses, stroking a cream-colored frock.

Daniel offered Sarah an apologetic tilt of his head and crossed to his daughter.

Sarah watched the two of them, sure they were having a discussion about the purchase of the dress, something she wasn't part of.

She wandered among the fashionable dresses, drawn to the new designs, and stopped next to a striped street suit. The two-tone green camel's hair was simply trimmed, without the grand flounces that had been the rage last year. It was draped, not bustled, like the dress she'd worn Monday night.

"You should try it on."

Sarah started and took her hand away from the fabric she hadn't even realized she'd been fingering.

"Try it on," he urged again. "The girls went to the toy section so there's plenty of time."

Sarah shook her head. "No, that's all right. I'd have no need for anything that impractical."

"Plain brown work skirts, only."

Always, comments on her work skirts. "What's wrong with work skirts?" She stood among the ready-wears, feeling trapped.

"Oh, they're fine. It just seems like you'd want a few fancy things, dresses as pretty as you are."

Sarah bristled. "For what? So men can concentrate on my dress and my hair and my shape instead of listening to what I have to say?"

Daniel stared at her and shoved his hands into his coat pockets. "Is that what this is all about?"

"I will not be defined by what I look like."

"Like your mother was? Is she the one who told you that you shouldn't let yourself be beautiful?"

The comment stung. He didn't understand, couldn't understand. She took a step forward and glared up at him, ignoring the concern in his expression. She didn't need his misdirected pity.

"You won't leave it be, will you?" Her hands gestured without direction. "All week long, you've kept digging for some buried comment my mother made. Let it alone. She never once insisted I behave any certain way, and this week doesn't have anything to do with whether or not I wear fancy dresses." She paused, fighting the feeling of exposure that stormed inside her. "My challenges were about controlling things, remember? Isn't that what you said? Why do you keep at it?"

She stalked away, farther into the ladies-wear section, unwilling to let him see how worked up she'd become.

He followed, cautious and quiet. "Because I think this has more to do with who you are than you realize."

Sarah sighed, controlled her breathing, and turned around. "All right, here it is." She kept her voice measured, focusing on control. "I don't wear fancy dresses because I will not be reduced to being any man's ornament. I want to be seen for what I am. I watched my mother struggle every day to be heard for her intelligent comments and her capable understanding, but no one, no one, ever paid attention to her. All they ever saw was what she looked like. I will not allow that to happen to me."

He reached for her. "Sarah, there's not a chance in the world that would happen to you."

She moved away from his touch. "It shouldn't have happened to her."

"And your father? Surely, he—"

She turned back to him. "Is there a point to all this?"

He opened his palms. "What was it you said last night? With your father, it's not what you do but how you do it? What's that mean? If you're not being the perfect ornament, then you have to achieve perfection at something else?"

Her hands flew out in a flamboyant gesture of dismissal. "Oh, now that's just about the most—"

"Is it?"

She turned away from him and started toward the stairs. This was going nowhere.

Daniel followed, his longer legs keeping easy stride with her short ones. "If you control things, you can shine, can't you, Sarah?" he said beside her. "You can know you've achieved something, you can win acceptance and glory. And if you never take a chance on anything you're unsure of, including opening yourself up and this relationship, you never risk failure."

His words clawed at her, opening the uncertainty that had lingered in her heart since last night. She'd let him in, and it had opened vulnerabilities she preferred not to bare.

"What relationship?" she asked him. "There is no relationship."

Frank Bates sat in the telegraph office staring at the logbook. Voices of a few afternoon travelers reverberated from the waiting room, distracting him for a moment, then quieted.

It wasn't enough that Jim had been called to some big meeting and he was pullin' double duty, but he was smack in the middle of a double shift on top of it, just so Sarah Donovan could rehearse her little play at the school and get ready for tonight's performance. Miss Clay had sent a note over, special, and he figured there'd be trouble if he didn't let her go.

Still, fate was smiling on him. Donovan was a slick one, all right. He'd searched the logbook through and through and still couldn't find the evidence Uncle Walter needed. She'd hid it that well. Her leaving for the school was the opening he needed to fix things up, help the evidence along. If she was so hell-bent on ruining his life, he figured it weren't no sin to strike first. Not in his book.

Frank stood up, crossed the room, and peeked out at the ticket counter to make sure things were under control. Two old farts were waitin' on the next train along with some old biddy in a lace bonnet. If none of 'em died from old age, he reckoned they'd be all right a bit longer without his attention.

He rummaged around the small office, looking for the bag of peanuts he'd hidden day before yesterday.

The way he figured it, Sarah was fixing to ruin a whole lot of lives besides his. There was that undertaker. Sarah had been seen all over town with him. Not that such activities were bad in and of themselves, it was just that, well, they'd been seen *doing* things that were better done in private.

Frank found the peanuts behind the coal bucket, pulled out a handful and stuck one in his mouth. He paced the small room.

Now, from what he'd heard, Sarah and that undertaker were doin' a whole lot more than just spooning. Folks, if you talked to the right folks, of course, were saying they'd been seen groping at each other right out there on the river on Sunday afternoon. And last night, they'd been drunk over at one of the beer halls, randy as all get-out. And Lavinia herself had seen them half-naked in a butler's pantry a couple months back.

Yessir, that little Sarah was nothin' but a cockteaser, dragging a professional widower man down. 'Course, most folks was too polite to talk about anything like that.

He spat the soggy peanut shell out onto the floor and stuck another one in his mouth.

Then, there were the telegrams he'd fished out of the waste barrel and Lavinia's tip about old Jim Wilson, the stationmaster. Those wires just about proved Sarah was settin' up illicit meetings. Offerin' her wares to Wilson explained how she'd been hired on here in the first place and sure did account for Jim always speakin' up on her behalf. All that was missing was the proof itself. Not that most folks would need any.

Just his Uncle Walter.

Frank fingered the logbook and thought about what Uncle Walter had said about the log entries reflecting only refusals on Sarah's part. Hell, anybody with a lick of sense could have figured that out. She didn't record anything that would give her away, and she'd told the boys on the other end to do the same. That's why there weren't no record of it.

He spat out a peanut shell and grinned.

Shit and hellfire. There weren't no sense puttin' it off, not when he had the perfect chance to protect himself. He was here covering her shift. Covering it without any official record he was doing so. There wasn't an entry in the damn logbook under his name, not yet. It'd be her word against his. He'd go back, look up those nights she got the telegrams from her friends and ink a few things out, just to raise suspicions.

Just for good measure, he might send out a few more wires as Lark, like he did a few days ago. 'Cept this time, he'd make the logbook entries under her name.

He guessed there'd be a record then, all right.

Sarah sat on her bed, a half-eaten box of fudge on her lap. Her cheeks were wet, her hands sticky, and her spirit sagging. Heavens, why couldn't Daniel just let things be?

A quiet knock sounded on the door. "Sarah?" Elizabeth called. "Open up. I know you're in there so there's no sense pretending you're not."

Sarah sniffled. "I'm busy."

"Busy, my foot," Elizabeth said from the hallway. "I saw you storm out of Joslin's. You open up this door and talk to me." She paused, waiting, then continued. "I can always get a key from your landlady, but then she'd be in there, too."

Sarah sighed, knowing Elizabeth would make good on the threat. "Hold on." She slid the candy onto the patchwork quilt and wiped her palms across her cheeks. She stood and crossed the room, turned the key, and opened the door just enough to talk. "What?"

"What? Isn't that my question?" Elizabeth stared at her, frowning. "Gracious, girl, you don't just march out of a store looking that way and not expect anyone to notice, do you? Get out of the way." She pushed the door open and stepped forward.

Sarah took an inadvertent step back, then scowled.

Elizabeth raised her eyebrows. "Scowl all you want, dear. It doesn't bother me." She closed the door in one soft motion and shook her head. "Now, let's sit down and eat some more of that chocolate you have smeared all over your face."

"I really don't want to talk about it."

"I know you don't. But you will." Elizabeth crossed the room, tossed her wrap over the footboard, and plopped unto the bed.

Sarah followed behind. She tucked a stray tendril of hair behind her ear and stood at the foot of the bed. "Look, I really don't want to involve—"

"Sarah, I am your friend. I am involved." She patted the bed. "Besides, Bill and I have been discussing you and Daniel all week. Did your little tiff today have anything to do with the kiss last night?"

Sarah shook her head. "No private life in Denver, I see." She sat down beside her friend and reached for a chunk of fudge.

"Amazing how many people there are in public places. I figured Daniel would be the one fretting over this, not you."

"Oh, twiddle. I couldn't care less about being seen. I just . . ." she frowned, "I just don't really care for the speculation."

Elizabeth stopped chewing. "That's unexpected from someone out to show the world who she is."

"I don't think anyone is talking about my accomplishments." She pulled her legs onto the bed, tucking them under her skirt. Saying she was worried about what others thought wasn't something she'd ever expected, either. Still, there it was. Folks were out there, talking about how foolish she was behaving.

Elizabeth considered the comment for a while, savoring a piece of candy. She glanced at Sarah and offered a benevolent smile. "So, you afraid the real Sarah is being exposed?"

Sarah's skin prickled and she shifted on the bed. "I don't really think we need to talk about—"

"How deeply *do* you hide yourself?"

Sarah glanced away. "I don't hide."

"Don't you?" Elizabeth gave her arm a gentle squeeze.

Sarah turned and drew a deep breath. Daniel had said the same thing, and she'd shut him out, as if denying the truth would make it go away. Lord, how she hated feeling insecure. Yet, there it was. Her eyes filled with tears, and she nodded. "Daniel said the same thing."

"So you ran, sweetie?"

"I ran and I shoved a pound of chocolate fudge into my mouth and nothing got any better."

"I figured as much." She stroked Sarah's arm and offered a quick hug. "Daniel hit a few nerves?"

"Hit them and then some."

"Want to tell me about it?"

Sarah shook her head. "No, not really."

Elizabeth pulled away and reached for more chocolate. She nibbled at it, then pinned her gaze on Sarah. "What was it Kate and Molly said the other night? Daniel must do things that aren't stuffy and that stretch his code of conduct? Why?"

"Daniel hides behind his rules." Sarah picked up a coconut bonbon and bit into it. "I think because he never made his own."

"Makes sense, from what I know about him." She wiped the corners of her mouth with delicate fingers, then turned to Sarah. "And what about you?"

Sarah swallowed. "Me?"

Her friend nodded. "Your challenge is to do things that are not related to causes, things that are simply fun?"

She shook her head and flopped back onto the bed. "Daniel says I use my causes so I can keep control."

"Is he right?"

Sarah stared at the ceiling, avoiding comment.

"Do you feel like you're in control when you're working toward some bigger cause?"

"Well, yes. Of course. I know what needs to be done, and I do it."

"And nobody demands anything deeper of you, do they?"

She sat up. "Why would they?"

Elizabeth ignored the question. "You know what to do and how to act and even how to feel about causes, almost like your role is scripted. No one ever sees you might be afraid underneath?"

"I'm not afraid." Sarah slid forward, slipping off the bed, and crossed to the dresser. From the pitcher in the washbasin, she poured a half glass of water.

From the bed, Elizabeth spoke softly. "You're not afraid as long as you stick with the script, stay in control."

Sarah's hand stopped. When was the last time she'd allowed anyone to see how frightened she was underneath her composure? So long ago that she didn't even see her fear herself anymore, it was so deeply hidden. She set the glass down. Daniel was right.

Elizabeth continued speaking. "And when you're in an uncomfortable position? Ice skating, perhaps?"

Sarah shrugged. "I don't like it."

"Why?"

"Because I'm horrid at it. I can't do it." She spoke into the mirror.

"And someone might see you be less than successful?"

She nodded.

Elizabeth rose from the bed and crossed to the dresser. She stood behind Sarah and hugged her shoulders. "And why is that such a bad thing, sweetie? What happens if someone sees the real Sarah? Is it necessarily a catastrophe?" She smiled and caught Sarah's gaze in the mirror. "Honey, what happens if they don't get the chance to see what's inside?"

"I don't know." Her voice sounded small, distant.

Elizabeth smiled, hugged her again, and kissed her chocolate-covered cheek. "Well, I think I've poked and prodded more than my fair share here. I'm going to leave you to your chocolate and let you sort some things out." She reached for her cloak, then crossed the room. At the door, she paused and turned to Sarah. "Being vulnerable takes a great deal of courage, sweetie, but it can be extremely satisfying. Just imagine what you're missing."

That evening, inside the Odd Fellows Hall, Sarah lit the last of the kerosene lamps she'd borrowed for footlights, fastened on a polished tin circle to reflect the light, and set the lamp on the edge of the stage with the others. The mingled voices of the children, sounding from backstage, created a comforting din, a vast improvement over the eerie quiet of her room at the boarding house where she'd spent the last several hours in miserable self-reflection.

Her head ached and her stomach was woozy from nervousness and too much chocolate.

She glanced around the makeshift auditorium. The chairs were arranged in tidy rows, and Miss Clay's splendid dessert table beckoned from the back of the room. She groaned and clutched her abdomen, hoping she wouldn't throw up.

Taking a deep breath, she turned and nodded to the little boy sitting next to the door. "We're ready, Jimmy. Tell the stage manager we're opening the house, then unlock the door."

She slipped backstage for a last check, even though she knew it was unnecessary. Still, doing so gave her an excuse to avoid the crowd for a bit longer. And a little more time to wallow in her self-pity, perhaps?

Heaven help her, she was a complete idiot. She'd walked out on Daniel not once but twice. And what had he done, after all, except to think about his wife and point out a few truths? If he was as confused as she was at that beer hall, who could blame him for not being sure about that kiss. And as for this afternoon, well, Elizabeth's gentle guidance and four hours of eating chocolate and mulling over his words had left only one truth at the bottom of it all. She *was* afraid of failing, of being completely herself. Failing hurt.

She was more than a bit chagrined that she'd spent so much time and energy avoiding that truth. Perhaps, there'd just been no point to confronting her fears before, no reason to think about it, and no reason to be anything other than the person she pretended to be. But avoiding everything uncertain in life, things like having fun and caring about others, didn't make much sense either, and the thought of not having Daniel in her life was as painful as the possibility of failure.

She'd talk to Daniel, tell him she was sorry, and maybe they could talk about everything. Like he'd wanted her to this afternoon.

She passed a backstage mirror and grimaced. She looked wretched. It startled her that she cared one way or another. Or was it just that she'd never admitted it before?

"Miss Donovan?"

"Over here, Jimmy."

"The place is crowding up fast and there's a fancy lady out there wanting to talk with you."

"Tell her I'll be right out."

Jimmy disappeared around the stage and Sarah gave a last look around. There was Molly, still running lines with one of the actors. Other prompters were doing the same, while a few of the children with major roles had isolated themselves into solitary corners, concentration filling their young faces. At the far end of the room, Kate paced, her lower lip between her teeth. There was nothing more Sarah needed to do, nothing she could do. It was their show, now.

She stepped around the stage and stopped. The hall was full. For a moment, she thought the whole town of Denver had turned out for the show. Her stomach knotted again.

"Miss Donovan?"

She turned. "Yes?"

An elegant young woman with striking black hair coifed high above her finely chiseled face smiled and extended her hand. "I'm Amelie Parsons. I serve on the speakers committee for the Denver Suffrage Association."

Sarah nodded. "Yes, I think I recall Elizabeth Byers mentioning your name."

"I'm terribly sorry to disrupt you at such a time."

"Actually, distraction is good right now."

"The association would like you to speak at the rally next week, about your experiences as a female telegrapher."

"Me?" Sarah knit her eyebrows together. "You'll have to forgive me, but I'm a bit surprised. I'm not on particularly good terms with your president."

Amelie Parsons crossed her arms and extended a knowing smile. "Still, the committee feels you'd be a tremendous asset to the orators."

Sarah's thoughts flew to Lavinia's bitter threat. "Miss Morgan had no problem with this?"

"She said she had confidence in our selections. Please, Miss Donovan. There aren't many women willing to take such risks, or even that many who pursue a career. Whatever the differences between you and Miss Morgan, it doesn't diminish your example, and the committee felt it important to include you. It would be one small speech, next Saturday."

"There were issues about gossip, some fears that the movement itself might be hurt by my involvement."

"Sarah, look. We're not asking you to take leadership, just to speak. Besides, more than half the women in the movement have been the target of gossip at some point or another, some of us more than others. What do you say?"

One speech, at the invitation of the association, hardly seemed enough to threaten Lavinia. It would be such a chance to share her accomplishments. Sarah closed her eyes and reminded herself to avoid haste, then smiled at Amelie. "I'd like to, but . . . could you give me until after the performance to commit?"

Amelie nodded and slid into one of the few remaining chairs.

Sarah scanned the room, seeking Daniel's trim figure, and finally found him with the Byerses. His brown serge suit was all business, but her memories of his solid biceps, hidden under the fabric, brought a smile to her heart. She stepped forward, negotiating the crowd.

The sharp clang of a handbell rang through the room. Miss Clay stepped onto the stage and beamed at the audience.

Sarah groaned, realizing it was time, and turned toward the stage to join Miss Clay, as they'd rehearsed.

Daniel watched Sarah make her way to the front of the room. She looked tired, though he realized few other people would notice it. Puffy circles surrounded her eyes, and her forehead was knitted with worry lines. Her skin was paler than usual.

He wondered if her pallor was due to nerves or if she'd had a wretched afternoon, too.

He'd returned home and spent the day working on a coffin, sanding out his anger and remorse on a piece of cedar. The woman was so stubborn that she couldn't see what was right in front of her. She had no problem hounding him, but she resisted like a wild animal when forced to look into herself.

Oh, it didn't really matter whether she realized she was burying her beauty because she was afraid she wouldn't be noticed for anything else. And it didn't really matter if she wanted to take on every cause in the world. What really bothered him was that she was pushing him away.

Dammit, did she think it was easy for him to challenge his conventions, to let his heart out of the box he'd kept it in for so many years?

He sighed. Applause echoed through the audience and he realized he'd missed the introduction.

The curtain opened to reveal Kate and her classmates clustered around a makeshift fireplace, discussing Christmas and their lives as the March sisters. Within moments, he was stricken by his daughter's self-confident defiance. In Kate's performance, he saw the Kate she'd never revealed, but somehow she had always been.

The play unfolded with Jo's constant questioning of life. Although Sarah had warned him, he hadn't expected deeper meanings to emerge. Jo's rebelliousness faded into the spirit of self-reliance that Sarah had told him about, the same confidence that Kate herself was beginning to display in her own behaviors.

He'd been wrong about so many things.

It wasn't exactly a comfortable thought. He shifted in his chair and watched his Kate, the independent Jo, express her love to the young boy playing Professor Bhaer.

The play ended in rousing applause, which evolved into a standing ovation. Daniel leapt up with the others, pride surging through him like a wave. His eyes found Kate and caught her gaze. He blew her a kiss and her smile filled her face.

Then the cast called for Sarah, and she appeared on the stage, tears in her beautiful eyes. Daniel smiled.

The woman projected self-confidence like no other he had ever met yet she hid a fragility he was only just beginning to understand. Her radical ideas were, time and time again, proving to make sense.

Bill poked him in the ribs with his elbow, drawing his attention. "That little girl of yours is quite an actress," he said as the applause wound down.

"She was wonderful," Libby added.

"Thank you." Daniel glanced at the stage and grinned. "She was, wasn't she?"

"And this from the man who didn't want his daughter in some radical play?"

"I was wrong, Libby."

She tossed him an "I told you so" look and moved to join the crowd waiting to congratulate the cast members.

Daniel waited with Bill, giving Kate time to enjoy her admiring fans. Molly popped out from behind the curtain and waved, a huge grin on her round face. Daniel waved back, then sought Sarah.

She stood at the far edge of the stage, beckoning to an attractive young woman in a fashionable gown.

"I see Sarah's circle of friends is pretty wide," Bill commented.

Daniel glanced at his friend, the dry comment poking at him. "Who is she?"

"Amelie Parsons. She's new in town, works in Mattie Silks's fancy new brothel over on Holladay Street."

Discomfort crept though Daniel and he swallowed against it. "She's from the Row?"

Bill tipped his head and winked. "Not a common whore, Daniel. Mattie Silks serves high-class customers only."

At the front of the room, Sarah and the stranger spoke with animation. Sarah nodded and Amelie clapped her hands together then extended her hand. Sarah clasped it, chatting all the while, then stepped back.

Daniel watched the interaction, apprehension knotting his gut. He shooed it away. "You know Sarah," he said. "Warm to everyone."

Bill shrugged. "Crowd's thinning. Let's go offer our congratulations."

They worked their way through the small groups of lingering audience members and approached the stage. In front of it, Kate and her fellow cast members were still surrounded by fans,

Daniel hurried forward, recognizing faces among the group, adult business associates, classmates, a few strangers, and Amelie Parsons. He frowned.

Molly spotted him, waved, and said something to Kate. Kate grinned and the girls moved toward him.

Daniel grinned back and opened his arms to enfold them.

"I am so proud of both of you." He kissed their cheeks, then sought each of their gazes in turn. "Kate, you were amazing. You are my inspiration. And Molly, your coaching must have been the best. I didn't notice a single mistake."

The girls beamed and he hugged them again.

"Now, where's Miss Sarah? I have a few things to talk over with her, too."

Molly turned and pointed to a group near the exit. "She's over there. Oh, Papa, wait till you hear." Molly jumped up and down, her brown ringlets bouncing. "Miss Sarah got invited to go to some fancy gathering Miss Amelie and her friends are putting on and she's gonna be the featured guest. And Miss Amelie's gonna take Miss Clay's whole class out for ice cream."

Daniel's heart skipped a beat and a sense of dread crept up his spine. Exposing Kate and Molly to new ideas was one thing. Exposing them to prostitution was another thing entirely.

He stared at Sarah as the dread mutated to protective anger. His jaw tightened and a lump filled his throat. He glanced at the girls and swallowed his urge to confront Sarah.

"Let's go home, girls." He nodded to the back door. "I don't think I need to talk to Miss Sarah, after all."

Chapter Seventeen

Lavinia perched on the edge of the horsehair sofa in Mrs. King's parlor, wishing Frank would hurry back with whatever it was he wanted to show her. She had three days until the rally, and her agenda was overflowing with important items that far outweighed Frank Bates and his constant complaints.

She picked at the ratty brown velvet and frowned.

Frank had been part of her life for close to twenty years now. Gracious, how she put up with the little gopher was beyond explanation. If it weren't for his fawning adoration, she would have dismissed him long ago. In recent weeks, though, his once petty worries had mutated into unpredictable outbursts that made her skin prickle.

"I'm awful sorry you had to wait, Lavinia." Frank stood in the parlor archway, his eyes drawn into dark slits. "I was takin' care of business, protecting myself, you might say." He approached with quick, uneven steps and handed her a crumpled piece of paper.

Lavinia unfolded the worn sheet. One quick look and she'd be gone. When he'd asked her to wait in the parlor, she'd thought it might be something important. She glanced at the paper, then stared at Frank in disbelief.

The semblance of the letter was clear, it was a business offer, extending the personal favors of one Sarah Donovan in return for a position in the Kansas Pacific telegraph office. It was also clear that it was not written by Sarah Donovan.

Lavinia smiled in spite of herself. It was a brilliant stroke and she was surprised Frank had thought of it. Combined with the remnants of the telegram messages Frank had dug from the garbage at the station and wires he sent last Thursday while posing as Sarah, it was all the proof Frank's uncle could want.

"Well?"

"Who told you to do this?"

"Nobody. I thought of it all on my own, just like I done with them wires and the logbook." He paced the worn carpet of the parlor, scratching the back of his left hand with short jerking movements. He stopped, pivoted, and glared at her. "I told you I wasn't gonna let nobody push me around. I ain't gonna take the fall at work this time and I ain't gonna let that woman do me in. No, sirree." His black eyes glinted.

Lavinia drew a breath. "Well, my gracious, Frank. You truly never cease to amaze me."

"Really? I done it for you, too. She's tryin' to mess things up for you, too."

"Yes, Frank. I know that."

"Of course you do. I just wanted you to know how I know it, too."

Lavinia's mind raced. Only Frank would use a tattered scrap for something this significant. It was not something a woman like Sarah would have done. Nor would she have sent a message this poorly crafted. If it weren't fixed, no one would believe any of it. Still, it was a genius move on Frank's part.

She offered Frank a dazzling smile. "Frank, dear? You are such a clever man. Would you let me make a suggestion?"

He nodded, eager as ever to please.

"We need to polish this up a little, maybe put it on nicer paper. You don't want anyone just tossing it away, now, do you?"

"No, ma'am. That's one of the things I love about you. You're a lady, through and through."

"Go on over to Mrs. King's desk and get me a piece of staionery."

"Right out of her desk?"

Lavinia rolled her eyes. "Just get it."

"But ain't that stealin'?"

"It's paper for goodness' sake, not anything of value. Besides, when did you get so concerned about doing right?"

"Mrs. King's never done nothin' to me. It ain't like *she's* trying to ruin my life."

"Calm down, Frank. You can replace it later." She stared at him, uncomfortable with his rising volume. Though she'd mocked his docile subservience, she preferred it to this strange, erratic raging. She was tempted to leave. Still, Frank was on to something here, something that might prove very valuable indeed. She patted the sofa. "Sit. We won't worry about the paper now."

Frank plopped down beside her, sullen. "It ain't like I can't do it on my own, you know." He paused, staring at her, and his jaw quivered. "I just like makin' you a part of it. Seems like the right sort of thing to do when you're courtin'."

Lavinia's hand froze on the sofa. "We're not courting, Frank."

"Aw, you're just saying that 'cause you don't want nobody knowin' till after the rally." He grinned and winked. "It's all right. I understand."

Lavinia shifted against the chill creeping up her spine. Just a few more minutes, that was all she'd need.

She pulled a pencil stub from her pocketbook and scratched a few corrections on Frank's note, rewording it to sound like the educated woman Sarah appeared to be. It was too bad Frank hadn't thought of this sooner. While his efforts would remove the troublesome telegrapher from her job, she knew it wouldn't happen before Saturday. She'd still have the little upstart at the rally. But, it wouldn't take long after that and she'd be gone for good, provided Frank did things right.

She handed Frank the paper. "Here, I've made corrections. This sounds more like something Donovan would write."

He clutched the paper and peered at it.

Lavinia leaned closer to him and touched his hand. "You might consider getting that rewritten, too. Use a sample of Sarah's handwriting, something from the depot. Someone over on the Row might do a good job making it look like Sarah's hand."

Frank grinned, then kissed her on the hand. "I reckon I could bring home one of the logbooks."

Lavinia fought back a wave of nausea, deciding Frank wasn't so much a gopher as he was a ferret, a greasy little ferret, and he was beginning to give her the willies.

Sarah looked up from her desk at the depot and rubbed her temples, glad the Wednesday afternoon crowd had thinned and the place was quiet. For once, the quiet was preferable.

She should be happy. She'd achieved success, after all. It was a week of accomplishments. The play had gone off well, bringing her plenty of praise in all of Friday's papers, even though the accolades really belonged to the children, not her. Then, on Sunday, the *Rocky Mountain News* had published an article on the upcoming suffrage rally, with her name listed among the dignitaries and featured speakers, right up there with Susan B. Anthony herself. This morning, she'd passed the primary operator's test, and Jim Wilson would promote her as soon as he returned from his two weeks in Kansas City.

She laid her head on the table and sighed, drained and empty and devoid of satisfaction.

Daniel had left without a word the night of the play, taking the girls with him. And who could blame him? She'd insulted him by walking away, twice. No wonder he was cool.

She just hadn't expected his coldness would matter so much.

Her eyes grew wet and she laid her head on her arms, wishing she knew when the thrill of success had ceased to matter as much as one man's desire and two little girls' smiles.

She wiped her cheeks with her sleeve and sighed again. If she'd given them half a chance, Daniel and the girls would be sharing in her accomplishments now. But they'd do so because they cared about her, not because she'd done anything remarkable.

"Miss Donovan?"

Sarah started, then pasted a smile on her face and turned toward the voice.

Amelie Parsons stood in the doorway, once again clad in fashionable attire. "The man in the lobby said I'd find you here. I hope I'm not interrupting." Her voice suddenly cracked and her eyes filled with tears.

Sarah rose and rushed across the room, instinctively pulling Amelie into the office, away from any prying eyes in the lobby. She grasped the woman's hands and squeezed gently, unsure of what else to do. "Miss Parsons? What is it?"

Amelie blinked and took a deep breath. "I'm sorry. I just didn't know where else to come."

Sarah pulled her into the office and led her to her stool. "What happened?" she asked.

"Mattie sent me to get Silverman but I couldn't. Dora hated him."

Sarah shook her head, confused. "Mattie? Dora? Amelie, what's going on?"

Amelie's teary eyes widened. "Oh, my. You didn't know, did you?" She sobered. "Sarah, I work for Mattie Silks. Dora is . . . was . . . one of the other girls. She's dead."

Sarah's mind scrambled, fitting it together. "Mattie Silks? From Halladay Street?"

"Yes. I should have told you before, but hardly anyone in the association knows. I haven't been here long enough for word to leak out and I'm so used to keeping it secret. I . . . will you help me, Sarah? I don't know who else to ask." Her eyes pooled again and her lip trembled.

Sarah folded Amelie into a hug. "Shhh," she offered. "Now, this Dora, how did she die? Maybe we need to get the marshal."

"He's been there and gone." She sniffled and looked away.

Sarah patted her shoulders. "You and Dora were close?"

"She went out of her way to make me welcome. I liked her a lot. That doesn't happen much in my business." She pulled out of the hug and stared at Sarah. "Please, I can't bring Silverman, I can't. H-he was rough with her and she hated him. She wouldn't want him pawing her, laying her out."

Sarah envisioned Silverman's distasteful attitude and shivered. "No, I don't think she would. But what can I do?"

"None of the other undertakers will do business on the Row." Amelie hesitated, then continued. "You know Daniel Petterman. Can you get him to come?"

Her thoughts drifted to Daniel's stony principles and she offered Amelie a weak smile, unwilling to make any promises. "I don't think he will, but I'll try."

Sarah had left Amelie at the depot, sitting in the office, with a gawking Ernie covering the wire. Now, approaching Daniel's coffin shop, she was glad she had. Convincing him was not going to be easy, and having Amelie along would make his agreement even more unlikely.

She opened the door and entered the shop. The acrid scent of embalming fluid filled the air. She wrinkled her nose and spotted a pile of shattered glass and the still half-wet remnant of spilled liquid on the otherwise tidy floor. A side window had been opened, the cold winter air obviously meant to diffuse the lingering smell.

Daniel stood at the counter, stocking bottles of colored liquids into the cupboard. His white shirt stretched across his shoulders and Sarah's breath hitched.

Good Lord, what that man does to me.

He looked up at the sound of the door. The pleasant, businesslike smile on his face dissolved into stony intolerance.

"Miss Donovan?"

Sarah's heart tumbled at his distant greeting. She closed the door and approached, feeling skittish and unsure of herself. She hadn't expected him to be this angry. She should have come over last week and apologized, no matter what it cost her pride.

"I'm sorry, Daniel." Her voice quivered and she fought for control. "I shouldn't have just left like that. I . . . sometimes, I don't want to face things. I'm sorry for my words."

There, it was out. Days late and far from adequate.

"Doesn't matter." He turned back to his assortment of bottles and resumed organizing them.

Sarah choked back the sting of his dismissal. "Oh."

The clunk of a bottle hitting the wooden counter filled the silence and Daniel again looked at her. "Is that it, or was there something else you needed?"

She swallowed and stepped forward. "There is something."

"Look," he crossed his arms in front of his chest and stared at her, "I've resigned from the committees, the play is over, and I don't think there's anything else we have in common."

"A friend of mine needs an undertaker."

His eyebrows lifted. "And this friend couldn't come?"

"She's very upset."

"And you can give me all the information I need? How long the body's been dead, where it's at, what type of coffin, when to schedule the funeral, how elaborate the arrangements?"

"Well . . . no."

He shook his head and resumed stocking bottles. "Then your friend needs to be the one I'm talking to. Or is this just another ruse to interfere in my life?"

A surge of anger poured through her. "That's uncalled for, Daniel, and you know it. First you dismiss my apology, then you throw accusations." She marched to the counter and caught his gaze. "As I recall, you do your own fair share of interfering."

He sighed. "All right, I'll give you that one. I *did* poke and prod. But what I didn't do was expose your children to people and things they don't need to know about."

"What are you talking about?"

His jaw dropped open and he stared at her. "I'm talking about your friend, the one whose guest you're going to be on Saturday?"

"Guest? Saturday?" Confusion swept through her. "Daniel, the only thing I'm doing on Saturday is making a speech at the suffrage rally. You *know* my views on suffrage and you also know I am doing my utmost to respect the fact that you don't share them. Did agreeing to give a speech cross the line so far that you feel you need to bring that up again?" Lord, she was gesturing like a mad puppet. She took a deep breath and waited.

"Suffrage rally?" Daniel looked confused, too.

"Yes! What in the world were you thinking I was doing?"

He turned away from the cupboard and ran a hand through his hair. "Something with that Parsons woman?"

Sarah stared at him, unsure what he meant. "She's on the committee for the suffrage association."

"She is? A woman like that?"

So that was it. Morality. Sarah sighed. "Yes, a woman like that." She shook her head. "There are no rules about the various members' characters. As a matter of fact, most of the members don't even know about her background, which is what

I assume you're talking about. I didn't, not until a half hour ago."

"You didn't know?"

"No." The question stabbed at her and, incredulous, she finally grasped his implication. "Is that why you're upset? Because you think I have some link to what she does for a living? Oh, Daniel, how could you?"

"That's what it sounded like," he insisted.

"And you didn't even ask me? Do you have so little trust in me that you can't even ask if you're unsure about something?"

His confidence wavered and chagrin filled his eyes. "I didn't even think. I just reacted."

"You assumed, based on what people might think?" Her heart sank. He hadn't moved past his narrow world at all.

He shook his head. "To what I thought was something I didn't want Kate and Molly exposed to."

The comment made sense, at least partially. His reaction wasn't *just* based on worry about appearances. She weighed her words, not wanting to drive him into a corner, but knowing they needed to be said. "Still, your response was based on what someone said, wasn't it? Did you even think that it might be better to let the girls enjoy the praise someone from the community was offering, with no reference to that person's background, instead of teaching them to fear and exclude someone because she's not socially acceptable?"

"Morally acceptable." He paused. "There's a difference."

"Is there? Morals are individual, remember? Or are you back to judging everyone?"

"But, she's—"

Sarah shook her head and let the words pour out. "You don't have to like what she does, but maybe you ought to recognize the difference between the person and the action."

"Are you preaching at me, again?" A defensive tone had crept into his voice and he glared at her.

"No," she insisted, then paused. Fighting would get them nowhere. "Yes. Would you expect anything less of me?"

He thought about it, his gaze probing her face as the moments stretched. Then he smiled. "No."

She smiled back. It was as good a breakthrough as she was likely to get. "So, are you speaking to me again?"

He nodded. "If you'll accept my apology. I shouldn't have assumed the worst."

An image of Amelie intruded and, much as she would have preferred to dismiss her promise to help the woman, Sarah knew Amelie's request would have to be dealt with. "You might want to wait until after I've told you about the friend I came for."

"I'm not going to like this, am I?"

"Amelie Parsons showed up at the depot a little while ago. One of . . . the girls . . . is dead. She doesn't want Silverman involved. Apparently, he got rough with her once."

Daniel processed the information for a moment. "You want me to prepare a prostitute for burial?"

"I didn't know who else to ask."

He shifted and leaned against the counter. "After the conversation we just had?"

"I didn't know you felt that way when I told her I'd ask."

He shook his head. "Would it have stopped you?"

"No." She glanced up at him and waited.

"You don't see anything wrong with me laying out a woman who sells her body? How would that look to the girls?"

Sarah shook her head, her palms lifting in a gesture of uncertainty. "It would look like an act of Christian charity." She paused, unsure whether she should push, then plunged forward, keeping her voice gentle. "Have you forgotten about the woman at the well, about Mary Magdalene? Not everything is black and white."

"But—"

She touched his arm, drawing his direct gaze. "Preparing her body for burial is not condoning her way of life. You'd be showing you care about people in spite of their everyday life and maybe even trying to understand what brought them there."

Daniel lifted his palms to his face and drew a deep breath, then looked her in the eyes and shook his head in reluctant acceptance. "Why does what you say always force me to see things I don't want to see?"

"That particular skill is one you possess as well." She offered him a gentle smile, then waited.

He nodded, still sober. "I didn't mean to cause you pain," he said. His hand cupped her cheek.

She leaned into it. "I know. You've gotten under my skin, Daniel, and it scares me half to death that you might push me away. Pushing first was easier."

"It scares me, too, Sarah. You know more about me than I know about myself, half the time." His thumb stroked her face.

She stilled his hand with her own. "Maybe we can be scared together?"

"Maybe." He grasped her hand, brought it to his lips, and kissed it. His hazel eyes were soft, atoning. He let her hand go and smiled. "Is the body still on the Row?"

"I don't know. Most likely."

"Then I guess we'd best get going." He reached for his jacket and a small brown satchel. "I'd rather my first visit there not be at night."

Daniel followed Amelie Parsons up the stairs of a well-kept brick house. She pushed open a scarred oak door and they stepped inside. A small but tastefully decorated parlor bade them welcome.

"She's upstairs. Please, wait here. I'll get Mattie." Amelie disappeared behind a dark-green velvet curtain, leaving Daniel alone and nervous as hell. He hoped she wouldn't be long. All he wanted to do was make arrangements to retrieve the body and get it back to the shop. The less exposure he had to this place, the better.

He glanced around the room. There were no gaudy mirrors, no ladies' unmentionables draped over the furniture, not even a lewd sign describing the house offerings. Except that he knew better, he'd have taken the parlor for that of any respectable Denver family. The realization jarred him.

"Not quite what you expected, huh?"

Daniel turned and found a short, stately beauty with light brown curls piled above her flashing blue eyes. Framed in the late afternoon sunlight that poured through the stained-glass windows of the parlor, she looked every ounce a lady. Her sultry tones lingered in the air. She smiled before her expression clouded.

She stepped forward and offered her hand. "Martha Silks. Call me Mattie."

"Daniel Petterman." He took the offered hand and shook it politely. He wondered how many men had felt its soft touch and kicked himself for the thought. He wasn't here to judge.

"I'll show you to her room." Mattie led the way up the stairs.

Daniel watched her graceful movements, increasingly more uncomfortable. Somehow, he suspected it would have been easier to deal with had Mattie and the house been as seedy as the picture he'd had in his mind.

Below them, Amelie emerged from behind the green curtain, her eyes red and puffy. "Mattie? Should I come?"

Mattie paused on the stairs, and looked at the younger woman, then shook her head. "I think it's best you don't. Get some money out of my cache and go buy Dora something nice for the burial."

Amelie's eyes pooled with more tears. "Oh, Mattie . . . I don't think I can face the questions—"

"Get Sarah," Daniel interrupted. "She'll field the questions." The advice was standard. Find a trusted friend to assist the grieving family, but he almost wished he could take back the remark. Sarah was sure to hold it over his head after all his fuss about her association with Amelie.

Amelie hesitated, then nodded and slipped out the front door.

"That was a good thing to do, Mr. Petterman," Mattie said.

"Giving her something to do was the right idea. She and this Dora were obviously close." In fact, it was the sort of distraction he'd have offered a grieving sister. Odd, seeing as he'd always thought the girls on the Row were fierce competitors.

"Closer than most of my girls. Amelie took Dora under her wing. She'd been awful melancholy of late."

Daniel digested the words, and the implication behind them. "Suicide?" he asked.

Mattie nodded. "The holidays were real rough for her. Made me feel there was someone important she was missing, but she never said." She paused before a door at the end of the long hallway. "Marshal's been here and gone. He left a release on the bureau." She led Daniel into the small bedroom.

A body lay on the rumpled bed, curled into a fetal position. An empty bottle sat on a small table next to the bed. Daniel's heart went out to the girl. Poisoning was a hard way to die. Curled up like that, it must have hurt a whole lot. He approached the bed, set his satchel on the floor, and stared down at her. "How long ago?"

"Her last visitor left at four this morning. Most of the girls sleep late, so we didn't miss her until luncheon, about two o'clock. When she didn't answer the door, Amelie came in. I sent someone for Marshal McCallin first."

Daniel nodded. Long enough for the body to stiffen. He peered at the girl and shook his head. It was always easier when they died peacefully. He offered Mattie a sympathetic smile, wondering if she'd been close to the girl, as well. "Is there family or . . . ?"

"Just us, that I know of."

He nodded, wishing he was better at comforting folks, softening the questions that were part of his business. He touched Mattie's arm and waited for her to acknowledge him with her glance.

"I guess there are a few things I need to know before I start," he said, "so I can decide whether to do things here or at the shop. Have you thought about whether you want her embalmed or if you're going to have a viewing?"

As with most families he dealt with, the questions seemed to confuse her for a moment. Then, she waved her hand. "Oh, Dora wasn't much for science. I think she'd prefer to let nature take its course but I do think some of her customers might want to see her before she goes."

Daniel debated his options. Nobody liked having the body hauled away if it wasn't necessary. He'd be here longer, but he hated to move the body to his shop if he was just going to send it back in an hour. He offered Mattie a soft smile. "I can lay her out here so you can have the viewing as soon as possible. Without embalming, she'll need to be buried tomorrow."

Mattie nodded. "We can do that tonight. The girls won't feel much like working anyhow." Her voice drifted away for a moment before she brushed her hands across the front of her dress and straightened her posture. "What do you need me to do?"

He smiled again, in reassurance, and inclined his head toward the door. "Why don't you go downstairs until I'm done."

Daniel waited until he heard the echo of her shoes on the stairs, then turned to Dora. He slid back the coverlet and sighed.

She was such a tiny little thing, almost like a doll, lying there in an innocent white cotton chemise and drawers. If she wore any fancy silk underthings, she'd hidden them away.

Lifting his bag from the floor, he rummaged for a wooden mallet, hoping he wouldn't need it, then gritted his teeth and began the distasteful task of straightening the stiffened body.

He moved with quick forcefulness, ignoring the all too familiar sounds as he broke past the rigor and moved Dora's delicate limbs to a restful position. Silverman probably would have enjoyed himself, the bastard. Amelie was right to have avoided him.

Once uncurled, Dora's beauty was evident. Though her skin was beginning to sag, her bone structure was light and fragile. Daniel wondered at her, at the sadness that caused her to take her own life. He pulled a small cloth from his bag, dipped it in the washbasin, and wiped dried spittle from her once pretty face. Her high cheekbones would make it easy to restore the shape of her face, and he figured the powder and rouge in his bag would hide the purplish hue where her cheek had lain against the pillow.

A knock sounded at the door. "Mr. Petterman? Are you finished?"

"Yes, Mattie, come on in." He covered Dora with her sheet, hiding most of her death-stained skin.

Mattie stepped into the room, washcloth and towel in hand. "I'll help clean her up and get her ready for the new dress. I think she'd want that."

"She's a fragile little thing, isn't she?"

"Dora had a way about her, an extra softness that most of my girls don't have."

Daniel moved away from the bed, giving Mattie room to sit down next to Dora, and began to draw needed supplies from his bag. "She's not quite what I expected to see," he said.

Mattie raised her eyebrows. "Not all hard and worn and old before her time?"

"I guess. She looks so pure and innocent."

"Dora had a pure heart, I think. Made her men feel again."

Daniel put down the container of rouge and the roll of cotton batting and stared at her. "Feel? I don't think feeling has much to do with it."

Mattie shook her head. "More than you think."

Curious, Daniel sat down opposite and began reshaping Dora's face. "How so? Men come to places like this for one thing, don't they?"

"Men go to the cribs at the end of the Row for that, Daniel, or get it in the alleys. They come here for lots more." Mattie rose and moved to the dresser, setting the washcloth and towel down, then rummaged through a drawer until she found a chipped tortoiseshell hairbrush.

"Specialized services, you mean?" He kept his eyes focused on Dora's face, wishing he hadn't asked the question.

"Comfort, adventure, love."

He shook his head and began powdering Dora's face, evening out her coloring. "Love doesn't exist here."

"But for those who need it, they get to feel it while they're here." Mattie sat on the bed again and reached for Dora's flaxen hair. She brushed it from the girl's face with her hand, then began to brush through the tangles. "Dora was real good at making a man feel like he was loved, like he was the center of the universe. There's going to be some real tears, come the viewing."

"So she made men fall in love with her?" Sarcasm crept into the words and he waited for Mattie to take offense. When she said nothing, he regretted his harshness. He opened the jar of rouge and dabbed his forefinger into it.

Mattie's hand closed around his. "Just a little," she advised, "to take the paleness away. Dora didn't make herself up."

He blended a small spot of rouge high on Dora's cheek and Mattie nodded. The girl looked more like a Sunday school teacher than a soiled dove.

"She didn't make them fall in love, she made them *feel* loved. She could make a widower forget, for just a few minutes, that his life was empty. She could make a gawky boy feel like he was something special. She made the rejection disappear for the man whose wife turned a cold shoulder. Dora made it more than just the act itself, if that's what a man needed. And if all he wanted was a good time, she was pretty accomplished at that, as well."

Daniel frowned. "And none of you think it's immoral?"

"Morality is a word we each gotta define ourselves." She set the brush down and caught his gaze. "Passion is a good thing, Daniel. I won't offer apologies for what my girls do. It's not for every man and I respect that. It's not the kind of life for every woman, either. Most of my girls know themselves well. They aren't needy themselves, or running from their pasts, like a lot of the women in this line of work. They approach this as a business. Meeting the needs of customers is part of successful business."

He shoved his supplies into his bag, Ebenezer's strong lectures filling his mind. "Seems to me as though most of us grow up learning that passion is best kept under control," he mumbled.

Mattie chuckled. "Most folks do just that." She stood and crossed to the bureau, returning the brush, then turned back to Daniel. "But how much better to give rein to it, express it. Goodness, if a person feels strongly about someone, why not share it? Not just some bland announcement but by making wild, sensuous love."

Daniel's thoughts tumbled to Sarah and the images he'd so

often had of her, thrashing and naked in his arms, images he'd never had of Mary, not in all the years they were married. She'd been good and kind and loving, but had never stirred his passion the way Sarah could without even trying. Would it be so wrong to give in to it?

Mattie smiled and crossed back to the bed. "The act becomes what you make of it. Callous sex, sensual pleasure, an expression of comfort, an offering of love. If you know what you want of it and are willing to take a chance on what you're feeling, you don't have to be afraid of it."

He busied himself with the satchel, uncomfortable that Mattie seemed to be able to read his thoughts. "There's not much more I can do here. Where do you want her placed?"

"I think the back parlor would be best. I'll fix up her hair a little more when Amelie gets back with the dress."

Daniel nodded, relieved the conversation was back to business. "If you cut it in back, it's easier to get on. Or you can wait until I deliver the coffin and I can do it."

"I'll dress her."

He moved toward the door. "Plain wood casket?"

"Something simple but nice, maybe with a lining." They left the room and Mattie closed the door.

"What about the burial?" Daniel asked.

"No service, just bring the hearse to take her up to the cemetery. Get her a plot in the City Cemetery, not Potter's Field."

He nodded. Most of the prostitutes ended up in small, unmarked graves among the unknowns in Potter's Field. "Yes, ma'am. I'll be back around to move her downstairs as soon as I load up the casket and get someone to give me a hand."

Mattie reached for his arm and he jumped. "Thank you, Daniel. Your coming here means more than any of us can put into words. There wouldn't be a proper burial otherwise."

He glanced at her, feeling her gaze, struck by her wisdom and unexpected dignity. How many times had he sat in church, listening to Ebenezer point his finger at the fallen?

Well, old man, the proof's in the pudding, isn't it? Mattie Silks has far more character than you ever did.

He glanced away, realizing it wasn't Mattie's character but his own that was in question.

Chapter Eighteen

A soft knock sounded on Sarah's office door and she turned to find Amelie there for the second time in one afternoon. Sarah knitted her brow, her surprise shifting into concern.

"I hate to bother you again," Amelie said. Her voice carried a note of desperation.

Sarah's heart caught at the sound. "Oh, no bother. I was just finishing up." She glanced at the lanky man on the other stool. "Ernie's already elbow deep into the rest of my shift and he's kicked me out." She grinned at her coworker as a blush crept across his boney face. "What do you need?"

Amelie stepped further into the office, glanced nervously at Ernie, and sighed.

Sarah set the papers in a wooden box and approached Amelie. The young woman's elegant composure, so evident the night of the play, was gone. Sarah touched Amelie's arm, uncertain of what she could do. She suspected Amelie had lost her only good friend.

Amelie bit her bottom lip, then said, "I need to buy a dress for Dora. I can't . . . will you come?"

"Well, I'm not much good at that sort of thing—"

"Please. The minute I walk into Miss Abernathy's shop, she's going to ask questions, and I just can't . . ."

"I'll come." Sarah offered a cheerful smile and patted Amelie's arm. "If seeing Dora's seamstress is too stressful, we'll just go somewhere else."

"But Dora's so tiny, she needs things specially tailored."

Sarah ushered her out of the office, nodding to Ernie on the way, and out into the gray January day. "Miss Abernathy's won't have time to sew something special, anyway, and it won't matter if the hem's too long or even if the dress is loose. Daniel will fix it so it looks like it was made just for her."

"He will?" Amelie's eyes widened.

Her reaction caught Sarah off guard, and she wondered if undertakers skimped on the services they provided the girls of the Row. She nodded and caught Amelie's elbow, guiding her toward Sixteenth Street. "Of course he will. Let's try one of the mercantiles. We can be anonymous."

Amelie brightened slightly as they made their way through the busy business section. The crowd thinned and Amelie stopped on the boardwalk. "She killed herself." The statement came out flat, as if just uttering it might make it go away.

Sarah's eyes pooled. "Oh, Amelie, I'm so sorry."

Amelie sniffled and resumed walking. "She's been miserable since the holidays but I never thought she'd take her own life. Lots of us girls get a little depressed this time of year."

"Was she missing her family?" It sounded weak, and Sarah wished she had said something more substantial.

"She never told me."

Sarah nodded and searched for a response. "Well, I guess the holidays might have been pretty lonely."

"They're rough. Those of us with families get hit hard. Some of us have regrets, some of us get afraid."

Sarah nodded, weighing the fears she'd only just discovered in herself. She squeezed Amelie's arm and smiled at her. "I didn't much realize it before, but I think we're all afraid."

"You're afraid?"

"I am. But don't you dare tell anyone."

Amelie offered a weak smile in return.

They approached the front entrance of the new two-story Daniels and Fisher dry goods store and Sarah turned the conversation back to Dora. "Why'd she come here?"

"To Denver?"

"To the business."

Amelie shrugged. "She never talked about that, either. She was awful closed up about things. Most of us are." She opened the door and slipped into the building.

Sarah followed. "So why do you stay?" She hoped the question wasn't too forward and breathed a sigh of relief when Amelie didn't take offense.

"I'm good at what I do and I have enough business sense to have my own house one day." She paused. "Dora could have done that. She had a good head on her shoulders and the men loved her. She lit up the room." She stopped and turned to Sarah. "I'm going to miss her terribly."

Sarah offered an understanding nod. Once again unsure, she led the way through the store until they found the ready-made dresses. Like Joslin's, the store had a fair number on display. "Then let's find something to really set her off. Tell me about her coloring."

"Fair. The lightest colored hair and porcelain skin."

Sarah nodded and pointed to a brocade day dress. "Then something regal, a dark blue, perhaps."

Amelie wrinkled her nose. "Too presumptuous. Dora wasn't a brocade kind of girl."

Sarah glanced around and spied a pair of frilly organdy concoctions. "Maybe a pastel to accent her delicacy?"

Amelie fingered the breezy material. "What would you choose?"

"Me?" Sarah shook her head. "Oh, I'm mostly a brown-work-skirt kind of girl."

"Why? You have gorgeous hair, and those eyes."

She shrugged. "Telegraphers don't need fancy frocks."

"Every woman needs pretty dresses." Amelie turned back to the racks and stared at the variety, perplexed.

"Did she have a favorite color?"

Amelie's eyes misted. "She liked strawberry red."

"Strawberry?" Sarah wandered to a group of frivolous looking walking costumes. "Like that shade?" She eyed the striped concoction of red satin and black velvet. It was at once both elegant and gaudy.

"That's perfect."

"You're sure?"

"Absolutely. If there was one thing Dora was not afraid of, it was fashion." Amelie stepped forward and caught the attention of a sales clerk, then arranged for the purchase.

Sarah hung back as the clerk placed the stylish dress into a box and realized she would have been afraid of the dress, of being fashionable, just as she was afraid of being herself. Daniel knew, knew so much more about her than she wanted to admit.

She was only hiding from herself, and they both knew it.

After the funeral, Daniel returned to work. He gave the horses a final pat, checked their oats, and turned to leave the musty barn. An unexpected satisfaction filled him. Though Dora's burial had been quiet and sparsely attended, most of her gentlemen friends having paid their respects at the visitation, it had been dignified. He passed the shining hearse, glad he'd polished it up proper, and exited into the cold midwinter air.

Sarah had been right about the girls from the Row. She understood so much that he didn't. He crunched across the snow toward his shop and shifted through the tangle of Sarah-thoughts that somehow never left his head anymore. He'd let things stew long enough. The apology he'd offered yesterday had been a start, but he knew it wasn't enough. He'd assumed the worst and hadn't so much as acknowledged her success with the play until yesterday. She hadn't even told him about passing her primary operator test—he'd read it in this morning's newspaper.

His gut clenched. He should have shared it with her.

He opened the shop door and entered, the warmth of the small Franklin stove surrounding him. Shedding his coat, he glanced around at the tidy counters and frowned. He pulled a few bottles from their assigned places on the cupboard shelf and set them at random on the counter, then sighed. It only made him miss her more.

She belonged in his life, a cool breeze after years of stagnant, proper inactivity. All he had to do was open the window and let her in, before she blew right on past.

"Damn," he muttered, and sank into his desk chair.

Any way he looked at it, it added up the same. He was smitten with Sarah and it was past time for him to get off the fence he'd been sitting on and declare his intentions.

He just wished he knew where to start.

He'd never really courted Mary. A faithful member of his father's congregation and daughter of a theology professor, she'd always just been there. In fact, he couldn't remember ever socializing with anyone else.

Heck, he didn't even know how to court a woman.

He knitted his brow and scanned the bookshelf over his desk for Thomas Hill's guidebook. *Hill's Manual of Social and Business Forms* would have an example or two of a well-written letter. He'd just copy one and use that.

And Sarah will shake her finger at me the minute she reads it.

He shook his head and leaned back in the chair, chagrined. He might as well forget about sending any letters. His mind scrambled, exploring other obvious options. Flowers were out; it was January for God's sake, and poetry would turn out as bad as any letter he might try to craft. Besides, he didn't even know if Sarah liked poems.

His Sarah liked beer and sausage, letters to the editor, and telegrams. She liked Joslin's candy and suffrage meetings and dinner parties. His chest pounded with the memory of the dinner they'd shared at Libby Byers's house, Sarah's soft lips closing around ripe strawberries, her tongue catching a stray bit of powdered sugar.

The image etched itself into his mind and he smiled, then stood and reached for his coat.

He had arrangements to make.

Sarah watched the last remaining passengers, a young mother and two mischievous toddlers, board the train. They'd left behind breadcrumbs, bits of candy cane, and a soiled hanky. Sarah smiled and began to sweep the litter into a dustpan.

Goodness, whenever had she begun to think of soiled hankies and crumbs as worthy of a smile?

Dumping the garbage into a waste-tin, she set the broom aside and made her way to the office. With Jim gone, there had been a mad rush, taking telegrams and selling tickets at the same time. Now that it was over and the passengers were loaded up and on their way, the depot had turned silent. She dreaded the quiet times the most.

She sat down on her stool, her thoughts drifting to Dora's burial and Daniel's solid presence. He'd offered only polite conversation to her since their brief discussion yesterday, but he'd smiled from the other side of the grave this morning, his gaze capturing her own and holding it.

And if she hadn't been a fool, it might have been his arms enfolding her instead. She wished she knew what thoughts had lain hidden in the intensity of those hazel eyes.

She picked up a pile of telegrams, folded them with care,

then stuffed them into envelopes and labeled them. The youngster Jim had hired for afternoon deliveries would arrive soon, and she hated to keep him waiting. Besides, work took her mind off Daniel.

Out in the lobby, the main door squeaked open and Sarah made a note to have Ernie fetch out the oilcan when he came in. She stood and peered out the ticket window.

A lad of sixteen or so stomped his feet on the worn buffalo hide that served as a floor rug. He glanced around the office and shifted his wool cap back on his head. His dark hair scraped the collar of his plaid jacket. The kid spotted her and crossed the lobby. "You Miss Donovan?" he asked.

"I am. What can I do for you?"

"Got a package for you." He extended a small paper-wrapped box. "Sign here."

Sarah eyed the package, bristling with curiosity, and placed her signature on the form. It was from Joslin's Dry Goods. She fished into her skirt pocket for a couple of pennies, tipped the boy, and waited until he crossed the lobby and shut the door behind him. Then she set the package on the counter and stared at it.

She didn't recall anyone ever sending her a package before. Warm pleasure crept through her, as satisfying as any public acclaim she'd ever received.

Careful not to tear the wrapping, she slit the paper open and pulled it away. A hinged cigar box beckoned her to open its lid. She savored the suspense for a moment, then lifted the cover. Inside, layers of tissue paper waited. Sarah smiled, stretching out the anticipation, and reached into the box.

Beneath the layers of tissue lay a perfect white chocolate rose. A small paper note lay beneath it, filled with Daniel's strong lettering. *Roses in January are not easy to find. Please accept this one, along with my heart, and join me for dinner.*

Delighted champagne giggles rose in Sarah's throat.

She picked up the paper and turned it over. It was blank.

She lifted the rose from its resting place, careful not to break it, and shuffled through the tissue. Finding nothing else there, she turned to the box itself and searched it for another note, then rummaged through the outer wrappings.

God in Heaven, of course she'd join him for dinner. She just needed to know when and where.

She sat down on her stool and shook her head. Giddy with excitement, she tried to sort everything out. This was like opening just one present at Christmas and having to wait for the rest. A sense of excitement filled her at Daniel's calculated whimsy.

. . . *accept this one, along with my heart* . . .

Her skin prickled, and she swore she could feel her heart pumping. From Daniel, the simple words meant more than a whole volume of love letters. She shivered.

The clatter of the telegraph key shattered the moment, calling her back to work. Her reluctant mind deciphered the assorted dots and dashes and she translated them into letters. The wire quieted and she set about translating the letters into words, humming to herself as she did so.

From Mr. Daniel Petterman to Miss Sarah Donovan STOP

Sarah's breath caught and her hand stilled. This time, she knew her heart was beating with abandon. She hurriedly translated the remaining letters.

Friday evening at seven at the Grand Central STOP I promise to leave all ghosts behind STOP

Once the five o'clock rush was over, Frank set his official envelope to the Kansas Pacific Railroad on the counter and sneered at Sarah's stool. The packet contained copies of the allegations, a description of the evidence and his pledge to send it upon request. The forged note had already been mailed.

Frank smiled to himself. He'd done a pretty fine job on the note. He hadn't even needed to find a forger. He'd done it all himself, real careful-like. Yessir, she couldn't ruin him anymore. He'd played his hand first this time, and she was in for one mighty big surprise. Just to be on the safe side, he'd copied down the information about the telegram that Petterman had sent setting up the tryst in the hotel. Leave it to Sarah to record it in the logbook. Frank reckoned it was nothing but bragging on her part.

Lavinia had favored him with such a smile when he told her about Petterman. She'd clasped his hands and told him he was wonderful. Frank guessed it was about as close as she'd ever come to professing her love for him, genteel lady that she was.

Yep, he had all his ducks in a row, now.

Sarah Donovan would be out from under his skin, he'd get his promotion back, and tomorrow night, he intended to ask Lavinia for her hand in marriage.

Once he finished the favor she'd asked of him, he had no doubt she'd be his.

Hadn't she said as much when she cooed at him and touched his cheek? All he had to do was make sure their fellow boarder Harry Bowers heard all about Petterman's mushy telegram. He wasn't sure he understood why Lavinia wanted Bowers to know, but she'd asked special. It was an easy enough thing to do, but it seemed to mean so much to Lavinia.

Yessir, it wouldn't be long now.

Chapter Nineteen

Daniel sat at a secluded corner table in the Grand Central dining room and tugged at his tie, nervous as a schoolboy. The starched white tablecloth was crisp and elegant, the silver gleaming, and the chef had assured a memorable meal. He sighed and motioned the waiter, then requested a brandy.

For a brief moment, he worried she might not show up, but he knew she would never have telegraphed her acceptance if she didn't mean to come.

The waiter returned with a snifter of amber liquid and set it on the table. Daniel lifted it, sipped heartily, and settled his thoughts on the night ahead.

The soft tinkle of Sarah's laughter floated through the room, drawing Daniel's attention to the lobby entrance. The maitre d' slid her wrap off her shoulders. She stood in the golden glow of the gaslight. Her lush blond hair was piled high on her head, with a falling mass of delicate curls.

Daniel's mouth lifted into a smile.

She wore a new dress, a concoction of burgundy hues. The skirt draped in simple folds across the front of her hips and its square neck revealed a hint of cleavage above a form-fitting bodice. The effect, suggesting a corset, took his breath away.

There wasn't an ounce of practicality about the gown.

Sarah's gaze drifted across the room, lighting on Daniel.

He stood, widening his smile with deliberate slowness.

She mirrored the action, briefly, then broke into a full-fledged grin. She moved through the room, male gazes lingering on her as she passed.

Warmth filled Daniel, an unexpected satisfaction in the reaction she'd stirred. His loins tightened and he shifted his stance.

Good God, she's beautiful.

She neared the table, the waiter holding her chair until she was seated.

Daniel waited until the waiter had eased Sarah's chair forward then sat himself.

Sarah's violet eyes were full of fiery sparkle. She took a deep breath, her breasts rising against the snug fit of her dress, then exhaled. "Thank you," she whispered.

Daniel fought to keep from staring at her bared skin. Instead, he caught her gaze and gave her a languid half smile. "You're entirely welcome."

She laughed, her curls bobbing slightly, then sobered. "I didn't think you'd give me another chance." She paused and a slight pink blush crept across her cheeks. "I'm glad you did."

"I'm glad you came. As judgmental as I was, I didn't know if you'd give *me* another chance."

Daniel watched her lips rise into a soft expression of absolution and knew they'd both crossed the first hurdle of the evening. "The play was incredible," he said. "I regret not telling you that night. I wish I had."

"Thank you, but it was the children who did well, not I."

Daniel shook his head. "The script was well chosen and well written. The cast was perfect and you pulled a marvelous performance from those kids. I learned a lot." He stared at her, waiting for her to deny it.

"Then we both did well, didn't we?"

He nodded, knowing she was right, and let his gaze drift over her while the waiter appeared with the first course.

Her white skin, usually hidden, drew him and he experienced

a small thrill that she'd forsaken her usual clothing choices.

"Daniel?"

"I'm sorry. My mind was a thousand miles away."

"I thought as much." She lifted a spoonful of watercress soup to her mouth. The edge of her tongue flitted to the spoon for the briefest of moments before her lips touched it.

Daniel shifted in his chair and concentrated on not spilling his own soup until the silence became too provocative. "So, how does it feel to be a primary operator?"

"Good. Really good."

"It's a pretty major accomplishment, from what I hear." He waited for the waiter to clear the soup bowls, then leaned forward. "I'm pleased for you. I wish I'd told you that earlier, too."

She mouthed a quiet "thank you," as the main course of beefsteak and steaming boiled potatoes arrived. The waiter served glasses of deep red wine, then disappeared.

Sarah cut into her steak and glanced across the table. "So, are we starting over?"

Daniel shrugged, her directness no longer surprising him. "Yes and no, I guess." He supposed they could go on all night, making small talk about nothing. His stomach knotted. The moment would disappear if he didn't seize it. He set down his fork and laid his hand on the table.

Sarah grasped it and waited.

He caressed the back of her hand with his thumb, drawing confidence, then looked into her violet eyes. "I think we're way past starting things, aren't we?" At her tentative smile, he continued. "Sarah, you're not the woman I would have chosen, but you are impossible to ignore. Truth be told, ignoring you is the last thing on my mind. It's time to let myself take a risk on life for once."

Sarah swallowed and nodded.

"I'd like to see where this takes us."

"I can't live within the boundaries of propriety that you're accustomed to. You know that."

"I know, but maybe I need to set new boundaries, or at least not worry so much when the old ones are crossed."

She nodded again and squeezed his hand, then pulled away. Bringing both hands together to her mouth, she sighed, then lowered them and looked him in the eye. "And you'll expect the same of me?"

He nodded. "I'd like to know the Sarah that's underneath the telegrapher and suffragist and do-gooder."

"I'd like that, too."

"Here's to a fresh start, then." He lifted his wineglass.

"To taking chances."

"And all that they bring."

They clinked their glasses together and sipped, the moment heady in all they had not said.

Daniel watched her, letting the silence play out. Her face filled with satisfaction as she savored each bit of tender steak and he marveled at how such a simple act could stir him so much. "Have I ever told you how beautiful you are?"

"Beautiful scares me."

Her words were light but he knew better than to dismiss them. He debated about how to answer her, afraid of scaring her away, afraid to let them go without saying anything. "It shouldn't. There are very few people who are self-confident, intelligent, and talented as well as beautiful. You shouldn't have to hide from any part of who you are."

She caught his gaze. "Words of wisdom from a man who keeps his passion under wraps?"

He smiled, allowing her retreat. "Passion scares me."

"It shouldn't." She smiled, an acknowledgment of the lightheartedness in his voice, then sobered. She stared at him, her chest rising and falling. "Passion is so much a part of you. What you did yesterday, the chocolate rose, the telegram, and the incredible anticipation you stirred in me, was full of passion, very deliberate passion."

Traces of her sultry tones hung in the air and Daniel grew hard at the images they suggested, the passion that was Sarah. He ached with the need to let go of his restraint and follow the images, but, first, he needed her to understand.

"When I was a boy," he began, then paused and drew a breath. "When I was a boy, my father used to take a switch to me if I lost control. He'd beat me until it bled, as my penance. Passion had no role in correct behavior. By the time I was six or seven, I had smothered whatever passion I felt and quit trying to live any other way. I avoided temptations and accepted Father's narrow life. I never really knew anything else."

He lifted his gaze and caught the smile Sarah offered, thankful it held acceptance and understanding, no pity.

"I knew Mary from the time I learned to walk. She was a gentle guide, the perfect contrast to my father. Somehow, she always made me see things in a different light, kept my passion in check in her own way, but never killed it. I needed her for that. Otherwise, I think I would have turned hard and bitter and rebelled until I destroyed myself."

Sarah nodded. "You loved her?" she asked.

Daniel recognized the unasked question in her tone, her need to know if his heart was free. He caught Sarah's hand and held it tightly. "Yes, I loved her, and a part of me always will. But I don't think I was ever *in love* with her. Until now, I never even realized there was a difference."

"I think there's quite a difference."

He raised her hand to his lips, kissed it, and let it go. "Tonight's not about my father, or about Mary. I think we're done with them now. I'd like to let them be."

"I think I'd like that, too." She dawdled with her remaining food, one hand drifting to her abdomen, and she sighed.

Daniel leaned forward. "I meant what I said, earlier, about you being beautiful. The dress is perfect."

"It's tight and it's impractical. You don't know how hard it was to walk into the store and pick this out."

"Yes, I do." He sobered and lowered his voice. "Do you have any idea what it did to me, seeing you in it?"

"I think so." A glint lit her eyes and she also leaned forward until he had a clear view of her cleavage. "But maybe you ought to tell me, just in case."

Daniel stared, his body tensing. He glanced around, assuring himself of their seclusion, then raised his eyebrows at her. "You are wicked, you know that."

"I know that. Call it passion. You were going to tell me, weren't you?"

He smiled at her teasing and danced around the question, forcing her to wait. "You know I don't much like bustles, don't you?"

"I know, but tell me anyway." The words were a challenge but her eyes had partially closed and her breasts strained against her bodice.

Daniel's breath quickened, matching Sarah's. *Let go.* Under the table, he was hard as a rock. *Let go.* His heart pounded. It was time.

"You promise not to slap me?" he asked.

She nodded her head, her lips parted, waiting.

He leaned even farther forward and stared into her eyes, feeling her breath on his face. "I love the way the front of the skirt hugs your thighs every time you step forward, teasing me, before your step changes and I have to imagine again. I love the way your breasts threaten to spill out the top of that thing when you take a deep breath. Hell, I love waiting for those breaths. I love how you can be fashionably dressed and still look like you're wearing nothing but your corset and I love thinking about what I'd do to you if it were just your corset."

Sarah exhaled audibly and swallowed. "And you were also going to tell me what it does to you?"

"It makes my heart beat hard enough so I can feel it. It makes my own breath stop. It makes me throb until it hurts." He held her stare, waiting.

"All that?"

"All that." He glanced at the door, then at Sarah. "Now, do you want dessert here or shall we go somewhere more private?"

Less than a half hour later, Sarah and Daniel stood, shivering, on the worn side path of the Petterman house. He squeezed her hands and nodded in the direction of the back door. "You head on into the kitchen and warm up. Blast the cold."

His words echoed Sarah's sentiments and she fought to keep her teeth from chattering. Daniel's offer was tempting. Her feet, in their silly evening slippers, were numb and her shoulders very nearly frozen. Drawn, she eyed the house, and frowned at its dark windows. "I'd hate to wake the girls."

"They're spending the night with Abby Thompson, so you've nothing to worry about." He gave her a slight push toward the door. "Now get in there and warm up. I'll be in myself just as soon as I get the buggy ready. No sense freezing."

She watched him disappear into the barn, then made her way into the unlit house. They'd left the Grand Central, intent on a slow, passionate stroll home under the bright stars, only to discover the evening's earlier unseasonable warmth had fled on a bitter west wind. They'd made it the four blocks to Daniel's house, but he'd insisted on hitching up the buggy to take her the rest of the way to her boarding house.

Glad for a few minutes out of the cold, Sarah fumbled in the dim moonlight, searching for the matches and lantern she suspected were somewhere within reach. Her hand located the metal match holder, then the lantern. Lighting it, she stood in the soft glow and waited for her eyes to adjust, then made her way into the kitchen. She dropped another log into the stove and poked at the embers until the log caught.

The fire sparked, crackling in the silent room, and she jumped. Laughing at herself, she realized that though the icy gusts might have shifted her priorities for a while, she was still wound up tight as a watch spring. She'd suspected for a long time that Daniel would be passionate but, Lord, did that man make her pot boil.

A few extra minutes together sure wouldn't bother her.

She shed her wrap and moved around the kitchen, seeking ingredients for cocoa and humming to herself. Within minutes, a pan of milk simmered on the stove. Sarah searched the cupboards, discovered a few peppermint sticks to add to the cocoa, and gathered two heavy white cups.

She was standing at the stove, stirring the mixture, when Daniel entered the house.

"Brrrrr." He rubbed his hands together and shook his head with vigor, as if trying to shake off the chill. "What happened to our heat wave?"

Sarah turned and gestured to the stove. "Cocoa's almost ready."

"Good. Buggy's waiting for the horses. Figured I'd warm up first, then get them hitched. That cocoa will hit the spot."

She poured the cocoa and handed him a cup. Their fingers touched and a molten shiver ran down Sarah's spine. Shocked by the intensity of her reaction, she pulled her hand away.

Daniel shifted his weight, his gaze focused on Sarah while he absorbed the heat of the cookstove.

She sipped at her cocoa, feeling his eyes devour her.

After a few moments, he took off his jacket and hung it next to her wrap on a hook near the door. His footsteps echoed in the quiet house as he returned to her, stopping so closely behind her that she could feel his peppermint-scented breath on her neck. "I'm glad you thought of this. I wasn't quite ready to say goodnight."

She shivered again and felt her heartbeat quicken. It was almost as if the walk home hadn't interrupted the night at all. "You haven't said much of anything since we left the hotel."

He touched her upper arms, his hands hot and sensual in their very stillness. "Nor have you," he said.

Knowing his words were true, she nodded.

"Guess I wasn't quite sure where I stood."

Sarah turned and faced him, his fragile admission surprising her. "You're worried about where you stand?"

He nodded, his gaze soft and slightly vulnerable. "I've never said anything like I did back there before. I wasn't sure I did it right. I didn't mean to insult—"

"Oh, Daniel." She touched his cheek and shook her head. "You didn't insult me and you most certainly did it right. You turned my legs to jelly and my thoughts to mush."

He kissed her palm, a slow smile creeping across his face, and he breathed in, as if savoring the words. "Then you wouldn't slap me if I took you in my arms and kissed you in the middle of my kitchen?"

She pulled her hand away and threw him a seductive smile of her own. "I guess that would depend on the kiss."

"Let's try this one," he whispered and drew her close. His hands danced across her back and his mouth descended on hers, touching softly against her lips. She opened her mouth to him and the kiss deepened, then he pulled away and raised one quizzical eyebrow.

"Mmmmm, not bad," she murmured. "Of course, if I had

something to compare it to—"

He ended her words with another kiss, so probing and intense that it numbed her. He pulled back again, sending a thrill of anticipation coursing through her. "Do you have any idea how I've been dying to run my fingers through your hair?"

Lord, the intensity in his eyes.

Sarah swallowed. "Be my guest."

His fingers slid around her head, pulling her close yet again as he touched her hair with near reverence. His lips played upon hers, making her his own.

Sarah's heart hammered in her chest. She drew Daniel's hand, placing it over her heart, sharing it with him until she felt his breathing match hers and knew his heart pounded in sync. His fingers brushed the bare skin above the top of her bodice, caressing it, while the base of his hand cupped her breast. She arched into his palm and he touched her nipple, hardening it between his fingers.

"God, Sarah, what you do to me." The words were ragged, uttered on his hot breath.

"Show me," she told him, and laid her hand against his chest, kneading it.

He leaned his forehead on hers and drew in a breath. "I should take you home."

She sagged against him, moved by his honor, knowing he was right. If she didn't take her heart and run, now, it would no longer be hers. She drew back, weighing the risk, and realized it was too late.

Heaven help me, I love this man.

The thought seeped through her body inch by incredible inch until her skin tingled with it. Tonight was passion's gift, waiting to be seized. To end the evening now was an option she was not willing to consider.

She slid her hand over his rock-solid pectoral muscles and

down his lean stomach, then paused. "Show me."

Daniel groaned and his breathing slowed. "God how I want you, Sarah."

She nodded, caught in the deep intensity of his gaze. "And I, you."

He closed his eyes and sighed, then resumed eye contact. "We should—"

"No more *shoulds,* Daniel," she touched his lips with a single finger, quieting him. "Just us." She validated the words with a smile and lowered her other hand until she surrounded his straining hardness. "Take me to your bed."

"Sweet heaven."

"Now."

He shifted, moving away from her, and lifted her into his arms, then strode out of the kitchen and up the stairs. Each movement sent a wave a pleasure racing through Sarah's body and she pressed against him. He kicked open a door, moved into the dark room, and set her gently on the bed.

"You're sure?"

"I'm sure."

Daniel kissed her hand and moved away. Seconds later, the scratch of a match sounded and he lit the bedside lamp, lowering its wick until a subtle golden glimmer surrounded them.

He shed his shoes and tie, then loosened the studs on his shirt with agonizing deliberation, a playful sparkle in his eyes.

Anticipation gripped Sarah and a small smile tugged at her lips. Could he possibly know what it did to her when he made her wait?

He answered her question with a lazy smile of his own, tugged his shirt open and dropped it to the floor. His stunning muscles gleamed in the lamplight, his chest and biceps toned by years of carpentry work.

Sarah's smile broadened at the perfection he kept so hidden

under his starched white shirts.

"Come here," he whispered. "You have something I want."

She slid from the bed and moved toward him, eager to touch his skin.

He caught her hand, kissed it, and placed it at her side. Touching the hollow at the base of her throat, he slid his fingers deftly across the swell of her breasts, light as butterfly kisses, then reached for the top-most of the tiny pearl buttons that ran down the front of her basque. He slid it open, moving downward until the garment was loosened.

He kissed her, once, and slipped his hands under the straps of her dress until the whole of it melted into a pool at her feet.

Her heart hammered but still, she waited.

Daniel loosened the tie of her single petticoat and it crumpled to the floor with her dress. He unbuttoned her low-cut chemise, untied her drawers and let both items drop.

"My God, Sarah, you are exquisite." His voice was heavy with tension. He shifted, loosened his pants, and stepped out of them.

Sarah's breath caught and her knees weakened. "So are you."

He stepped forward and lifted her from the puddle of clothing.

Flush against him, her skin met his. She felt his heartbeat, a mirror of her own. His skin, hot under her fingers, was slick with desire, every pulsating inch of it.

He carried her to the bed and placed her on it. He slid her slippers from her feet and removed her stockings, then trailed tiny kisses across her toes and up her legs.

She thrashed as he touched her inner thighs then stilled as he rose above her and kissed her on the mouth. The delicate kisses gave way and he consumed her, probing with his tongue until she returned the action in kind. His mouth covered her, moistening her breasts, and his fingers stroked her until she moaned.

She kneaded his chest, feeling his heart beneath her hand and she brushed her fingers across his nipple. He shivered and she kissed him there before moving her hand down his stomach. He shivered again, gasping, as she surrounded him.

Daniel's fingers stroked her, gently at first, then with gathering intensity. She fell back, panting, and her fingers left him. Her heart roared in her ears and she fought to catch her breath, thrashing at his touch.

"You are so perfect," he whispered, then entered her, matching his movements to hers, carrying her past the tightness until she arched, her senses exploding, and she cried out. He called her name and shuddered with his own charged release.

They lay, ragged breaths mingling in the lamplight, until Daniel shifted and pulled her close. Lazy contentment surrounded her and she smiled against his broad chest.

He cupped her chin and tilted her head. "I thought I felt a smile," he said, offering one of his own.

"I never knew, not really," she told him.

His smile widened. "Neither did I, Sarah. Neither did I."

Chapter Twenty

Just after eight the next morning, Sarah slipped through the alley entrance of the Guards Hall, given over for the weekend to the Colorado State Suffrage Rally. Her thoughts were as far away from equal rights as they could get. She pressed her hands to her face. Lord, her skin still felt warm, despite the brisk morning air. She blinked against the hall's sudden dimness and tried to refocus but all she could think about was the lingering tingle of Daniel's touch.

They'd made love a second time before reluctantly rising so Sarah could return to her boarding house for a few hours of needed sleep before her speech. She'd have found no rest had she stayed in his arms. Hours later, her senses still prickled with new awareness. Outside the window, the morning sun shimmered on glistening icicles, a reflection of the glow in her heart. She smiled at them and unbuttoned her coat.

"Oh, good, you're here. We were beginning to worry you might not get through the crowd."

Sarah turned to find a stout middle-aged woman tucking an errant gray tendril behind one ear. She extended her arm for Sarah's coat and placed it on a hook next to the door.

"It's a wonder they haven't discovered the alley door."

"That it is. We've had two fistfights already this morning and the noise level has been incredible. We'll be lucky if we make it through the day without calling the doctor."

Concern nipped at Sarah. She'd seen plenty of violent rallies back in Saint Louis. "Are they hitting our ladies?"

"There's a group of drunken men out there hitting anyone who looks at them sideways. Imagine, drunk at this time of day. They must have been at it all night long."

"Our ladies?" Sarah insisted.

The woman offered a dismissive wave. "A few snowballs and rotten vegetables, as expected. So far, the respectable folk have kept the others back."

"How's the group inside?"

"Very receptive. You'll have a rapt audience. I've heard a number of the ladies express interest in your presentation."

Anticipation leapt through her. She'd waited a long time for the validation that would be hers today. Her constant efforts to prove herself as capable as male telegraphers would be embraced and understood. Her accomplishments would be recognized and today, being a woman wouldn't hinder her. Her efforts would encourage others and she would make a difference.

"Come, let's get you backstage. I know you have a bit of time but I feel better knowing where you are." The woman smiled and tucked another loose section of hair behind her ear. "It's a madhouse, so take care." She beckoned to Sarah, then led the way out of the side hall and into the main lobby.

A rush of sound and movement accosted them. Busy voices filled the room. Nearby, a trio discussed the angry crowd assembled in front of the building. Another group chattered about their dissatisfied husbands. A brightly garbed matron ran by in search of a hatpin and jostled a pacing young suffragist practicing an introductory speech. Women seeped through the front door, smoothing skirts and sighing with relief.

"See what I mean?"

Sarah smiled at her, comfortable amid the bustle. "Is the auditorium this wild?"

"Not since the speeches started." She ushered Sarah into another hallway and pointed to the end of it. "Wait there with the others. You're scheduled to go on at nine. Good luck."

Sarah's stomach churned for a moment. She hadn't practiced her speech since yesterday afternoon. She reached into her pocket, searching for her notes. She pulled the paper out and unfolded it, refreshing her memory. Everything was in place, all the details. There was nothing to be nervous about.

She drew a breath and exiled her anxiety. This was what she'd been waiting for. She strode down the hall, determination and confidence rising with each step. In less than an hour, she'd share her story. The months of struggling for acceptance would disappear and her accomplishments would be recognized.

She could taste the fulfillment already.

Lavinia pushed her way through the swarming crowd in front of the Guards Hall. She noted the strong line of women and their hand-made signs advising voters to support suffrage in next week's referendum. A few sported bright red spots from the tomatoes that had sailed out of the crowd. Others were wet from well-aimed snowballs. Catcalls and threats filled the air.

It was all she had hoped for, and more.

She noted the familiar scowl of a disgruntled woman-hater and jabbed him with her elbow in passing.

He turned, his face crimson.

"I'm so sorry, Mr. Sullivan," she said. "The crowd—"

"Bitch," he muttered with a threatening tone.

Lavinia gasped and allowed her face to register shock. People reacted to the situation with open stares and comments of their own and a reporter jotted down notes. A group of stalwart suffragists surrounded her and moved her through the crowd while Sullivan and the others ranted. She smothered the smile of satisfaction threatening to spoil the picture of her injury.

Up ahead, Marshal McCallin and the two deputies Lavinia had arranged to keep the peace stood at the main entrance. The three would be sufficient to keep the crowd from storming the building but would have little effect on the protesters outside. The rally itself would experience few, if any, disturbances, and the press would publish all sorts of sordid details about the rabble-rousers who threatened the peaceful gathering.

It was exactly as she had planned.

She mounted the steps, offered a sweet smile to McCallin, and entered the building.

The lobby teemed with women. Women in common housedresses mingled with those wearing their finest walking suits. More experienced suffragists issued orders to new recruits, directing them with gestures and exasperated sighs. Enthusiastic young women with clipboards and lists moved through the room, eager to please. Lavinia paused for their acknowledgment.

"Oh, Miss Morgan!"

Lavinia turned and recognized Fern Jacobs, a pale, inept young woman who was forever attempting to ingratiate herself. She took a deep breath and offered Fern a smile. "Yes, dear?"

"The raffle prizes are here. We were able to get a lace tablecloth, a lavender parasol, and a bottle of French perfume. I set them up on a table, just over there, next to the refreshments, and we can draw names whenever you're ready."

Lavinia patted the girl's arm and beamed at her as if she'd accomplished a major feat. "That's fine, dear. Let's wait until the end of the day, though. After all, the more tickets we sell, the more money the association makes." She hoped Fern had enough sense to keep the raffle proceeds in a locked box.

"Oh, and there's a Mr. Bates waiting to speak to you." Fern fidgeted with her hands. "I put him in the sitting area next to the cloak room."

Lavinia sighed. She did not need Frank and his ever more erratic behavior right now. What in heaven's name was he doing here? Whatever the little ferret wanted, it would have to wait. She entered the sitting room and glared at him.

Frank jumped up from his seat on the leather settee. "Lavinia, you're here."

"Of course I'm here. This is my rally. I'm supposed to be here. You, on the other hand, are not."

"Now, Lavinia, don't be angry." His mouth twisted into a lopsided grin. "I just wanted to top things off. Make your special day into one you'll never forget."

Lavinia shivered and took a step backward. Something about his eyes wasn't right. This was not the docile Frank she was used to. "I'm busy, Frank. Can't we talk about whatever it is later?" She turned toward the door.

Frank's hand shot forward, clenching her arm. "No, damn it." Fury filled his eyes. "I done everything so you'd be pleased."

Lavinia swallowed. What in heaven's name was going on? She smiled and forced herself to be calm. "And I am, Frank. It's just that—"

"Then you're happy with me?"

She nodded, discomfort knotting her stomach. "Of course."

He dropped his hand and began pacing. "I knew it. I knew it. All the time we was courtin', I knew it."

Lavinia frowned at him, worry dissolving into anger at his insistent belief. "We have not been courting, Frank."

"Yes, we have." He nodded his head, frantic, and stepped toward her. "And now you're gonna marry me."

She stared at him. "M-marry you?"

"Aw, shoot." He pounded his fist into his hand and began pacing again. "I was gonna get down on my knees and do it all sweet-like. You got me all flustered and I ruined it." His voice rose. "You made me ruin it."

Lavinia made an inadvertent sound of disgust. "I am not going to marry you."

"I'll ask you pretty." He licked his lips and looked around the room with darting glances. "I didn't mean to say you ruined it. It was me. I'll make it right. I'll—"

"I am not marrying you, Frank. Not now. Not ever."

His face paled. "But what about us?"

Lavinia shook her head. "There is no us, Frank. There's never been any us."

"But I done everything you wanted."

She stepped forward, determined to put an end to his delusions. "That's right, you have, and I've tolerated your sniveling far longer than I wanted to. But I've had enough. Enough! Go away and don't ever come near me again."

"But—"

"You are a rotten little ferret and I find you despicable. I always have." Men were nothing but ungrateful, incompetent fools, and Frank Bates topped the list of them. Besides, he wasn't behaving the way he was supposed to, and this new Frank scared her. She took another step forward, until her face was mere inches from his, and narrowed her eyes. "If you so much as look at me sideways, I'll tell your uncle all about your forgeries at the station. And then, I'll march on down the street and have a talk with Marshal McCallin."

Shock filled Frank's face. "You bitch," he yelled. "You ungrateful, worthless bitch. You used me!"

Confusion rushed through her at the unexpected outburst. She calmed her own voice and reached for his arm. "Frank, I—"

"That ain't right." He shook off her hand and scowled at her. "Not after what I done. You're just like all those other suffragists, after all." His face clouded for a moment then exploded in fury. "You'll regret turnin' me away. You all will. I ain't gonna be anybody's errand boy no more."

He stormed past her, shoving her to the floor.

Lavinia struggled to her feet and smoothed her dress. How dare that little fool accost her? Why in all the years she'd known him, he'd never been anything but subservient. What had caused him to explode was beyond her. She certainly hoped no one had heard his outburst.

She peeked out the door. Down the hall, the hustle and bustle continued in full force. She doubted anyone had noticed Frank's little fit. She straightened and entered the hallway.

In the lobby, Fern demonstrated the merits of the lavender parasol and sold two more raffle tickets. A pair of elderly women debated the merits of Susan B. Anthony's most recent speech, their faces animated above the pristine white lace collars of their somber black dresses. Past them, the side door creaked open and two girls stepped into the crowd.

Lavinia stared at them. She'd told all the women to leave their children home. Someone hadn't the good sense to listen. She shook her head and approached.

"And what may we do for you, ladies?"

The taller girl stopped and smiled politely. "We're here for the speeches, ma'am. Where might we find the auditorium?"

"I'm not sure you girls should be here. We discourage children from events such as this."

"Oh, that's all right," piped up the younger girl. She tossed her brown curls and grinned. "We're just gonna listen to Miss Sarah and then we'll go. We won't be no bother."

Lavinia stared at her. Heavens, thanks to Frank, she'd forgotten all about Sarah Donovan's little speech. She let her eyes roam over the girls, no doubt Petterman's daughters. Perhaps, she just might be able to stop Sarah's speech, after all. She glanced at the watch pinned to her bodice and smiled. Not quite nine o'clock. Sometimes, good luck just happened.

"Do come in. I'll need you to wait here in the lobby for a few minutes. Fern has cherry pie on the raffle table. You may have a piece while you wait. Someone will let you know when it's time to go in to the auditorium."

She pointed to a bench and waited until the girls were settled, then made her way through the crowd. She had a few things to do, and if fate was smiling on her, she'd have just enough time before Sarah's speech.

Daniel sprinted up Blake Street, dodging patches of fresh ice. Already, his chest was tight from the frigid air that filled his lungs with each breath. He'd left the Thompsons' house some five minutes ago, immediately after Abby Thompson's admission that Kate and Molly were headed to the rally. They'd assured her he'd given his approval.

In those few minutes, his thoughts had jumbled. If the girls had been at home, he'd have never allowed them to go to the rally. He couldn't chase away the fact that he'd left the girls in someone else's care last night, someone they'd easily manipulated. Or that he'd selfishly spent most of that night making love to Sarah. Remnants of guilt prickled at him and he knew he'd have to stand up to his culpability later, but first he had to make sure Kate and Molly were safe.

His heart thundered with anxiety. He'd heard enough rumors of premeditated violence yesterday at the barbershop to justify his worry. He hadn't even wanted Sarah to go, except that he knew better than to insult her independence or take away from her accomplishments. Besides, if anyone started anything with Sarah, she'd hold her own.

But Kate and Molly . . . He just couldn't imagine them coming out of a riotous mob without harm. What in the blazes were they doing at the rally in the first place?

He rounded the corner of Blake Street and turned toward

the Guards Hall. The crowd in front of the brick-faced auditorium moved with threatening force, surging forward, then back, with each shout of opposition. People shook fists, arguing the merits and follies of suffrage. Daniel's stomach lurched.

He searched the periphery of the crowd and realized he wouldn't find them unless he made his way to the steps of the building. Two little girls would be lost among so many adults. He took a breath and began to slide his way through the suffocating bodies.

Tommy Sullivan, well known for his frequent violence toward his wife, shouted slurred threats and waved a near empty bottle of whiskey. Daniel frowned and dodged away from Sullivan's erratic movements. Closer to the front, angry voices rumbled as vehement women attempted to convince skeptics that they deserved the right to vote. A fistfight broke out as two men pummeled one another over their differing opinions.

Sweet Heaven, where are they?

Daniel struggled forward, ignoring elbow jabs and muttered curses. He mounted the steps and peered out at the mob, each second of his search seeming to take a lifetime. Kate and Molly were nowhere to be seen. He turned and edged his way to the front door of the hall.

"Got a pass?" asked Hanks, the balding deputy who protected the entrance.

"I'm looking for my girls. Could they be inside?"

Hanks shrugged. "If they had a pass or an official invite. Otherwise, I'm not supposed to let anyone in."

"May I go in and check?"

"You got a pass?"

Daniel shook his head in irritation. "If I had a pass, I'd be in there already." He glanced around, seeking someone with more authority. "Where's McCallin?"

"Handling a fight." Hanks gestured helplessly. "Look, when

he gets back up here, we'll see about letting you in." He pointed out at the crowd and indicated McCallin making his way forward. "Right now, I got better things to do than argue with you. Looks like Hanson's having problems at the other door. Just hang on until McCallin gets back and let me do my job."

Deputy Hanson stood in front of the other door in a heated argument with a group of husky men. Their voices rose, demanding entry to seek their disobedient wives.

Daniel shook his head at their hostile insistence. Their wives were probably better qualified to vote than they were. He glanced back to the crowd. McCallin had stopped again.

"Shit," Hanks muttered.

At the other door, one of the belligerent men had downed Hanson. A second man reached for the door of the hall. Hanks's attention shifted but he didn't budge.

Daniel watched with growing unease. McCallin would be needed at the other door and he'd be waiting here forever while Hanks enforced his useless rules. Damn. He stepped forward. Hanks shifted with him, a solid wall.

Hanson yelled and Hanks turned toward the sound.

The second his head turned away, Daniel swung. His fist hit Hanks squarely on the jaw and dropped him. Daniel stepped over him and slipped inside.

The lobby was in as much disorder as outdoors. Daniel made his way through the busy enclaves of women, searching for his daughters' brown ringlets.

A scream sounded through the room and he turned. Near the raffle table, Lavinia Morgan faced an angry young man with the broken neck of a beer bottle in his hand. A pale young woman cowered behind the table, still screaming. Two diminutive old women in lace collars rallied in front of the table. One of them snatched up a parasol and swung it at the man's head. He ducked, cursing. The second white-haired woman grabbed a bottle from the table and aimed it at the man. She squeezed its atomizer and the heavy scent of perfume filled the close air.

The man coughed and turned away. A handful of cherry-pie filling flew from the crowd. It landed on his face, dripping onto the floor. Seconds later, Molly scrambled forward and flung a second handful of pie at him, then kicked him in the shin. Kate floundered after her and tossed a glass of punch at the man as he dropped to the floor.

Daniel's heart skipped a beat.

Dear God. He lunged toward the girls only to have the crowd close around him. He clawed his way through the mob, hoping Kate and Molly had sense enough to back away in time.

The hostile men who had downed Hanson were flooding through the other door, bringing their violence with them. They poured in, rushing hell-bent for the auditorium. Kate's brown curls bobbed in the midst of them, swept along with the crowd. Molly yelled. Frantic women shouted after them and converged behind them just as others began to push toward the auditorium.

Daniel rushed with them. His jaw tightened and a chill raced down his back. He elbowed his way through the crowd, dodging fists and praying.

Sarah approached the stage wing and peered out at the audience, waiting for her introduction.

An explosion of sound erupted from the back of the auditorium and the rear doors burst open. A group of angry men staggered into the room. Women screamed. Supportive husbands, attending with their wives, jumped up. A tussle began among the men and shouts rose. The crowd made its way through the doors.

Sarah watched with concern. She hadn't expected the violence to find its way inside. Surely, Lavinia had arranged for security.

The mousy woman at the lectern pounded her gavel and called for order before motioning wildly for Sarah to come on stage. "Start your speech," she urged. "They can't hear me. You'll grab their attention."

Sarah took a deep breath and stepped forward, accepting the assignment, her eyes on the back of the auditorium and the rising upheaval. Two small figures emerged from the melee and stumbled to the floor.

Sarah recognized Kate and Molly and gasped. Panic prickled on the back of her neck and she stepped back.

"Start your speech."

Sarah choked back the urge to run forward, knowing she was too far away to save the girls. She could help them best by taking charge. People were depending on her. Besides, this was the moment she'd been waiting for, wasn't it? She banged the gavel with force, cleared her throat, and began to speak.

From the aisle, Kate and Molly turned toward her, their eyes wide and hungry for comfort. Kate's lips mouthed her name and Molly raised her arms, beckoning.

Sarah's breath hitched and her speech suddenly seemed petty. She paused, stepped back, and fled down the front steps of the stage. She rushed forward, toward Kate and Molly.

A handful of women had surged from their seats, holding the throng away from the girls. The crowd split around them like buffalo diverted by a clump of trees. Sarah clawed her way toward them, only distantly aware of Lavinia's commanding voice urging control. She reached the girls and sank to the floor, clutching them in her arms.

"Shhh, it's going to be all right. You're safe." She rocked them, brushing their tear-soaked hair from their faces, kissing their foreheads.

Daniel emerged from the crowd and dropped to his knees, pain and worry etched into his face. "Are they all right?"

Sarah nodded. "Shaken up but safe."

"And you?"

"I'm fine."

"Then let's get them out of here." He scooped Kate into his arms. "Can you bring Molly?"

Sarah nodded, gathered Molly up, and followed Daniel down the aisle, away from the melee. They crossed in front of the audience and burst through a side door, into the dark hallway.

Daniel stopped and set Kate on the floor, then searched her tear-streaked face. "You're not hurt?"

She shook her head. "No, Papa. But we're awful scared."

Molly clung to Sarah, sobbing.

Sarah kissed her and pulled her close. The dizzying rush of energy dissolved into numbness. With it came the realization that Kate and Molly had not come here with Daniel. Lord, whatever had they been thinking? She glanced at Daniel, unsure of what to do next.

He sat back on his haunches and examined Kate. She sported a blossoming bruise on her cheek. He touched it and she flinched. "You are hurt," he said.

Kate offered a weak smile. "I think it was someone's elbow. It happened when we fell."

He hugged her, then pulled Molly close. "Let's have a look at you."

Kate drifted back and Sarah gathered her into her arms.

Molly sniffled and stood before Daniel. Her face, like Kate's, was soaked with tears. She wiped her nose with her sleeve. Splats of bright red cherry-pie filling dotted her dress, but no blood. Aside from scraped knees, she was unharmed.

Daniel hugged her as well then leveled his gaze at both of them. "You girls know you could have been seriously injured here, don't you?"

"Yes, Papa," they chorused solemnly.

"But we didn't know that when we came," Kate added. "We didn't have any idea."

Daniel nodded. "I was scared to death, girls,"

"Us, too." Molly's bottom lip trembled.

"What in heaven's name were you doing here?"

They didn't answer immediately. Kate shuffled her feet and glanced up at Sarah. Molly looked at Kate.

"Girls?"

Kate stood up straight and took a breath. "We—"

"Sarah invited us." Molly uttered the words in a small voice.

Sarah stared, words escaping her.

Disbelief flooded Daniel's face. "I don't think Sarah would do that, Molly. You must have misunderstood."

"But she did. It was when Miss Amelie asked her to give her speech. She said the rally was somethin' nobody should miss and that she'd be honored to have us listen to her."

The memory tumbled back to Sarah and her stomach tightened. They'd been quick words, uttered without thought. She hadn't expected they'd really want to come, and had all but forgotten they'd discussed it. Lord, what had she done?

Daniel's jaw clenched. He stood and crossed to the end of the hallway without saying a word.

Sarah swallowed. She hadn't considered for a moment that the girls would take her words seriously. She glanced at their teary faces and disheveled clothes. What if they had been injured? Tears filled her eyes and she bit her lip.

At the end of the hall, Daniel checked the door, found it safely locked, and returned. "Kate, Molly, you two go wait by that door. Don't open it up for anyone. I'll be there in a few minutes." He waited while the girls moved down the hall, then took Sarah's arm and led her to the other end of the hallway.

Her heart pounded in the silence.

"Did you tell them that?"

She nodded. "But, I didn't—"

"How could you?" he whispered. "Good God, Sarah. What were you thinking?"

She shook her head. "But I didn't think they'd—"

"They're just girls." He stared at her. "And after I gave you my trust. Or was last night just a game?"

Pain slammed through her. "Your trust?" She stepped forward, her voice barely controlled. "What about trusting me now?"

"You just admitted doing it. How in God's name can you ask me to trust you? I told you those girls are my world. I let my guard down and left them vulnerable. I should have thought with my head, emotions and passion be damned."

Sarah reached for him. "You're wrong, Daniel."

He ignored her plea, and moved away from her touch. "I'm taking the girls home now. Don't ever talk to them again. Stay out of my life, Sarah Donovan. For good."

She watched Daniel and the girls disappear out the side door and sank to the floor. Her heart shattered and she leaned back against the wall, immobilized by guilt.

Chapter Twenty-One

Disbelief and dejection knotted together, shifting into a deep sense of resentment.

Sarah slammed her fist against the floor, damning Daniel for his ready breach of faith and refusal to listen. The invitation had been nothing more than a polite comment, made in passing, one any other person would have dismissed as meaningless conversation. Any adult.

Good lord, she'd forgotten they were children.

Surely Daniel would understand that. She jumped to her feet and strode down the hall to retrieve her coat. She pushed away her nagging apprehension. All she needed to do was catch him and talk to him about it. It would take only a few minutes and he'd realize the truth.

Except that he should have realized it all along. The thought jabbed at her, poking holes in her analysis. She closed her eyes, willing her emotions to bow to common sense. It was the situation she needed to respond to, not Daniel's hard-won passion.

She marched across the lobby and into the other hall, grabbed her coat and turned to leave.

"Miss Donovan?"

Sarah sighed and turned toward the familiar mousy voice. The timid young woman who had introduced her approached. "There's a man here who wants to speak with you." She nodded toward an elderly gentleman at the other end of the hall.

"I'm just on my way out," Sarah hedged.

"He says it's important."

Sarah sighed again and nodded.

The man approached, but didn't offer his hand. He stopped and peered at her, his baby-blue eyes startling under his bushy white eyebrows. "Miss Donovan."

"Yes?"

"I'm Harry Bowers. I'm a member of the Denver Chamber of Commerce."

"How do you do?" She raised her eyebrows and waited.

Bowers tipped his head and took a breath. "This isn't a social call, Miss Donovan," he said. "I'll get straight to the point. Over the past few weeks, I've overheard bits and pieces of gossip concerning you."

Annoyance crept through her. She didn't have time for this. "Gossip is often misleading, Mr. Bowers."

"Quite true. That is why I normally ignore it."

Sarah crossed her arms, forcing her voice to stay level. "Yet, you've stopped me in a hallway to discuss it, so I presume this is not one of those times?"

His mouth twitched with momentary discomfort, then thinned into a determined line. "I dined at the Grand Central last night and couldn't help noticing you were there with Daniel Petterman. Petterman is a fellow businessman and the newly elected president of the Chamber of Commerce." He sighed. "The gossip now has a potential to impact others."

Sarah rolled her eyes. "Oh, for heaven's sake—"

"I'll be blunt, Miss Donovan. I've overheard several discussions at my landlady's table concerning you. I've heard that you procured your job because you granted favors to the station manager and that you are being investigated for conducting illicit transactions via the telegraph."

"What? I've never . . ." Shocked anger roiled inside of her. What had Frank Bates done now? "That's ridiculous." Heavens, had she been so wrapped up in other things that she'd missed something important at the depot? She turned to Bowers, hating that anyone would believe Bates. "Have you ever stopped to consider that the people saying such things might have motives for doing so?"

He nodded, his mouth again twitching. "I have, indeed." He regrouped and leveled his gaze at her. "I don't come here lightly. I wired the main office of the Kansas Pacific and they verified that you are under investigation."

Her annoyance skittered to a halt and a strange sense of dread swirled in the bottom of her stomach. "And how does that even begin to concern you?"

"Because you are involved with Petterman." Bowers paused and took another breath. "I watched you last night and saw a great deal more than I should have. If you haven't seduced him by now, I doubt it will take you much longer. If even a few other people saw what I did, his name will be linked to yours. I will not stand by and allow the Chamber of Commerce to be dragged through the mud because its president has been duped by a woman like you."

Sarah shook her head, unwilling to believe what was happening. Her hands clenched and the knot in her stomach tightened. She swallowed and stared at Bowers. "With all due respect, you're intruding into things that are none of your business."

He stepped forward, wagging a finger in indignation. "Oh, but it became my business the minute you targeted a Chamber member. Scandal is bad for business. I've no doubt the papers will get wind of this before much longer. After all, everybody at the boarding house has heard. I suggest you take your little games on to the next town. If you choose to stay, the Chamber will use its influence with the Kansas Pacific to assure that you are fired. You won't find a job anywhere else in town."

The impact of his statement worked it way into her understanding, crashing into her heart. She stared at Bowers, unable to find the words she wanted. She steadied herself and took a deep breath. "And if it's not true?"

"It appears true. That's all that matters." Bowers shook his white head. "You need to leave, Miss Donovan, the sooner the better. In the meantime, you stay away from Petterman. He's a good man and doesn't deserve to be brought down by your actions. But if you soil him with your continued attentions, the Chamber will have no choice but to revoke his membership and disassociate ourselves from him and his business."

Frank Bates paced the tiny office at the depot, oblivious to the cold wind blowing through the empty lobby or the half-open door that had failed to latch behind the last departing passenger.

His world was spinning out of control. He'd trusted Lavinia, given her everything. She'd turned out just like all the rest, plotting against him, setting him up for the fall. A wave of fury blended with the desperation he'd felt since leaving the rally. He plopped onto the stool in front of the counter and stared at the wall.

Lavinia's words stung as they echoed through his mind. She'd called him a ferret, said she despised him, made him out the fool. Well, she could just go to hell, too. Christ, the things he'd done for her.

He shivered and glanced through the ticket window toward the open door. Shit, how long had that been standing open?

He pulled his jacket shut and thought about getting up to close it. In the end, he figured it didn't matter, no how. He might as well leave it open for the marshal. It'd be just like that bitch to go runnin' to tattle on him. She knew everything. He pulled out Uncle Walter's letter, received yesterday, and unfolded it. The official investigation was underway and the head office was awaiting the original papers. He read through the list of items he was to send, then slipped off the stool and pulled the tidy bundle of papers from the wooden box he'd hidden them in. He plopped them on the counter. They stared up at him: the wires he'd found in the garbage, the fake letter to Jim Wilson, and the page he'd ripped from the logbook with the poorly forged entry under Sarah's name that day he took over her shift. It was all here, all the evidence he needed to solidify the scandal. It was also everything Lavinia needed to reveal his guilt.

Hell and spitfire!

Bile-like malice rose in his throat and he slammed his hand on the counter.

Damn her.

He'd have laid down his life for her and she'd shunned him, over and over, all in the name of her almighty important suffrage. She'd shut her heart to him, and all the adoration in the world hadn't made any difference. All his efforts to please, everything, had been for naught.

Lavinia was nothing but a warped old hag.

He marched out of the office, his footsteps echoing as he crossed the lobby. He slammed the door shut and stomped back, his anger rising with each step.

He should have let Sarah take Lavinia down. Then they could have battled it out for leadership of the suffragists. If he'd had more patience with Sarah in the first place, instead of letting his concern for Lavinia take over, he could have proven himself better than her without the forgeries. He'd gotten ahead of himself and look where it landed him.

He kicked a box out of his path, then grabbed the metal bucket that served as a garbage pail and hurled it across the room. It hit the wall with a resounding clang, its contents spewing through the room, and clattered to the floor.

Lavinia and Sarah and every other suffragist on God's green earth could go to hell, for all he cared. Even that Susan B. Anthony woman for starting all the hullabaloo to begin with. Someone should have done her in long ago and saved them all. Then there wouldn't be no women telegraphers and no suffrage rallies. And Lavinia would've married him in the first place.

Frank watched the bucket bounce, an idea sprouting in his mind like an overwatered weed.

He could stop them all, just as easy as pie.

He pulled an envelope out of the drawer and set it beside the bundle of papers. He addressed it to his uncle and stuffed the papers inside. He'd send them out with this morning's mail, finishing what he'd started. That would take care of Sarah. He was in too deep to turn back now.

As for that Anthony woman, she was due on the noon train. If something happened to her, it would all stop. Women would keep to their places instead of threatening the livelihoods of decent men. They'd quit their plotting and manipulating.

And Lavinia, Lavinia would have nothing left to strive for, her life would be the waste she'd made his.

All he had to do was send the yard crew home, then walk away and ignore the wire instructions to divert the inferior train to the siding. Two trains headed straight toward each other on the same track would pretty much take care of things.

That would fix them. Everybody would know Frank Bates was nobody's fool.

He glanced at his pocket watch, grabbed the envelope, and went to tell the boys they had the rest of the day off.

Daniel strode up Blake Street, Kate and Molly straggling behind him.

"Papa, wait for us," Molly called.

Daniel sighed and slowed his step. He'd almost forgotten the girls. There was no sense taking this out on them. He paused, squinted at the sun, and waited for them to catch up. They shuffled through the snow and stood before him, downcast. He scooped Molly into his arms and offered a thin smile to Kate. "Let's get you two home."

Molly buried her head against his shoulder while Kate grasped his arm in a brief squeeze but both remained silent.

He almost wished they'd start chattering, anything to occupy his mind. He felt ill-used, drained from worry, downright weary. Or maybe it was just that he was so stunned that Sarah had put the girls in danger. Last night, she'd lain in his arms, offered him her body and her passion, and taught him the earth could shatter. The earth, and his heart.

They neared the house and he set Molly down, then opened the door. The girls entered without a sound. Molly's eyes were moist and full of regret. She crossed the front hall without shedding her coat and climbed up the stairs to her room, still silent. Kate followed, pausing halfway up the stairs, and turned back toward him.

"Papa?" she said.

"Hmmm?"

"You didn't even listen to her. Are you sure this is what you want?" She dropped the words and continued up the stairs.

Daniel closed the door, not at all sure. He paced through the house, listless. Finally, he stepped into his shop and plopped into his desk chair.

Damn it.

Sure? Hell, no. He wasn't sure about anything. He wasn't sure about what had happened back there at the rally or about how he had reacted or about any of his jumbled-up emotions. He wasn't used to dealing with emotions at all. It had always been easier just to label them inappropriate and shut them off.

Now, they wouldn't stop and he couldn't even begin to sort them out.

He leaned forward, his head in his hands, and closed his eyes. Visions of Sarah exploded through his consciousness. Sarah, lecturing him about taking a stand on the things he believed in. Sarah, surprisingly afraid to step out onto the ice. Sarah, learning to laugh at herself at a German beer hall. Sarah, making things happen and teaching his daughters to express themselves. Sarah, full of passion, coaching him to experience life in ways he'd never dreamed of. Sarah, hiding herself behind brown work skirts so no one would reject her.

Oh, God.

He jerked up in the chair and his blood all but stopped moving.

Last night, she'd come out from behind that facade, and today he'd turned his back on her, cutting off her explanation before she could even offer it.

Guilt and remorse flooded through him followed immediately by realization. *She didn't mean for them to come.*

The thought thundered through his mind. How many times had she said she didn't know how to talk to children? She spoke to them as if they were adults, but always with concern and protectiveness.

She wouldn't have endangered the girls, not for all the glory or equal rights in the world.

Daniel shoved the chair out of the way and rushed out of the office.

He couldn't lose her, not now, not when he'd finally discovered he could love.

Sarah walked into the depot and shut the door. An eerie silence accosted her. For once, she welcomed it.

Bowers's words weighed on her, heavy and unyielding. It

didn't matter if she explained things to Daniel or whether he believed her. If what Bowers said was true, if Frank had set her up so well that there was an investigation, then things had changed. Bowers had made it clear that consequences reached much farther than she'd imagined.

She entered the office and stopped suddenly. The station was completely empty. There was no delivery boy, no freight crew, and no Frank Bates. On the counter above the empty stool, the telegraph was rattling wildly.

Sarah ran forward, deciphering the dots and dashes as she moved. She grabbed a pencil and scratched the letters on the first paper she could find.

Where in heaven's name was Frank?

The message ended and she shuffled in the drawer for the proper day letter forms, amazed anew at the mess Frank always seemed to create out of her tidy organization. She laid the form on the counter and reached for a pen and the paper she'd scribbled the message on. She dipped into the ink well and began to copy the words then paused and set the pen down.

Her hastily written words were at the bottom of an official letter from the main office of the Kansas Pacific advising Frank Bates that the investigation of Sarah Donovan was underway. She picked up the letter and scanned it, finding verification of everything Bowers had told her earlier along with instructions to Frank to mail the supporting documents as soon as possible.

Sarah's heart sank. She wasn't sure what Frank intended to send for proof, but she suspected it wasn't good. She glanced at the clock. Almost noon. He was likely at the post office with it right now.

A nagging, unwelcome thought wormed its way into her mind. It appeared Frank had set her up very well. The main office might indeed find her guilty of every allegation, and Denver would turn its back on her.

She slammed the paper on the desk and fought the urge to fire off a complaint to the main office. She glanced toward the door, knowing there was a narrow chance she could catch Frank before he mailed his package. She could fight this and win, proving herself both innocent and worthy. But at what cost?

She'd already unwittingly endangered the girls. If she fought this, here in Denver, how much disgrace would she bring on Daniel? Depending on what Frank was alleging, the scandal could damage everything Daniel held valuable. Her defense would very likely destroy the man she loved.

And that, she wouldn't be a party to.

She glanced around the office, her chest tight, and spotted a small wooden box. She emptied it of its contents and began to fill it with her own belongings while searing pain ripped at her until there was nothing left but a vacant hole.

Tears welled in her eyes and she shook her head to clear them away. She wouldn't cry, she wouldn't.

She stared at the wall, feeling the emptiness begin.

Chapter Twenty-Two

Packing didn't take long. Sarah dropped the last of her personal belongings into the box and sighed. An old knitted hat, her chipped bone-china coffee cup, and a few assorted knick-knacks that the *Little Women* cast had given her as gifts didn't seem like much of a life. Another unwanted tear formed in the corner of her eye and she brushed at it with her palm.

Lord, it was quiet today. January was slow, anyway, and with most of Denver up at the rally waiting to see if any riots erupted, the station was deserted. Perhaps that was where the crew, along with the company horse, had disappeared to.

She ran her hand over the logbook and fingered the telegraph key.

At least she had her primary operator's status. Strange how it didn't seem to mean much anymore; not beyond being a professional advantage. The achievement just didn't hold the fulfillment she'd expected. What had mattered most was holding Kate and Molly when they needed her. Safe or not, they had needed her. That and being wrapped in Daniel's arms, sated by love.

Her heart squeezed and she closed her eyes, savoring the fullness of her memories, and dreading the emptiness to come.

Fighting her battle alone against Frank's allegations was a bleak prospect, and proving him wrong would be no more fulfilling than the fight. She sank onto the stool and wiped away a tear.

All these years, she'd hidden behind her struggles to be the best, to make a difference, to win admiration, when all she had to do was quit hiding. Daniel and the girls hadn't needed her to achieve anything. They'd loved her sitting on the ice, misstepping on the dance floor, and making hot cocoa. Seeking women's suffrage and knowing how to send a telegraph were just part of her, not her whole substance.

She sniffled and shook her head. Lord, how she wished she hadn't mucked things up so badly, that there was a way to bask in all they'd given her without ruining their lives. She hadn't even given a thought to how her grandstanding might embarrass Daniel or lead the girls into situations they didn't understand. And now it was too late to fix things without making the mess worse. She swiped both palms across her cheeks and sighed, forcing away the tears that still lurked behind her eyes.

The click of the telegraph arm broke the silence and she leaned forward to decipher the message. Where was Frank, anyway? This was his shift, not hers.

The brief wire was a reminder about the twelve o'clock Special. She'd almost forgotten about the extra noon train from Cheyenne and its load of suffragists, Susan B. Anthony and the other dignitaries Lavinia Morgan had invited to the rally. She jotted down the message, recorded it in the logbook, then glanced at the switch log to verify the dispatcher's orders.

Frank's scratchy handwriting had recorded the order. The northbound Express, with its load of freight, would be nearing Denver at the same time the Cheyenne Special was due. As the secondary train, the Cheyenne Special was to be routed to the siding. The column next to the order was empty. No one had logged in the corresponding action.

A cold wet finger of fear crept up Sarah's neck.

She pushed the foreboding away and cleared her thoughts.

Just because Frank hadn't recorded the action didn't mean the two trains were headed into Denver on the same track. It didn't mean two massive locomotives were steaming toward one another nor that every life on board was in danger. It didn't.

Sarah rushed across the room and grabbed the master log. Fumbling through the pages, she found the current day and checked the last positions of the switches.

Good God, no one had thrown the switches.

Her breath caught and goose flesh rose on her arms. The main line *was* open at both ends. In moments, the Express would arrive, moving at full speed through the station while, a half-mile away, the Cheyenne Special would top the hill and descend into the yard along the same track. She ran her finger down the page again, willing it to say something else. It didn't.

She dropped her pencil and dashed out of the office, hoping she was wrong. She rushed across the lobby, ignoring her coat on the hook next to the door, and raced through the door facing the tracks. Outside, the rail yard was still empty. She turned northward, toward Cheyenne, and began running, slipping willy-nilly on the ice with each step. Her heart thumped.

Where in God's name was the yard crew?

Passing the first switch, she assured herself it was in the open position, then ran on. Cold air filled her lungs, stinging them. The second switch, the one that would route the Special onto the siding until the Express passed, was further north, at the bottom of a small rise.

Sarah stepped on her hem and her feet slid. She landed on the rail bed as the skirt tore, rocks stinging her palms. She righted herself and drew in a ragged breath. Images of others' injuries flashed in her mind. How many bodies would there be if she didn't stop those trains?

Panting, she neared the switch. She'd move the tracks first, then run up the line to the far side of the hill and flip the signal lever at the edge of the track, the engineer's cue to take the siding and stop. She grasped the cold iron handle, shivering, then stepped forward, pushing the lever. It grated in the cold, reluctant to budge.

Sarah threw her weight against the handle, feeling the strain in her shoulders and upper back. The switch groaned and moved forward a foot and a half. With just half the weight and considerably less strength than most of the yard crew, it often took Sarah several attempts before the switch moved into place. She took a breath, threw her entire weight into it, and shoved.

The swinging rail section refused to move further. She peered at the rails, looking for the source of the stall. A huge boulder sat on the siding, blocking the switch's path.

Sarah's heart pounded. The yard crew was supposed to check for such obstructions on a regular basis. She wrinkled her eyebrows at the unexpected size of the boulder and a shiver ran down her spine. She stepped in between the rails to examine the rock. It was anchored in a bed of setting ice. Realizing she'd need to get a crow bar, she kicked at it in frustration. She didn't have time for this.

A few feet away, the lever jumped, then swung back with a resounding click, and the tracks shifted back to their original position with her misplaced foot wedged between the two sections of rail. The boulder settled into the slight hole left by the dislodged ice, firmly against the rail that held her foot.

Damn.

She grimaced in pain, realizing she'd forgotten to lock the lever into position before she'd left it. She stared down at her trapped foot and tried to pull it free. It moved slightly but the rail refused to budge. Throwing her weight against the boulder, she tried to shove it out of the way.

It, too, was stuck.

Sarah glanced up the track and forgot about the pain. Her

skin crawled and a slow, cold sense of doom wormed its way through her body. She shivered.

"Oh, God. The trains."

His heart pumping from exertion, Daniel ran around the corner of Depot Street and approached the station, figuring it was the most likely place to find Sarah. He'd been irrational and hurtful, and he sure didn't want to waste time running all over town when he needed to be apologizing to the woman he loved. He sidestepped to avoid a section of ice, and slowed as he neared the slick spots near the door. Stepping with care, he entered the depot.

A dismal silence lingered in the room and a chilly blast of air assaulted him from the open door on the track side of the building. He moved across the lobby and into Sarah's office. Aside from the odor of stale coffee, it, too, was empty.

A sharp twinge of disappointment struck him. He should never have left her in the first place.

A wooden box, sitting next to the telegraph key, caught his attention. The figurine Kate and Molly had given Sarah as a director's gift topped the contents. Daniel approached the box, uncomfortable with its implication. His gut tightened.

On the counter, next to the box, Sarah's penmanship graced the bottom of an official letter. Spying her name elsewhere, curiosity picked at him and his gaze drifted to the body of the letter. He skimmed its contents, looking for an answer he wasn't sure he wanted. Addressed to Frank Bates, the missive confirmed an investigation into allegations against Sarah and requested documents to support that she was using the telegraph to prostitute herself. It also indicated questions about her relationship with Jim Wilson, the stationmaster.

Daniel slammed his palm onto the counter and swore aloud.

Christ, no wonder she was packing. He'd all but accused her

of unscrupulous intent himself and now this.

They'd fight it, together. It wouldn't take much. Who would believe Frank Bates, anyhow?

"Sarah?" His glance swept across the office and into the main lobby, settling on the open door to the tracks. Maybe she was outside. He strode across the room and exited. Once on the wooden platform, he scanned the yard until he saw her, hunched over the tracks not too far from the bottom of the hill.

His pulse quickened and he moved forward, anxious to clear the air and offer his apology. He just hoped she'd let him get it out before she started scolding him.

What a fool I've been.

He trotted down the platform stairs and began to jog across the wide rail yard toward her, slowing for each patch of ice. A quarter mile ahead, Sarah struggled with something. "Sarah?"

She turned toward him and her shoulders slumped. "Oh, Daniel, thank God you're here."

The strange desperation in her voice caught him by surprise and he ran the last hundred feet to her. Once there, he saw her face was knotted in pain, tears welling in her big violet eyes. Following her glance, he found her foot stuck tightly between two rails, a large boulder wedged against one of them.

Worry jabbed at him and he bent down, touching her foot with care. "Sarah, honey, hold still. I'll get this thing moved." He braced himself and tried to lift the rock, only to have his feet slide out of control on the ice.

The whistle of a train shattered the air. Daniel's heart jumped at the sound, pounding in his chest as the meaning became clear. He regained his footing, glared up the tracks for a split second then shoved at the boulder. *Jesus.* Where was the pick? Didn't she bring a pick?

"Daniel, listen to me. They're going to collide." She pointed northward, at the small rise and its drop into the train yard.

His breath stalled. "Who?"

"The Northbound and the Special."

"Good God."

"You need to signal the Special."

He shook his head. "Let's get you out. We just need to pry this rock up and—"

"No time. There are people on board. You need to stop that train before it tops the hill. It's their only chance."

Daniel eyed Sarah's position on the track and shook his head, her full implication finally hitting him. "But the Express—"

"I can signal the Express myself. It's flat ground, the engineer will have plenty of time to stop."

Over the hill, the Special sounded its second whistle blast and a cold chill grabbed at Daniel's heart.

"God, Sarah. That train's too close." He turned and saw the calm assurance in her eyes shift to panic, intense enough to confirm he might not make the run in time.

"Run, Daniel," she commanded. "Wave it down, before it tops the hill."

He glanced at her, his pulse pumping hard against the fear. She was wearing red. "I need your clothes," he blurted, the words forming as fast as the thought registered.

She stared at him, uncomprehending.

He grasped her red plaid skirt, ripped it down the front, and tossed it into her arms, certain she would know what to do. Ignoring her confused squeal of protest, he reached for her red flannel petticoat, tore it away, and sprinted up the hill. Behind him, he heard the imperative warning blast of the Express's whistle. The engineer had seen Sarah. He resisted turning, forcing himself to trust the makeshift flag and that there would be enough distance for the train to stop. The screech of grinding brakes filled the air.

His legs pumped harder, straining against the incline of the hill. The churning roar of the unseen Special grew louder and the clack of its wheels against the rails became distinct. His lungs protested in the icy air.

Oh, God, please let me get there. He topped the hill and saw the train. Billowing smoke poured from the encroaching engine.

Daniel stepped onto the track and swung Sarah's red petticoat into the air above his head. A warning sounded, filling the air. Brakes ground, straining against the rails. The locomotive loomed, huge and powerful, as it slid toward him.

Sarah pivoted southward, Daniel's fleeting form giving her renewed hope, and watched the Express roar into the station.

She lifted the plaid skirt and waved it overhead, shutting her mind against the pain radiating from her trapped foot. The garment arced across the tracks, the icy wind making it billow with each sweep. In front of her, the Express whistled a warning and began to brake.

Lord in heaven, what if it doesn't stop?

Cold sweat formed on her bare skin. She hadn't considered that the train might not be able to stop. She moved her arm faster, then realized it didn't matter. The engineer had already seen her. There was nothing left to do except wait.

I should have told him.

Her heart trembled. By now, Daniel would be on the other side of the hill, standing in front of his own fast-approaching train. And if either of them failed in their efforts, he would never know how much she loved him.

The screech of grinding metal crept across the rail yard and acrid smoke filled the air. Sarah held her breath as the train neared, grinding to a halt with agonizing slowness.

Less than thirty feet away, the engine shuddered to a stop.

Sarah stared at it through the smoke, slowly becoming aware of her cold, tear-stained cheeks and bare goose-bumped skin.

Good God, she was standing in her drawers!

Sparks sprayed across Daniel's shoes as the train slid past him. Heat filled the empty air as the engine strained toward the crest of the hill. He coughed in the swirling coal dust and turned.

Sarah.

He dropped her red flannel petticoat on the pale snow and scrambled after the locomotive. Near the top of the hill, he realized it had stopped. He slowed, exhaling his relief, and looked out over the tracks.

She was there. Safe.

He released a pent-up breath, closed his eyes, and offered a whispered prayer of thanksgiving.

Behind him, the engineer had climbed from the engine and was crunching across the snow.

"What the Sam-hill is goin' on here?" he demanded.

Daniel nodded downhill. "See for yourself. I've got something that needs to be done." Leaving the puzzled engineer standing there to figure it out on his own, he jogged down the hill, intent on seizing life before he lost the chance.

"Sarah?"

She turned, all soot and grime in her ragged plaid bodice and a pair of white drawers with lace trim, and burst into fresh tears.

Pure relief bubbled through him. He swallowed her in his arms and kissed her dirty face. "Oh, God, Sarah, I thought I'd lost you. I love you."

"I was so afraid I'd never get a chance to tell you that I love you. I never thought it'd come that close." She stared past him, her eyes huge.

He turned and saw the engine from her perspective, close and monstrous.

Daniel's heart thumped wildly and he kissed the top of her

head. "Me, either, darling. Tell me you'll let me make you an honest woman."

"An honest woman?"

"I figure it's the best way to fight Bates. Besides, I'm standing here holding a half-naked woman while a whole trainload of suffragists looks on from the top of the hill."

She turned and followed his gaze. A crowd of women peered down at them.

"What d'ya think? You ready to take a chance?"

"I am, Daniel."

"Good. Now let's give those ladies something to talk about." He lifted her chin, slid his hands around her body, and kissed her.

Epilogue

August 1878

Sarah stepped out of the depot and squinted into the bright afternoon sunshine. Her hand moved to her lower back, nursing the steady ache that had settled there during her brief stint at the telegraph key. Next time Jim needed a fill-in operator, she'd have to decline. Thank goodness she'd given up her permanent position last month. She stretched, patted her growing girth, and waited.

Across Depot Street, a crowd of kids had gathered in the empty lot, brewing trouble. Sarah shook her head and glanced up the street. Daniel approached, his easy stride sending a shiver of desire through her. Beside him, Molly and Kate bounced in animated conversation.

Daniel grinned and lifted his eyebrows, then kissed her, full on the mouth. "You are radiant, Sarah." He pulled back and stood silently, a teasing smile on his rugged face.

Molly tugged at his arm, thrust her chin forward, and tipped her head toward Sarah.

Kate laughed softly and shook her head.

Sarah's hands opened in a gesture of expectation. Those three couldn't keep a secret if their lives depended on it. "What?"

Daniel steered her up the street and onto the boardwalk, making her wait. "I wrote a letter to the editor," he finally said.

"All by yourself?" She grinned, teasing him.

He shook his head in mock exasperation. "Figured it was

time to get folks talking. Those same kids are here, day in and day out, doing nothing."

Sarah paused, her hands moving to her hips before she could stop them. "Haven't I been saying the same thing?"

"Every day, if I remember right." He strode on.

She followed with quick steps, enjoying the game. She glanced at Kate and Molly and raised one eyebrow. "*He* wrote a letter?"

Molly nodded. "It was his idea and everything. But we helped."

"I see."

"That's not exactly true, Molly," Kate added. "It was Papa's idea to write the letter but it was about our idea."

"Our idea? The club?"

Kate nodded.

"I proposed our good citizens organize associations for our young people." Daniel stopped and faced her.

"You didn't?"

He tipped his head and lifted his hands in a gesture of helplessness. "You've been excited about the idea ever since Kate and Molly brought it up. How does the Denver Girls' Association sound? I suggested a boys' club, too."

"It sounds well considered and refined."

"I can get the letter back."

"And ruin your moment of spontaneity?"

He shrugged, a sheepish grin filling his face. "Kate gave me the notes she took."

Sarah's laughter bubbled out. She should have known. "So did you write your own letter or just copy our notes?"

"A little of both, a balance of passion and restraint."

"You don't mind, do you?" Kate prompted.

Sarah smiled at Kate's concern. "No, honey. I think it's a wonderful idea. I never really thought about sharing it with anyone beyond your circle of friends, but why not? I'm sure there are plenty of girls who would join."

"We told Papa that it's important the girls get to do lots of different things, not just needlework and cooking. Girls gotta learn about bein' leaders, too."

"And forming their own opinions."

"Daniel?"

He nodded and grinned again. "And vote."

Sarah stopped and stared at him. "I'm going to have to read this letter."

"Only after we get our chocolate," Molly said. She grabbed Kate's hand and pulled her across the street, toward Joslin's.

Sarah leaned her head on Daniel's shoulder. "I hope you added something about nurturing. Sometimes, that gets missed."

"I suggested someone to lead the effort, too."

"I'm happy being at home with the girls. They're teaching me so much about life and how empty mine really was. I don't need to create and lead another group."

"You don't need it, but maybe it needs you, the new you."

"And you wouldn't mind?"

"I'll be embarrassed as the dickens every other day, I'm sure. But, no, I don't mind."

She shook her head and slid her hand into his, comfortable in their give and take. "Jim heard from Frank Bates today. He's out of jail, wants his job back."

Daniel squeezed her hand, offering silent support. "Think he'll get it?"

"Jim said he'll never telegraph again. Word got around fast. I still shudder to think of what might have happened to me if I hadn't had such a distinctive keystroke. It still surprises me how rapidly the other operators realized it wasn't me sending those suggestive messages."

"Character and style, that's my girl."

"Frank told Jim that Lavinia is still in the sanitarium." Losing her position in the suffrage movement was apparently more than she could handle. The woman had nothing else in her life.

He stopped, catching her gaze, no longer teasing. "But you don't miss it?"

"I wish we'd gained the right to vote, but leadership?" She shrugged. "No, I don't miss it. Too empty."

He touched her face and offered a satisfied smile. "Funny how we needed each other to realize how narrow our priorities were, huh?"

She nodded. "And amazing how full life truly is."

"That it is." His hand drifted to her abdomen, a brief caress. The baby shifted, tumbling under Daniel's touch, filling Sarah with contentment while Daniel's hand lingered there, completely oblivious to what anyone else would think about it.

AUTHOR'S NOTE

Many of the events in Sarah and Daniel's story were inspired by history. There really were female telegraphers, many of whom faced problems similar to Sarah's. The women of Colorado did campaign for a state suffrage referendum in January 1877. William Byers rose to prominence as editor of the *Rocky Mountain News* and his wife Elizabeth was known for her leadership in multiple social endeavors. Mattie Silks did indeed run a fashionable house of prostitution on Holladay Street. Hop Alley, Joslin's, the City Ditch, the Kansas Pacific Railroad Depot, and many other places mentioned existed, as did James Archer and Marshal McCallin. If I have made errors in my representation of these people, events, and places, the mistakes are unintentional and entirely my own.

ABOUT THE AUTHOR

Pamela Nowak has loved both history and romance for as long as she can remember. She graduated from South Dakota State University with a BA in History and has taught classes at both the high school and college level as well as adult basic education and GED classes at a state penitentiary. She served as a historic preservation specialist for the Quechan Indian Tribe at Fort Yuma (Yuma Crossing National Historic Landmark). Currently, she serves as director of a homeless shelter. Her interests include reading, historic research, directing community theater, and visiting historic sites. She lives in Cheyenne, Wyoming, with her husband and daughter. She invites you to visit to her at *pamelanowak.com* or *myspace.com/pamelanowak* or e-mail her at *pamelanowak@pamelanowak.com.*